Mortar Transformation

by

Alexandria May Ausman

Book cover illustration by Alexandria May Ausman
Editor: Jon M. Ausman

Library of Congress Control Number: 2024914059

ISBN: 978-1-963335-19-4 (ebook)
ISBN: 978-1-963335-18-7 (paperback)

Published By:
Ausman & Cousins LLC
1700 North Monroe Street
Suite 11, Box 284
Tallahassee, Florida 32303-0501

For author interviews: ausman@embarqmail.com

FOR
CARY

Cary: The Shadow King

Das Kaiser Haus Series

The Collar King Series

The Most Brutal Man in Europe Series

Book 1 (Coming soon)

The Psycho Series

Cemetery Kid (Chapters 1 to 20)
Stop Calling Me Psycho (Chapters 21 to 33)
Motor-Psycho (Chapters 34 to 44)
Delusion of the Collar and the Key (Chapters 45 to 53)
Brutality's Prisoner (Chapters 54 to 64)
Aesthetic Akathisia (Chapters 65 to 74)
Metallic Burden (Chapters 75 to 83)

27 Masters Series

Anita the Benevolent (Chapters 1 to 7)
The Beast and the Witch (coming soon Chapters 8 to 16)
High Priestess of Schizophrenia (coming soon)

Book 7 Characters: Mortar Transformation

Aara: a Haus black collar
Almut: a black collar Torture Master
Altergott, Dr. Reese: a clinical psychiatrist
Amanda: the original name of Motte, a silver collar
Annette: a Haus black collar
Barnum: a deceased Haus Elder
Bladrick: a deceased Haus Elder
Blume: a black collar, spouse of Almut
Borlan, Dr. Attila: a Haus doctor
Byron: a Haus Dominant, a Voting Council member
Cary: a black collar door guard
Chenoweth: a deceased pedophile
Christian: the anger and lust shard
Christian Axel: a Haus Dominant, the Priceless
Claus: an Elder of the Haus
Cora: a FemDom of the Haus, the Fur Queen
Debbie: mother of Meine Liebe, a psychopathic sadist
Der Goldene Hund: the Voice or the Boss shard; the Conscious shard
Der Makellos: Leo and Christian's German Shepherd
Egon: a Torture Master
Felicity: a lamb
Friedrick: a Haus Dominant, friend of Byron
Geraldine: a hard working lamb that cooks for Maxximillian
Gerard: a deceased sadistic stepfather to Christian Axel

Ghanzi: a Haus black collar

Gisela: a Haus FemDom

Gretta: a Haus FemDom, the Silk Queen

Helga: a deceased Dungeon Mistress

Hermann: a rapist friend of Peter, a non-Haus person

Henner: Gretta's German Shepherd

Hubertus: a black collar Torture Master

Ivan: captain of the Russian Guard (outdoors)

Jäger: a Haus Dominant, boyfriend of Jakob

Jaison: Almut's son

Jakob: a Haus Dominant

Jonas: an Elder of the Haus

Karstin: a Haus FemDom

Kilian: an Elder, psychiatric rehabilitation counselor

Kloe: Marc's deceased big sister, a black collar, also the name of Marc's lamb

Leo: an Elder of the Haus

Lucus: a Haus Dominant, a royal

Mad Max: the sadistic shard of Maximillian, aka the Heart and Judgment

Mad Maxx: husband of Meine Liebe; a Haus Dominant

Mad Maxx: the masochistic shard, aka the Brain and Guilt

Magnas: a Haus Dominant, a Wolf

Malfred: a Haus Elder

Marc: a deceased Haus black collar

Matz: a Haus Dominant, a pimp and loan shark

Max: the Soul shard

Maximillian: the submissive name given to Christian by Peter

Maximillian: the seductive shard, aka the Libido
Maxximillian: the submissive adopted by the Elders
Meine Liebe: submissive and spouse of Mad Maxx
Motte: a silver collar submissive
Noethan, Dr. Anselm: a deceased Haus doctor
Olga: a Dungeon Mistress
Osvin: a first floor Haus Dominant
Peter: a Dominant of Der Kaiser Haus; best trainer of submissives
Rolf: a Haus Dominant
Roland: a first floor Haus Dominant, a violinist
Roselina: a Haus black collar, spouse of Cary
Rudolph: the black collar Stable Master
Russell: Meine Liebe's pedophile stepfather
Ryker: a deceased Haus trainee
Samual: a black collar Great Hall attendant
Sebastian: a deceased Haus Dungeon Master
Sigerd: a Haus FemDom
Stephan: a deceased Haus Dominant
Tadeas: a deceased Haus Dungeon Master
Valitin: a Haus Dominant, a Wolf

Preface

Unbeknownst to the residents of Das Kaiser Haus, their Mortar King is being eaten alive by a mysterious illness. While the disease robs him of his mental acuity, Byron secretly makes his move to take possession of the ailing monarch. This once seemingly 'love-sick' but harmless nuisance in Mad Maxx's life has managed to do the impossible. Misled into believing his beloved Felicity no longer loves him. The Mortar King falls victim to the brutal Byron's clever brainwashing techniques.

Slowly, Mad Maxx discovers he's unable to imagine surviving his hellish journey without the Silk Prince's mystical pain killing potions. Under the influence and out of control, the shards begin to lash out at those they feel have wronged Mad Maxx. The sudden demonstration of brute strength by the Mortar King elicit fear among the men that lay claim to his body and soul. Jonas, Peter, and Mad Lucus are forced to work together in a last ditch effort to try to save the Mortar King…from himself.

Chapter 47: Silence of the Lamb

I sat there staring at my Felicity in that doorless birdcage unable to understand the sight of it. Byron kept his eyes on me with a humored smile on his face. Several moments passed before at last the brute's voice broke the silence in that room.

He chuckled. "Are you not happy to see that Felicity is safe and sound, Maxx? Look at her. Not a single mark on her perfect white coat. It has been my pleasure to protect such a sweet little girl. She is the modest eater and never gives complaint. I can see why you adore her like you do. I confess I have falling for her charms too." He reached through the bars and petted her with one of his nasty fingers.

I whimpered as I watched him touching my innocent lamb. "I uhm, thank you for looking after her Byron but I am here now. Can you please led her out of that cage. I want to take her home with me when I return to Lucus this afternoon. I also would like a bit of privacy to speak to her about things."

Byron pulled his finger from that cage with a startle. "Huh? You think she wants to be out of this haus I give to her? Nein. Felicity was the frightened mess when I rescued her from that uncaring woman Birgit. She was seeking you Maxx, but I had to break to her that her father left her behind. I didn't dare lie to her, though I admit I thought of doing it to protect her from that sad knowledge."

I gasped in fear as I kept my eyes on Felicity. "Sad knowledge of what Byron."

He scoffed. "Really Maxx? You going to sit there in front of this poor little lamb and tell lies. How dare you expect me pretend that I didn't just fish you from the banister. You did intend to abandon this gentle soul and still would if I didn't promise you the moon to keeping you from it. You didn't ask Birgit if she wanted a lamb. More than that you didn't bother to speak with Felicity about what she wanted did you? Did you?"

I cried out in terror as the big man came barreling at me. He grabbed me by the coat and dragged me off the bed like a rag doll to the cage. Byron then grabbed the back of my hair and held my face to stare at my lamb behind the bars.

He growled out as he held me tightly like that. "Listen to her. Do you hear her weeping? Do you know who caused her that hurt? You did Maxx. You left her to fend for herself in the cold cruel world. You're a selfish bastard to think only of your own pain. This little lamb counted on you, and you failed her. Beg her forgiveness for what you have done, Maxx. Maybe if you are lucky, one day she will find it in her heart to show you the mercy you didn't give her."

I could hear Felicity sobbing like he said she was doing. through the bars I could see her tears of agony over my leaving her behind, well planning to anyway. I felt my

3

own heart break in two that I had injured the only thing on Earth that ever really loved me.

I suddenly realized I was no better than any of the perverts and criminals that I had ever known. They all took what they wanted then left me to be used by the next monster. I couldn't deny this was exactly what I had done to my own sweet lamb. I didn't consider what would happen to her when I was gone.

I led out a wail of anguish. "Oh, My Gott. Felicity, I apologize, my love. I am the bastard. Forgive me please. I beg your mercy. I will do anything to make this right. I will never leave you behind again. I swear it on my honor." I broke into bitter tears of regret while Byron kept me pinned to face the one I had betrayed.

Byron snorted with disbelief. "She doesn't believe you, Maxx. She thinks a man cannot change nor should the evil he has done be forgiven or forgotten. You know like you don't trust me because in the past I did wrong. What do you think? Is it possible to make up for all the bad one does in this life if they are truthfully sorry for it?"

I nodded with vigor as I looked up at him, the tears falling fast and hard. "Ja, ja. A man can be good after he has fucked up. Felicity will forgive me. She knows I didn't mean to hurt her. I swear to her I make this better and I will do what I say. Please led her out Byron so I can prove I am sincere to my lamb."

Byron shook his head with a look of pity in his expression. "Nein, Maxx. I want to do what you ask but I

4

promised Felicity I would keep her safe since you wouldn't. She asked to be in the cage where no one can harm her. This is her safe haus for now. Ask her. She doesn't want to leave this room or my apartment."

I shot a look of desperation at Felicity and heard her repeat what Byron told me. My lamb said she was afraid and no longer trusted that I would look after her. I was devastated to know I had lost her love. Now, I utterly understood what it meant to be all alone in the world. Everyone had turned their back on me, even my beloved lamb.

I broke Bryon's hold on me when I fell face first onto the floor at the foot of that bird cage holder with suddenness. I laid there in prostrate before Felicity wailing in pure misery. Byron stood there watching the show appearing unsure what to say or do as I wept like the lost soul I had become. I had thought dying was the answer, but I found my bid for it only caused a worse hell than I could have ever imagined.

Byron allowed me to do this for quite some time before he eventually tired of my woeful antics. He finally reached down and dragged me back to my knees with great force. I couldn't even look the man in the eyes I was so damned ashamed of all the dreadful things I had done. That shit in the palace, the gruesome killing of those men, that selfish attempt to commit suicide, and the worst of it, allowing the monster Byron to gain possession of my sweet Felicity. I was nothing but a useless loser. I deserved whatever horrors that happened to me and I fucking well knew it.

Byron blew out his breath. "Maxx, listen to me. I know things seem dark right now, but if you are willing. There is a way to redeem yourself."

I sniffed while I wiped my tear drenched cheeks. "How Byron? I am the nothing, nein worse than nothing. I am the foolish scum under the nothing. Maybe suicide isn't the answer. I haven't earned the honorable death. I deserve to die like the criminal I am."

Byron gasped and dropped to his knees next to me with an expression of shock. "Nein, that's not true Maxx. You are not a nothing. You merely made a mistake or two. It is okay. A man will make many in his life. That is where wisdom comes from brother. If you never fuck up then you never learn anything."

I shook my head. "If that were the truth of it Byron I would be the fucking wisest man on earth by now. Instead, I sit here with my lamb hating me, and Mad Lucus waiting to tie me in his cock bed. Well, I suppose that is all too good for me. Evil people get what they have coming to them eventually. I suppose I should accept my fate as the pincushion and stop trying to pretend I can be more than that."

Byron reached out and wiped my face with gentleness. "Hush, no more of that kicking yourself Maxx. I won't hear of it. Ja, Felicity is pretty pissed at you, but I think she only says she hates you because her feelings are hurt. I bet if you

6

work hard at it, show her you are a changed man. She will come back to loving you once more. The lamb is a forgiving creature you know. Come on brother. Give her some time to heal. Don't assume it is all over before there is clear evidence to that fact."

I shuddered and whispered back. "You really believe she can love me again for truth, Byron? After what I did, I cannot blame her for never trusting me again."

Byron smiled with friendliness. "Sure, I believe she can Maxx. I mean look at you and me, ja? You see that I am your friend. I am not attacking you as you were sure I would do. I give you your own place, protect your lamb when she was helpless. I will even help you get free of all these foul creatures like that Lucus. One day soon brother, we will be in our very own Haus. Believe me when I say the sun will rise in the morning and Felicity will love you again. Tell you what. I will even help you win her heart back."

I gasped and looked up at him with a shred of hope building in my broken heart. "You will? How will you do that? Why would you even care?"

He patted my back vigorously. "Well Maxx, I think you are not listening to your buddy Byron. I told you I care about you. Nein, I honestly love you. I will speak with Felicity. You know, explain the situation to her. I think with some time, and my encouraging her to watch the two of us developing the loving friendship when once we were harsh enemies. That should show her you are capable of changing. How could she not love you once she sees how wonderful you are to me. It is the brilliant plan, ja?"

I shrugged as the sensation of fear tugged at my spine for some reason. "I guess so. I suppose it makes sense, yet I cannot lie Byron. I do hate you. You are not my friend, nor do I ever think it possible you will be. I think Felicity will see I am faking. If she sees that I pretend with you then why should she trust I tell her the truth?"

Bryon grabbed my face with harshness his eyes lit up with fire. "Then if I were you I would work fucking hard to make the lie a truth. I tell you with honesty if you are unable to find affection for me as your trusted buddy then that lamb of yours will never love you again. Are you ready for a hard life in the clutches of the heartless creatures Jonas, Gretta, and Lucus without Felicity? Or are you going to stop your stupidly hating the man that can give you all you ever dreamed of and more."

I gulped down the lump in my throat feeling I may weep again. "It is not that easy Byron. I honestly don't want either choice you give me. Do you expect me to know how to do the impossible? I need you to tell me what to do to fix all this. Say what you want from me and see it done. I will do anything to get Felicity to love me. I want her to come back to me. Please I need you to direct me to seem that I am your truest friend despite my deep hate for you."

Byron scoffed and shook his head. "I cannot tell you what to do, Maxx. From here on out anything that happens is up to you. I cannot make you do anything you don't honestly desire to happen between us or that is the lie isn't it? This time I am the helpless victim of your decisions. whatever you want me to do or not do I will do. Afterall you are the Master of this Haus, ja? Am I not merely a servant to the metal crown, a lowly prince kneeling at his feet? You have all the power, Maxx. I can only hope you use it wisely. Raise me and Felicity to be your family or let Lucus and the others subjugate you to meet there greedy needs. What is it going to be? You tell me, Sire."

I nodded. "Okay then I say to you to keep your fucking hands off me. I don't want you fondling or molesting me anymore. Don't be touching me like that ever again. If you can learn to treat me like a man and not your fucking sex toy maybe I can find true affection for you as a friend. In fact. I will try with all my might to forget all that has happened and move on as your honest brother."

He smiled with happiness, "Okay now we are getting somewhere. I swear to you I never touch you again unless you ask me to. Is that fair?"

I scoffed. "Ja, since I won't be ever asking you to."

Byron chuckled. "Ja, okay but there is something special about the best friend brother relationship that you forget or maybe never knew."

I shrugged. "I confess I don't know much about it. I guess Jakob, Rolf and Leo, they are my friends. Maybe Matz a bit. I did have a kind of brother once, but he is dead." I trailed off as I thought of the Prince Ryker.

Ryker's voice floated through the air. "The Dominants they play the mind games brother. They lie to you to confuse you and get you to do what day want. Then they make you think it was all your idea."

Byron noticed my distraction. "What just happened there, Maxx? What did they tell you?"

I flinched when he said that. "Huh? What did who tell me? I don't understand your meaning."

He frowned at me. "That is what I mean. Brothers don't keep things from each. other. Secrets are things they share between them and guard from the world outside. Now, tell me what did you just hear?"

I looked at the floor. "Ryker told me that you are playing the mind games with me. Trying to get me to believe this is all my idea when really you mislead me." I braced for the backhand I was sure he would level on me for that confession.

He began to chuckled with humor, which surprised the shit out of me. "Ah, that Ryker always was the shit stirrer. I liked him though. He always had the cheerful smile."

I gasped in surprise. "You know Ryker? How? He, uhm, he is dead."

Byron nodded. "Well, that is true, but he still speaks to you, ja? The boy was a good boy but this place and her evil people, well they didn't stop until the destroyed him. Ryker thought he knew how to survive this hell Haus. He was wrong. You are takin advice from a boy that lost the game,

Maxx. You on the other hand have made it to the ripe age of seventeen. Vow, that is impressive that you can claim wearing the silver but almost an adult. You add that you did break that bat collar and stand as the Mortar King today. That my friend is really something. So, you going to take that advice loser Ryker gives to you? Do you really think I am playing mind games? If so, what the hell am I getting from it but achy knees from kneeling next to you and a wet carpet from your tears."

I looked at the floor in a sudden stun from what he said. "I guess I never thought of it like that before. I mean Ryker he helps me keep from making mistakes. He has always been there to give the advice."

Byron began to laugh with heartiness. "Well, shit. That sure explains a few things. No wonder you are always getting the short end of the stick Maxx. You take your orders from a boy that was your fucking competition. Didn't it occur to you he wants to see you fail? It would be the perfect revenge on the one that made it where he desired to be."

I groaned in misery. "What you say makes sense. I am the fucking fool to listen to his advice. I guess I will need to try to make decisions on my own from now on."

He nodded as he stood back up offering his hand to aid me. "That's my boy. You don't need to be listening to a dead failed Priceless to know right from wrong. Maybe it is time you seek out the living with experience to find wise counsel for your tough questions, ja?"

11

I stood up wringing my hands looking at Felicity with longing. "Ja, which is what I will do. Wait, I don't know anyone that will help me like Ryker did, does. Everyone I know tells me to do what they say or like the black collars wants me to tell them what to say."

Byron stuck out his chest with pride. "That is what I am here for Maxx. I am happy to take the place of Ryker. You can trust my judgement. Look at me, the Voter without a fortune to back my name. I am well liked with no serious enemies in this Haus. I had a mother that loved me and can boast knocking a grown man out with one punch. More than that, Felicity trusts me. Look at where she chooses to hide from the brutality of the world. She knows I am the right man for the job."

I looked at the floor with shame burning my ears. "Ja, she did come seeking your protection when I let her down. If my lamb thinks so highly of you then I am the fool to deny you the same respect. I thank you for the mercy of it."

Byron appeared stunned, faking I am sure looking back on it now. "Really? You mean that Maxx?"

I nodded as I winced. "Ja, I think so."

He laughed. "Well, that didn't sound too sure, but it will do for the moment. Okay, let's try out this new arrangement shall we? I think you are too skinny. This frailty is a weakness the fiends of the Haus will use against you. From this moment on you are going to eat three hearty meals a day. You can do that in the Great Hall or sneak up to see your buddy Byron. You must gain some weight and

12

get back to working out like we used to. In fact, you know what? I give you a week to heal from that shit down below, then next Saturday we will start to hit the weights together. It will be like the good old days, ja?"

I shivered with the memories of those good old days. "Uhm, if you say that is the thing to do I won't argue with you over it. That said, I have to get back to work soon. That is likely what Matz came to visit with me about. Are you going to tell Gretta about that dishonorable thing?"

Bryon crossed his arm and stared at me with sternness. "You have Lucus to pay the bills why would you need to return to the prostitution shit? Is Matz blackmailing you or something? I know you don't like the sex with the man. There must be some reason you even consider such a risk."

I shrugged. "I, uhm, you won't like what I say to you. Maybe I better not say anything. I speak too much already."

He glared at me with mild anger. "Listen to me Maxx. If this friendship is to work you must tell me everything. I cannot defend, protect or even help you if I don't know everything going on in your life. I am going to be your Guardian soon. You tell me anything and find that I will not judge you for it. I am here to make your life easier not to hen peck you to death like Lucus or Jonas or even that fucker Peter does."

I shot a look of fear at Felicity and wrung my hands faster, "Uhm, well I need the money to buy the silver children that are slated for death. I pay for their contracts then paint them black. After that, I pay Karsten to keep them till of age."

Byron grabbed his chest and his face melted to one of sudden admiration I hadn't seen since the day he first saw me naked in the closet. "Oh, my Gott. That is why you sell yourself? Not for your own gain but to save the lives of the lost. I didn't think you could be anymore wonderful, but then you drop this bombshell on me? Matz, does he know what you do with the money he collects for you?"

I nodded. "Ja. He and the wolfpack aid me in seeing the children to safe care. I give them a small percentage to protect them and me during the dangerous jobs."

He smiled and then startled me by reaching out to caress my face with gentleness. "Well, I don't like that you do this dark business, but I cannot deny why you do it is brilliant. You can be assured of my silence on the subject. I will never tell, long as we are buddies your secret is safe with me. However, I make one minor suggestion."

I shrugged. "I am listening Byron."

Byron sighed. "These idiots will pay for any kind of sexual contact with you they can get, ja?"

I nodded and kept my eyes to the floor feeling quite uncomfortable with this discussion and with this guy in particular.

He blew out his breath. "I would say that you knock the intercourse off. Stick to the blow or hand jobs. Don't do

14

anything fetishy. Let them see you naked or watch you pleasure yourself but don't let them have you all the way."

I gasped and looked up at him with disbelief. "What? I am fine with striking out the fetishes. Yet, you say not to allow them to couple with me. But that is the most popular thing on the menu. I would have to see twice, maybe three times, the clients to make up for the loss of income if I deny them the one expensive thing they all buy."

Byron nodded with vigor. "Oh, I bet you have them lined up clamoring to fuck you Maxx. However, listen to my sound advice on this. You come home to Lucus with bruises from a thudding or seed where you cannot get all of the evidence evacuated for sure and you will get caught. Better to give ten blow jobs and go undiscovered. One mistake is all it will take, my friend. Lucus is a pretty clever guy. Mark my words, he will eventually catch you. Then what will happen to those black collar children, or Matz and the wolves?"

I dropped my head back down realizing now that Lucus was around watching, he was right. "Ja, okay, I understand this you say is a smart thing to consider. I suppose I could find a way to work every day instead of only a few a week. Then I could make enough money to keep purchasing the children without taking the elevated risk of getting us all caught."

Byron smiled widely. "There you go Maxx. Compromise is always the best way to go. You see you always been working with an all or none attitude. Nein, you must start to see the middle and there you will find comfort."

I shuddered. "You say it is comfort to work every day sucking cock rather than two or three enduring a few brutes nasty lusts? I think you are not sexually experienced enough if you truly believe that brother. However, I do see what you are saying. I don't desire to lose all I have worked to build. If Lucus found out I was still doing this, well he'd never let me out the door again no doubt."

Byron startled, "What? Did you just say? Lucus knew about this? He lets you whore. No way."

I shook my head. "He found out about it. Likely the same way you did. Anyway, he had put a stop to it or so he thinks. Matz, Roland and I found a way around him. I admit though, I got put in the palace before I had the chance to try out the new plan. I think you are right. Lucus will be looking for signs of betrayal pretty close. He is very hands on if you know what I'm meaning. I doubt I will be capable of hiding it for long if I don't end the full intercourse. There are too many chances and signs of it will be left behind." I looked up with a sudden startle realizing I had been just sharing confidential information with Byron while not even thinking. Shit!

Byron scoffed. "Hands on you say. What exactly does that mean? I already feel sorry for you if half of what I have heard about that pervert is the truth."

I began to tremble. "I don't think this discussion is proper with you, Byron. I beg your forgiveness, but I would rather not say any more about it."

Byron shot a look at Felicity. "Oh? You don't think telling your buddy Byron about your personal woes is proper. Maxx do remember Felicity is watching our interactions. If you desire to show her you trust me, then you need to let go this barrier you have between us. I want you to tell me everything you endure at the hands of Jonas, Peter and that pervert Lucus. Once I know what you must suffer, then I can offer advice to ways to either avoid it or at the very least cut back on the assaulting. I can't help you if I don't know, remember?"

I felt helpless to fight his insisting on this humiliation. I wanted Felicity to forgive me, and Bryon swore she would if I could prove a person changeable. Bryon told me to sit on the bed and he took one in the chair next to my lamb.

For the next hour he quizzed me, and he listened to the most intimate of details regarding my special services to the men that sexually assaulted me on a regular basis. I wanted to lie or stop answering him, but I felt compelled to speak with honesty and held nothing back.

By the time I was done bearing my soul to him, I felt drained, shamed and depressed as hell. If talking about your problems with friends is supposed to make someone feel better than apparently I was doing that shit all wrong. I had never felt more violated or been more disgusted with myself than I did after saying all that horrific shit out loud to the Voter.

Byron sat there drinking in every foul description and revolting act I had been forced to do for these men. When I finally finished he leaned back in the chair crossing his arms as if in deep thought. I kept my eyes to the floor as the guilt bore down on my fatigued shoulders with fresh heaviness.

The brute cleared his throat then said, "I thank you for the honesty Maxx. I had no idea, okay that is not the truth, I had some idea of how bad things were for you. Now that I hear the story of it from the one that suffers it, I am at a loss for words brother. I can understand why you wanted to end your life. Who the fuck wouldn't rather die than put up with that nasty shit from those disgusting bastards for all these years."

I shrugged. "So, you are saying I should end my life then?" I was kind if relieved to hear he was agreeing with that idea if he was since I was again thinking suicide the proper course to end my pain.

He shook his head with vigor. "Nein, I don't say that Maxx. Stop putting words in my mouth. I can speak for myself you know. What I wish to say is that I am even more resolved to get you the fuck out of this hell hole as fast as possible. I cannot just sit back while these fiends tear you apart like they do. Especially, now that I know the whole truth of it."

I wrung my hands in anxiety and paced slightly. "I hope you mean what you say, Byron. I don't think I can do this shit I tell you about anymore. It was always hard but now after that bad thing down below, I just cannot keep taking this every fucking day." I began to feel the freak out starting within. Probably over the stress of saying the truth of my dishonorable life out loud to Byron, you know. It was really bothering me that I told him that horrible stuff.

Byron put up his hands motioning me to calm myself. "Easy there Maxx. Let's slow down and take a deep breath. Look at me boy. Stop the walking like a trapped animal and wringing and focus your attention to your buddy Byron. Hear only my voice." He grabbed my wrist as I flew past him to turn and walk back in the pacing.

I wailed. "Let me go, dammit. I told you not to be touching me." Byron tightened his grip as I pulled with desperation to escaping his hold.

Byron spoke in almost a whisper, "Hush, I repeat to you. Focus on my voice. Hear what I am saying to you and nothing else. I know of a way to keep that pervert Lucus from forcing you to his lust for a couple days. I know it is only the temporary solution, but it will buy you some time to heal both physically and spiritually."

I struggled despite what he was saying. "Nein, that man won't listen. You don't listen. No one ever listens to Maximillian. Christ, someone please kill me. Why cannot I be dead? People die every day, all the time. What have I ever done to deserve such torment as to not even be grants the favor of death?" I began screaming and twisting like the loon in his grip.

Byron jerked hard on my captured arm. "Stop this shit right now, Maxx. Felicity is watching you act like the ass. No wonder she doesn't want to go anywhere with you. You bring her shame. I can understand her desiring my protection from a father that is unstable and cannot control himself."

I shot Felicity a frightened look as I whimpered out, "Nein, I am not unstable, Felicity. Please come with me and I show you I can care for you properly. Don't ask to stay here with this man. Don't you remember what he did? You were there, my heart. He couldn't even protect you from that monster Kilian when he threw you into that bucket of chemicals. Byron sure as hell cannot look after you now. He is the pervert."

Byron reared his arm back to backhand me but held it midair while I cowered and braced for the blow. "Dammit Maxx. You bring up things you swore that we would leave in the past. I almost forgot that I am the changed man and struck you for it. However, you see I am in control of myself unlike you. I won't hit you for betraying your swearing to me, but I do think at this point your word is not good enough to trust anything you promise. I want you to sign the contract stating all we agree between us this afternoon. I want it in blood too. I was willing to accept your word only as the honorable man, but you insist on being the lying snake at every turn. I have done nothing to you since we came to the understanding of friendship to

20

earn that insult of being called a pervert. You on the other hand, intend to leave this apartment to service the sexual needs of that revolting Lucus, work as the whore and do Gott knows what else. I did fuck you but only with permission and not half the men in this Haus like you do daily. You of all people have no right to be calling another what you really are."

I hear that loud and clear. I fell to my knees pushed there by the unbearable weight of his true words to me. I looked to the floor and shook my head trying to stop the uncontrollable urge to scream. I couldn't stand the chest wrenching pain within but somehow I had to convince Felicity that I was. Byron refused to let go of my arm as I knelt there taking deep breaths with my eyes closed.

He whispered out calmly. "There you go Maxx. In through the nose, hold, then out through the mouth. Calm that fit for your buddy Byron. You are in the safe place for the moment. This attitude you take is irrational and hurtful to those that love you. It is time to get ahold of your inner demons and make them work for you, not against you."

I nodded. "I hear you Byron. I apologize for my offensive words and ugly acts. I will sign your contract with blood without quarrel. You are right. I am the perverted, not you. No one should trust the soulless whore called Mad Maxx. I don't deserve Felicity's love nor yours."

Byron blew out his breath. "Well, that is the truth of it today Maxx, but with my help we are going to change all that, ja?"

I winced as I finally accepted I was the worthless bastard that had everything bad coming and more. "If you say so Byron. I don't understand how you can make the silk purse from the sow's ear though. I am the little bitch and that is the way it is."

Byron demanded I look up at him. "You stop that negative thinking, Maxx I told you that already. I am going to help you find redemption and get you off your snake belly to stand on your feet like a man. All you have to do is listen to your Byron's voice. Despite your disgusting nature I still love you. I accept you as you are, and I see the true potential that lurks under the surface."

I stared at him in disbelief. "I don't understand you Byron. You know all my darkness and still find me someone you desire to aid? I would think you would be angered to realize that prize you thought you were getting was really nothing but trash. Instead, you stand here and say you see goodness in the gross thing kneeling before you? That simply makes no sense. Even Felicity finally realized she fooled by the worst of creeps."

Bryon smiled at me. "You are mistaken Maxx. Sure, I am a bit perturbed to find out I was in love with a fantasy, but I realize in time you could still obtain that lofty spot of perfection. Actually, I am most proud of you my boy. You have taken the first steps toward the cure for what ails your nasty little soul. You admit you are the twisted up foul creature. Now that you say it, see it, understand it, you have the power to rise up from it."

I scoffed. "I do? How is that? Quit the whoring and let Matz and the silvers suffer? Oh, maybe I tell that Vampire no more of his blood couples. That should go over like the lead balloon. I know, you want me to march down to the torture chamber and tell Peter I am through with his bullshit Dominating me, oh I mean, Dominance training sessions. Right after that I go back to Mad Lucus, cut off his gold collar and say, suck your own asshole, motherfucker. Then if I am lucky and can run really fast in my weakened state, I maybe will make it to see the front door. just before Gretta and others have me arrested and sent directly to the Palace where you, my friend, are banned from seeing me for life. Any of this sound like the plan to you?"

Bryon chuckled. "As I said earlier, you are a funny guy. Nein, you need not go that far to find yourself clean of the sin your currently wallow in. We are going to take this one small step at a time. If you do too much too fast, the ones that keep your demons well fed will notice the change. That will not be a good thing. They maybe will try to beat out of you the reasons for your suddenly being a decent human being. Then where will you be?"

I looked at the ground. "Alone in the Palace again without Felicity."

Byron snorted, "And?"

I sighed. "And without the wonderful advice of my friend Byron."

The Voter crossed his arms. "That is not what I wanted to hear, but it is a strong start I suppose. Okay it is nearly six Maxx. I am going to get the empty contract. We will write down our agreement, then you sign it in blood with me. After that I will tell you how to manage Lucus. He will be expecting you to fall for his attempts to raise you from the bottoming he and Gretta set up in the Palace."

I interrupted him with a startle, "What bottoming? Huh?"

Byron shook his head with an expression of irritation. "Those two idiots pushed you beyond your limits so they could brainwash you into do everything they tell you to do. You are no novice to that technique of the bottoming, Maxx. I shouldn't have to explain that process to you."

I nodded. "Ja, I know what the bottoming is, but what I don't understand is why would Gretta and Lucus try that shit on a Dominant? I broke my metal. I am not going to just fall back on my knees and call Lucus Master, uh oh."

Byron nodded with a sly smile. "Uh oh is right. Lucus and that bitch been working on you for months now boy. You had no idea? Really? I just assumed you were aware, but they managed to find your weak spot with that sport with the hounds. If they figured it was the way to break you by accident or design I cannot say."

I groaned with misery. "Oh, my Gott I am stupid. I didn't know that he was doing it, I swear it. How could I be such a moron. I have been through that shit before. I fell for it like the idiot child. Christ, I am not only the pervert, but I am also retarded too. Shoot me please." I covered the boy's eyes with my hands in honest embarrassment at my missing the obvious.

Byron patted me on the back appearing truly sympathetic to my feeling like a dummy. "Ah, don't be too hard on yourself, brother. That fucking Lucus is an intelligent foe. Anyone could have missed what he was really up to. I only know cause I overheard him bragging to Gretta of the conquest."

I gasped with shock. "He is really in with Gretta. You are not funning me? You heard him say this like you overhear what I spoke to that bitch about for truth?"

He smiled sheepishly as he nodded. "Ja, I confess I tend to listen to shit that really isn't my business. However, in this Haus one can never allow themselves to be out of the knowing. That is a dangerous place to be you know. Men end up dead that way."

I nodded back. "Ja makes sense when you put it like that. So, now what do I do that I know about his attempting to hijacking me? How can I stop him from finishing the job that he surely is almost completed. I seem to remember wanting to jump from the banister the last time I went through this with Peter. I almost fell for it that time, but I got sick. They put me in the dungeon and Peter's spell was broken. This time they will send me to hell in the dungeon. Plus, I have to go back to him or that Palace is my new home."

Byron headed for the bedroom door as he called back, "I have been trying to tell you Maxx I have a fail proof plan. We are going to make Lucus think he is doing a decent job, keep that pervert on a leash with his attempts to seduce you to feed his revolting desires, and while at it work on getting us both the fuck out of this nightmare place, ja?"

I watched him rush from the room completely fascinated by the ideas of all that he said could be possible. I must confess I didn't think I was enjoying that disgusting shit Peter, Jonas and Lucus forced on me, but other than that I thought Byron had valid points. I did need help thwarting Gretta and Lucus's trying to submit me to their will. I also wanted out of that Haus so bad I would have believed the lies spun by the Devil himself if he could assure me of that freedom ticket.

I maybe should have realized the tricks Byron was using on me to keep me confused, but honestly, I didn't. I was at the end of my rope and the man was saying everything I needed to hear. Felicity had for whatever reason decided the Voter was to be her champion and I trust her judgement. I may not have liked Byron yet. Okay, I hated him. I couldn't deny he had been nothing but the gentleman.

Truth was, he could have assaulted me and gotten away with it clean. I couldn't have been angry with him either. I told him I wouldn't quarrel about it, as long as he was quick and careful. I said that because I realized with all he was offering in service, I did owe him some in return. He gave me the sanctuary room, was offering to get me out of the Haus, and giving me good advice on ways to survive long enough to see our plan to escape happen. More than that, he was keeping my confidence about that horrible thing down below and his discovery of the prostitution business. Then there was Felicity. He had been there when I had failed her most miserably.

I was deep in thought about my poor opinion of my unexpected savior Byron when the brute came back into the room. He carried the paper contract and a shiny silver straight razor in a fancy case. Byron sat that razor in front of me still kneeling by the bed as he took a seat in the chair. He began to feverishly write out the contract between us appearing quite distracted by the details of it.

I kept my silence as I listened to him speak aloud to no one while listing the things he wanted to include, you know. I didn't dare to interrupt him during such an important task. I stole a look at the clock to see my time of freedom from Mad Lucus was nearly up. The idea of returning to him immediately made me desire to jump again.

For a moment the fatigue of living washed over me, but I forced myself to stay calm with that deep breathing like Byron told me to do. Now that I understood this bullshit suicidal stuff was what Lucus and Gretta wanted, I was strong enough to fight back the urge to do it. I was going to be damned if I would let them break me so bad I would be easy prey for their cruel brainwashing.

I looked to the floor trying to collect myself to a state of calm. A sudden flash caught my attention. It came from the razor case laying in front of me. I peered into the box with curiosity. The thing seemed to emit a beautiful but unearthly glow. A quick visual examination revealed this shaving blade's handle was encrusted with glimmering diamonds. The stones looked a lot like my China Geraldine's eyes.

I was completely captivated by the glimmer of the blade and those jewels. Before I could think better of it I reached into the case and ran the boy's fingers over that beautiful hygiene tool.

Byron looked up from his work and saw that I was fully enamored with his razor. "Ah, you like that do you? Well, you certainly have great taste. Go ahead Maxx. Take it out of the box and get a better look at it."

I gasped as I withdrew my hand with an expression of shameful embarrassment. You are not supposed to touch another's tools for their personal grooming, you know. "I apologize brother. I have no excuse for such bad manners. I was trained to know better." I dropped my gaze to the floor.

Byron scoffed. "Normally I would have to agree you behave as the rude bastard but not this time. I bring that razor for the blood contract and as a gift to you Maxx. You

28

can touch your things in your own room all you want. Tell me, do you like it? I had it made just for you."

I narrowed my eyes as I flashed a confused glance at that razor. "Huh? Why would you have a custom made razor created for me? That is fucking weird don't you think."

Byron got up and approached me with a grin on his face. "Nein it is not the least bit strange. I saw you're growing the beard down in the Palace when I visited you. I know that you normally wear no hair on your flesh other than that pretty head of yours. I thought maybe you would appreciate such a gift. However, I never got the chance to give it to you." He frowned as he knelt down and handed the contract to me.

I took it with a nod. "Oh, I see. Ja, that does make sense I suppose. It is a good thing you never brought this beautiful thing with you though. One of the Dungeon Masters would have taken it from me. Then likely stole it for their own."

Byron snorted. "Of that I have no doubt, now you read it. Make sure you agree this is what you want. If so, then I ask you to baptize that blade with your blood. Sign it and be quick about it. We still have to discuss how to keep that pervert Lucus from talking you into shit you need to stop doing with him."

I wanted to argue with him that I often was helplessly bonded while Lucus or any of the men raped me. That means I am not the willing. I said nothing about his error in

29

thinking I liked that shit though men pulled on me. It was just best to let it go.

I mean he was wrong to say that nasty shit, but he was right to say my time was short. Six o'clock was coming fast. I decided rather than wasting time with a needless argument I needed to get this man on the hook. I desired to make damned sure he was keeping his word of sneaking me out of the Haus. I knew it was in my best interest to get this over quickly before he changed his fucking mind, ja?" I scanned the page with rapidness, reached into the box and with speed cut my fingertip.

Byron watched me sign that contract and likely saw my hands trembled. It was not fear of him that caused it this time. I can honestly say I was excited. One of the things on that page that stood out loud and clear was the sentence: "Byron promises to bring Maximillian out of Der Kaiser Haus and aid him to function within the society outside her walls." I had waited all my young life to see those words on a legal contract. I admit I was thrilled to have the dream of freedom within my grasp at last.

The Voter took the razor from me and cut his own finger. He signed below my own name, the one on the guardianship papers, Maximillian Weiss. I let out the breath of relief the second I saw this bond was completed. I wasn't sure how the fuck we could dare to file it with the Hall of Records.

Byron heard my sound and shot me an adoring smile. "There it is. We are the legal partners for truth Maxx. What a beautiful day ja? Well, I would love to take you down to the Great Hall to celebrate our new association of true brotherhood, but I do believe you have a prior date ahead of me. The party will have to wait till another day. Here take this gift blade I give you and cut yourself in all your intimate spots. Only the shallow slices not so bad you need stitches. But make sure to do it deep enough that it is likely to leave scars if not allowed to heal to completeness." He pushed the blade at me.

I stared at him unsure if I was hallucinating what he had just said. "Uhm, Byron forgive me for saying this, but I thought I heard you say I am to cut up my personal areas of flesh. I think I misunderstood your instruction. Can you repeat your advice on this preventing Lucus from the raping shit? I thank you for the mercy of it." I thought for sure this would clear up that most disturbing interference from that fucking DJ. Sometimes he says things to me in another's voice you know that bastard.

Byron pushed that razor at me with stern vigor. "Nein. You didn't mishear me Maxx. It is known to me that Lucus hates the beautiful scars on your flesh brother. He will do anything to avoid you collecting any more than you already sport. You are covered from head to toe in these gorgeous signs of your many battles to survive. I notice there are two places that so far are nearly free of them. That beautiful backside of yours and that amazing cock. You cut them up like I tell you and Lucus will avoid the intercourse for fear of causing those wounds to open further. He won't molest your manhood for that same reason. It won't prevent the demand for oral services or a hand job but hell, those are

31

nothing. He won't get what he really wants which is to be inside you or force your orgasms. Stop wasting time and get to it. You have to trust me Maxx, this plan will work. You'll see."

I stared at his outstretched hand eyes wide in terror. "You have got to be joking. I am not cutting up my ass and cock like the dinner goose just to keep Lucus from fucking me or fondling my parts. Christ Byron, I have enough Gott damned scars as it is. This is the most insane shit anyone has ever said to me and that is really saying something brother given my history."

Byron's expression grew dark. "You listen here Maxx. I just signed a fucking contract with you that said you would trust my judgement. I do believe I said I don't want to argue with you over everything I need you to do to see this plan of ours goes smoothly. If I tell you to cut your fucking hodensack off you should do it without quarrel or hesitation." He grabbed my arm and forced the blade into my hand.

I felt the sweat breaking out on my brow. "Uhm, okay. Byron I say to you this is the one thing I cannot do even for the chance of freedom. I uhm, am afraid of the cutting. It is a phobia."

Byron sat there staring at me in disbelief. "Now I am going to ask you if this is your idea of a joke. Look at you Maxx. You have thousands of scars from far worse cuts then I ask you to do this moment. How the fuck can you be fearful of such an action."

I shook my head and shivered. "It is because I have so many I am afraid. Please don't ask me to do this brother. I am already disfigured to disgusting. I will have a hell of a time finding the Frau that can overlook this ugly man as it is. The lack of scars on the parts that matter for making the children is really all I have left going for me. I cannot chance fucking that flesh up as bad as the rest. Even if I could find the bravery to bare the blade with my own hand, what if I cut too deep. Then more scars forever." I dropped the razor on the carpet and covered my face with the boy's hands feeling I may come unglued yet again. I had never told anyone that sorry truth before and I was not feeling real good about blurting it at that moment either.

Byron's face took on the expression of pity as he reached out and picked the razor up. "Alright, I understand Maxx. I didn't realize that you view those beautiful badges of courage with such disgust. I personally find scars very sexy, and many other people do as well. Of course, we are not the ones that must wear them all our lives, ja? Tell you what if you cannot do it you don't have to."

I uncovered my face. "You mean that? You have another way to keep that pervert at bay then?"

He shook his head and blew out his breath in frustration. "Nein, I do not. I guess you are stuck with the non-stop pincushion intercourse in that very sore spot that truly needs the time to heal. Oh well, that is too bad. I know this idea would have worked but hey, if you cannot do it, you just can't. I respect that." He started to get up to leave with that razor still in his hand.

I gasped and moved forward. "Nein, wait. I do need a break from the penetration sex Byron. Real bad. I also don't want that nasty creature jerking on me or forcing the enema. Are you certain this plan of the cutting would work?"

He smiled brightly. "Ja, I am real sure. Lucus is the prissy bastard. He doesn't appreciate the work of art that you wear on your skin like I do. If you were cut up pretty good he would refrain till you healed, maybe it would take a week or more even."

I sighed. "He would want to know how it happened. If he thought I self-mutilated he maybe will punish me severely for it. That could be worse than enduring his perverted lusting."

Byron nodded. "I thought of that already. Everyone in the Haus knows of your all night torturing of though idiots that hurt you down below. Tell him that you went to confront the bastards, but they got the drop on you. They tortured you sexually, but Almut, Hubertus and Cary showed up and rescued you. That incited your most justified cruelty that all were the witness to."

I looked up at him in surprise. "Ah, that lie may actually work. It would also cover the real reason I was so violent, if he doesn't already know the truth of it." I felt my ears burning with the shame again.

Byron chuckled as he tried once more to hand me the razor. "Nein, he doesn't know trust me. If he did you would already be without that ugly gold around your neck brother.

I told you that pervert is the smug priss. He may be into the edge play and turned on by the foulest of the natural processes. Yuck, by the way. I never would have thought that of him. Never mind that, but he would never get over what the Haus views as one of the only three forbidden acts of this Gott forsaken place."

I groaned. "Ja, I know you are right in what you say but I tell you once more I cannot cut myself as you ask me to Byron. Just because I say your plan is valid, doesn't mean I can ignore my phobia for it."

Byron frowned and stared at the razor. "Oh, I see. Well, I guess I will let you have a little peaceful time with Felicity before you go back to endure what you must. Maybe Lucus will let you out of that bondage bed long enough another day soon. I see you then, ja?" He nodded and began to head to the door.

I closed my eyes and trembled as I called out to him "Wait Byron. I tell you I cannot do what must be done, but maybe you could help me with it?"

Byron stopped and shot a confused look at me, fake I am sure. "What do you mean, Maxx? You know I am happy to do whatever you need to find comfort. Yet, I am not sure what exactly you are meaning at this moment. I offer you the tool for the deed. What more can I do to see you free of that horrible man's lust?"

I whispered with my eyes tightly closed in terror. "You could do the cutting that I cannot. Please I beg your mercy Byron. I am too weak to do it myself."

He walked back to where I knelt and leaned down close. "I didn't hear you Maxx. What is it you say to me?"

I took a deep breath and braced for the words I never thought I would ever say. "Please cut me up Byron. Make sure Lucus doesn't desire to lay with me for at least a week. I beg of you to do this."

The Voter tapped on my forehead till I opened my eyes to look at him. "Listen here Maxx I will do this, but only if you are sure this is what you want. I don't wish to have you accusing me of assaulting you tomorrow or another day after the deed is done. I must say in order to do this thing I will need your permission to touch you. I cannot very well cut your intimate parts with careful skill unless I do. Are you willing to release me from that promise to keeping my hands off? Or do you wish to risk I make the serious mistake with the blade?"

I felt my stomach rolling with disgust. "I won't be angered tomorrow for your doing what I ask of you today. I recant my order that you not touch me anywhere. Please hurry this up before I lose my nerve Byron. I am really afraid of that straight razor."

Byron opened the blade to fullness as he nodded. "This is the instrument that made all those other, ja" I nodded as I kept a baleful eye on that weapon in his hand.

He scoffed. "Figures. I should have realized it was the handy straight razor that did all that by the patterns and shapes of the artist's skill on your flesh. Okay, I need you to take off your breeches and do everything I tell you. I will treat the wounds the moment I am finished with putting my marks on your fresh skin. Until then I ask you not to flinch if you can help it. You can, however, yell or wail all you like. No one can hear you in here. Don't be ashamed to cry too if that will get you through the pain of it. I want to hear you say once more where I can hear it this is what you want me to do. Give me your permission to touch and cut you up Maxx. Otherwise forget this. I only do this cause you ask me to."

I whimpered and trembled as I began to unbutton my breeches to remove them. "I am begging you to cut me up Byron. I ask you to touch me in the places only the lover should behold. I thank you for your mercy. This that I say is good enough to satisfy you that I am the willing participant, ja?"

He nodded with a smile. "Ja, which is what I needed to hear and you too. Now let's do this shall we?"

For the next several minutes I endured his cruel stoke with that blade. I confess I did flinch, wail and weep a great deal. The flashback from that day in the barn with Gerard plagued me through the whole ordeal. Byron had to hold me still with force several times to keep me from trying to flee.

I begged him to stop right after he laid his first mark on my sensitive parts. He refused to stop. He told me that I didn't mean what I was saying that it was the phobia speak not Maxx. Byron kept on cutting into the last few square inches of my unmarred flesh. I could see the expression on his face showed he was enjoying his task a great deal and my terror of it even more.

Deep inside, I knew this man had tricked me into granting him the permission to put his personal marks on me. It was always his plan to coax me into begging him to do this backdoor act of claiming me for his own. You see this brutality he did was not really much different than the brands Malfred, Peter, Jonas and Claus already burned into the boys flesh.

Byron didn't use the light superficial cuts but as you can clearly see My Liebe he slashed me with abandon. I carry the scars of that stupid mistake to this very day. It is truly a humiliation that I didn't learn the lesson from that horrific scene. Byron was not interested in becoming my buddy, my heart. He was intending to become my new Master. I say with great sadness, despite his cruelty with that blade, I was fated to fall under his spell.

Jou see, the man had had only just begun his reign of terror on this idiot Mann of yours. The truthful nightmare of this story is so shameful, I almost find it hard to confess it to you even now. Ugg, well like it or not, I am going to be honest about this Byron business once and for all. I refuse to keeping the secret any longer. After all, it is through secrets predators like that motherfucker keep their victims held as the prisoner. I am finally ready to be set free of the chains that held me his hostage within my head.

I nodded with a sigh. "I understand, Master. That happened to me with that Chenoweth guy. That didn't turn out too good either."

Master Maxx chuckled. "For you or Chenoweth, Meine Liebe? I seem to recall that nasty bastard found himself hanging by the sharp end of a knife, oh wait, I meant rope, ja?" He kissed my head.

I groaned. "Gosh Master I put up with a lot of nasty men with their stinky boy parts every day, but no one says anything. Then one of them gets himself stabbed to death and I never stop hearing his name brought up."

Master Maxx laughed even harder. "Stabbed? Wait I thought you said he hung himself as a suicide, Meine Liebe?"

I gasped and sat up straight in his lap. "Oh, I meant one guy hangs himself and..."

He interrupted me. "Let it go Meine Liebe. Whatever happened to that motherfucker was too good for him. You don't seriously think me the Mad Maxx would judge you for that messy business after all I have already told you I have done myself? There are few on this Earth this pervert can point a finger at and call worse than me. In fact, if the truth of it be told, I deserve to be hanging from your knife too for the things I have done and will do to you."

I turned around in shock to stare at my Master and Husband. "How can you say that, Master? You are not like

Chenoweth and the other mean people around here. Not to me anyway."

Master Maxx picked up his cane then pointed to my many stripes that he left on my thighs from it. "Oh? I am not like the others you say. Well, I can safely say one thing about Byron. He sure taught me how to be the perfect sexual predator. I hear my victim saying to me that I am different when I believe I do far worse to her than many of the men her mother sells her to. I am not the proud man for what I have done to you, my heart. I feel the shame of it to my black soul but that doesn't make me do the right ding. If I were half the man you truly deserved I would get up this minute, call the law and throw myself off that fourth floor banister with speed. I tell you that I used the same techniques that Byron did on me, and even with that evidence written on your flesh you defend me. Amazing!"

I glared at him angrily. "You are wrong, Master. You are not like Chenoweth or Byron or any of them. You want to save me. I love you and you love me. The other bad men don't feel guilty for what they do or do no say sorry for it either."

He sighed deeply. "You are a wonderful heart Meine Liebe, but you are misguided and under my spell. It makes me even more shamed to be the pervert I honestly am. You see, I believed that I loved Byron, and he loved me too in time. That is how this works. The victim falls for the offender and once seduced the predator can do whatever they want without quarrel from their prey. I will go on with

40

this story and see if you don't recognize the things Byron did to get his hooks into my soul."

I frowned as I snuggled back into his lap comfortably. "I will listen to what you have to say Master, but it won't change anything. I know you love me, and I really love you. Byron didn't marry you and he didn't help you escape like he promised either or you wouldn't be here with me now."

Master Maxx scoffed. "How do you know he isn't the one behind my being here with you tonight, Meine Liebe? He was a secret I never told a soul. You are the first to hear the truth of it. Not even your Master Peter or Leo know of these things I am going to tell you. Maybe he still is in my life, controlling my every move. Don't you fear that is what I will tell you?"

I shook my head. "Nope. I know he is gone, or you wouldn't be telling me about him, Master. Besides, the predators don't let you get married or have a life. They want to keep you locked up forever in the basement where no one else can save you. Byron didn't help you get away. He probably tried to put you in a different prison than the Haus."

Master Maxx squeezed me tightly. "Damn you are a smart little thing. Where the hell have you been all my life? I sure as hell could have used your unearthly skills at seeing the truth of things many times in my fucked up past. It would have saved me a lot of pain."

I snorted and laughed. "I was right here waiting for you to find me, Master. Debbie made sure I never went

41

anywhere else. She is like Byron not you. You are going to help me get out of here and you are coming with me. That is just the way it is going to be."

He ruffled my hair playfully. "Spoken like the true Mistress of the Haus. You are not even the woman yet and already the Queen of my heart. Okay, where were we? Oh ja, that awful cutting up of my manhood. Yikes!" I shot a quick look at his boy part and winced with a shudder at the sheer number of scars. Byron really was a dirty motherfucker for doing that among other things, just for the record.

I endured Byron's harsh sexual torture that he had convinced me was to prevent a worse sexual torture. What a dumbass I am, damn. When he finished I was a weeping, bloody mess. He got the alcohol to treat the wounds. The man got a second helping of wailing, kicking and crying out of me as he lit me up in places the sun don't shine with that unforgiven antiseptic. Fucking ouch.

Byron helped me get my breeches back on, though to be honest I would have rather gone without them thanks to the horrendous pain the rubbing material caused me. He allowed me a few moments to beg Felicity to forgive me for my transgression against her, then he aided me to his front door. I could barely walk at this point.

He stood there appearing sheepish as I braced myself for the short walk downstairs. I wasn't sure what was worse. The movement required to get to the fourth floor apartment or having to submit myself back into Mad

Lucus's control. Byron saw my hesitation and reached out to stroke my cheek.

I flinched at his touching me like the lover. "Stop that, Byron. I only give the permission to touching me for that horror cutting business. I didn't say you can keep on rubbing me anytime you please."

Byron pulled his hand back as if I bit him. "Oh, I apologize Maxx. I forgot myself for a moment there. It won't happen again. I was merely grief stricken that you are not going to be here to speak with or hang out is all. I was overcome with pity for your rough situation."

I groaned. "Made rougher still by that razor you held Byron. You act like I am never coming back fool. You know I will have to. Felicity lives here. I don't know how I am going to continue without my lamb with me. I will be back the second I can get away from Mad Lucus. I want to try to get her to relent her refusal to come home and live with me."

Byron frowned. "If only I were a fucking lamb. Ja, okay I hear you. I am sure if you keep at it Felicity will get over her anger. You have the key. Remember you are welcome to come here anytime day or night. I want to say that it would make me feel better if you could understand that Felicity is already home. You are the one that is lost to us. Well, never mind. Soon you we will all be one big happy family under the same roof."

I glared at him with irritation, mostly because my parts were burning like fire. "We are already under the same roof

Byron. It is the address I hope to be changing with swiftness."

He laughed as he opened the door and looked out to make sure no one saw me leaving his Haus. "You are really a comic. I love that about you. Okay coast is clear. Remember what I told you. Pretend you are despondent, lost and follow Lucus around like the baby chick. He has to believe your falling for his grooming, or he will send you back below to bottom you out again." I walked past him slowly headed for the stairs.

Byron reached out and swatted my slashed backside with force. I let out wail of agony as he laughed with great humor at his sadistic act.

I turned around my face red with anger as the sweat poured down the sides of my head. That really fucking hurt. "You motherfucker. I told you to keep your hands off me. What the hell is wrong with you, fucking pervert. Do you get your rocks off by torturing the tortured? Huh? Speak up, you asshole." I noticed that Byron was grinning with an evil expression on his face, but he wasn't focused on me.

I turned around with a startle when a voice said, "Hello there, Mad Maxx. Fancy meeting you here. You are just the young man we have been seeking all afternoon. If Byron is finished with his sport with you, I would request you come with us. We would like to have a visit of our own."

I let out a wail of horror as I found myself face to face with Kilian and his brother Reece. With Byron at my back and Mad Lucus just one floor down waiting for me to return to him or make sure I got a one way trip back to the Palace, I really didn't have time for this shit nor was I in any condition to fight off any of the growing number of bastards looking to take more chunks out of my ass.

Chapter 48: King of Perverts

I backed up in terror right into the waiting arms of Byron standing behind me. He immediately wrapped his huge arms around my waist. I gasped as he tightened them holding me to the spot. I had no choice but to face the deadly duo team of the Elder Kilian and his sadistic, psychiatrist brother Reece.

Kilian grinned with evil as he watched the brute Voter take possession of their quarry. "Well, thank you, Byron. You have always been my best buddy. I swear to you I will see you are well rewarded for keeping Maxx here still for our visit with him."

Byron chuckled with a diabolical tone. "No problem brother. You say what you need, and I can assure you Maxx is all ears. Aren't you boy?" He jerked me hard demanding I answer him.

I nodded with a shudder. "Sure, Honored Elder Kilian. I am listening. I beg you be quick with the discussion though. I need to be somewhere shortly."

Reece came forward slightly with a mild look of irritation breaking out in his expression. "Too bad for you, little cunt. You aren't going anywhere for a bit. Your date will have to wait. I am sure he will understand. If he doesn't, not our problem anyway now is it?"

I gulped down the dryness in my throat. "I am unsure what I can do for you fellows that would require more than a few moments of time. As you see I am unwell. If you are seeking your thrills, I would ask you to give me a couple days for the healing then maybe we can work something out?" I trembled feeling my bladder was going to let go when I heard myself say those words of fear. I was hoping to buy a bit of time for that contract with Gretta to go into effect you know.

Kilian sneered. "A couple day you say. Seems you were well enough to see to our brother's wanton needs. I know Byron. If you are leaving his bed, you cannot be too fucking ill. He is the beast in the lustful arts. You forget I was there in that closet not so long ago boy."

Byron chuckled and nodded as I whispered out. "Ja, which is true. That is why I am too worn to attend to you guys at the moment. Byron sees that I am the wrecked man. Please, I ask of you to let me be for a bit." I lied about being the spent lover of Byron but shit like these bastards would never buy the truth of it anyway, ja?

Reece frowned. "I have had enough of this banter, Kilian. Take the boy and let's go. I am aching to try out this new drug that I just got my hands on plus that contract isn't going to cancel out itself. If anyone hears of it, there is going to be trouble and you know it. Byron, again, thanks for the help. We will be taken the boy from here."

I whimpered in fear as I realized Gretta had contacted the brutes and told them of my demands. It was becoming obvious that bitch did file it. Instead of seeing to the details with rapidness, she sent her goons to beat a recanting of it out of me. I couldn't believe my bad luck. I had fooled around with their childhood buddy Byron long enough to be caught off guard and without a fucking weapon or chance to survive. I knew I was beyond screwed. These boys were not going to stop their brutality on me wherever they were takin me until I relented my demands to see them punished for this very same shit day were pulling.

Byron sighed loudly and tightened his hold a bit more, causing me to gasp for air. "Gosh Reece, I don't know if I can let you have Maxx. I kind of wasn't done with him. I don't know what it is about the boy, but I feel like the helpless man every time he flashes those baby blues of his at me. I know I am not the kind to let my head get away with me, but Maxx here is so damned insistent. He is so bad for me, being the pervert that he is, but I think maybe I have fallen for his bad boy charms. My mother warned me not to fool with his type, but I didn't listen to her wise advice. Yet here I am. A slave to his wicked seduction and cruel love."

Kilian shot a look of confusion at Reece then said, "Huh? You are speaking like a psychotic, Byron. That boy you hold is an idiot. He couldn't enslave the heart of a fucking corpse. You feeling okay brother? Do you have a fever or something?" He looked him over with concerned curiosity.

Byron shuddered and then kissed me in the ear which made me want to gag but I dared not piss him off for fear he'd hand me over. "Tell them Maxx how you will not take nein for an answer from your target Byron. Go ahead, no

48

need to keep secrets from my oldest friends on Earth. I don't want them thinking I engage with the perversion you are of my own free will. I beg you for mercy to clear my good name of such a horrible dishonor." He whispered into my ear.

In the past I wanted to argue that this shit he said was the other way around, but he tightened his grip menacingly. "Byron says the truth of things. I make him my bitch and he loves it. He runs but I hunt him down and take what I want from him. There is nothing he can do. I am the Master of this Haus. I take what is mine without excuse nor boundaries." I couldn't fucking believe I just said that lying shit to these fiends.

Byron nodded with his head still on my shoulder. "You hear that shit? The boy is a fucking monster. I beg of you brothers, help me. If I hand him over to you do you promise me you will end my torment by taking his life. That is the only way I can ever be free of his spell." I almost broke out in tears thinking this was some weird mind game the three played to justify murdering me.

Kilian smiled with thrill as did Reece. "You know we cannot do that, brother. We can, however, beat him to an inch of his life for you. Killing the King is illegal, and death follows swiftly on its tail. You hand him here and we will make damned sure he never bothers you again. Hard for him to assault you from the Palace cell, ja?"

Byron sniffed loudly as if about to cry. "Oh, you intend to fuck him up to near death then see him locked

49

back below. That is good to know. I worried you merely were here for a bit of 'catch and release' sport with him. This changes everything." I felt his grip start to loosen and I began to panic that he was giving me over to the brutes.

I wailed, "Nein, Byron, nein. Don't let them take me. I want to say here with you. Please, you have to do what I say. I seduced you, remember. You are my love slave." Byron let go enough for me to turn in his grip and embrace him in a death grip of terror. Yikes, that shit I was doing sure looked and sounded real bad, you know.

Byron appeared shocked by my hugging him like that. "Whoa, let me go Maxx. I cannot do this anymore. This love affair is sick and twisted. I cannot bear it if you keep on this cruelty. I must be free of your entrapment anyway possible. You are the heartless bastard. I know you don't love me for real. You merely tease and torture me at every turn. Go with Kilian and Reece and haunt me no more, damn you."

I gripped him with vigor and wailed even louder. "Nein, I am not heartless. I do love you, Byron. Whoever told you different is the fucking liar. I never teased you, I swear it. Please tell them you love me too. That you won't let them take your lover away. If I go below we will never see each other again. Think on that." I buried my face into his huge chest like the whiney bitch I had become.

Byron grabbed me by the upper arms prying my desperate flesh from him. "Stop this Maxx. You are not going to fool me anymore. Only a moment ago you told me to never touch you again. Now you present we are the lovers for truth. Bullshit. You say you hate me, and we are not even friends. Gott damn you are the moody sonofabitch."

I shook my head eyeing him with pure fear running through my veins. "I was a tease, I confess it. I shouldn't have played the head games with you Byron. You have the right to be angry with me over it. I take all that I said back. You can touching me anytime you like anywhere you like. I don't hate you. I love you and we are true friends for all time. I beg your forgiveness for being the moody bastard. It won't happen anymore. I learned my lesson. Please take me back inside your Haus. I show you this minute I have changed my ways." I forced a passionate kiss on his mouth. Well, let's say a terror driven kiss that appeared eager. Ja, eager to get the fuck out of there.

Byron at first appeared to fight my attempt to woe him to save me, but quickly gave in. He began kissing me back. He wrapped his arms back around me and the two of us stood their engaged in what appeared to be the heated lovers embrace. It only then occurred to me that in all the time I had endured this brute's lustful actions we had never kissed. Byron was definitely eager to savor this little victory while he could boast of it.

That terrible tongue bathing may have continued on forever if it had not been for Kilian clearing his throat loudly. "Christ Byron, are you stupid? I don't believe this insanity. You allow this little nothing to lead you by the hodensack. Holly hell, man. You are not kidding that you have lost your head. Give the boy over for your own good, brother. You deserve better than this trash you are fawning over. Damn, and I merely thought you were getting the free sport. I had no idea this devil had managed to mislead you so badly. Come on Maxx. Byron, I mean it. Hand him over, dammit." He taped on my back with harshness.

Byron pulled out of my feigned adoration of him appearing red faced and sweaty with thrill. "You mean what you say, Maxx? Really mean it. Swear it to me and see that I'm ready to prove my worthiness as your helpless lover."

I panted in pure fright. "Ja, I swear all that I say to you, Byron. You help me escape these bastards, then we can be lovers for truth." Hell, I would have promised to put out my eyes with red hot pokers if it would have saved me from the Altergotts and the second stint in that Mortar Palace.

Byron smiled with the moon in his eyes at me. "If that is what you want Maxx. I can deny you nothing lover." I wailed in shock as he tossed me with force to the wall behind him.

I collided with it as I had earlier below. Thanks to my weakened state I crumpled to floor unable to get up. I thought for sure I was finished, and that Byron had betrayed me. I assumed he stunned me to make it easier for the three of them to haul me off for their foul designs. Luckily, and unluckily, I was way off base on this action this time.

I watched in disbelief as Byron tackled Reece like a bull that saw the red flag of the matador. Reece led out a yell and stagged back unable to tolerate the force of his blow. The two flew backwards toward the banister railing.

Kilian didn't expect that attack from his old buddy any more than me or Reece did. He backed away blinded by shock. He tripped over his boots and fell to his ass just as the two brutes speed past him. He sat their appearing too confused to figure out what else to do.

Meanwhile, Byron had managed to back Reece into the railing. He grabbed the psychiatrist around the throat and began to throttle the man. Reece grabbed Byron's huge arms, but it was useless. Reece was no match for the bodybuilding Voter in his prime shape. I watched in a fascinated trance along with the stunned Kilian as Reece's face turned blue.

I thought for sure Byron was going to either snap his neck or strangle him to death. Apparently so did Kilian. He tried to get to his feet while yelling out pleas for Byron to let Reece go. Byron seemed to listen to the snake. The brute released Reece's throat. He grabbed the swooning mental doctor around the chest, just under his arms, as if holding him up from the faint that seemed to be overcoming the man.

Then in an action I won't forget till the day I die, Byron turned and flashed me an evil grin. He looked back to Reece and in a single, smooth, rapid movement let him go just as he pushed the psychiatrist backward with force.

Reece opened his mouth and emitted a blood curdling scream, but then disappeared from sight. Gravity is the unforgiving bitch, and that snake didn't have wings. He fell over the side and fell to the first floor from that fifth floor railing. Buh-bye Reece Altergott.

I let out a gasp as I whispered. "Holy hell. You killed Reece, Byron." I shot a look of shock at Kilian that had found his feet but was frozen to the spot in a full stun. He didn't seem to believe what he just saw any more than I did.

Byron turned around and smiled at me with adoration. "I did it for you, my love. I told you I can deny you nothing. I am your helpless slave. I am deep under your spell. I sell my soul to the darkness, even kill one of my oldest and best friends all because you command me to. I ask you now, what of Kilian? Do you desire I send him after his brother?"

Kilian let out a sudden wail of grief and fell to his knees. "Reece! Oh, my Gott. My brother. Please let this be a fucking dream. I want to wake up. Nein, not Reece. Reece, speak to me. You cannot be dead." He began to blubbering like a lost soul. It was sort of pathetic and sad too. I admit for a moment I almost felt sorry for him, almost.

I braced on the wall getting to my feet and led out a groan of agony. That Byron's slashing did a number on me, ja? "Nein Byron. I desire only to see my contract with the Silk Queen fulfilled. Reece got the mercy compared to what I had in mind. Kilian though, he started this shit with me. I say take him to the Mortar Palace. I give you the Key. Lock him up, chain him down as I was. Then seek out that contract filed in the Hall of Records I made with Gretta. I ask that the Dungeon Masters follow their King's orders to the letter. This snake has earned nothing more and nothing less." I reached into my breeches and took out the key to the Mortar Palace.

Byron grinned as he took it from my outstretched hand. "As you wish Maxx. I think you better be getting downstairs to that rat bastard Lucus. Otherwise, he will punish you for arriving late despite his commands. Do remember what we discussed. I see you soon, lover." He reached out and caressed my cheek for a second.

Byron sighed as he tore himself away from his most inappropriate attention to me. I watched him haul ass to subdue the grieving Elder still on his knees staring over the railing at the corpse of his dead brother below. The snake gave him no quarrel, which surprised me, as Byron grabbed him by the upper arms pulling them behind his back. The brute forced Kilian to his feet. Then he pushed him along in front of him headed down the stairs to the Palace below.

I could hardly believe my eyes. Only fifteen minutes or less had passed. In that time, one of my mortal enemies found his grave and the other found himself my prisoner. All this was thanks to my saying a few lies to the love-struck Byron. The world felt like it was spinning far too fast for me to gain my location on it. I was sure I was going to be lost soon if I couldn't get the insanity around me to stop.

I began to head for the stairs to turn myself over to Mad Lucus when a female voice halted my feet. "What the fuck is all this racket? Why the hell are you here, Maxx? Aren't you supposed to be with Lucus? Am I to assume you are ignoring the orders of your Gold contract with him? I am glad to hear of it actually. I can now have a valid excuse to send you back to your Palace where you fucking belong."

I turned around with fury building in my chest. "Hello Gretta, just the bitch I was hoping to visit with. Well, that racket you heard was merely the sound of our contract being sealed. I must tell you that it was not as we agreed but the deed is done, nonetheless. Reece has paid for his crimes against me and all the mentally ill he harmed. That snake Voter that was the Elder is on his way as we speak to pay his debt as well. I wonder though, are you packing? I certainly hope you are. Otherwise, maybe Kilian won't mind the roommate other than the moody Florian. Humm?"

Gretta glared at me trying to appear the stoic though I saw the fear in her eyes. "You speak nonsense as usual Maxx. Nothing you say ever is to be taken with seriousness. I just saw Kilian and Reece. They were on their way to the gym."

I laughed at that. "Well, I can say that Reece did make it to the first floor with speed, but he no longer requires the fine build. Kilian is left behind and you can be assured he will be attempting to lift the weights shortly. If you don't believe me, take a peep over that banister. Go ahead, I will wait for you to see even the psychotic can tell the reality from fake every once in a while. I ask you again, are you packing my beauty? I do believe moving day is here. It is not in your best interest to making me inquire of your eviction notice a third time. I am not the merciful man."

Gretta narrowed her eyes but went to the banister. She looked down. I heard her gasp as she grabbed her bosom in shock. I limped over and took a spot next to her. I glanced over the edge too. Reece was there at the bottom alright. He had not faired any better than Barnum had so long before when Bladrick pushed him over. The psychiatrist was unrecognizable and laying in a widening pool of blood. The residents below surrounded him, and a few looked up.

I heard one of the black collars shout, "It is the Mortar King that did this. Mad Maxx die Brutale has passed a death sentence on another Dominant. Woe be it to any high or low that offend the Master of this Haus." The whole lot of onlookers gazed up then all fell to a kneel.

I chuckled full of demons. "You see that my love? The residents recognize the will of their Master. I wonder why my future Frau doesn't mind as well as her fucking hound Henner? Humm? Well, no worries my heart. Soon enough I will be using you for my base urges. Once I drill my desires into you a few times, I am sure you will train up real nice. Ja? I hope you are ready to endure my most perverted and dark desires. I have had many, many years to dream of the horrible, oops I mean, sexual things I plan to do to you. I swear to all the is holy when I am done with you, you will never need a mirror again. You won't be able to stand the reflection that looks back with her accusing eyes. I will show you the true definition of dishonor. You made sure I have been completely infected with perversion, and I can barely wait to pass on my disease to the right woman." I reached out and put my arm around her shoulders.

She shuddered and shook me off her. "Keep your fucking disgusting hands off me, Maxx. The day you and I are the lovers is the day this Haus falls though the earth right to hell."

I nodded with a gleam in my eyes. "You are indeed the eager bride. I worried you would need a little breaking in, but you seem to have the moves and words that turn me on down to an art. Tell you what though, I will offer you a bit of advice. Try to sound more convincing when you demand I let you go, stop touching you or get my cock out of you. Tears of pain and humiliation also go a long way with pleasing your Maxx. Why don't you follow me around for a bit, and I will give you a visual lessons in suffering. That way when my turn comes to return the service to you, you'll at least know why, oh I mean, how to behave or should I say struggle for your dignity."

Gretta backed away with terror in her expression. "You really are mad. Or perhaps you speak to the wrong people if you think the brutality you have endured had anything to do with me."

I chuckled with cruel delight at her fear. "There you go sweetheart. Tell yourself the lies. If you are lucky one day maybe you will even believe them. See, you are a natural at the ways to please this man of yours. Soon Gretta, my love, I am going to give you a private demonstration of why you all realized you made the mistake leveling me the Priceless. I am the thing that hides under your bed. I live in the darkest places of your mind. When you hear me yell in perverted thrill that means I am coming for you. I really mean it." Gretta turned and ran away with speed observably trembling from my cryptic words.

I gasped, "But Master. You haven't killed Gretta, have you?"

He kissed my head gently. "I will kill the woman most brutally, my heart. The only reason she lives is because at this moment I need her to see your collar broken. Better the devil you know, or in this case the devil that owes you. One day, I will make all my promises to that bitch come to truth. She wasn't the truthful designer of my fall, but that bitch's greed robbed me of my dignity and left me open to attack from the jackals of the Haus. When I go to end her days, it will be slow, painful, and she will beg for death a thousand times before it finds her. Equal service for equal service, Meine Liebe. I want her to know what it is like to be helpless while others use you for their garbage can."

I nodded. "I don't blame you for doing it either Master, but can I ask one favor?"

He chuckled. "Sure you can, my heart. It will cost you dough. What are you offering in return for it?"

I turned and looked at him with curiosity. "Don't you want to hear what I am asking for first, Master?"

Master Maxx shook his head. "Nein. I want to know what you can give me that I don't already take at will. You wish for me to do something nasty no doubt, but you are too poor to pay me back for the cost of my soul, or am I wrong?"

I narrowed my eyes at him. "I will give you healthy children on my knees and love you for all of my life, Master. That is something you can't take from me against my will."

He flinched when I said that. "That is indeed a prize I am willing to bargain for. Name your price for such a wonderful service. You wish for me to murder Debbie and Russell no doubt?"

I shook my head with an evil little smile. "I am not supposed to tell you when you are wrong Master, but I will say this time you are. No, Debbie and Russell deserve to be punished, but death is too good for them. If I get the chance, I will do it, but only if I have to. I would rather find a way to make them suffer like they did to me. My favor is that you look the other way while I get rid of Master Peter."

Master Maxx nearly fell over when I said that. "Huh? You speak of killing my father again? What the hell Meine

Liebe. You think it is your right to kill your parents for the evil they do to you? Isn't it the same for me? Your Master Peter has done nothing to you. It is his own son, Christian Axel, that he has defiled."

I stared at him hard. "Okay, then why haven't you killed him yet Master?"

Master Maxx shrugged. "I need him to aid me in watching out for you, Meine Liebe. You know that I must return six months of the year. Plus, if Peter came up dead at this moment it would likely set off the suspiciousness. Then the Haus would maybe come after me and bring you to the Dungeons to finish the training. Even as the Master of the Haus it is forbidden to kill the Voters or Elders without good reason."

I snorted. "You mean Leo or Jakob or even Rolf couldn't do what Master Peter does? Well, as to Peter accidents happen. Cars run off the road, people fall downstairs, they hang themselves with knives."

My Master looked at the mattress with a sudden sad expression on his face. "I cannot kill Peter, Meine Liebe, because if he ends up dead and I am the suspect then Jonas can recollar me. I believe I told you that. I cannot kill the man or be accused of having anything to do with it. He assumed I would be seeking the revenge. That clever bastard made sure I could never raise a hand to him, not ever."

I smiled sweetly. "Yeah, I think you did say something about it Master. But no one would suspect a little girl could make the pervert Peter disappear. If you give me permission to do it if and when I get the chance, then I will do what I swore I would do for you. Do we have a deal?"

He groaned. "You wouldn't give me those things for truth without this promise then? You only are with me over a deal?"

I sighed. "Master, you said to never give a service without getting a service. I am learning what you taught me. I will love you forever. That is free. You want me to have kids willingly as your legal wife and be a real family. That is going to cost you. I have been thinking lately that having babies is going to hurt a lot. I want something for it. I want to make Master Peter go away before he ends up in our house and our bed. If you can't do that, I sure as hell can. I hate that sonofabitch for all he has done to you and what he is going to do to me."

Master Maxx caressed my cheek and looked at me with love in his eyes. "I take your deal, Meine Liebe. It is the fair deal you offer this unworthy husband of yours. I only asking you to leave that bastard alive till after the collar selection. He has reason to see you break your metal. I cannot be assured any other that would replace him could be swayed to vote ja. You accept this stipulation, then you have my word to offer no further quarrel other than to be cautious. That man is tougher than you think. If he gets the drop on you…"

I interrupted him even though I assumed I could be punished for it. "He won't even know it is coming, Master.

You are willing to do what you have to do to keep us safe. It is only fair I do the same for us. If I live to collar selection, I swear Master Peter won't live to see his grandchildren."

He nodded with a sigh. "I look forward to the day with eagerness, Meine Liebe. I have dreamed of the day he can no longer hurt me for so long. To think I hold my champion in my arms and in the flesh of a little girl. It is both breathtaking and scary at the same time."

I laughed as I turned around in his lap. "I know what it is like to be a hostage, Master. I love you, I really do. I want to be free someday, and I want you to be free too. The only way we can live in the world is to make sure anyone that can tell on us for the nasty stuff they made us do, are shut the hell up. That includes Master Peter. I know it won't make all the bad things go away, but it will be nice to have nightmares without being afraid that they are going to find us and hurt us some more."

Master Maxx wrapped his hands around my chest in a hug. "I am glad you understand even if we manage to get free our lives will be hard for the cursed. There is no coming back from the personal hell for us. A life without our past chasing us other than in our brutal memories, well that is the best we can hope for. Okay, on with the story, ja? Where were we, oh ja. Gretta was running away like the scared little bitch."

Gretta didn't look back even once. I chuckled with bitter thrill at her fearing me for a moment. I stopped when I realized happiness over another's terror was further proof

I was the perverted sadistic bastard Byron pointed out that I had become. This made me wince with discomfort. I didn't want to be one of those demon's like that fucking Gretta or Kilian. I looked back over the banister for a moment.

I confess I was thinking of jumping after Reece you know. It seemed to me the easier route to ending the monster everyone called Mad Maxx die Brutale. Plus, I was tired of dealing with the sexual shit with the men. I knew that Byron told me I secretly liked the things they did and made me do to them, but I wasn't ready to believe that was truth, not yet anyway.

I had always thought that I was not the schwuler, but I couldn't deny I was the male prostitute. I still realized that the lack of women in my life was by a design that was against my will. The cruel judgement he leveled at me when he managed to pump the dark confessions of the bedroom antics I endured for five years, well it was starting to get to me. I turned away from the railing and limped slowly for the stairs. The worry that somehow I had asked for all that sexual abuse, you know wanted it to happen, like Byron told me plagued my troubled mind. What if he was right?

I mean even the brute Voter didn't deny that prior to the collar breaking nothing that I did was of my own will. He said that after I became the freeman though, I was not the helpless victim anymore, yet I still engaged with the perverted same gendered sex with multiple partners. He pointed out that as the grown man, I had the choice to say nein but let them all run over me. This was the single most important fact he used when explaining that I was indeed the schwuler that enjoyed the rough and perverted sex, or in other words I was the gay slut.

His valid sounding argument was perplexing me a great deal. I stumbled down the steps deep in confusion. Try as I might. I seem to be unable to find evidence that Byron had made an error in his thinking. I made it to the fourth floor with the feeling that I was losing control of the wheel despite the fact that I was holding it fast and tight in my grips. I flashed a frightened look at Mad Maxx.

He shrugged. "I am sorry brother Maximillian, but Byron has a point. You didn't wear a collar when you allowed Jonas, Peter, Kilian, Reece, Hermann, Matz, Osvin, okay going to stop there since I don't have all fucking day. However, you didn't stop any of them is what I am saying."

I growled in anger at Mad Maxx. "That is not fair brother. Sure, maybe I wore no collar, but those men promised that if I refused them I would be sent away or worse never get out of the fucking Haus. You know that. You were there. Chains are not always made of metal fool."

Mad Maxx glared at me with an accusatory expression. "Okay, Maximillian, let's assume you win that argument. May I offer another piece of the budding proof you are the schwuler slut? There are two prime examples of the boy's sexual preference: Leo and Cary. Neither of them were forced, were they? You go and let them fuck you as the willing. You even look forward to Leo."

I shook my head with anger. "That is not fair. First of all, Der Hund said it was okay with Leo. I didn't choose him either, Mad Max did. As for Cary, there was a reason for seducing that man. Again, I add I didn't choose him. Der Hund did. I am not a schwuler slut, dammit."

The voice of Mad Lucus broke me from my argument with Mad Maxx. "Well, that is certainly good to know Christian Victor. I am afraid if you were, you and me would be having a long talk with you behind bars below. I am the jealous man. I already told you this."

I flinched and looked all around. I had managed to get to the fourth floor, walk to the apartment and never once noticed I was doing that action. I quickly fell to the kneel realizing that I was more than fifteen minutes late for the appointment with my Master.

Mad Lucus crossed his arms and sighed sounding irritated. "You are late, Christian. I was just about to give up on your ass and call Gretta. I said six not six-thirty. Did you mishear the fucking time? Give me one reason I shouldn't have you sent below for the whipping. This is insolence and you Gott damned know it."

I gasped and began to tremble in fear. "Nein, Master. I swear I was on my way to be on time, but I was jumped by Kilian and his brother Reece. They held me the hostage and prevented my return to you on time. I did as you commanded and paid them back for daring to fool with my actions as the Master of the Haus. My revenge on the ones that dishonored me in the Palace is complete. I returned to you the second I was finished."

Mad Lucus appeared to startle. "Did you just say you were assaulted by Reece and Kilian? How long ago?"

I chuckled but kept my eyes to the floor in reverence. "Oh, about five minutes before I sent Reece to give me a report on how the first floor carpet smells."

Mad Lucus gasped. "I saw you coming down the stairs from the fifth floor?"

I nodded. "Ja, I had business with Gretta. Seems the Silk Queen decided to move up to the sixth floor. She desired Kilian's apartment. Kilian didn't care much for being leveled down so she could have it. I ended up having to remind the three of them who is the Master of this Haus. Kilian is below in the Palace re-thinking his attachment to his apartment and facial flesh. Gretta is packing to move and Reece, well he found out why they leveled me Priceless. I think maybe you saw him only a few moments ago as he fell off his high horse, ja? I assume you were standing out here in the hall. You couldn't have missed the man. He is the drama Queen, always announcing himself." I giggled into my hands with an evil sounding tone.

Mad Lucus stepped back as if afraid. "Ja, I saw Reece. He was in a big hurry, to make it to the first floor face first. I guess you threw him from the banister?"

I shrugged. "I didn't save him from falling from it if that is what you want to know Master. He is a problem for me no more, nor is his fucking snake brother. I dare say the Haus has four empty apartments and one full Mortar Palace. I suppose that is enough laying down my law for the day, however, I am more than ready to add to the open rentals around here if anyone else were to cross me." I raised my face to glare at Mad Lucus with hatred.

Mad Lucus frowned as he looked back with a bit of fear in his eyes. "Are you threatening me, Christian?"

I shook my head slowly. "That depends if you threaten me first, Master. I heard what you said. I am the Mortar King and Master of the Haus. I will no longer allow others to simply victimize me without equality of the service, not even you. Treat me fairly and I give you no quarrel. You dare to pull what any of the men I have sent to hell did, or close to it, you too can be assured a swift judgment followed by a painful execution."

He gasped and fire began to burn in his eyes. "I don't like your tone nor the things you are saying to me. I am your fucking Master, Christian. You cannot speak to me like that."

I stood up with swiftness g him to back up in defense. "You may hold the right to my collar Master, but you are not going to treat me with inequality. You don't care for what I am saying? Too bad for you. I never liked a fucking thing you say to me, but I do my Gott damned job as the submissive anyway. You do yours with honor or I will make fucking sure to balance the tab between us."

Mad Lucus backed up another step "To your knees, you brute. I mean it. That is a directive." He sounded afraid.

I gracefully returned to the kneeling without quarrel and lowered my head. He stood there a few moments appearing unsure what the hell just happened. When I didn't offer to move or be aggressive in any way for several moments more, he slowly approached watching me like the hawk.

He cleared his throat. "You minded me?"

I nodded. "You said to kneel, Master. I do what I am told."

Mad Lucus took a deep breath appearing relieved. "Oh ja, you did it beautifully. Then I am to assume you are not going to fight me on this D/s relationship? I mean I assumed based on the things you were saying you intended to demand I release my collar on you."

I kept my eyes to the floor hating myself for saying what I was about to say. "Nein Master. You misunderstand. I merely remind you that in a D/s both sides have to be respectful of the other. It is not one sided. I will grant you all the services of my station at your feet with perfection and grace. You will provide the services as the protector, decision maker, and provider of all the things needed to keep me safe and healthy. I will tolerate your bullshit. I can swear to make all your perverted and dark dreams of pleasure come to truth, but you are going to earn every Gott damned bit of my adoration. I will take nothing less than your sweat and blood. You can give it to me willingly or like the four that are dead and one that wishes he were, I will take what is owed me without your consent. The sonsofbitches that call themselves my Master before you forgot the true power of the D/s lays in the hands of the submissive, not the fucking Dominant. I will not allow you to forget that fact. If you try, then I will forget you. But the worms sure as hell won't."

Mad Lucus smiled with thrill. "You have been listening to your Master. You left me the broken victim but return to me as the Master of the Haus. I am now your Lord, and you are indeed my King. I couldn't be prouder of you Christian."

I glanced up at him with storm clouds in my eyes. "As you wish my Lord. Are we to linger out here in the hallway for the entire Haus to witness our private affairs or shall we retreat to the sanctuary of our home." I wanted to vomit at calling that apartment, which was mine Gott dammit, our anything.

Mad Lucus grinned like the cat that ate the canary. "Oh ja. What am I thinking. Rise my love. Let's go home. I've been missing you in my arms. I am eager to satiate the desire I have to hold and strengthen our bond through the couple." I winced as I rose hoping the pain I suffered at Byron's blade skills would prevent that fucking coupling shit that idiot was blathering about.

I followed Mad Lucus through the front door. I looked about the room noticing it had been moved around a bit.

There were tons of books and notebooks with scribbling laying all about the floor next to the couch. I decided this man simply had too much time on his hands. He would have found distraction as the college professor or maybe the researcher. I wish he had taken up such an occupation. Had he done that, I would not be left with the bad memories of my time serving under his gold collar and in his stupid cock bed, barf.

Mad Lucus went right to the bedroom door and turned to me. "Are you coming with me on your own power, or do I need to re-attach my leash to get you to mind?"

I scoffed. "I think I am trained well enough you need not insult me with chain leashes or questions that are underhanded threats my Lord. If dragging your non-argumentative submissive around behind you on the leash is something that brings you pleasure I give no quarrel. Otherwise, tell me what you want and see it done with experienced skill."

I thought the man was going to squeal like the excited frau. "Ah, this is better than I could have imagined. I knew deep down you wouldn't fail to meet my high expectations of you. I am grateful to see that I have lost the bet with myself. You didn't kill yourself as I feared you may."

I sneered at him. "And deny so many others the thrill of the hunt? Nein, my Lord. I have no reason to end my life. If I wait a minute, someone else will do it for me. Call me the lazy man if you want, but I think perhaps I am merely happy to serve a purpose of value for a change. If you cannot be appreciated as the human, then be feared as the beast, ja?"

He frowned at he pointed into his bedroom. "I am not sure I agree with that dark thing you just say Christian. Something about you is, I don't know, not right."

I shrugged and limping badly pushed past him into the room. "Be careful with the complaining my Lord. You are Doctor Frankenstein, and I am the monster you created. You do recall what happened to Victor don't you? He suffered through life the same fate as his creature did he not? You are the selfish pervert, and I have become what you want me to be. Too bad you tried to play Gott. You are only a mortal, ja? They say only the creator is perfect, but I think you did manage to make the unblemished nightmare without the mythical powers of the Gotts. You are getting exactly what you asked for. I give you no more trouble in your demands of me. If you don't like anything you see in me, then you have only yourself to blame." I laughed insanely as I approached that ugly cock bed and knelt with swiftness to await his command.

Mad Lucus approached with an irritated look on his face. "You are calling me a pervert again? I told you to stop doing that. I am not a pervert. I am a normal gay man with healthy appetites in the bedroom."

I giggled at that bullshit. "Is that so, my Lord? I was unaware that it is normal for any man or woman that is thirty seven to be seeking a sexual relationship with a sixteen year old boy. I suppose all over the world it is okay

72

to force the underaged kid into the sexual relationship with an adult even when they told the bastard nein how many times?"

Mad Lucus growled. "You are seventeen. That is nearly the man, Christian."

I nodded with a vicious gleam in my eyes. "Ja almost, exactly my Lord. I was sixteen when you began stalking me, and demanding I meet your sexual desires. No matter. Here I am. What can I do for you to assure that I am paid up for the services that you surely will grant me back with equality in the near future?"

He snorted. "You are twisting this entire situation all out of proportion and I simply don't like it."

That made me chuckle. "Most people don't enjoy hearing the truth spoken aloud, my Lord. Tell you what, I will refrain from such trivial realities, ja? Not my strong suit anyway about reality or so I am told. I beg your pardon for my rash attempts to impress you with my intelligence. I obviously was mistaken when I assumed you would find that sexy. I suppose I can lower that bar from this moment forward. You need me to do the dumbass striptease, or perhaps just lay there and moan while telling you how great your huge cock feels in me?"

Mad Lucus came forward with his arm raised to strike me. I sat there glaring at him in hate. I wasn't afraid of his backhand. I was actually hoping he would go through with that swat. I was pissing him off but in reality nothing I said should have.

Sure, it was sarcastic as hell, but it also was honest about all the shit he made me do for him in the other encounters. Seriously, if he dared to punish me for merely asking him to give me the commands to see that I attended his desires the way he liked, well I wouldn't want to be him. Hahaha.

He held his arm in check and glared at me angrily. "Strip down Christian. Keep that fucking mouth shut till I tell you what to do with it. I have heard enough out of you."

I nodded and began to disrobe with smooth quickness. Mad Lucus watched me undressing in silence. I held my breath as I removed the breeches. I heard him let out his breath so loud it sounded like someone left the tea kettle on the stove too long.

He shouted out sounding horrified, "Christian Victor, what the holy fuck has happened. You are cut up. Oh, my Gott, your cock, turn around." I did as I was told. "Nein, the backside too. This is a motherfucking nightmare. Who did this foul thing to my property.

If I could have smiled I would have, as I sighed. "Well, my Lord, I went to visit with Sebastian, Noethan and Tadeas. You know for the revenge you commanded. The fellows were too much for me to handle alone. I was the dumbass that didn't bring back up. Anyway, they were most unhappy to hear of my reason for the visit. The three of them decided to use the opportunity to have a little more fun with me. They cut me up like this. Thankfully, the

Shadow King and King's men came along and caught the criminals while at their dark deeds. The men saved me, and I fed them to the yard dogs for their cruelly dishonoring me and marking up my flesh, including the head wound." I looked to the floor feigning remorse.

Mad Lucus's eyes went wide. "Oh, well okay, that explains your torturing the men all night like you did. I wondered exactly what the fuck they could have done so awful to earn them such a gruesome punishment from you. Were Kilian and Reece involved in this too?"

I shook my head. "Nein. They intended to do far worse though. My Lord I don't mean to appear overly eager, but I am very tired. I have not slept much in two days. Can we hurry this special services call up a bit? I really would like to lay down for the slumbering."

He stared at me in disbelief. "Christian honey, I cannot dare to have intercourse with you as torn up as you are."

I looked down at the wounds. Somem were bleeding again. "I don't understand why not, my Lord. Didn't you tell me you care nothing for my comfort any more than the ones that caused this did?"

Mad Lucus crossed his arms with a look of frustration. "You throw my own words back at me, Christian. Okay, I will say it like this so you can understand me. If I dared to handle your intimate parts in anyway in that condition your present to me, I risk not only causing you further infection, but it will encourage scarring. You know I hate those scars. Thankfully those beautiful blue eyes, and pretty boy face make up for the horror that disgraces that gorgeous flesh of yours. You go right to the bathroom and wait for me. I go for astringents and bandages. I will also demand you use the lotions with vitamin extracts after you heal a bit. I want to minimize the possibility of allowing blemishes to set upon two of your greatest assets. I know you have the contract with Peter, until I can find the loophole out, and Jonas is the Guardian I cannot control. I command you to tell those brutes I have ordered you to be chaste to the intercourse below the waist for the next ten days. Tell them I know I have no right to deny them access, but I am asking them to do the gentleman thing and gain there thrill from you without breeching my wishes. This you understand?"

I nodded trying to not appear happy about his orders though I was fucking ecstatic to mind that command to be honest. "As you wish my Lord. I will tell them. I don't expect them to respect your desires. Peter and Jonas are many things, but the gentlemanly behaviors is not something you can accuse them of engaging in with any frequency."

He nodded with a scoff, "No doubt Christian those brutes will have no respect for my boy. Perhaps I will take this opportunity to provide you proof of my honest interest in granting the service return for the ones you will surely give to me the moment you heal?" He smiled and reached out to caress my chest.

I stared at him without flinching at his foul touching. "I look forward to seeing your prowess as my Lord and

Master. You can be assured such a mercy will be returned with equal vigor."

He shot me a coy look. "Now that sounds very promising. It would be of great thrill to hold you as the willing lover ready to see to all my fantasies."

I took off for the bathroom. "That is why I am here I believe, my Lord. You can be assured when another gives me something of theirs, I never forget the favor of it. You give me your soul Lucus and I will make sure to give you my own to replace it with." I went inside leaving the grinning brute thrilling at words of promise he truly didn't understand.

You see Meine Liebe, Max was no more. I had no soul at all. It had become part of the shard called Mad Maxx die Brutale. Essentially I just promised Lucus nothing but anger and sadistic cruelty in return for his forcing me to serve him. I, as Maximillian, would see to all his stupid base sexual and pleasure needs but he could never take from the boy what no longer existed. Sex and service without love is to chain up the unwilling angry dog.

Sooner or later, I would turn on my Master and when this hound bit it would be deep. I had lots of time to think of ways to injure this man. I was inside his private world. All the information I needed to gather to do evil to him was going to be made available to me. A Dominant should always be aware that if you force a submissive into the collar against their will, it can only lead to disaster. Any idiot that thinks the submissive can be bullied to accept them deserves every nasty thing they get from the dishonor of it.

Peter, Jonas, Malfred, and even this motherfucker Lucus, thought I was not intelligent enough to understand the truth of how the D/s partnership works. Gaining the submissive to accept your collar by misleading manipulation, coercion, and not granting choice to say nein is not D/s. Peter, he misled me. Jonas, he manipulated me as did Malfred. Mad Lucus, he used a form of coercion and didn't grant choice. They all failed to gain my honest and mindless following them as my Dominant. I did what I did for them out of fear and all I did other than try to survive is seek the escape route or think of ways to kill them.

Leo and Byron, that Meine Liebe is a different story. Leo manages to keep a true D/s relationship with me to this very day because he allowed me to choose. He granted equal service for return of my own. His honesty in our relationship earned him the coveted position of being one of two that can truly claim ownership of me at any time in my life despite my long years at expert training to be the pleasure submissive.

Byron, well that is a horse of a different color. We are getting around to how that sonofabitch managed to get me to engage with him in the true D/s relationship. He was far cleverer than any before him or since. Not even my Leo can boast of the kind of power and control that man eventually took over me. I was the sitting duck that needed almost no bullets pumped in to find me his mortally wounded victim.

As Mad Lucus attended my cuts all I could think of Byron. He was there to save me from the Altergotts. No one, not even the so called loving Mad Lucus, had lifted a finger to stop those two from abusing me at their will.

Instead of truthfully protecting me from them, he used it to his advantage by forcing his gold collar around my neck. To make matters worse he had sat there while Kilian nearly brained me to death. We can include him leaving me in the Palace to rot as the brothers made fine sport of me. Hell, for all I knew, he was with Gretta in granting them permission to do as they had done.

When I was at the end of my rope without a single friend or anyone to care, Byron swooped in like the buzzard to make a dinner of the dying calf. He was able not only to tell me what I needed to hear, believe and hold on to, but he also managed to make me question my own role in all this horror I suffered. He knew all he had to do is put a voice to the secret fears that I hid from my consciousness that I deserved or asked for these terrible people to do this shit to me.

The words I yelled out to Reece and Kilian about Byron being my helpless victim kept looping through the wheelroom. I wondered if there wasn't some truth to it. Byron had been chasing me for years by that time. He seemed both angry and enamored by the thrill of that cat and mouse game we played. I thought of Felicity and her seeking him out to protect her when she believed I had abandoned her. I seriously began to consider there was more to Byron than I had ever noticed before.

He killed his oldest, and one of his best friends Reece for me. He took one of the others closer to him still to be disfigured because I asked him to. I could no longer doubt his love for me was real, at least to him. He didn't rape me when he could have, and he even minded me when I told him not to touch me. The Voter had claimed he was willing to do anything for me because I had seduced him first, not the other way around. It started to make sense to me that if I were indeed a perverted sicko, like he told me I was, then that would be something I would do. Enslave the helpless Voter for the sadistic pleasure of it. Not sexual, but psychological sadism, you know.

The more I thought of that fake kissing him, and how he melted in my grip, the more I feared maybe I wasn't lying. Did I truly love Byron in my usual psychologically perverted way but never realized it before he pointed it out to me?

I trembled as the panic took hold of my spine. It had to be the truth. His explanations made all the confusion of my sorry life for the last five years make sense. Right there and then, while Mad Lucus finished his patching me up, I had to find a way to stop my sadistic demons from harming Byron, or anyone else. If I had learned to become the psychopath, there had to be a way to undo it, ja?

Mad Lucus ordered me to get to that horrible bed. I didn't quarrel with him as he bound me naked to the headboard. I hated the bondage shit, but I was so tired I could have slept on a rock in the middle of a stormy sea. He laid down next to me. He looked me over with a sigh and longing in his eyes. I braced for him taking back his swearing to keep his hands off me for ten days.

To my surprise he laid down on his pillow and laid an arm gently across my chest without making any grabs for me sexually. "You said the Shadow King aided you with the brutes that cut you up like that? This is that backdoor guard Cary, ja?"

I groaned. "Please my Lord, I can guess what you are about to say. This Dark Bonding is not of the lovers' kind. He gained the third-floor apartment and free meals for his family and him in the agreement, not the right to my favors." I lied, which is the proper thing to do with Dark Bondings. You never admit to sex with a black collar, ever.

Mad Lucus lifted to lean on his elbow staring at me. "That is what I was going to ask. Third floor and free meals? That is a lot for what in return?"

I glared at him. "You are quite rude my Lord to ask of the private affairs of me and my chosen Shadow King. However, for your information, you just treated the return service he provides. Had Cary not been doing what I bonded him for you would be putting the flowers on my casket rather than bandaging my cock."

He nodded. "I suppose I should thank him for that."

I growled out angrily. "I think not. That bastard gets the good housing and fucking food in the Great Hall for his troubles, my Lord. Thanking him is not your place. I tell you I will mind your commands but don't ever insult me again, damn you. I attend my bonds and contracts without need of your sticking your nose into them."

Mad Lucus shot a look of surprise at me. "Okay, my heart. I will refrain from bothering Cary if you insist. Speaking of your men or ex-men in this case, I ran into Matz earlier today."

I held my breath thinking Matz told Lucus of my trying to jump earlier. "Ja? Small world isn't it or more likely small Haus. So? Why should I care about Matz, my Lord. He and I are through, you know that. Are you about to try to insult me again by claiming differently? I hope not for your sake."

Mad Lucus shook his head with vigor. "You misunderstand, Christian. I tell you about this because Matz asked me to give you a message about a couple friends the two of you shared. Do you know a Ghanzi and Aara?"

I jerked my head up in a startle. "Matz sent a message through you about those two? What the fuck? Why would he do that, my Lord?"

He frowned. "You don't think these two important enough to bother your Lord with is what you are saying?"

I took a deep breath and nodded. I was of course lying. Those two meant the world to me but I couldn't let Lucus know it. "They are just a couple of black collars that used to help the wolfpack out sometimes is all. Not important at all."

Mad Lucus laid back on his pillow blowing out his wind. "Oh good. I worried what he said would upset you. Anyway, Matz said they both have been put to the yard nearly three days now. The killers are unknown, and the wolves are in mourning over the affair."

I felt the world pull me inside of it as my heart broke into two. I held back my tears but closed my eyes pretending to have fallen asleep. Mad Lucus laid there waiting for a response. When none came he lifted back up and looked me over. He watched my breathing which I was forcing to stay even and slow. The man laid back down once he was satisfied I had slipped off to slumber.

He turned off the light. I heard his breathing become deep and then he started snoring. Only then did I led the tears of grief fall from my eyes. I ended up finding my own fitful rest after silently and internally wailing for the two little black collar children that I had failed to save from their fate.

Felicity had chosen Byron. Marc, Ghanzi, Kloe and Aara had all gone to their eternal dreams in the green fields. There was nothing left for me to care about, or care back for me. The honest loneliness I felt in that crowded Haus on the overpopulated Earth brought me to a deeper misery than I thought humanly possible. For the first time in all my life I can say I was truly lost and no longer desired to be found.

When the sun kissed my eyelids with her warm lips, I opened them to find Mad Lucus standing next to the bed smiling at me. Not something I wanted to see first thing in the morning. Yikes!

He chimed out with happiness, "Good morning, Christian. How are you feeling?"

I shrugged. "Like the welcome mat at the Haus front door, my Lord. Thank you for asking. And you?" He reached over my head and unlocked my cuffs from the headboard.

He chuckled. "Your humor is maybe one of your finest qualities, my heart. I feel fit and chipper. I think maybe you need a little coffee and definitely a hearty meal. Peter sent me your dentures while you were away. I ask you to put them in. Let me see how they look. Then get dressed. I am taking my lover to breakfast at the Great Hall." He leaned down and forced a deep kiss onto my mouth.

I endured it without feeling, expression or fight until he let me go of his hold. "My Lord, I do hope you actually intend to see me consume more than the twenty-five calories you allow me last time in the Great Hall visit."

Mad Lucus's eyes went wide in humored shock. "Christ, which was crass to bring up Christian. Nein, this time we order a meal. You accept your place in my home and bed. I have no power move planned. Only the morning meal is on the agenda this time. Here, show me. I am eager to see something I haven't since you were fourteen." He grabbed a box off the nightstand that held the fake teeth.

I glared at him. "Do you mean a mouth full of teeth or the hope of a better life in my eyes, my Lord?" I took the damned things and put them in, with a bit of a struggle, as the Dentist taught me.

Mad Lucus gasped and grabbed his chest appearing pleasantly stunned. "Oh, my Gott. You are so beautiful, my heart. I love these teeth. Come, hurry up and put on one of the outfits I had made for you. I desire to show off my prize today to everyone in the Haus. They will all swoon with jealousy when they view this handsome man Mad Lucus sports on his arm."

I rolled my eyes when he turned around. "As you wish, my Lord. I assume Geraldine didn't come by to leave me any food. I guess she has decided I am not worth the effort like everyone else has."

Mad Lucus spun around in a startle. "Huh? Everyone else has. Nein. It is true Geraldine has not been cooking but she did tell me she would leave a plate down at the Great Hall for you. Wurst, bread, oatmeal the works. That way whatever you choose she has you covered. What is this you say about not being worth the effort?"

I shrugged. "It is nothing, my Lord. Just grouchy I guess. My wounds hurt and I don't feel well. Maybe you would show mercy and allow me to sleep a little longer. I am most fatigued for some reason." I put my legs over the side of the bed knowing the bastard wasn't going to let me out of the pony show. I had many years of experience with all the bastards who did that the second they thought themselves the winners you know. Stupid ego stroking over nothing.

He shook his head. "You know better Christian. The reason you feel so poor is partly due to your lack of nutrition. You are not going to skip anymore meals. Geraldine sent word she is ready to get back to work cooking for you. Now you don't want to upset that hard working lamb do you?"

I grimaced. "Of course not, my Lord. May I remove the bandages so I can bathe before I dress?" I looked down with a sigh at that mess Byon made of me though it did work.

Mad Lucus chuckled "Nein. Tell you what. This morning, I give you the sponge bath service."

I flinched "Thank you for the mercy of it but my Lord I don't desire to be a bother. I can do that for myself."

Mad Lucus grabbed the back of my head with firmness. "No bother at all Christian. I really like the way those teeth improve your looks. You were already the handsome boy, now you are very sexy. I listened to what you said about the D/s relationship. I give you the bath with a sponge, and you can return the service to me with your tongue. You can give me the oral services on your Lord with the addition of those teeth. You have to practice keeping those weapons off the triggers, ja? Well, get to it Christian. You can call this the first course of your breakfast. Twenty-five calories isn't much, but you need all you can get." He pushed my head down as he demanded I get to my knees to sexually service him.

Well, that was that, for the so called time off of the special services. Mad Lucus did keep his hands above my waist, but he was as disgusting as ever in his demands. That motherfucker insisted I used everything above Byron's handiwork on everything he had head to toe. By the time I was finished I was happy to get that sponge bath. I brushed my fucking teeth several times.

I dressed rather quickly and was limping to the door when Mad Lucus stopped me. "Here, I bought you a new cane, Christian. As I told you before you acted an ass with the other one. You better never led me catch you trying to walk without one. It is hard on your bones, boy. The only one around here allowed to rough up those hips is your Lord and Master Mad Lucus." He chuckled at his stupid sexual inuendo.

I nodded and took the walking stick from his outstretched hand. It was not as nice as the one Matz bought for me, but it was handsome enough in its own way. The top was of the Falcon in silver. His beak extended to allow for my firm grip of the cane. He smiled and offered many compliments that I ignored.

He opened the door, and I followed him out in the high protocol without the leash thankfully. I was behind him, but I could tell by his gait he was beaming with pride to all who could see us traveling along. The blacks, silvers and even the Dominants knelt or bowed as we passed them in the hallway then the stairs. Mad Lucus was without a doubt in seventh heaven.

At the bottom of the stairs, I could see my men and Shadow King kneeling together. That made me raise an eyebrow as Mad Lucus walked by them appearing unaware of their presence. Almut stood up with suddenness and grabbed my wrist. I shot a look of fear at Mad Lucus noticing he had not seen my man's attempt to gain my attention. I hand gestured for him to quickly speak. He whispered out loudly, "Please Master, my son Jaison, they painted him silver yesterday. I beg of you, can you find a way to paint him black like you did for Marc and his sister.

Chapter 49: Demonic Possession

Almut fell back into a kneel after delivering his plea to save his son from the fate of the silver. I continued following Mad Lucus down the hallway toward the Great Hall. I did hear the King's man request, but even Almut realized there was not a fucking thing I could do about the situation right at that moment. I was still within his, Hubertus and Cary's sight when I lifted my hand without turning around to look back at them. I rapidly signaled I would attend to his request shortly. Even from the distance I had put between us, I could hear the three men led out their loud breaths of relief.

I was well aware of the importance of a son to his father. Well, unless you were mine, hahaha. I confess, the last thing I wanted to do was get involved in purchasing another silver kid. I assumed like the other four I would literally work my ass off, get attached to Jaison and then have the heartbreak when the Queens found a way to murder him. I assumed at that time Cora got to Ghanzi and Aara too.

However, I couldn't just turn my back on Almut. If for no other reason than it would likely put a rift between me and this loyal follower. I knew with all the enemies I had managed to collect, I would be a fool to throw away any ally. No matter how high the price Almut had demanded to keep him on my side, I had to find the way to paid it.

Mad Lucus and I arrived at the Great Hall entrance in quick time. I was surprised when the man turned around to look at me while we stood there waiting for the black collar attendant.

He looked me over with a dreamy expression and goofy smile on his face. "Come here my love and take your Lord's arm. I want to enter as the lion with my mate clearly marked as being my willing partner." He put his right hand on his hip awaiting me to wrap my own through his elbow.

I held back the urge to wince at this request for the public humiliation, but I did as he told me. I knew everyone thought me the schwuler, but to be the lover of Lucus, yuck! "I wasn't aware you gave a damn what these nothings around here think or don't think, my Lord. Since when you become the slave to popular opinion," I said rather offhandedly.

Mad Lucus's smile melted to a frown, and he tightened his arm around my own. "You are the novice at holding power, Christian. If I desire to get the riff raff of this Haus to bow to my authority, I must demonstrate unity with my Mortar King. One day soon, I will be the voice of this Haus. My words will be the law. There is no reason not to give everyone the notice that I hold the heart of their Master in my hands." He snorted as the black collar attendant nearly fell over as he spotted the identity of his next customers.

The twenty something brunette male Haus sub gasped and grabbed his chest with awe in his eyes. "Master! Oh, I beg you to forgive my slowness at coming to serve you. I didn't see you or I would have attended your needs with swiftness." He fell at my feet in a sloppy kneel.

Mad Lucus stood there appearing somewhere between stunned and angry. "What the fuck. Get off the floor you idiot. Your Lord and King are hungry, Gott dammit. You are wasting more time with this stupidity." I put up my hand to silence him which stunned him so much he actually did shut the hell up for a minute.

I glared at the black collar attendant. "What is your name worm?"

The man nearly choked as he stammered out, "S...s...Samual, Master." He kept his eyes to the floor and was panting in all out fear.

I scoffed. "Sssamual, you say? Huh, that is the strange name. Did your mother have the stutter?"

He shook his head and barely whispered out. "Nein, Master. It is only Samual. I admit to you I am frightened and didn't speak clearly."

I nodded then said with gruffness. "Well, let's see. You are the slow bastard and attend the needs of the low level scum of the Haus before getting to me. You kneel like the clumsy goat nearly ruining the shine on my boots. Then you further insult me by not clearly answering the simplest of inquiries of your Lord and Master. Humm, that is three strikes I do believe. Sssamual, who is your trainer, boy?"

Samual gasped and trembled. "I had many Masters."

I chuckled with evil rising within. "Oh, you did? So, this insolence you show to the Master of the Haus is the fault of all the black collar trainers for the Great Hall staff. Is this what you are saying then?"

He whimpered near coming to tears at this point. "Nein, Master. This worthless man is responsible for the shoddy service, lack of grace and speech impediment."

I leaned down and demanded he look at me. "Ja, it its Sssamual. You will seat me and my partner with skill and speed. After that you will head down to the torture chamber. You will wait till Hubertus has a moment to see you receive five lashes by tawse the moment you are able to demonstrate to him that you can fucking kneel without slobbering on your Master's shoes." I hand motioned Samual to rise.

He kept his head bowed and was clearly weeping. "As you wish Master. I thank you for the mercy of it. Follow me, Sire." He took off with speed.

Mad Lucus stood there with his eyes wide in shock as I pulled him along after me to follow Samual. "Christian? Five lashes for nothing? That is a bit much, isn't it?"

I snarled at him as we moved with quickness behind Samual. "You said you desired to demonstrate the power of the Mortar King. Well, that is how it is done, my Lord. Not this bullshit pony show designed to cause nothing but the wagging of tongues and drive the fevered fantasies of the wicked that reside under this roof. I told you already Lucus, be careful what you wish for. You just may get it and so will everyone else."

Mad Lucus gasped. "Call off the order for punishment of this poor black collar, Christian. You surely know it is unfair treatment for the minor infraction. I would think you of all people in this horrid place are aware of that."

I stopped my traveling with suddenness which halted Mad Lucus that I held by his arm and shot him a vile look of disgust. "I will have to insist you shut the fuck up, my Lord. I am warning you only once. You are not the regent of the Mortar Throne yet. In fact, other than this fucking gold you hold over me you are a nothing in this Haus. I am the Collar King. You ever question my authority over my subjects in public again, you will be down below sharing the chains with Sssamual." I heard Samual led out a small whimper and dropped to a more graceful kneel waiting for me to finish dressing down Mad Lucus.

The eyes and ears of every Dominant and FemDom diner in the Hall was locked on me and Mad Lucus. You could have heard the mouse heartbeat; the place had grown so quiet. No one dared breathe a word or even scraped their China plates the moment the two of us had appeared at the entry. I could see the fear in every expression. Not a single resident had not been the unwilling witness, at least by audio, of my torturing Sebastian, Tadeas and Noethan in the most gruesome of ways. It was clear my plan to put all the Haus on notice of my brutality when angered had worked perfectly. No one wanted to catch the attention of Mad Maxx die Brutale that morning.

Mad Lucus shot a glance around the room at his neighbors and equals. "Christian I uhm, ja okay, I am hungry. Let's just allow Samual to seat us. Maybe we can discuss this later?"

I scoffed at him. "There is nothing to discuss, my Lord. I said all I am going to. Next time I show you. Sssamual, I wish to have that table over there, to the left. You may seat us now." I pointed at the table where Cora, Gretta, Peter, Jonas and Claus were sitting.

Samual gasped and whispered back, "Uhm Master, that table is already occupied. Please allow me to give you the cleaned one with a fabulous view."

I bellowed, "You dare to deny you Master? Guards, remove this motherfucker from my sight. Take him below to await my pleasure. You, ja, you. Get over her and show this worm how to serve your better with skill, or do you desire to join your brother?" I glared at a red headed black collar of roughly thirty that was standing next to Gretta serving the Elders and Voters their plates of food.

The man dropped everything and came running while hand motioning for other servers to "clear the table." You should have seen the look on the Elders and Voters faces when the Guard came rushing into the room and drug the wailing Samual off. If that expression was classic, you would have really howled to see their expressions of stun when the black collar staff practically threw them out of their chairs. Within only minutes that table was clean and ready to receive its new occupants.

Gretta, Cora, Jonas, Peter, and Claus were "rounded up" and escorted to another table far from the one that I wanted. The red headed black collar pulled out the chair and immediately knelt while waiting for me to sit down. Another black collar did the same for Mad Lucus. He sat down next to me with the confused look I can only compare to that of a cat that missed the mouse after the pounce.

I shot a look of caution at him. "Do not forget what I show you here this morning, my Lord. All of you play me for the daft fool. I am putting you on notice that I am well aware of the truthful power I can command if I want to. I mind you only because I realize that I can exercise this control till you rat bastards panic that I am going to give all of you everything you truly deserve. Don't bother wasting your threats to see me sent back to the Palace. I already know that too, Gott dammit, and hearing it is already getting fucking old. All I will say is that if pushed into a corner I can and will make it worth my while before I am hauled off to rot in a cell. I swear if you demonstrate unfair abuse to the gifts I grant, you will not live long to regret it." I picked up the menu and began to look over the selection as if nothing had happened of interest in the last five minutes.

Mad Lucus blew out his breath. "I don't know what to say Christian. I am unsure if this new you turns me on or horrifies me. One thing it sure has done is cause me to worry about your mental state. Is there something I should know, my love? What has happened to cause my sweet boy to become the demon almost overnight?"

I dropped the menu and leveled my hate filled eyes on him. "You never cared about what turned me on or horrified me before now did you? As for that anxiety you feign over the state of my mental welfare, I would politely request you keep that bullshit to yourself. You didn't care when I was coming apart and needed honest comfort. Lucky for you I no longer am in need of the mercy that always seems denied me. If you suddenly are nervous about my psyche I would hazard a guess it is only because I seem a little too sane. Easy to fool the confused psychotic, ja? Not such an easy task to trick me when I am not shattering from all the stress I have endured. Well, I will make this real simple for you, my Lord. I am fine. I am better than great. I never felt better in my whole shitty life. So, if you are done with the small talk, I am hungry. I am going to have the wurst and sauerkraut that I can finally chew with these fake teeth. I suggest you order your own fucking breakfast and stop trying to pretend to be my honest loving partner. You and I are D/s, my Lord, and you are not my father confessor."

Mad Lucus sat there appearing unable to figure out what to retort. I ignored him without effort. I raised my hand to gesture for service. Almost every black collar in the place practically ran over each other in an attempt to rush to attend my desires. I didn't bother to show any expression nor interest in them. I told them the food I wished from Geraldine's plate she fixed for me. I have to say of all the five years I had been dragged to the Great Hall, which was the speediest, smoothest and finest service I had ever received.

My coffee cup barely would have a sip taken before a black collar rushed to replace it. My food and Mad Lucus's arrived within ten minutes. Hell, those poor Haus subs practically wiped my mouth and spoon fed me the breakfast. I took the moments of leisure, since I really had nothing to do with all that fawning, to steal glances around the room.

I found what I was looking for rather quickly. The evicted Elders and Voters had been moved across the room to a large table. All five of them were glaring at me and Mad Lucus with expressions of open anger. That made me chuckle a bit. I was glad they felt slighted having been put in their places with such wanton abandon as I had exercised against them.

It was not that I was truly the power hungry as Mad Lucus, well all of them, are. I merely saw the opportunity to show everyone, including Mad Lucus and the Haus subs, that Mad Maxx die Brutale was no longer the door mat they could just wipe their feet on.

I truly thought that eventually Gretta would find a way to send me back below anyway. I decided before that happened I was going to hand a few asses a bit of return service for what they had done to my own.

I finished the meal and ordered a coffee to go. Mad Lucus appeared rather surprised that I was getting ready to leave. He was still eating in no hurry to get anywhere. Likely he was enjoying the newfound power, that idiot brute. He watched me picking up the fresh coffee in the Styrofoam cup while grabbing my cane. I stood up to leave.

Mad Lucus reached out with vigor and grabbed my wrist to hold me still. "Hey, where the hell do you think you are going Christian? Do you not see I am not finished with my breakfast? sit down and be still till I am ready to take us back to the apartment."

I jerked my arm from his hold with a violent pull, near forcing him forward from his seat. "Unless you have further need of my pleasure services, my Lord, I have other shit to attend. I will be back to see to you when I am through with my list of personal duties."

Mad Lucus steadied himself, his face twisting into an expression of fury. "Your duty is to your Lord and Master Mad Lucus. I have not granted you a release, boy. You cannot just run free through the hallways without care."

I glared at him with the blazes of hell fire rising in my eyes. "I am not running free anywhere and I have a shit ton of cares my Lord. Go ahead and verbalize the release from your side if it makes you feel powerful. I was in that pit for a month dammit. Many things that are of importance to me were left undone during that time including meeting the requirements of contracts that were in action long before you rudely butted your huge nose into my business. I am going to get my books, deal with Peter, and pray at the Chapel for my tormented soul whether you agree to it or not. Try to stopping me, I dare you."

Mad Lucus gasped as he saw that there was not the boy Christian Victor standing there before him, but a wraith that wore his scarred skin. "Uhm, okay ja. I had forgotten about Peter and my agreement that you could attend to that silly religious belief of yours. I give you release till, uhm, how long will all that take you to, do you think?" His lack of confidence tickled my perverted demons a great deal.

I leaned down and engaged him in a heavy kiss with much tongue. The man nearly passed out, as did half the diners sitting at the tables around our own. I pulled out of it and softly caressed his cheek while looking deep into his eyes. Mad Lucus panted out appearing to have difficulty catching his breath.

I narrowed my eyes with a gleam of mischievousness in them. "You need not worry lover. I will be back in time to get my low calorie supper. You go home and rest up. I intend to enjoy your cooking a great deal. Ohm by the way, while I am on the subject. You are really going to need to brush up on your culinary skills if you intend to keep your Christian Victor the well fed happy man. You wouldn't desire to see me left hungry, would you? Surely you have heard the rumors of my boredom with the common cuisine. You don't expect me to ignore my tastes for the exotic meal do you? I hope not. If so, then I may have to resort to checking out the menus of other far hotter kitchens, ja? See you soon, my spatz. Promise you won't start without me, ja?" I let go of his face and took off with speed for the door of the Great Hall leaving the confused, and very turned on, Mad Lucus to stew in his juices.

I rushed for the staircase and practically ran up them headed for the third floor. I ran into Cary and Roselina along the way. The two were hauling a pathetic looking sofa between them. I saw Almut, Hubertus and two black collar females, that I assumed were their wives, lugging other bits of shoddy furniture items. All six of them fell to a kneel the second they saw me hauling ass toward them.

I motioned them to rise. "Almut, come here for a moment please?" I said while checking behind me that Mad Lucus had not followed me up the steps.

The huge Torture Master approached me with his head down. I saw the small brunette with him flash an adoring look at me. "I am here Master. Ask and see your command done with swiftness."

I nodded with a chuckled then backhanded the fuck out of him, nearly knocking him to the floor. "You fucking idiot. Don't you ever bother me when I am in the protocol again. Your forget your place. Do it again and I will see you have no other children to worry about being painted silver. I will have your manhood removed and fed to Ivan for his supper. You understand me, you stupid sonofabitch?" Almut trembled and the other five black collars backed away in fear.

He held his reddening cheek and nodded. "I beg your forgiveness Master. I wasn't thinking. I thank you for the mercy of your generous reminder. It won't happen again I swear it."

I growled in irritation. "You're fucking right it won't, I mean it. You brutes all think you are above anyone else in this Gott damned hell hole in my eyes? Well, you are not. I will see any of you suffer far more pain than one whose name is unknown to me. I pay each of you with favors usually reserved only for the top level of this Haus. You will serve me without expectation of favoritism, or you will find yourselves in hell thirty minutes before you realize what has happened."

Hubertus, Almut, Roselina and the other two Frau's bowed their heads low, but Cary gasped loudly which caught my attention. I glared at him for a moment then rushed at him and punched him in the stomach sending him to his knees gulping for air.

I stared at him without pity in my expression,. "What did you say, Cary? I didn't quite hear you. Can you repeat the words? What is that? Oh, I know you said nothing. Nein, you make the noise like someone knocked the air out of you when I give you the rules of minding your King. Well, that is not the correct response. I gave you the demonstration of the proper action for when such a noise is appropriate. Do you have anything else to say, or sounds you wish to add brother? If not, then I suggest you get back to your feet and find another to aid you with carrying heavy shit to your new haus. That Frau you are unworthy of, is heavy with child. She should not be lifting shit. You brutes, all of you. Release your females to your homes. You boys carry the weight. They are to attend the less physical labors of your castles. Damn, not a fucking gentleman among you. I am ashamed to call you bastards brothers."

101

While this correction of the bad behaviors of my men was occurring. All around us the silvers, black, Dominants and FemDoms of that floor, and those traveling along the stairs, fell into the kneel. Many eyes and ears witnessed my laying down the law to the brutes and their women. I meant for this little scene to be embedded into the minds of as many of the residents as possible. Once again, in less than twenty-four hours, I was seen to be cruelly engaging with people that everyone thought were my closest friends and allies.

I know all this I tell you of my brutality toward Samual, Almut and Cary seems simply because I was the angry man. That is not the honest truth of it. Sure, I wanted the residents to believe Mad Maxx die Brutale was just a nasty fellow. That is not the only reason I showed such evil to these men. I also wanted everyone to think none of them mattered to me.

I had learned a painful lesson the hard way, and so had four innocent souls. It was clear to me that showing favor towards those I truly cared about was a sure fire way to send them to their graves. I realized that love, though I didn't believe in it anymore at the time, was a weakness that others could use to exploit me, and force further indignities upon my person. From Felicity to the poor little nine-year old Aara, I had found myself trapped in a nightmare thanks to my observed fondness for each of dem.

Well, no more. Mad Maxx die Brutale had come to clean up my Haus. Everything had to go. I knew I wasn't loved by anyone for truth. I saw no reason to risk the lives of the few left around me that had at least been merciful from time to time. It seemed intelligent to show no further public kindness to anyone.

This planned coldness toward my men and other associates, I believed, would end this hole in my hardening psychological armor.

I was surprised at how this new me was not causing distress. I felt completely numb and blind to the terror I seemed to be causing these people that served me. In reality I confess it initially seemed easy enough to do. The whole process was made even simpler when I realized I had been the fool. I had been stupidly wanting to believe everyone really cared about me, but I finally understood that like everything else I had ever been told it was a lie.

After all, I didn't even know the names of my King's men's wives, children, nor did I know much about Cary other than what turned him on in the intercourse. I stood there standing in a menacing stance above my Shadow King. I noticed a sinking feeling as I began to accept Byron was right about me. I was nothing but a perverted schwuler slut that loved to be tortured, raped and beaten to a bloody pulp.

The part of me that knew better than to buy into the bullshit, well he skipped town apparently. I listened hard from the wheel and to my deepest heart break, yet I heard no voice that argued for my honor.

I sighed with regret as I shot Mad Maxx a look of sadness. "We could still jump from the banister."

Mad Maxx shook his head and kept his eyes down. "Nein, too late for that cure, brother. The boy has done a lot of really bad things, though none of us knew all of it was because he is evil. I think it best we take our punishment for living like the pervert. It is not going to be fun to endure but I for one cannot bear the thought that we find the peace of the grave. At least not until we can undo all the wrong we caused."

I nearly fainted when he said that. "You do know we are faking being the Catholic, right brother? What is this shit about undoing the nightmares that we apparently caused? You cannot go back into time and fix mistakes, stupid. We kill the boy now, well then the disease of perversion is contained. We don't, then soon enough far worse than we already do is going to happen. There is no cure for the demons that live in our blood. You heard Jonas. The boy was born with them swimming in his veins. I must kill this beast the only way available. End of story."

Mad Maxx die Brutale came off the back wall shouting with suddenness. "Shut this pussy suicidal talk. Shut the fuck up. We already took the vote on it, remember? I say that Mad Maxx is correct, Maximillian. You wanted to live so bad you didn't think of the consequences of existing without a soul, like Max, in the brutal world of the pervert. Real what you sowed, motherfucker. You bend over and take it and you learn to love it, little slut. Stop wasting time with useless introspection when your victims, uhm, oops, I apologize for that slip. I mean audience awaits. I hope that is not tears I see in your eyes you stupid cunt. What is there to cry about anyway? Look around you, brother. They fall to their knees all scrambling to knock you to yours. You lucky boy. Get back to work Mister popular." His cruel laughter echoed throughout the wheel room.

I wiped my eyes. I wasn't crying, I had dust in them, and they were watering, I swear it. "Who the fuck are you. I hear the air stirring but I don't recognize the voice that assaults my ears. Speak quickly or find yourself beaten to an inch of your life woman." I suddenly realized while I had been discussing the situation with my brother shards a woman had fallen to kneel and was trying to hail me.

The plump brown haired frau looked at the floor and whispered, "I am called Blume, Sire. Almut is my Mann. He asked your favor to save our son Jaison. I am here to offer whatever services you desire of me to repay the debt of gratitude he and I owe you for the mercy you show us."

I blinked in total stupidity at her words. "What? Almut, your Frau, is she daft? This shit she babbles is making no sense."

Almut stood there with his head bowed. Everyone else was on their knees in the kneel including Cary who was still trying to catch his breath. "I assure you my Blume is of the sound mind, Sire. She speak for the both of us. If you desire her favors she will be happy to attend you with my blessing anytime you request it. We offer you this mercy in return for the favor of saving Jaison from the life of the pleasure submissive."

I shot a look of sheer shock at Almut then looked back at the trembling Frau at my feet. "You are both out of your fucking minds. You offer to let me fuck your wife, Almut? Christ, that is fucked up on so many levels even this pervert cannot wrap his mind around the idea of it. However, we can start with the fact that it is forbidden to have intercourse with the black collars."

I saw Cary led out his breath in relief, silently this time, as Almut nodded. "Ja, we are aware of the law Master. However, Sire, we have no other way to repay this debt. Blume will use extreme discretion in her service return to you. There are many secret arrangements among the Dominants and FemDoms of the Haus of this sort."

I glared at the man I was sure by this point was touched in the head. "Oh, is that so? She going to keep her riding my cock a secret from her Mann too? Tell me Almut, will you merely lay there in the bed with us pretending to be asleep while I fuck your wife half to death?" I watched the Torture Master wince as if I backhanded him again.

He took a deep breath. "Sharing my wife's skills with you is my honor, Sire. I can assure you no quarrel will come from my mouth."

I nodded as I shot another look at Cary. "Well tempting as this trade of service sounds, I must tell you Almut you surely realize you offer the wrong flavor to your Master. I am not interested in the women. I assumed you knew that, or do you not listen to the rumors in the halls?"

Almut nodded still appearing quite subdued and most unhappy with the discussion subject. "Ja, I hear what the wagging tongues spew. I know better though, Sire. You are the straight man for truth no matter what anyone wants to believe. I can assure you if the interests was truthful in the male I would offer to take my Blume's spot in this service return without hesitation."

I chuckled full of evil. "Oh, is that so? You would be willing to let me fuck you, would you Almut? A big old brute like you, crying like the little bitch as I break your man cherry. Ha! Now you are tempting me brother. Tell this woman to get the fuck out of my sight. I am not going to use your wife as my sperm pocket no matter how much you both beg me to."

Blume gasped and whimpered out as she grabbed my wrist with desperation filling her pretty brown eyes. "Please Sire, tell us what we can do to sway you to save Jaison like you did Marc and Kloe. I will do anything and so will Almut. We love our baby. I am begging you. I have no dignity, no hope without my boy. I must believe you are the King of lends sent her to save us all."

I pushed her off my arm with force and grabbed her by the back of her long hair. She squealed and for a moment Almut stepped forward to defend his Frau. I turned my head at him and shot him a hateful look daring him to come any closer. The huge man shuddered and then backed up to where he had been standing. Cary stared at me wide eyed with his mouth open as I pulled Blume's head back till she couldn't avoid my furious gaze.

I leaned in close to her and said in a menacing whisper, "You ever touch me again Blume I will see you burned alive for it. I care nothing for your or Almut's comfort outside what I already pay for his loyal service to me. I may choose to purchase that little nothing you call a son, but if I do it is he that will owe me the debt of gratitude, not you. I will take my payment out of the flesh of my silver that I can assure you. Why the fuck would I settle for the old used up cow and bull when I can thrill at the fresh calf. I bet that little boy of yours, with a bit of training, will warm my bed for many years to come. You forget your place. That boy belongs to the Dominants and FemDoms now, not to you anymore. I give you this one warning to keep your distance from your King Mad Maxx die Brutale or next time you will be sorry you ever caught my attention. Do you hear me woman?" I flung her to the floor with a sudden jerking of her mane.

Blume wailed and rolled into a ball for all the nosey passers bye to see. I stepped over the female and continued down the hallway without saying another word to any of them. I didn't even bother to release them from the kneeling. I was headed to Matz and Roland's apartment. I didn't want to seem too merciful, and I feared if I heard another whimper from that loving mother over her son I would break. I honestly felt horrible for her.

I will tell you Meine Liebe what I never confessed to anyone before. Hearing the pure love for their kid that Almut and Blume spoke was the most beautiful thing I had ever heard. This poor, uneducated black collar couple that had likely been forced into the arranged marriage cared so much for Jaison, both were willing to compromise their flesh to see him remain innocent of the nightmare himself.

You see Almut was completely straight, but he had said without a wince he would play the bottom in schwuler sex with me to protect his boy. He was willing to turn the blind eye to my sleeping with his own wife for that same reason. Then Blume, well that lady offered to be my whore all in the effort to hold her son in protection at her bosom. It was touching to hear their pleas, but I must also say I was a bit jealous. I wished for a moment that I had parents to care half as much as these two wonderful heart did for their young.

I did have the misgivings about purchasing Jaison's silver to paint black, but after that scene, I couldn't bear to say nein. I realized I had to hurry before Jaison was either snatched up by a cruel FemDom/Dominant or soiled to shit by one of the brutal Dungeon Masters/Mistresses. If he was of the black collar heritage and chosen silver I already knew something more important than the name of his parents. The boy was uncommonly handsome and graceful.

When the black collar children are pulled into the dungeons, before I got that law changed, only the most gorgeous, talented and uncommonly gifted are selected silver. That is because the Dominants/FemDoms fear choosing the black collar children to slowly molest to death. If you think on it you would understand. The servants of the Haus would rise up in revolt if too many were condemned to such a horrific fate of the silver. The parents of that boy or girl are right there watching every fucking thing they do.

They usually stick the silver collar on the children bought off the human trafficking market or, like me, by the Dominant's unwanted sons or daughters. The Elders wisely realized better to fuck to death the children that no angry father or mother will come forward to try to defend.

Anyway, I was brutally cruel to Almut and Blume so that when and if I purchased Jaison no one would assume I thought anymore of that boy than as the disposable cock warmer. I was a natural actor for that role since I had been exactly that until I broke the bat collar. That said, I had to cut the drama short to keep from losing the window of opportunity to try to salvage this unfortunate black collar boy that was cursed with good looks.

I knocked with vigor on Matz and Roland's door feeling the frozen lips of fear nipping at my spine. I wondered with his selection being the day before if maybe I wasn't already too late. The Dungeon Masters and Mistresses move with speed on the pretty ones. Those that escape the molestations of their handlers are often snatched up by the coyote Dominants and FemDoms.

Those are the first-floor residents that troll the dungeons weekly looking to get first dibs on the "cream of the crop." It is most uncommon for a very good looking boy or girl silver to survive to the third day after the slave collar selection before their metal is already sold and sometimes sealed. Sometimes in secret like Stephan had done to Annette you remember.

Matz answered my hailing him on the second attempt. He seemed surprised to see me standing there in the hall. His eye was swollen and turning purple from Byron's sucker punch the day before.

I growled out in anger. "You going to stand there like the dumbass or invite me in Matz? I am going to need an old man walker rather than the cane if you make me wait much longer."

Matz gasped and seemed to come back to himself. "Oh, where are my manners. Ja, come in brother. Forgive me. I was, well I thought maybe, doesn't Mad Lucus hold your metal now? How the fuck are you even here without that weirdo?"

I rushed passed him into the apartment. "First, you are not forgiven Matz so don't ask again. As for that shit about Mad Lucus, that is none of your business, is it? I would smack you around a bit to remind you of your fucking place, but I am in a bit of a hurry. I will kick your ass next time I see you when I have more time for such pleasures."

He stood there his eyes bugging out in shock. "Huh? What the fuck is going on Maxx. You come here in a rush and threaten me for what? Enlighten me please."

I turned around in full on fury and grabbed him by his shirt collar with malice. "Listen to me you little bastard. I need to purchase a high quality silver down below right this minute before the coyotes find out he is up for grabs. How much money do you have on you? Is Roland here? How much does he have on him?" I pushed him back nearly sending him to his ass.

Matz shook his head in disbelief. "Holy hell Maxx, you have lost your mind. You come barging in here demanding money, babbling about high quality silvers. I fished you off the banister only yesterday and now you demand to buy yet another kid to see murdered with viciousness. Did Mad Lucus not tell you about Ghanzi and Aara, brother? Didn't he tell you that those two babies were ripped apart by hand until there was nothing left of them but a blood spot on the stable floor? Neither were raped brother, just dismantled with more gruesomeness than I even ever heard of until that shit you pulled the night before last. Wait, you were in the Palace three days ago, ja?"

I raised my hand and backhanded Matz without holding back any strength. He fell to the floor, and I raised up and hit him again. His mouth busted open as he flailed helplessly trying to protect his face from my assault.

I yelled out in fury, "How fucking dare you to accuse me of harming my babies. You are the Gott damned rapist and thug around here, not Maxx. Maybe it was the wolves and you that saw fit to destroy a little nine year old girl and her ten year old brother, ja? They say the guilty dog barks first, you know."

Matz wailed out in terror, "Maxx, stop this please brother. I apologize for even insinuating out loud that you would commit such a dishonor. I beg your forgiveness for

112

being the stupid mad. You are hurting me, Maxx. If you cannot see it in your hear to overlook my insult I ask you to accept my offer to finance this request for the high quality silver you are seeking." I backed away and ended my attack when he said dat.

He lay there flinching at the sound of every word I said, "Now you say something I can hear clearly, Matz. Get your ass off the floor and get dressed. Bring all the cash you and Roland have handy then follow me to the Dungeons. Hurry the fuck up. You are wasting my time."

Matz sat up wiping the blood off his chin. "Okay, I put on my shoes Maxx. I am ready to go. just led me grab Roland's wallet." I watched the skinny man rush to the coffee table and grab his boyfriends money pouch.

I scoffed "Where is that cocksucker you live with Matz? Off rubbing his bow across another set of strings I bet."

Matz shot a look of cautious confusion at me. "That is not very nice to say Maxx. Wow, you certainly lost a few manners down below, among a few other fine qualities you used to possess." He quickly forced a boot on his sockless foot.

I nodded. "You obviously are referring to my tendency to lay there and cry while you fuck me over, ja? Well, if so, then ja. You can say I was forced to my feet by those trapped on all fours."

Matz pulled on his other boot with a quizzical expression. "I don't follow you, Maxx. What is this you are saying? Is there something you need to speak about with a friend? Did something happen below that has you trying to kill yourself one day and beating the shit out of your buddy the next?"

I laughed maniacally. "Course not, brother. You know me. I am Mad Maxx die Brutale. I am the same indestructible, perverted, and moody bitch I have always been. Are you coming on your own power or do I need to put a leash around your neck and drag your skinny ass behind me. I already told you I am a day late as it is asshole."

Matz stood up still appearing unsure what to think of this oddly aggressive Mad Maxx. "You are trying to turn me on with threats of the kinky shit are you (he laughed nervously). I like that. However, Maxx I must tell you that silver you are seeking is going to break the bank for Roland and me. I mean I give you the money without quarrel, but I need to know when and how you intend to pay it back? We have to pay the rent you know."

I went to the door with speed. "Christ Matz, you know I am good for the loan. I suck your dick when we get back with the pink slip to this collar in hand. Come on. I am ready to go now."

Matz came rushing up and followed me out of the apartment nearly running to keep up with me. "Okay, sure I am most happy to enjoy your oral service favor, but Maxx getting my thrill isn't going to pay the rent. You have to tell me how the fuck you are going to attend to the money flow issues. That silver is going to need a place to stay too. Karstin isn't going to have a haus to keep him if you don't…" I put up my hand to interrupt his prattling.

I stopped the fast pace and glared at him with anger. "Matz, it is not my fucking job to book the clients. You are the pimp, and I am the whore. You told me before that mess with the coronation that you had many lined up waiting for their taste of the forbidden. Is that a lie?"

Matz shook his head. "Nein, it is the truth. I still get phone calls every day from the first-floor trash looking to buy a front row seat to your show. So, am I to assume you are ready and able to come back to work for me? I mean I thought with Lucus, that Master of the Haus business, you maybe are no longer willing to sell your services to the unwashed masses?"

I snorted. "Are you kidding me? Where else can I sate my unnatural desires? You know it takes at least ten men a day to keep the Mad Maxx from pitching the fit of sexual frustrations. Set them up Matz for noon to three each day down in the Chapel or first floor apartment. I will handle the Lucus issue, and you do your fucking job without questioning me ever again. Let's go motherfucker. You are worse than a Gott damned old woman with all the nit picking. No wonder I traded you in for a less pushy roommate."

Matz nearly fainted when I said that. "What? Are you funning me Maxx? Sonofabitch did they change your medication down below? Maybe it is that head wound you have there. You are out of your mind."

I chuckled as I rushed down the steps forcing him to jog to keep up. "I was never in it to begin with Matz. I want to know what you found out from the black collars that may or may not have witnessed what happened the day Ghazi and Aara were murdered. Also, I warn you. When we get below you keep your mouth shut. I will do all the talking. If you disobey that command, I will use these nice strong new teeth to make sure Roland has the bottom lover without having to pay me to play his mare." I opened my mouth and pointed at the dentures.

Matz fawned over the improvement in my looks thanks to having the teeth for a moment until I threatened him. He then told me that all the black collars acted with suspiciousness when questioned about the gruesome death of my little children of Middle Eastern Decent. He ended his description of his and the wolves interrogation of probable witnesses by voicing his belief that identity of the killers would never be known.

He and I were nearly to the steps that led below to the Dungeons when I sighed and said, "You think Ghazi and Aara were killed by their brother collars don't you Matz."

He nodded but didn't look up from the floor. "Ja, brother I do, and so do Roland, Valitin and Magnas. Look the evidence clearly points to their co-workers this time.

Unlike Marc and Kloe these two were so little they had to stay with the older black collars. There is no way they were killed with such cruelty, and no one saw nothing."

I stepped off into the dank, dark stairwell with him following close on my heels. "Could maybe the Silk or Fur Queen have done it and threatened all them with death if they spoke?"

Matz sighed with sadness. "Nein, Maxx. I mean sure it is possible but unlikely brother. You and I both know why those sweet babies were put to the yard. They didn't belong here, and it matters not silver, black or Dominant, they were doomed. The hatred for their natural tanned skin runs deep. Many families are in this Haus thanks to that fucking world war. Our country is divided inside and out over the lack of tolerance for anyone that isn't the white, western European. The children were Muslims to boot and Ghazi, poor baby, he was vocal about it. I tried to tell him to keep that shit private, but he was such a proud little man." Matz trailed off and sniffed loudly. He was trying to wipe his eyes to hide that he was weeping.

We made it to the bottom of the stairs. "Are you absolutely sure about this thinking, Matz? I mean I am going to go question those black collars. Rudolph was there, right? If I find out you boys didn't kick over every rock, I wouldn't want to be you."

He sniffed loudly. "Look Maxx, you have no reason to threaten me on this, Gott Dammit. I loved those babies and I dare say knew them far better than you did. Losing them and Marc and Kloe has nearly killed me and all the wolves. I admit to you I don't even want you to buy this silver you consider this minute out of sheer fear this kid will finally send me to my grave with heartbreak. If I knew the names or had the chance to find out who the fuck hurt our children, I would do to them what was done to our lambs in the effort to get the offenders."

I stopped my fast travel once more and looked at him to see if the man told the truth. He stood there wet eyed and definitely in despair. I had not been too fond of Matz after that whole raping shit he pulled when we lived together. That day though in the dark, dank dungeon hallway I saw the truth of the man.

He was just a normal guy, that sometimes made mistakes he was not proud of. I decided to forgive him for all that he had done against me, but to never tell him of it. I mean anyone that can love a child that is not their own as much as Matz loved our black collars, is an angel in my book. Of course you have to consider the source there. *Master Maxx squeezed me while chuckling at that statement.*

I nodded. "Okay Matz, let's assume the black collars killed Ghazi and Aara for being the non-European. I will tell you in all honesty the ones that sent our babies Marc and Kloe to their reward dispatched their loyalists to kill them. There is only one enemy in this Haus to any black collar that I lay claim to, and that would be yours truly. If I am able to lobby this silver into my possession I want you to keep the secret of his association with me. If anyone asks, I bought this boy for my perverted interests."

Matz nearly choked on his spit. "What? Why would you want me to tell people you fuck a kid? Are you insane. Wait, how do you know that the killers of Marc and Kloe are to the yard?"

I chuckled. "If you answer the second question correctly then you know the answer to that first one, ja?"

He nodded slowly appearing to finally understand everything he thought he saw. "You are one clever bastard, Maxx. No wonder I fell in love with you so hard. Roland, he is my world, but I confess sometimes when I lay in his arms I wish I had met you in a different time and different world. What I wouldn't have given to be yours and have you be mine."

I nodded with a look of mischief twinkling in my eyes. "Well, no worries there Matz. You pull out the cash and you can rent my adoration for the whole hour anytime you wish to live the fantasy."

Matz frowned. "Ja, always the illusion Maxx, never the reality."

I motioned him to follow me. "You still haven't broken that code have you, brother? I am not real, and this is all a nightmare that this boy cannot wake up from. Therefore, I cannot be anything to anyone but the fantasy that will never come true. Hurry up, the clock is ticking, and we are not getting any younger." I took off headed for the office of the Head Dungeon Mistress.

Matz and I approached the aged Olga the Dungeon Mistress that had risen to replace the fallen Helga. *Excuse me a moment Meine Liebe, hahaha, sorry about that but I am still thrilled that beast found her grave. Thank you, Leo.* The ugly ole lady saw us coming and dropped the magazine she had been peering at to watch us approach through her thick glasses.

I stood straight as possible and walked with purpose, while Matz tried to hide behind my tall frame. I had been rapidly approaching six feet, three inches, by this time. The Mistress grabbed a tissue and blew her mushroom shaped nose with a loud honk just as we made it to her desk.

I bowed slightly in politeness. "Good morning, Mistress Olga. I am here to inquire about the purchase of one of your recent lot."

She nodded as she leaned her huge frame back in the chair and crossed her arms over her sagging boobs. "Ah, what a fine day it is. The Mortar King himself comes to see me, trying to cut a deal to possess one of my little silver fishes. Okay, tell me, Sire, which lucky kid do you have your regal eyes focused on?"

I looked at the top of my cane trying to appear bored with the conversation. "One of no obvious worth. A silver male, around ten years old with black collar lineage. I do believe the boy is called Jaison, but I may be incorrect. I didn't really bother to hear of such triviality. I am merely interested in the flesh not the moniker the dog comes to."

She nodded with a wicked smile on her face. That made me want to puke for the record. "Well, Sire, I must say you do have fine taste in your selection for the pleasure submissive. Ja, I know the boy you are asking after. He is a fresh one. Not trained for shit and insolent as hell. Maybe you should think of gaining the possession of one that has already been broken to the whip. This one is currently in solitary thanks to his fighting his paint."

I secretly began to like this boy already. He was not going to take that silver collar without giving them hell, good for him. "You are too kind Mistress to worry about my troubles. However, I am enticed by the resistance a young boy offers when broken to his metal. The more they squeal the more the thrill, ja?" I said with evil in my tone.

Olga really grinned at that horrible thing I just alluded to. "You are the bad boy, Sire. You know the law says you are not to take a bite until the silver is fifteen."

I nodded with a cruel chuckle. "You need not concern yourself with such insignificant rules, I know I don't. As long as the boy has the penetration virginity at collar selection I have done no serious harm. I can assure you he will be intact, at least enough to seal his lock. Besides Mistress, I don't believe it is your place to warn me, the Master of this Haus, about what is permitted in my own bed with my own playthings."

Olga snorted and sat forward. "This is true, Sire, however, that silver is not your plaything yet, now is he? Tell me Mad Maxx, what do you think a handsome black collar legacy is worth to the right buyer?" She batted her wizened eyes at me.

I leaned in close to her face "Why Mistress, a fresh pretty boy like that, it would be hard to place a price on his maidenhead. I think maybe if we are bargaining I am willing to offer whatever it takes to have him for my own dark thrills. In fact, I do believe the boy's worth is Priceless, ja?" I reached out and caressed her drooping jowl.

Olga swooned and panted. "Oh well Sire, I do believe we can work something out to see this collar land in your lap, oops, I mean your hands. How soon would you be desiring to take possession of him for his training to serve your needs?"

I leaned in closer and engaged the old hag in a deep kiss. The woman melted as I explored her nasty cave like maw with mine tongue. I pulled back when I felt her begin to paw at my chest with wantonness. The woman still had her eyes closed and was fish face kissing the air.

I heard Matz behind me stifle a giggle as he said, "Uhm Maxx, I am going to take a quick nature break. I be right back." The wolf practically fled to the restroom just a few feet down that stone hallway.

The Mistress opened her eyes when she heard Matz speak. "Oh my, I seem to have forgotten what it was we were discussing? I apologize, Sire. I suppose an old woman does have the memory issues."

I nodded as I kept my head. I was now leaned over the desk just out of her lustful reach. "We were discussing your retrieving that beautiful boy for me. I think we had only to settle the purchase price for him."

She nodded with an expression of bliss on her face. "The price is three thousand plus, a private demonstration from you on the secrets of your Priceless skills."

I stood up with fire building in my eyes. "You drive a hard bargain Mistress, but I am sure that boy will be worth the price I pay in cash. As for the other part of your request to seal this deal, my honey, I am more than happy to arrange that for you. Do you have time in your busy schedule to fit in that life changing lesson, Mistress?"

Olga nodded with eagerness. "Ja, I will make the time, Sire. You let me know the time and place. You can be sure Olga will be there."

I looked to Matz with caution as he returned from making his water, and his giggling at watching me seduce this old goose. "I send my man Matz by tomorrow afternoon with the information. Now if you would be so kind as to call your brutes. I wish to be on my way to enjoy the fruit of my bargain with swiftness."

I motioned for Matz to hand me the wallet. I took out the three thousand while ignoring the gasp of disapproval I heard from the Wolf and handed it to the greedy Dungeon

Mistress. She snatched the money from my hand (touching it far more than necessary while doing it) and took up the phone to call the Dungeon guards.

I had managed to safely procure Jaison in less than twenty minutes for a huge sum given that he was untrained with the promise of disgusting sex with Olga the Dungeon Mistress in the near future. I should have been rather proud of the fact I had at least bought Jaison the fighting chance but somehow like everything else lately, the victory felt hollow and unsatisfying. My outlook on the future was still just as dark as the shadows that haunted every hall of that stony hell below the Haus.

Matz and I stood quietly at the wall waiting for the guards to bring Jaison from his isolation cell. It wasn't long before I spotted two large brutes hauling a small blond boy between them headed our way. I watched the young man and saw even from a distance his handsome features were almost otherworldly. I gasped with sudden realization that this boy was still in a lot of trouble even with his silver about to be painted to black. This kid was too pretty to survive in the walls with so many perverts rutting and lurking, hungry for the finest flesh nature had to offer them.

I shot a look of terror at Matz and saw he too realized the problem. He shook his head at me and sighed while grabbing his temples. I winced at his nonverbal language of agreement with my assessment. Shit, how the hell were we going to keep this boy alive when he looked like a damned angel fallen to Earth.

The guards came up still holding that perfect little boy in their arms with stoic expressions on their faces. Jaison stared at me with what appeared to be awe in his expression. His eyes never strayed from me as I thanked the guards for retrieving my property. Matz tipped the brutes a few bucks and they quickly retreated, leaving Jaison with us and the Dungeon Mistress.

Olga chuckled with nasty humor. "A real beauty isn't he Sire? Well, try not to use him up too fast. If you spare his fine complexion you maybe can get a bit of your coin back out of him when you tire of your sport with him."

I nodded. "I thank you for the fine advice Mistress. I bid you good day. Matz will return with the rest of our agreement." She nodded as I told Matz to take Jaison's hand and follow me.

Jaison suddenly yelled out in excitement, "She called you Sire. You are Mad Maxx the Collar King. I knew it. I heard about the scar on your face. Oh, my Gott. My Master is the savior of the silvers. I am saved. Gott heard my prayers."

I turned around with a startle to see the Dungeon Mistress narrowing her eyes in suspiciousness. I panicked as I saw her looking at her telephone. I knew that bitch would call all her hen buddies to tell them of the silver boy that was relieved to be purchased by Mad Maxx die Brutale. I had to do something to end that rumor immediately.

I lifted my hand and backhanded Jaison with such force he fell to the stone floor. Matz gasped and backed up in shock. The boy wailed as he grabbed his reddening face. I reached down and snatched up his hair at the top of his head. Without hesitation I took off dragging the screaming, terrified boy behind me like the sack of potatoes. Matz stood there frozen to the spot disbelieving the horrific sight before his eyes.

I shouted out over the wailing Jaison. "Ah, scream boy. I love the sounds of it. You just wait till I get you home. When I am done with you this dungeon will seem like the gentle mother. You are right, as for being your savior, oh I assure you I will savor every second of destroying your innocence. Hahaha." I continued with speed doing all I could to ignore the pathetic pleas for mercy the boy made as I dragged him along.

When I made it to the steps I stopped and dropped the weeping boy on the floor. Matz had run to catch up with us. He approached with caution as I wrung my hands nervously staring at the boy that had rolled up into the fetal position at my feet.

Matz looked at him then to me in fear. "What the hell was that bullshit. You traumatized this little angel. How could you Maxx? Fuck, you are a monster."

I nodded with anger rising. "You Gott damned right I am, Matz. Now you listen to me you little twerp. Take this pile of garbage up to the first floor. You go right to the barber and have his head shaved bald. You hear me Matz. I don't want to see a fucking bit of fuzz left on that empty bowling ball on his shoulders. I am going to turn over his papers to the black collar Mistress. When you finish having him shorn, take him to the torture chamber. Do two things, drop him off with his father Almut for assignment to train for the Mastery of Torture at his father's hands. The second thing you need to do is make sure Hubertus has tawsed Samual from the Great Hall as I commanded. If not, then you come find me. I will correct that bullshit immediately."

Matz rolled his eyes and rubbed his face as if relieved. Jaison stopped crying when he heard the words painted black and return him to his father. "Oh, my Gott. You scared the shit out of me Maxx. I thought you flipped your fucking wig. Jaison, get up boy. Thank your Lord and Master for his mercy. He has given you a second chance to live to be the old man. Stop that fucking crying. You will learn to shut your mouth when around your betters. What he did is far from how bad it could have been you know."

Jaison slowly unrolled and took to his feet, keeping his head bowed. "I do thank you for the mercy, Master. I apologize for making you angry with me. Did you say I am to go back to my family?"

I nodded. "Ja, you little worm. I thought you would be fine for sport but seeing you up close, I think you are simply too common to keep my interest for long. I made the mistake buying your collar. I am too proud to admit that I foolishly made this deal. I send you back where you came and demand you keep your fucking mouth shut about even having laid your eyes upon me. I ever hear you admit to this farce sell, I will kill you in the foulest of ways. You understand me, boy."

He whimpered but nodded. "Ja, I do Master. I thank you for the true mercy you show me. I never say a word of you, but I want you to know the legends are true. You are the savior my parents prayed for." He then came forward and hugged me.

I pried him off me groaning out in feigned anger. "Get off me worm. Matz, get this nasty thing out of my sight. I have to go take a fucking shower. If I don't I will stink of beast all day, dammit."

Jaison covered his smile as Matz took him by the hand and led him up the steps. I tried not to look up and watch them go but damn me I did steal one glance. Jaison was staring back over his shoulder at me with a peaceful smile. It may have been one of the most beautiful sights I had ever seen. A little boy that had been stolen was returning to his family after three years of hellish isolation from the ones he loved.

I wish that could have been enough to get me to return to believing I was worthy of such a blessing as having dreams and love as Jaison did, but it wasn't enough. I watched that lovely young boy climb back up those horrid steps to rejoin the living with as deep a feeling of being the corpse. I looked at the door under the steps that led to my Mortar Palace. I wondered briefly if I didn't belong there as Gretta said I did.

Then I chuckled as I recalled that Kilian was at that moment enjoying the company of Reece, Noethan, Sebastian and Tadeas. I bet the smell of those fellows dismembered heads was quite the joy. If the snake was still able to smell without much of a nose left after the acid bath I ordered for his cruel games with me.

I know it seemed odd that I would choose such a punishment for that bastard. Well, Meine Liebe I never do or say anything for no good reason. I knew I couldn't justifiably kill the Elder now Voter level Kilian. I had to find a way to neutralize him from ever using his charm and good looks to seduce others to use me for his plans ever again. I used that disfigurement to assure everyone would see the truth of the snake. He would forever be as ugly on the outside as he is on the inside, ja?

Anyway, I headed up the steps clinging to Jaison's silver contract as if it were my own heart. I was in a rush to find the black collar Mistress and set the boy free. That night, Jaison would once more sleep in the grateful arms of his adoring parents. It only cost me my dignity and another tiny piece of the soul I no longer possessed, right?

I found the Mistress of the black collars with ease. She gave me no difficulty assigning the boy to his lifelong career as the Torture Master to be hand trained by his own loving father. I had Matz shave the boy's head because the tradition stated that any silver that was painted black then worked outside the stables or in the kitchens was to receive a week's worth of instruction from the Dungeon Masters.

129

I made damned sure the boy's beauty was temporarily marred during that time so none of those horny beasts took the interest in defiling Jaison before he began his life under the protection of his huge, scary father Almut.

As it was, that little trick of making him less attractive by being bald did work. Jaison made it through that dangerous trial without a single incident of molestation nor did he draw the attention of any Dominant or FemDom coyotes that happened by as he endured the final few days of his stint as a prisoner of the Haus. Sometimes a little cruelty is the only way to prevent a bigger trouble down the road, ja?

I left the black collar Mistress headed with speed down the first floor hallway. I intended to head down to the Torture chamber to visit with Almut and Hubertus. to give one the good news of his son's freedom and make sure the other didn't injure Samual too badly. I never made it to see the men.

As I rushed passed that closet from hell, you know the one, the door came open. I nearly pissed my pants as Byron rushed out and snatched me from behind. I struggled like the madman in his grips till I realized the identity of my abductor.

He held me tightly from behind panting from the fight to keep me from escaping him. "Hello Christian. Did you miss your lover Byron? I know I sure did miss you."

I winced as I realized this crazy man really did believe that shit I spewed to keep him from handing me over to

Kilian and Reece. "Oh, it is you brother. You scared the shit out of me. Next time you desire to speak to me approach me like a friend not the lurking fiend, ja?"

Byron chuckled as he ran his hands roughly across my chest and stomach with wantonness. "I will keep that in mind Maxx. Come with me to the closet for a minute. I want to speak with you privately."

I trembled as the memory of the things that man did to me in that fucking closet rushed through my mind. "Oh, uhm, there is no one around Byron. Maybe there is no need to hide in the closet like a couple of outlaws now is there?"

He breathed out into my ear. "I didn't offer you the choice. If you misunderstood, allow me to correct that error. You join me willingly or I tell Felicity you are treating me like an enemy again. She won't appreciate knowing you don't trust her judgement, will she?"

I gasped. "Nein, don't do that Byron. Let me go and I come with you without the need to be filling my lambs head with further reasons to hate me."

Byron let me free of his pawing grip and I followed the man into that smelly room. He closed the door and turned on the light. I stood there wringing my hands keeping my eyes to the floor as he eyed me head to toe. His silence was making me more than a little nervous. I thought maybe he intended to demand special service on that spare table, which was still there, like he used ta.

He leaned into the closed door and folded his arms over his huge chest with a catlike smile. "You are absolutely beautiful Maxx. I swear to Gott I couldn't love you more than I do this moment."

I raised an eyebrow "Why do you say that Byron? Did Felicity say something to cause you to think more highly of me than you already did?"

Byron laughed hard then shook his head. "She didn't have to whisper in my ear this time. I saw what you did for Almut. You saved that pretty first born son of his from becoming the meal of the predators in this Haus."

I nearly fainted as I shot a look of terror at the Voter. "How the fuck, nein. Whoever told you that is a fucking liar. I don't know anything about such a wild tale."

Byron laughed even harder. "Damn are you adorable when you attempt to wriggle out of the truth. Look Maxx I happen to be visiting with a friend when you came to paint him black. I overheard you order the Mistress to assign the boy to train under his own father. I have to say, you are kind beyond words. Though I wonder, Jaison is awful attractive, and a kid painted silver. How the fuck did you afford his metal, boy? Don't bother trying to deny what I already know. Simply answer the question that plagues me, and I will move out of the way and let you get back to whatever it was you were doing when I caught up with you."

I shrugged. "Oh, you know me. I sweet talked the Dungeon Mistress into cutting me a bargain."

Byron frowned with storm clouds appearing in his expression. "Maxx, if you and I are going to be friends and lovers, then you have to stop this bullshit story telling when I ask you a question. I repeat. What perverted thing did you do or promise to get that boy's high quality silver into your slimy hands?"

I closed my eyes and swallowed hard at his cruel description of me. "I uhm, took out a loan from Matz and Roland."

Da Voter nodded with his smile returning. "Ah, now we are getting around to the truth at last. A loan you say. A big one I imagine based on the fine qualities of the property you just turned over to the Haus for free. How much? Two maybe three thousand?"

I looked back at the floor as I nodded. "Three, but I don't understand why any of this matters to you Byron. I am sure Felicity would agree the boy is worth all that and far more. She would think me wrong to step away to allow that sweet boy to be slowly crushed under the cruel metal of the Masters."

Byron sighed appearing irritated. "So now you are speak for that lamb of mine. That is not the intelligent thing to do, is it? I happen to know you are dead wrong about what she says regarding Jaison."

I flinched when he called Felicity his lamb. "You speak to her about this, Byron? What did she tell you?"

He nodded. "Ja, I just left her in fact. Felicity says you can buy all the silver children in the Haus you want. You can set them free and burn down this hell hole. It won't change the fact that you are a perverted, lying, back stabber that she hates with all her heart."

I held my breath. "Please tell me you are teasing me Bryon. Felicity said that she hates me, for truth?" I had been afraid all along this was why my lamb didn't want to come home with me.

He looked toward the floor. "I am not funning you, Maxx. Felicity does hate you. She told me you buy Jaison with money you don't have. Then you will go engage in the shameful acts with half the Haus behind closed doors to pay back the debt you gained from the purchase of his metal. She says you call this mercy for the ill-fated children, but you left her behind to suffer. She can only assume you take on the silver bills to hide the fact you enjoy sex with as many strange men as you can manage. Is what Felicity tells me the honest truth of it, Maxx? I want to argue for you with her, but shit, I kind of have to wonder if the lamb doesn't have validity to her claims about you. I mean you are the pervert, so maybe thinking you the wanton slut is not a stretch, ja?"

I felt everything within me demanding I run away rather than toward Byron. Yet my legs began to head for his awaiting arms. I was in the imaginary tractor beam and unable to break from his spell. I reached him and he enveloped me in his huge grip assuring if I had second thoughts, too bad for me. He forced his lips to mine. I closed my eyes and let go of all my inhibitions. It was as if I were on autopilot.

Byron eagerly pawed and molested my flesh only stopping shy of grabbing the areas that he had cut up and only after I wailed out several times as he roughly handled me there. It seemed he was happy with this feigned display of superficial affection from me until he leaned into my ear with suddenness.

He whispered out with a moan. "Maxx hold still so my touching you is only half the equation. You are merely the compliant. Remember I want the willing. Touch me back the way you like to feel of a lover."

I groaned in true agony at that idea as I whispered back. "I don't think I can do that, Byron. I honestly don't like the way the man feels. It is not sexy to me. I mean no offense, but I am not turned on by you and I cannot pretend to be." I thought for sure I was literally screwed since surely Byron would tell Felicity on me for denying her champion.

He instead pulled back out of his groping with a smile. "Ah, you tell the truth to me at last. I am proud of you Maxx. I know how hard that admission must have been for you."

I gasped as he caressed my face gently staring at me with an expression of admiration. "You are not angry with me? I don't understand. I thought you said you wanted me to come to you willingly and be your lover. I tell you I cannot do that, what the hell Byron. Are you playing the head games with me? You are going to go tell Felicity I am a bastard, ja?" I was nearly yelling at him in total panic by this time.

Byron reached out and grabbed me by the upper arms and shook me with force. "Settle down, Maxx. You cannot freak out each time we are together, damn it. Look, only yesterday you were refusing to allow me to touch you at all. Today you allow it but are not ready to touch me back. We take this one step at a time. I merely ask you to take the steps as you feel comfortable towards our ultimate goal. You are doing as I ask you. You are the cold heart slut accustomed to being fucked without the sacrifice of caring for the one doing it to you. I don't expect you to suddenly become the hot honest lover overnight Maxx. We have time. Now, I am going to let you get back to your business. I brought you a gift that I think will aid you in calming that chronic anxiety that causes so much moodiness in you. You listen to your lover Bryon and take up this habit. I think you will find a little relief of your painful symptoms, ja?" He reached into his shirt pocket and handed me a pack of cigarettes and a silver lighter.

I stared at the smokes with a stun. "You want me to take up smoking? What? This disgusting habit is going to ease my symptoms of nervousness you say. That is the craziest thing I ever fucking heard. I am not taking those coffin nails from you."

Byron pushed them into my face. "Ja, you will Maxx if for no other reason than to give you something else to suck on other than the cocks around the Haus. You listen to my advice and see if I am not right. Felicity told me to inform you this was actually her idea. She would never suggest something to hurt you, now would she?"

I took the pack of cigarettes from the Voter with a sigh. "If smoking will bring her around faster than I will do it happily. I thank you for the mercy of it, brother." He took back the pack opened it and handed one of the cancer sticks to me demanding I try the damned thing.

I stood dare trembling while he lit the tobacco up. At first I just let it burn but Byron insisted I suck the thing and inhale the smoke. *Meine Liebe a quick warning here. Never pick up smoking.* The moment I took that first real drag of the nicotine I was hooked like the stupid fish.

I had no idea at the time the having the schizophrenia caused me to be far more likely to become addicted to cigarettes. The scientist don't understand the functions but there seems to be a connection between the nicotine and a calming of the schizophrenic's worst inner pain. All I can say of it, is don't. You cannot miss what you never known.

Byron watched with a thrilled smile as I lit the second cancer stick up with trembling hands. The moment the first one was spent I felt the euphoria that flowed over me with each drag quickly dissipating. I was in a rush to find that feeling again, no matter how minor it seemed to be. After many years of agonizing numbness, to feel anything was a feeling I never wanted to end.

The Voter told me he needed to be going as I went to light the third. He chuckled and told me to come see him anytime I needed a fresh pack. As he closed the door leaving me alone in that hideous closet I suddenly felt a rush of despair rush over me. I dropped to the floor on my ass and pulled the boys legs to my chest. I silently wept as I smoked that cigarette there on that dirty carpet.

I hated my life so much. Nothing seemed to be right. I didn't want to slap people around or bark orders. I didn't want to suck cock for pennies. I didn't want to be a chain smoker, Byron's secrete lover or a schizophrenic Mortar King, but I was all those dings and far worse. I was discovering I was also a twisted sicko pervert not worthy of life. I stood up and wiped my eyes eager to get the fuck out of that closet. I opened the door and began to flee that horrible place of bad memories when I heard a familiar voice call my name out in thrill. I followed the sound of his tongue popping and fingers snapping.

Chapter 50: Demon of Seduction

I stopped dead in my tracks when I head Jakob's familiar voice hailing me from down the hallway. My old buddy had been missing for months. Every time I had managed to sneak off to visit with him, there had been no answer to my knocking on his door.

I turned around to face the Queen and noticed that Jäger was trailing close behind him. I raised an eyebrow when I saw that this fourth floor Dominant was holding onto Jakob's hand being dragged along like the unwilling kid. It suddenly occurred to me the two of them must have finally become the lovers after a long game of playing hard to get.

Jakob's smile melted to the frown as he got within speak distance. "Oh, my Gott, Maxx. You look horrible my love. You are so thin and pale. What the hell has happened? Are you ill? Augh, your head. What the fuck. Who did this shit to you?"

I nodded as I leaned my weight on my cane and took a long drag of my cigarette. "Well, it is great to see you too brothers. It has been what? Weeks? Months perhaps? You see that is the funny thing about not checking on those you claim to care about. Things change and they move on, or below. Enough of the superficial bullshit attempt at polite pleasantries, you have proven to me you don't really mean you don't care.. Now, what can I do for you? Looking for an enjoyable time or maybe trouble? I promise whatever your poison, I am your man." I blew my smoke into Jakob's face with malice.

Jakob coughed and waved his hand around trying to dissipate the fumes. "Damn, Maxx, which is quite rude."

I nodded. "Ah, you are so correct. Enjoying your own pleasures while ignoring the comfort of your friends is one lesson I learned well from you. Equal for equal brother. I repeat, what do you want? I am in kind if a rush here. You are wasting my time. State your business with me and move along."

Jakob's eyes went wide, and his mouth dropped in a stun as he stammered out, "Uhm, I don't understand what you mean. Am I to assume you are saying you think I ignored you?"

I shrugged. "I don't think shit unless I am ordered to, Jakob. I am the mindless sex toy, don't you know. However, I do believe the last we spoke I voiced a fear that maybe I was the real boy. Lucky for you, oops I mean me, my mind shattered. You didn't want to be bothered with the troubles I make for everyone, ja? I seem to recall you dropped me off with Mad Lucus. You never came back to check on me like you promised. That is okay. He has cleared up that silly delusion of rights to be treated as the human being rather than the plaything real nice. I no longer question the truth of it. Are we done with this conversation yet? Or do you desire to inhale more of the spent smoke from the angry ghost of Maximillian?" I blew another lung full of my cigarette fog into his face.

Jakob coughed and stepped back frowning deeply. "That you say is unfair, Maxx. I didn't come back because there was nothing I could do for you. I stayed for the two weeks when you were held at Karstin's looking out for you. I guess you don't recall that though. You were pretty far gone."

I nodded as I dropped the spent smoke onto the carpet and ground it out with my boot. "Oh, I recall more than you think Jakob. If you were protecting me, then I think a career as the guard is not for you. The wolves were in the hen haus, brother. They got the rooster too, many times. That still doesn't explain why you make promises you don't keep. Oh, I get it. You think that the comfort found in knowing your friends are still aware of your existence doesn't mean much to the worthless psychotic, ja? Ha, that does make sense. I thank you for the mercy of clearing that up for me."

Jakob put his hand on his hip and wagged his finger into my face. "Now you hold on just a minute, Maxx. I am not going to stand here and take your insulting me like this. I am your friend, and I do care about you. I have no idea why you are suddenly so hateful to your Auntie like this but let me tell you something. You are not the only one around this Haus that was having the serious troubles at that time. I was having to run from one sick bed to another. I was exhausted. Thankfully, Lucus sent me and Jäger off for the much needed holiday to Tahiti before I ended up in a bed right next to the two hearts in this place that I love the most."

I shot a look of humor at Jäger. "Ah so that is where you been all this time. Tahiti on Lucus's dime, which was paid in full by my ass. I bet Jäger here is feeling much better now that you worked out all that ailed him. ja? I will call you Doctor Jakob, the specialist in proctology." I chuckled with diabolical humor.

Jakob popped his tongue and flounced. "You are not only the rude bastard, but you are also quite vulgar. I am starting to wonder how I ever thought the world of you, Maxx. You are not only looking foul, but your attitude has also grown ugly. I think maybe it is best you move on for a bit until the boy I adored decides to come see his Auntie and apologize for being an asshole."

I grabbed Jakob around the waist and pushed him into the wall before he could even think to struggle. "Now you don't really want me to do that now do you Auntie Jakob? Being the asshole is what endures me to everyone I have ever met in this Haus. I seem to recall you also were interested in me for that quality not so long ago. I admit back then I was not too interested in your claims to want your own taste of my skills. I have since turned over a new leaf sweetheart. I really have missed that delicious lip gloss of yours. Tell you what, have this man of the month Jäger bug off or hell, come into the closet with me and bring him to bugger on. They say three is the crowd, but I say threesomes are my specialty, ja?" I leaned in and forced a very seductive open-mouthed kiss on the man while groping him wantonly.

142

Jakob led out a squeal and tried pushing me off with vigor. That only caused me to pour on the charm with more strength. I reached up and ripped his blouse open while trying to drag him kicking and screaming towards that hell closet. Jäger that had been quietly listening and watching the interaction between me and his lover suddenly came alive. He grabbed me by the shoulders and pried me from his struggling boyfriend. I turned to punch him, but he flung me hard sending me flying.

I collided with the wall but didn't fall. Jäger didn't have the strength of Byron and as I said even thin as the rail I was already a large brute by then. I braced my weight against it and caught my breath a moment while eyeing Jäger's attempts to calm his very upset lover.

Jakob was still thrashing and yelping as if he were being attacked. The hapless Jäger grabbed his flailing arms and hushed him till the Queen finally realized that this man was helping not hurting him. I chuckled as Jakob fell into Jäger's arms weeping with much drama. I reached into my shirt took out another cigarette and lit it while watching the show.

The Queen heard the sound of my lighter and shot me a look full of confused agony. "Why would you try to hurt me like that Maxx. I thought we were the best friends and family."

I nodded while taking a deep drag. "Ja, so did I Jakob, but I was schooled. You cared for me when you thought I was available to warm your bed. The moment I was not, and you found another stud to fill your, uhm, heart, you dumped me. I would apologize for misunderstanding what you wanted from me, but you see I didn't make any mistakes in anything but the timing. You have another dog sniffing around your tree. You no longer need this one."

Jakob sniffed loudly as he began to weep. "I never thought of you as just a lay, Maxx. Take that back. I love you, Gott dammit."

I growled out with sudden fury. "Liar, the only person you genuinely love is Jakob. You can go fuck yourself now that you no longer desire to fuck me."

Jäger turned around with fire in his eyes as Jakob fell into a weeping jag at my words. "You heartless cunt. How dare you insult Jakob. He has done nothing but worry about you for as long as I have known him. I confess he speaks so highly and often of you that I was jealous of you. Not anymore thought. It is obvious my poor lamb was deluded. You are a nasty punk that doesn't deserve his admiration."

I chuckled. "Jealous of me were you? Well, Jäger there was no need for that. Haven't you heard? I am forbidden the pussy. I couldn't fuck Jakob here if I really wanted to." I winked at him with wickedness.

Jäger led out a loud roar and came at me with his fists ready. I stood there calmly until he was in striking distance. Without any feeling at all I ducked his right hook then plowed my own into his sternum. The man led out his air and his knees buckled. Quick as a flash I racked him upside his head with my cane. Jäger fell to the floor wailing in pain as the blood poured from the scalp wound caused by my blow.

I knelt next to the writhing Dominant and grabbed his hand. Then without a word put out my cigarette on his forearm. He opened his mouth and screamed. His thrashing about nearly knocked me down but I managed to get back to my feet before he could kick me again.

I shot a look at Jakob. He had fallen to his backside and pulled his legs to his chest. He was crying like a kid as he stared at his injured boyfriend. I shrugged at him when he shot a glance of horror at me and mouthed out, "why?"

Then without another moment's hesitation, I took off down the hall leaving the two of them to clean up my mess. I could hear Jäger's cursing and Jakob's weeping echoing down the walls for quite some time before at last the sounds of the rushing residents drowned them out. That closet hall was a sparsely traveled path you know, so I was in a hurry to get back to where ambushes from Byron or Jakob or worse were no longer possible.

Okay, I see by the look on your face Meine Liebe you didn't appreciate that cruel business I dealt to Jakob and Jäger. Normally, I would pop the hell out of you for daring to question my will. That said, this time maybe you do deserve an explanation. I told you that Jakob may be next to Matz, my best friend. Well, despite what I just confessed he is to this day.

I shook my head in disbelief. "How did you get Jakob to forgive you for doing that mean stuff to him and Jäger Master?"

Master Maxx chuckled,. "You think that was mean, Meine Liebe? I have done far worse to you and all within the first hour of meeting you. That attack on Jakob and his man was nothing."

I gasped. "Then you are saying he accepted you had the right to do it, Master?"

He nodded. "Ja, well nein, okay it is complicated. I will get to that part of the story. You merely have to trust me when I tell you I never do anything without good reason. If you are going to survive in the Haus the most important lesson you must learn is never believe what you see. There is always more to the story, and what seems real is not always the truth of it. I say to you that I had asked for Jakob's help to keep Mad Lucus off me. I had told him I was in desperate trouble many times and the man didn't listen. He said he wanted to be my friend, my best friend in fact, but when I needed him the most he was not there. He did abandon me. He dumped me on Lucus's floor and never came back to check that I was safe. Lucus raped me that night and the next morning. He was supposed to be guarding me down at Karstin's when I was tied up and acutely psychotic. He didn't do his job there either. He was off on dates with Jäger when the wolf pack used me for their sex toy. I couldn't defend myself. That was for my best buddy to do. I had given everything I had to see his ego restored when really it wasn't for me to do. I did it because

I love him with honesty and as my brother. I trusted him to return that deep feeling and trust. I attacked him like I did for two reasons. One to teach him what it felt like to have one you depend on take advantage and think nothing more of you then for what you can get. The second reason was because I knew acting out would scare him enough to go to Leo for aid. If Jakob didn't seek out my truthful lover, or at least find him since I could not, then Jakob really wasn't my friend. More than that, Leo wasn't truly my beloved. I could have asked Jakob for aid once more, but I had no luck there many other times. This time, I believed I made myself clear. Jäger was not too seriously injured, and only Jakob's pride was wounded. The sad fact is when you ask for someone to save you, no one wants to get involved when you are the lowly schizophrenic. However, you cause damage, shit they can barely wait to come running to subdue you. This making sense to you, Meine Liebe?"

I nodded. "Yes Master it does. I try to tell them about Debbie, and they ignore me. They don't want to hear what I have to say. I throw a fit at school and presto, I am sent to the office and suddenly everyone wants to talk to me about how rotten I am. So, really you were trying to get put in the Palace, weren't you? To stop yourself from being the pervert?"

He chuckled as he hugged me tightly. "Ja, I am glad you understand. That saves me trying to explain it to you. I wasn't able to kill myself. I thought maybe I should be locked up far away from everyone. Before I turned into the monster I could feel growing inside me. Really, I kind of hoped this time, Gretta would do me the favor of ending my

147

pathetic life. Well, I am here. That means my plan, like everything else I ever tried to do, didn't quite work. If you be still I tell you all about it. Are you ready to go on with the story to find out?" I nodded as he continued with his long tale of loss, despair, and brutality.

I tore off through the roaming groups of collars, Dominants and FemDoms feeling nothing. I knew that mean shit I did to Jakob and Jäger should have bothered me but to my horror I felt justified in doing it. I may have been doing that crap for a reason, yet that didn't make it right. Deep within I began to realize that the whirling vortex had started to consume the boy's heart.

It was sucking away all the empathy and hope of a better day faster than my Geradine could eat her oats. I felt the freeze of hell nipping at my chest. I wondered if maybe it was too late to slay the monster Mad Maxx die Brutale from consuming what was left of Christian Axel the boy.

I reached into my jacket pocket and pulled that horrible pack of cigarettes out. Though smoking is common today, do remember this is 1981, in the Haus few engaged in the filthy habit. Nein, the vices of the Haus are far more complex than the simple addiction to tobacco. There cocaine, acid, liquor, sex with minors, torture, and far worse is the rule of the day.

Only the lower rungs of the society in her walls gravitated towards the cheaper thrills such as nicotine. I looked at that package and damned Byron for giving them to me. I had only started the fucking pack and already I could feel the urge to light up every few minutes. It was as if I was born to smoke. I thought briefly about tossing those slave drivers onto the floor and walking away. Fuck me that I didn't. I could have maybe escaping the fate of helpless addiction to them if I had stopped right then.

However, the feeling of euphoria and calming of that infernal river of anxiety within was too enticing to the pleasureless Maximillian. All I knew was pain, terror and loss. If simply putting one of those nasty things into my mouth and sucking the smoke helped my agony even a little, shit I wasn't going to turn it away.

I stopped in the middle of all the kneeling residents to light up the cigarette. I noticed that usually one of the black collars walking toward me wasn't looking for a spot to fall to his knees. His eyes were focused on me, and more than that he moved with speed. I took a drag of the smoke while watching this insolent prick haul ass toward his Mortar King that was in a most nasty mood. I almost felt sorry for the idiot. Surely, he had a death wish, or so I was thinking at the time. Hahaha.

I was ready to stop this motherfucker when suddenly he dropped down to a graceful kneeling just within earshot of me. "Master, forgive me for interruption. I beg your mercy, but I have been sent to seek you for an audience with an Elder."

I snorted as I took another drag. "Is that so? Well, I don't know what the fuck mercy is so don't bother begging me for it, worm. Which Elder is seeking an audience?"

The black collar trembled while keeping his eyes to the floor. "The Honorable Elder Jonas requests you come to his home with haste. He says you have the appointment with him that you may have forgotten?"

I chuckled with an evil sounding tone. "Honorable you say? I think there is nothing that fucker does that can be classified as such. I would send you back to tell him to bite me but that is the problem. That is exactly what he desires to do, ja? I release you to your other duties. I am not going to thank you for doing your job though so best you move the hell off with speed before I take out my frustrations on the messenger." The black collar male gasped as he nodded, then scurried away on his knees like the hermit crab.

I had to laugh at that crazy bullshit. I looked around at all the people still in their kneel. Many trembled. Others were stealing awed glances at me. I glared at each one and they would look to the floor with suddenness. It was truly funny to think all these collars, Dominants and FemDoms were frightened of a sick, skinny teenager just because I fed a few assholes to the yard dogs, oh, and allegedly threw Reece from the banister.

It was then the realization of what that black collar said hit me. Shit, it had been two weeks already since Jonas had visited me for his blood couple in the Palace. He was obviously thinking now that I had a full day or two out it was time for me to return to feed his disgusting fetish. I shuddered at the idea of his sucking on me. I even considered briefly ignoring his request.

However, the horrors that he could enforce upon me, worse than the Palace or Heslach were even without fucking Reece there, caused me to rethink continuing my journey to the Torture Chamber. I took off for the back stairwell to head up to the sixth floor with much irritation.

I threw down my spent smoke. In the carpet yet again, hahaha, as I made it rather clear I cared nothing for the Haus. Just as I approached the steps. Cary was standing there at the back door guarding it. He saw me and his face broke out in a pleasant smile despite the nastiness of our last encounter earlier that day.

I tried to haul ass up the stairs pretending to not notice him, but he yelled out, "Christian, hey baby, come here a minute will you?" I stopped the journey with a wince but then turned around headed back his ay.

I glared at him as I approached. "What the fuck do you want, Cary? Do you not see I am in a hurry to be somewhere?"

Cary grinned and dropped his eyes coyly. "You are too damned romantic lover. How did I ever survive without your gentle words."

I scoffed. "Cut the shit Cary. I mean it. I have to be somewhere in a hurry. Being late to the appointment I am headed is to assure the outcome worse than it already will be. State your business and I will be on my way."

Cary looked around to be assured we were alone. Then quick as lightening he came at me grabbing me around the waist. I was completely caught off guard as he forced his lips to my own and engaged me in the lustful kissing. It took me a moment, but I managed to push the pawing Shadow King off me.

I growled out nearing fury. "Shit, you interrupt my schedule to slobber on me. Damn you Cary, if you want to fuck make an appointment, idiot." I wiped my mouth and began to tear off for the steps with speed.

Cary yelled out behind me as I head up. "I want to see you soon, Christian. Come by my apartment when you have a minute. Roselina and I will make you dinner. Then maybe after, don't you want to know why I just needed to kiss you?"

I was several steps up when I yelled back. "I have been enduring this nasty sex shit since I was twelve Cary. I know exactly why you kissed me. Tell Roselina I will be there for dinner tomorrow night after your shift ends at eight. Now fuck off, damn you."

He laughed loudly as he put his hands aside his mouth and yelled back, "You are wrong, my King. I kiss you because Almut is straight. He sent that message as did Blume. Now that I have become a 'Christian' you are my angel baby. I cannot wait for tomorrow night." I didn't turn around but lifted my middle finger and flipped him the bird as I continued rushing up the steps.

I could faintly hear Cary's laughter at that as he said, "Promises, promises. Tomorrow night I make you keep that threat you hand signaled lover."

I rolled my eyes at that. That fucker was incorrigible. I couldn't even insult him when I tried. I wondered of all the black collars in the Haus I could have Dark Bonded, why Der Hund picked this idiot? It seemed to me a real waste that our Master shard didn't choose the female. I suppose even our core shard was afraid of Peter's rule. I made a promise to myself one day I was going to ask Der Hund about it if I ever saw him again.

I made it to Jonas's apartment pretty quickly. I stood there at the door as I had many times as the boy dreading knocking. I didn't want to see that bastard for any reason but especially not for the bi-monthly blood coupling. I thought of the wounds that were still burning badly left by Byron. I knew that shit wouldn't affect the Vampire's resolve to see his lusts fed. I took a deep breath to brace my nerves and banged on his door.

He opened it without hesitation. The expression of fury on his face told me he was a bit sore. You know over that little display of power I demonstrated in the Great Hall only an hour or so before. I looked at the floor as he stood there flashing his fire filled dark eyes at me.

The silence between us was uncomfortable and finally broken as he stepped aside. "Come in here, Maximillian. I have a few things I wish to discuss before we get to my pleasure with you."

I shrugged as I walked past him. "Oh? I didn't realize you talking and me being forced to listen without input is defined as a discussion. I suppose I need to find the updated dictionary, ja?"

The Vampire was not impressed with my sarcastic response. "You will shut your insolent mouth the fuck up right this minute. I am going to tell you something. If you ever embarrass me again like you did down in the Great Hall, I will make you sorry I didn't let Ivan take you to the yard when Peter tossed you. You hear me?"

I nodded as he slammed the door shut in anger. "Sure, I hear you Jonas. But am I listening? That is the real question, isn't it?" Again, probably not the right thing to say to a pissed off Vampire.

He flew across the room and backhanded me with force. I took the blow but didn't flinch nor cower like I usually did. I stood there glaring at him full of hate. That surprised the Vampire. He reared back and hit me again. As before I took the blow without moving a muscle nor falling to my knees nor even demonstrating that it hurt.

Jonas's fiery eyes began to smolder as he backed up a bit staring at me in disbelief. "Do you want me to call the white coats, Maximillian? How dare you stand there like the dummy. Kneel, you big bastard." He pointed at his boots.

I scoffed. "Nein, I am not going to kneel, and you call them. You surely noticed I am bigger than you now. I am not the little boy you can throw around anymore. That means, you call for back up all you like. Yet, before they get here I will send you to visit with Reece. Better think on that a moment, dad." I chuckled with demons rising.

Jonas nearly choked when I said that. "You insolent sonofabitch. You dare to threaten me. I am your guardian and husband. Kill me and they will burn you at the stake."

I nodded as I took out my pack of cigarettes and lighter. "Ja, they will, but like father goes the son. I put that stake through your heart first. The way I see it maybe it would be worth the pain to know you wait in hell for me pops. just be aware of something Jonas. You really have no need to start this quarrel with me. I am here as you requested to keep my end of our bargain, fool. You can waste time trying to bully me, or you can take what I owe and be happy with it. This is your final notice that I am not going to let you push me around taking more than your fair share. You have been the unnecessary brute to me for years. In the end, you get what you wanted, and I limp away more injured than I should be. Try that shit on me from this day forward and I think I am ready to throw you from the banister. I will let the chips fall where they may. If it means I must be put to the yard then at least I won't have to put up with you or Peter or that motherfucker Lucus anymore. Beware father, that peace from all you is looking pretty fucking good to me these days. You want to test me? I think you better reconsider it if you are." I took a long drag of the smoke.

Jonas stood dare a moment watching me with a confused expression then fury re-entered his eyes. "You forget I have Geraldine, boy. You piss with me and find that lamb served up at the Great Hall for dinner."

I held out the cigarette and looked at the bright red cherry at the end of it as if bored. "Oh, you could Jonas, but I say to you again. The dead don't need to eat do they? Kill my lamb, I dare you. Find out I can be far crueler than you. Ask Sebastian, Tadeas and Noethan or perhaps your old lover Kilian. By the way, have you seen him lately." I locked my dead gaze onto his demonic eyes.

Jonas bellowed. "You have let power go to your head, boy. This will not be permitted. You are a nothing. A psychotic, a used up catamite. You are barely worth using as the sperm pocket anymore. Age is catching up with you, boy. Soon, all those pretty looks that kept you endeared to so many will wane. Then what good will you be to anyone?"

I sat down on his couch and flicked my ashes onto his carpet. "You bet I am all those things Jonas, but I beg to differ on that last statement. No matter how old I get I am still younger than you by many years. You are only getting older along with me, dad. Good luck getting another Priceless to give you that precious youth serum from straight from the tap. Tell me something. Do you have enough energy left at your advanced age to break in another if you could find him? I seem to recall I was quite the handful as the child. I am not the cutie pie little boy you thought you would hold in terror anymore, that is true. I am the calm, well trained donor that still possesses the thing you desire more than anything. I suggest you start treating me with the fucking respect I have more than earned, Jonas. You meet me halfway and find that taking your dark pleasure with me has become easy with less stress between us perhaps you will even enjoy that long life you expect. However, fool with me any further and trust me, I will make you sorry you ever stole that taste of the forbidden from my gunshot wound."

Jonas crossed his arms appearing to suddenly be deep in thought and less angry. "You really think I am going to allow you to behave as my equal. You shouldn't have been allowed to break the metal Maximillian much less walk around free of the leash. I am still having the tough time believing this idiot that sits before me rudely dropping his ashes on my expensive things is called the fucking Master of the Haus. Pure abomination. I have known you since you were the drooling, little bitch that couldn't even handle a fucking blow job without weeping about it for hours after. Gretta has sat on her throne and thumbs allowing the schizophrenic moron rise to be the voice of the Law. Insanity apparently is contagious."

I snapped my evil gaze at him. "Like it or not I am the Mortar King, Jonas. I am your better now and not your fucking submissive any longer. You will bow to my will motherfucker. Gretta had no choice but to back the fuck up. You go ask her. I put her in the corner as I will do to you this minute. As for my weeping over the tasks of my childhood enforced upon me, try me out Jonas. You may find you are the one weeping this time when I am through with you."

The Vampire pointed at his hallway. "Well, this threat I got to try out. Get your lazy ass off my furniture. Put out that nasty smelling shit you are smoking and go to the back room. If you want to behave as the unruly asshole then we can go back to the bondage while I take what is mine from you."

I stood up and dropped the cigarette onto his floor and crushed it with my boot. "Fine by me, Jonas. Just so you know, I am cut up severely. Mad Lucus told me to beg your mercy from the couple until I heal up, but I refuse to do such an indignity. You can leave your lancet in the black dresser. I have plenty of open wounds to choose from for your dinner. In fact, this time I will even enjoy your disgusting habit. It pleases me to know for a change you actually have to do what I have always wanted you to do. You see, no matter which place you take your infusion you are either sucking my cock or my ass. That is what they call irony, isn't it? Bon appetite motherfucker." I chuckled with dark humor as I took off headed for the room with the red door at the back of the hallway.

I entered the room and rolled my eyes that nothing about it had changed in all those years. The bondage bed that had frightened me as a boy still sat in the center. That impressive black dresser didn't seem as big or scary to me anymore. I saw that the chains on the headboard had not been used in a long time. There was rust in the joints of them and the whole room smelled stale. I chuckled as I sat down on the bed and began removing my boots.

Jonas appeared but lingered in the doorway watching me from a distance. "I see you laughing. What the fuck is so funny, Maximillian? I am about to cut you up then dry fuck you. That causes you humor, why?"

I shrugged. "I was thinking of this Vampire joke."

He scoffed. "Oh? You think Vampires are funny do you? After all these years being the victim of one I believe you are trying to act stoic. It is not working Maximillian. I know you are scared. I can see it in your eyes."

I stopped undressing and shot him a humored look. "Okay, you insist on my demonstrating I tell the truth of it. Here is the joke, well besides the one standing at the door. Three vampire brothers decided to hold a competition to see which one of them is the most powerful. The first brother is the strongest. He says, "Watch this." He takes off at nearly one hundred miles per hour. Two minutes later, he returns, with his mouth covered in blood. "What happened," his brothers exclaimed. "You see that mansion over there?" "Ja?" "Well, I went over there and sucked each and every last family member dry. They are all dead." "Wow," his brothers said. "We expected that though, for you are the strongest." The second brother to go is the oldest. "Watch and learn, boys," he said, and takes off even quicker, at 150 miles per hour. Five minutes later, he returns, both his mouth and his neck covered in blood. "What happened," his brothers exclaimed. "You see that village over there?" "Ja," they said. "Well, I went over there and killed every last person in the entire village. There is not one left alive." "Wow," his brothers say in awe. "As we expected, for you are the oldest and have the most experience." The third brother is the fastest. Not to be outdone, he said "Watch this and don't blink or you might miss it." He flies off, faster than the rest of them, going at least two hundred mph. In only ten seconds, he returns. His entire mouth, nose, and neck are covered in so much blood it stains the front of his shirt. "What happened," his brothers exclaimed. "You see that giant tree over there?" "Ja!" "Well, I sure fucking didn't."

Jonas stood there a moment and then suddenly he burst into wild laughter. "Holy hell, which is the funniest vampire joke I have heard in years. Very clever Maximillian. Now strip down and quit fucking around."

I went back to removing my clothing as I snorted/ "Don't I wish I could stop. That, however, is apparently my perverted cross to bear. There go making the insulting statements to you Jonas. your kind don't like the cross, ja?" I removed my jacket and blouse while keeping an eye on the Vampire that had slowly been coming a bit closer to me.

Jonas scoffed. "Shut the hell up, Christian Axel. You know that shit about crosses, sunlight and stakes to the heart are all myths. Total bullshit." He was looking me over with wantonness in his expression.

I pretended to not notice he was close enough to attack as I undid my breeches buttons. "You Vampires are a moody bunch. You cherry pick the things to believe. That blood sucking and being the mean natured is all very true, but eternal life. I think not." I reached out with suddenness and struck him in the face with a strong backhand. Jonas did not expect that. His head flew to the side, and he staggered a bit.

I stood there glaring at him topless and with my trousers undone but not down. "Come on you batty motherfucker. Show me how fast you can heal. Or is that a myth too? Well, only one way to find out, ja? By the way, I am not that pussy Christian Axel. I am Maximillian die Brutale, asshole." I leapt on him before he could regain his solid footing.

He fell backwards taking me down to the floor with him. I straddled the bat and began to backhand him repeatedly. I held nothing back. His mouth burst open, and blood poured from his fractured lips. Once I saw that, it was as if a flood gate busted within the boy. That monster that had been struggling broke loose of his chains.

I started to plow into Jonas with my fists. To my astonishment I even leaned down and bite the shit out of him with the fake teeth. I held the wheel with white knuckles doing all I could to stop the boy from signing our death warrant, but the flesh wouldn't listen. The monster of rage ran the show now, and I, Maximillian was his prisoner.

Jonas at first only grunted and cursed loudly. As my blows become more forceful and anger driven he began to wail. I had never heard the man make noises of fear before. The surprise of it stunned me just enough for him to find an opening to land a blow of his own. He struck me in the sternum knocking all the breath from the boy. I gasped for air but found my lungs paralyzed.

I rolled off him clawing at my throat trying to get the precious gas into me. Jonas managed to get on all fours. He crawled at me with speed and leapt like the angry lion with a roar. I grabbed him by the upper arms but without the oxygen he had me at the disadvantage for a moment. The old Vampire used his upper hand well.

He didn't hesitate to knock the holy shit out of me with his own series of harsh backhands. I rasped out curses while trying to knock him off me. Jonas held tight to his position of the top straddle. He probably looked like the experienced cowboy riding the crazed bronco thanks to my bucking with extreme force.

Jonas finally locked his clawed hands around my throat and began to throttle me. "You hold still you insane sonofabitch. I should murder you right this minute for daring to raise a hand to me. How dare you?"

I gasped and ripped at his hands with vigor barely able to breath led alone speaking. "Go ahead bat. Kill me. I am not scared of you. But you better be afraid of me motherfucker. Is the myth about fire true for ending the Vampire? Keep choking off the Master of the Haus's air and you are going to find out."

The fire in Jonas's eyes burned like the raging forest fire. "What the hell has gotten into you, Christian. Did you become the possessed down there in the dungeon? Demons

162

of the Haus foundation surely have made a nest in your soul. Stop fighting me, dammit. This is your duty to me by contract. I am forever your husband and your Master."

I roared out in fury managing to fling the winded Vampire off me onto the floor. "I will never stop resisting you. I hate you, Jonas. You tricked me into the blood bonding. You used ropes and lies to get what you wanted. Well, guess what? There is no such thing as forever, asshole." I jumped at Jonas who was panting on his knees next to me.

This time he was ready for me. He grabbed me by the hair and endured my fury driven blows. With much force he twisted my head and pushed me face first into the carpet. The Vampire quickly entrapped my left arm as I clawed at his hands holding my head. Quick as the flash he pulled it behind me to an agonizing position. I wailed and pounded on the ground while trying like hell to buck him off again.

Jonas didn't waste a moment. with his free hand he grabbed the back of my head. He then pounded it into the floor repeatedly nearly knocking me to unconsciousness. Only when he felt the boy go limp under him did he stop the forced head banging.

The room spun around, and I thought for sure I was going to vomit. For a few minutes I was weak, stunned and confused. I could feel Jonas's weight shifting on my back, but I couldn't get the flesh to respond. I was helpless to fight him off as he pulled down my nearly undone breeches.

I heard him gasp. "Who the fuck did this shit. Fuck, you are cut up. God dammit. No wonder you behave like a loon. I think you are ill and not necessarily the mental kind only. Shit, I cannot blood couple you if you're full of brain infection. Christian, you listen to me boy. Go immediately to the clinic and have someone assess all these open wounds. The minute you are cleared of any pathogens you come back here to me. I will not be denied what is mine or I will see it destroyed." He grabbed me by the upper arm and flung me to my back to face him.

I was sure I was going to faint as I mumbled out. "I killed the doctor haven't you heard, Vampire? Hahaha. You know something? All this time I thought it was you that had the fleas. Turns out it wasn't you at all that gave them to me. I should have realized the culprits would be down into the dungeon instead of up into the belfry, ja." I swooned and likely passed out for a moment.

Jonas left the room, I think. I came back to my senses when he forced a glass of water into my mouth. I stared at him unsure of how the fuck I had gotten onto the floor. I saw that my clothing was scattered everywhere. I assumed the bi-monthly blood couple was over since I ached everywhere and saw blood on his face.

Jonas leaned down and looked into my eyes. "You in there, Christian? Say something. If it is smartass, then I warn you Maximillian I will beat you more than I already have."

I winced as I nodded "Ja, Christian is in here Jonas. I don't desire any more punishment. If you are satisfied with your service then I must ask you for the release to clean up. I have other business to attend."

Jonas led out a gasp as if surprised. "If I am satisfied with your service? Wow, your mind is gone. I never have been interested in the masochism, fool. Beating me up and then being the broken sex toy when I finally subdue you is a far cry from decent service to your Mann."

I narrowed my eyes at him in suspiciousness. "Did you blood couple with me in front of the mirror or something?"

Da Vampire's expression became confused. "Huh? What kind of a question is that? That doesn't even make sense. Why would it matter if I couple with you in front of mirror?"

I scoffed. "Because you cannot see a Vampire cuming if you're looking in the mirror fool. get off me." I pushed him off and held my aching head.

Jonas sat there a moment staring at me in disbelief then suddenly broke out in wild laughter. "Oh, my Gott. You cannot see the Vampire cuming in the mirror. Where the hell do you get this crazy shit you say? I should beat you down and murder you for such insolence this afternoon but fuck. You are obviously out of your psychotic mind. I may be the fiend, but I am not Reece or Kilian. I don't take advantage of those who are unaware of their surroundings."

I groaned in pain as I tried to stand. "Since when did you stop kicking the dead horses, Jonas? I seem to recall no matter how far in the atmosphere I have gotten you are happy to be the astronaut and take this as you say, 'used up' spaceship for the perverted ride."

Jonas, also groaning, got to his feet and offered his hand to aid me to my own "Aw, now you are being unfair Maximillian or Christian or whoever the hell you are today. I only come see you in the Palace for what was necessary for me to remain youthful. I could have done far worse, and you know it. Plus, I saved Geraldine from those punks, or did you forget that?" I took his hand and stood up while pulling up my breeches with relief. It is not good to be without a barrier to the creepy man. Though garlic underwear would likely be better than the thin silk trousers Lucus gave me.

I winced as I buttoned up and rushed for my blouse and boots. "Ja, you do have the point there. Thank you for saving my lamb. However, you did that, so I don't starve to death. Hard to stay young drinking from the corpse, and I do believe fucking one is illegal in this Haus. Anyway, you don't care a fig for her otherwise."

Jonas shrugged while he watched me redress. "Doesn't matter why I do what I do. The issue is your health. Your complexion has a strange hue. I never seen you so damned skinny. Have you grown taller? Ja, you have. That head wound looks ghastly. I do believe those dark circles under your eyes are not normal either. I must say I believe based on what I am seeing of your behavior and overall

166

appearance, something is seriously wrong with you. I dare say this is more than that fucking schizophrenia you carry in your blood." He looked me over with an expression of curiosity and disgust.

I snorted as I buttoned my blouse. "Well, whatever it is I am most thrilled to discover the Vampire repellent at last. I for one hope the ailment gets worse. You know what? I wonder, if it drives you away, perhaps Peter and Lucus will also find it unattractive. If only I could get so lucky. I have dreamt for all my life of the joy it must be to sleep alone. I could go the rest of my days happily without having to endure the horny, hairy, snoring, farting male bed companion."

Jonas sighed and crossed his arms. "You better hope you are able to return to the pretty boy that drives me wild with thrill. We both know you are only alive right this minute because I keep Gretta from sending you to the yard. You know, despite the ugly shit that happened today it maybe was worth all of it to hear you are unhappy with Lucus and all other males. I had worried there for a bit you had turned schwuler on me."

I startled when he said that. "Oh, is that what you think? That I am sick of the men for my sexual partners? Ah, you misunderstand me. I meant I am sick of you, Peter and Lucus. You are all old news. You of course are older than the others, much older. I am interested in younger and wilder passions with the studs in this Haus. I need the strong, handsome male to scratch my perverted itch. The ancient bulls simply can no longer take me there. I thought maybe it was, as you say, I am overused. Yet, I think really the problem is I am ready to graduate from the primer classes to the more advanced studies. You geezers simply cannot keep up with my beastly demands." I chuckled as I tied up my boots keeping my focus on the floor so Jonas couldn't read the lies in my eyes.

Jonas growled out irritation. "You are pushing your luck, boy. I am willing to overlook that fit throwing you do, and even pretend you have not insulted me several times. That said, you hurl another negative criticism at me regarding my legendary prowess in the intercourse, I will forget you are daft. I think it best you finish dressing with that mouth of your shut before I find something to shove in it to still that sharp tongue of yours. Oh, and while we are on the subject of your soft parts, next time you see me take those fucking dentures out and turn them over. I cannot trust you with any weapon around me when I am exposed and vulnerable. How many times do I have to tell you that I am the only one allowed to bite around here. You would think you learned that when I knocked your Gott damned teeth out. Apparently, you are still not getting that lesson through your thick skull."

I shot him a glare of hatred but minded his demand to be quiet. I was in no mood to blow the man, when he was offering to let me out the door unmolested. In all the years I had endured his nasty interest in me he had never cut me any slack. I decided best not to push my good luck.

The truth of it was my standing up to him more than anything else, even the cuts, is the real reason he released me that day after I escaped the palace. He was unsure what had prompted my rage reaction against him since he was being his usual asshole self. I like to think he feared reprisal most foul, like the three fed to the dogs, if he pushed me too far. Though I can never prove this as the fact.

Ta this day Jonas never has admitted to why superficial cuts prevented his blood couple with me. Especially when you consider he intended to cut me up himself for the drinking of my fluids. He allowed me to leave his apartment, to my surprise, without even forcing the oral services or taking a single drop of me to drink.

As I walked into the hallway, and he shut the door behind me I was left flabbergasted. The Vampire's face was turning black and purple from our vicious battling. It was not like him to throw away the prize when he had soundly won the war. I thought maybe the bat was getting a bit of dementia or softening up in his advancing age. Hey, I was seventeen and Jonas at fifty-eight was ancient to me back then, ja?

Well, whatever prompted him to leave me for a while, far be it for me to not take full advantage of the mercy. I ran down that hallway as if chased by an army of Vampires headed for the stairwell at speeds the Olympics would have fawned over. I was half-way down the back steps before I realized I had beaten Jonas up and lived to tell the tale of it. I had waited five years to see that bat bleed. It felt awesome, for a minute anyway.

It was getting rather late in the afternoon when I was finally freed of Jonas clutches. I decided it was time to head to the Torture Chamber that I have headed to for hours now. I needed to check on Samual and speak to Almut. This time I saw that Cary was busy dealing with a second floor Dominant. He didn't notice me slip off down the first floor hallway. I held my breath hoping that I had managed to escape his detection. I had made it through an entire day without a single couple, not counting that blow job I had to give Mad Lucus that morning.

It seemed to me if I did manage to avoid all the wrong people I maybe could claim a single day in my life where I wasn't nearly on life support or locked in a mental hospital rubber room, of no forced sex with a man. If I did somehow manage that feat I thought may be one of the truly good days of my entire shitty life.

Well, except that Felicity hated me, I was Dark bonded to a sexually sadistic fiend, had beaten up all my friends along with the Vampire, been stalked by a sexual predator, believed I was a slutty, schwuler pervert, and let's face it was quickly becoming hopelessly addicted to cigarettes. Other than all that, well, it was nice not to be fucked. *Look Meine Liebe, when it comes to finding the good in life, the cursed cannot quibble about the details. Don't forget that important detail about survival.*

I was feeling a little better, less numb you know, when I headed down the steps into the torture chamber. I thought of the cigarettes and wondered if they were somehow giving me magic powers or boosting my confidence, you know. I took the pack out and lit one as I moved with speed down the stone staircase.

I reached the bottom and all around me everyone dropped to the ground. It looked like a bomb went off. There were people scattered everywhere in front of me all at the same time. I chuckled at that weird scene and began stepping over the prostrated residents. No one made a sound or moved a muscle even after I was distant from their spot.

It was actually kind if eerie and to be honest, though respectful, was making me feel further isolated from my fellow human beings. The tugging emptiness began to creep up my spine once more as I approached Almut's assigned door to electro playroom.

I opened it and rushed inside, grateful to be free of that hallway full of bowing living statues. I leaned into the door rubbing my forehead. I had one hell of a headache from that headbanging shit you know, while listening for the sounds of the residents to resume. Within moments of my taking off out of there sight I heard the noises of people speaking and moving resume as if nothing just happened.

I sighed in relief and looked around the room. No one was in there. The chains were empty of any victims awaiting punishment. I saw that Almut's tools of torture were all neatly put away in the lockers and the restraining table had been wiped to spotlessly clean. I groaned realizing the black collar Torture Master had not even bothered to come into work that day. Likely he was in the

Dungeons visiting with his newly freed son in the holding cell for the newly painted Haus subs. I didn't blame him. That is where I would be if Jaison were mine, ja?

At least I knew that Cary wasn't funning me. Almut and Blume had already heard of Jaison's good fortune. That was one less uncomfortable interaction I would have to suffer for the time being. I hate it when someone fawns over getting the favor granted. I am not sure why, but maybe because they always try to touch me. I don't like to be touched. *Okay, you Meine Liebe can touch me. Anyone else, yuck.*

I giggled as he tickled me in the ribs after saying that.

He kissed the top of my head then whispered into my ear. "Touch me often and in all the right places, then see the service returned with eagerness. I say to Jonas it is my dream to sleep alone. Let me tell you a secret, my little Frau. That was a lie. I desire to hold the soft, smooth, rounded flesh of Meine Liebe in the cuddle all my life and beyond. I beg of the fates to see we are buried together in that perfect union if we don't make it to the finish line. I could close my eyes forever without fear if I had you to hold." I shuddered as I felt a tingling rush through my spine and chest.

I gripped his huge arm tightly in my little ones. "We are going to make it, Master. It would be a blessing to sleep in your arms for all time. You taught me the cursed don't get mercy. I bet even when we get out of here and far away from the Haus, we will still have to fight to find peace."

He nodded as he sighed. "You are wise beyond even my own years, my little demonseed frau. There will be far more bad than good days, of that I don't doubt. Yet, I have to say I have already won that greatest of all prizes. I believe with all my soul, now that I have found you, I will never be alone again, and neither will you. Remember, apart or together, no matter where the winds blow us, we are in each other's heart. Not even the schizophrenia can take that away from us. That bond is unbreakable."

I nodded and snuggled into his warm flesh with a smile. For a moment I could almost believe in the green fields and baby lambs. My childish vision of Heidi and the kindly grandfather danced in my fucked-up head.

Then the memory of his disease came in to bust up the colorful images of a fantasy future with each other. I stole a look at his face. The scars of his traumatic past forced me to face the cold, bitter realities. It was far more likely I would die in that basement, and he would find his end in a dungeon cell. The hurtles we needed to jump seemed too numerous and high to ever overcome without one of us falling behind, hopelessly lost to the other.

If only I could find a way to join him in a place where the brutality was a dream, and the dream the reality. It maybe wasn't a sure answer to our vast issues (age, level of maturity, country of origin, status as prisoners to various offenders, lack of support system, and his debilitating illness just to list a few. Do recall I am not fully sick with the disease yet]) but it was a childish fantasy. I really believed if I followed him and Felicity, she would lead us to this wonderful place where everything is forgiven and forgotten.

Master Maxx giggled as he poked me in the ribs stirring me from my deep thoughts. "I ask you twice if you need to make water, Meine Liebe. Where were you just now?"

I sighed. "Heaven, Master, and you were there too. I don't need to go potty. I ask with respect that you tell me more of the story about the time Maximillian ran the wheel?"

He chuckled. "Well, I am truly apologetic to pull you and I from that lofty place. If you can forgive me for rudely interrupting your sweet thoughts and you are good with the nature calls, then your polite request is granted. Where did we leave off? Oh ja, I was about to leave the electro-playroom to find Hubertus and Samual."

I was about to leave the room when the door came flying open. I almost was hit by the damned thing the visitor was so vigorous with his bid to enter. I backed up just in time to watch my father Peter come storming in with his eyes full of the storm clouds of anger.

He looked me over than growled out. "I have been waiting for you to drag your lazy ass down here to see me all fucking day. here the hell have you been?"

I scoffed as I puffed on my smoke maintaining the eye contact leaning my weight on my cane. "Wish I could tell you, but you know me. I'd forget my head if it were not tied to my shoulders. Good to see you too Peter. How have you been? Read any good books lately?" I snickered at my making the small talk with the Voter.

He glared at me with those cruel gold eyes of his,. "You are not as amusing as you think you are, Maximillian. You know Gott damned well you owe me the training session, and you are a week behind in your studies too. I should have been the first thing you did this morning the second you got through playing big shot in the Great Hall."

I really howled at that. "First thing I did, you say, or first one you mean Peter. Well, I would beg your forgiveness for not rushing down here to fall on my knees begging you to allow me to suck your cock, but I am the busy man these days. I had a waiting list a mile long and sad to break it to you brother, but you're not as important to me as you seem to think you are. In fact, I can safely say, you are a nothing in my eyes." I blew my smoke into his face.

Peter smiled with evil humor, which was a bit unnerving I admit. "Well, well, well, seems someone has been practicing his Dominance training with vigor. That's good. I am pleased to see you have improved by leaps and bounds since last I saw you when you were the quivering weeping mess, only a few days ago down below." He leaned into the door and crossed his arms still grinning.

I didn't like the way he was not showing anger at my obvious insolent statement. "I am glad to hear you appreciate whatever it is you think you see, Peter. Now, if

175

you don't mind. I have other things to attend. Step aside, I am leaving."

Peter stood up straight and dropped his arms to his sides with a chuckle. "Nein, I am not moving, and you are not going anywhere. What are you going to do about that, big man? Go ahead and show me your balls that have finally dropped. It brings me great thrill to be the first to kick them so hard they flee screaming back where they belong inside you. Then when I am done with that, I am taking the services you owe me. I granted you mercy when down in the Palace. Your studies are not the only thing you have been neglecting for the last month."

I took a long drag then flicked the smoke at the Voter, barely missing him. "You know I don't get you, Peter. Is it not your job to train me to get off my knees and stand up like a man? Yet at every turn you are there trying to trip me each time I take to my feet. What the hell is with that? Another of your sick games? Is this how you get off or something?"

Peter nodded with a smirk. "Don't you know it. I love keeping you forever the bottom, Maximillian. You try to stand up like the stallion and I bend you over like the mare. The more you fight, the more I enjoy it. I am going to make sure you never become the top, not ever. I decided that long ago when I tied you up and made you my little bitch. These other men around here, they are the passersby thrilling only in the singular passion of using you as the toy. Not me. My interest in you goes much deeper than any cock in this Haus can get into you. I fuck your mind, along with your flesh. Thanks to that double pleasure, I will never tire of hearing your pleas for mercy or tasting your tears of defeat."

I didn't move as his hateful words looped around in my ears. "I am not the bottom anymore, Peter. I am the Master of this Haus. Fuck with me and see your good fortunes flounder."

He pointed at my neck. "Oh, you are the top now are you? A Master that wears a collar. Now this is truly a novelty. Does Lucus let you fuck him Maximillian, or is it still the other way around? Is he on his knees or are you, Sire." He began to laugh at his tormenting me with truthful words, damn him to hell.

I winced. "Shut up Peter. I don't have to answer to a worm like you about anything I do or don't do with my partner Lucus. Maybe today I make time to attend to those services you claim I owe you. This time you bend over that table, and I fuck you. Don't worry. I was trained by the best. It will hurt, ja, but it is the humiliation of it that really stings." I came at him like the madman.

Peter was ready for the outburst. We grappled each other pushing and punching like pro boxers. He got the upper hand for a moment and slammed me into the wall. My father tore at my blouse trying to rip it open. I kicked him with all I had in the hodensack sending him gasping to the floor. I rushed over and grabbed my cane that I had dropped in the beginning of the fray.

177

Before Peter could recover I swung it like the baseball bat across the back of his head knocking him forward face first onto the floor. I heard a loud snap just as the cane broke in two. I dropped the useless weapon and leapt on the nearly unconscious Peter with a wail. Once again I lost control of the wheel. The beast within broke the chains and he was hungry for blood.

I rolled him to his back and got between his legs. He was moaning in agony, swooning in confusion. I tore open his shirt and unbuttoned his jeans. I tugged at them trying to pull them down. Peter started to regain his head. I saw his eyes go wild in terror.

He yelled out in a distressed filled tone, "What the fuck are you doing, Maximillian?"

I stopped trying to strip the man and glared at him with cold brutality dripping from my eyes. "Why Peter, which is exactly what I am doing brother. I am about to teach you a lesson in empathy. When you raped away a twelve year old boy's innocence I bet it is similar to the seventeen year man raping you of your anal virginity without the comfort of lube, ja? I tell you what. Let's find out shall we. Oh, don't close your eyes. I want to see the look of pain, and terror it causes you. I find sadistic pleasure in it." I went back to forcibly disrobing my father.

Peter freaked out when he realized I wasn't funning him. He kicked, punched and bit me trying to stop me from the sexual assault. I totally had lost all understanding that I was about to become the very thing I hated the most. The rapist, and worse, my first victim was going to be the one that started me down this path to perversion, my own father.

I had nearly gotten him to the point of accomplishing such a feat when it became clear I forgot something. I am not turned on by the man and that is when he is not screaming and struggling, yikes! I couldn't do the dark deed thanks to being incapable of penetration. I couldn't believe my bad, or good actually, luck. I could believe myself the sexual pervert all I wanted, and Felicity could honestly think it too. That didn't make it true. I simply couldn't bring myself to rape Peter even if he did deserve.

When I found nothing I did could arouse my interest in the couple with him. He stopped struggling and began laughing at me. I punched him in the gut, but he continued to howl at my obvious defeat.

I got off him and readjusted my breeches glaring at him full of venom. "Shut up you fucking pervert. I don't see anything funny about this. If you saw your face in the mirror you would be more somber, there is no doubt." I kicked him in the boots.

Peter sat up still chuckling but wincing from his injuries. "Couldn't rise to the occasion there could you, Maximillian? I thought you were the Legendary schwuler. Ah, well maybe you are still the gay man like everyone things. I think ja, you really, really are. The sissy type you know. The female in every relationship with the man.

That's too bad for you. Looks like you will always be the bottom after all, won't you?"

I growled out as I kicked him in the leg harder this time. "Shut up. I am not a bottom. I am straight and you fucking know it. You always have known it. If you were a female you would be crying for your mother right now as I fill you full of my seed."

Peter howled. "Oh, what a big man you are. Pick on the little girls but cannot hold your own with the men. Ja, that's a sissy bottom for you. Now, if you are done trying to play a role you are not capable of I suggest you get back over here and grant me my services as the contract we have demands. You don't, then fine by me. I merely call Gretta and see that gold turned back to silver. Make up your mind if you want to be the doctor with a wife someday or the aging catamite forever chained to my bed. Up to you, but better hurry up and stop wasting my time. I need to go over your lesson plan after you suffer humiliation by relieving my tensions." He stood up though he did stagger a moment.

I dropped my head after looking longingly at the door. "You are never going to leave me alone are you, Peter? Nothing I do is going to stop this nightmare."

He nodded with a smile. "There you go. First honest thing you have said to me all day. Now, on your knees, boy. I am the wanton man, and you are about to be sorry that you pulled that stupid stunt." He pulled up his pant enough for him to limp to the door and lock it.

I frowned but dropped to a kneel as he came back. I knew I couldn't beat that fucking contract I had with him. To break it meant I belonged to him for life. I took a deep breath and hoped Byron's trick worked to keep Peter to the oral services only, but as I have said a million times, I am not a lucky man.

Peter decided that my idea of no lube would teach me a lesson about trying to literally fuck him. I was in pure hell from his forcing that dry intercourse and the open cuts that were irritated. I held in there in stoic silence for as long as possible, but eventually I began to wail from the agony of his thrusting into me as violently as possible. Again to punish me, he was also taking his sweet time about this humiliation.

It was most likely the sounds of my distress that caught the attention of the visitor that began to knock with vigor on the locked door. Peter ignored my would be savior and poured on his mount with more strength. I was nearly insane from the mind numbing discomfort by this time.

Suddenly there was a loud crashing noise. I couldn't believe my eyes. The knocker had decided he wasn't going to be denied entry to the electro-playroom. He had kicked the door in. I gasped in pure terror as Peter held my waist tightly preventing me from fleeing his couple and this embarrassing scene.

I whimpered in full on panic as the huge bodybuilder walked into the room as if invited. "Hello Peter. Did you not hear my knocking?"

Peter didn't miss a beat as he panted out. "What the fuck do you want Byron. Can you not see I am busy at the moment?"

Byron smiled at me with wickedness. "I do see that. Mind if I join in the fun?"

I dropped my gaze to the floor and felt my heart sinking as Peter grunted out. "You bet, Byron. I will be done in a minute here. I am reminding the little cunt of his status as the bottom. Your aid in that lesson will be most appreciated."

Byron turned and slammed the door shut and leaned into it still smiling with evil. "I am happy to be of service in teaching Mad Maxx a few things this afternoon."

I watched as he forced the lock closed on the wreaked door and approached the distracted Peter never taking his eyes off me. I trembled in terror wondering if he was going to do as Peter was and hurt me as bad as possible to gain revenge or just for twisted thrill. He winked at me which caused me to gasp in sudden realization what he was about to do. Just as he swung his big fist aimed right for Peter's head, I felt my father's mount break immediately as he fell unconscious to the floor. Byron had punched him the fuck out with only one hit.

Chapter 51: Sick as a Dog

Byron reached his hand to me. "Here Maxx, let me help you back to your feet sweetheart. Don't be afraid. Peter is not going to wake up for a bit. You are safe now." I trembled as I took the brute's offer for aid.

He pulled me to stand and reached around my waist with suddenness. I closed my eyes thinking he was going to begin finishing what Peter had started. I gasped in astonishment when instead of molesting me he pulled up my breeches with force.

I stood there dumbfounded as the man buttoned them closed with gentle patience. He was grumbling under his breath that Peter was a foul beast to attack his injured boyfriend. I gulped down the bile that rose in my throat at the idea this crazy man really believed me his truthful lover. I was sure when I couldn't find the honest interest in him he had gotten the hint. Surely, he didn't think somehow I was just going to turn schwuler because he had helped me out a couple times.

Once he got my breeches closed up he took off across the room and grabbed my blouse. Byron tossed it at me. I caught it and quickly put it back on. I was not willing to tempt him to change his mind about joining into the punishment session with my father, ja? He walked over to check on the unconscious Peter while I moved with speed to redo all the buttons.

Byron lifted Peter's bruised head. "Wow, I only hit him that single time. Did you do the rest of this damage honey, or did you find him like this?"

I winced when he used yet another pet name to address me. "Uhm, I confess Byron. I was not as compliant with Peter as you found me a moment ago. He demanded I give him service he believes I owe, and I disagreed with the bill. I am sure when he awakens, the punishment he was giving me will seem the joy compared to what that brute does over this insult." I sighed and held my temples. Damn, I had a headache from all that fighting, you know.

Byron chuckled and shot me a prideful glance. "Well, we will see about that Maxx. I must say you appear to have given him a real struggle. He is not going to soon forget you are not the easy mark you used to be. That beating you gave him will leave a scar or two I think." He rolled Peter's limp head from side to side to view the entirety of his injuries.

I nodded. "Ja, even more reason for him to see me suffer for daring to stand up to him. I confess it was the foolish thing to do, but I thought it would work like it seemed to on Jonas."

Bryon's head snapped up to look at me with surprise in his expression. "Are you saying you attacked Jonas too?"

I went to gather up my jacket laying in the floor and grab the cigarettes from the pocket. "I did. Jonas decided to let me go without getting his contracted special services. Peter though was far more persistent. I couldn't get him to

184

relent. In fact, the more I refused to comply the more turned on he got. I suppose I need not tell you in the end he was the winner and as always Mad Maxx was forced to his knees. You walked in to see the sorry truth of my worthless life. As you say, I am nothing but a schwuler slut. The overused sex toy. That is the way it is. It is never going to change. I am sure you are disgusted by what you saw and heard. I apologize for your having to endure such a dishonorable scene brother." I pulled out a cigarette and lit it up blowing out the smoke in bitter frustration.

Byron stood up and came toward me. I looked at the door nervously wondering if I should run. "I am proud of you Maxx." He flashed a smile of adoration as he approached.

I shook my head in disbelief. "What? How can you say that? Gott dammit, Byron. You saw the fucking truth of my perverted nature with your own eyes. I am the useless man that cannot prevent a humiliating couple when the man is persistent in his demands. I couldn't stop Peter even with a cut up ass and a wicked right hook."

Byron stopped just in front of me still grinning like the love-struck schoolboy. "Baby, you did all you could to defend yourself. That is what I see and hear of this unfortunate situation. You are the slut, but still you tried to deny your inner urge for perversion when Peter came at you. Just because you couldn't stop him on your own doesn't make it any less of a win. I told you with my help you can change your debouched ways. It is not going to happen overnight, honey. You been living like this for a long time. Finding the strength to be more than a slave to your inner evil is not going to be easy. I knew that when I got involved with you. As it is, I see you improving in leaps and bounds. In only one day, you start to show signs of affection for your honest lover Byron, stood your ground against your desire to be with Jonas, and attempted to foil that inner beast within you to be Peter's bitch too. Shit, Maxx, I am more in love with you now than ever before. I didn't realize that was even possible. Come here my love. Let me hold you. I want you to feel my heart beating only for you. I think in all the years you endured the harsh intercourse not a single one of these assholes thought to console your psychological pain caused by being thought of as nothing but the pincushion for their foul lust, ja?" He held his arms open vide.

I stood there staring at him completely in a stun at his words. "Huh? Console my pain? I don't think I understand you, Byron. You think a hug is going to make my ass stop burning or my heart mend? If you do honestly believe that then you are severely deluded and obviously never been raped." I threw down the cigarette with swiftness and turned to flee for the door. I had to get out of there. I realized this guy was the dangerous loon.

Byron apparently expected me to make that move. He reached out his long arms and snatched a back of my blouse before I could get even a few steps in retreat. I pushed forward with enough strength that I heard the material groaning at the seams. With almost no effort at all he pulled me back into his awaiting embrace. I let out the pathetic wail as he closed his huge limbs around me from

186

behind. I must be honest, I was frightened like that because I thought he was going to assault me despite his initially letting me free.

To my surprise his cuddle was gentle though too strong for me to escape. He laid his head on my shoulder and kissed my neck lightly. I led out another wail of terror believing this was his idea of the foreplay.

Byron clutched me more tightly and whispered into my ear "Hush baby, I am not going to hurt you, I swear it on my honor. I beg you to allow me to sooth your hurt and shame. Let go of your defenses. You can trust your Byron that loves you for truth. Think what would Felicity do if she were here? How does she provide you the comfort after being used as the whore? She does do the after care that is always denied you by the rapist, doesn't she. Pretend I am her. Show me how she makes the pain and guilt go away."

I began to feel my chest aching as I thought of my Felicity. The rain clouds burst behind my eyes. The tempest of despair began to flow down my cheeks. This weeping of shame always happens when I feel the sting of humiliation and degradation that my sorry lot in life burdens me with chronically. Byron was right. Felicity is always there to help make this terrible agony of the loss of my dignity calm down. Without her, I felt scared, and confused beyond anything I had ever known.

Byron felt me tense in his hold. "Felicity trusts me, Maxx. She chooses me as her champion. That lamb of yours tires of attending your constant sadness. She told me to take her place until she has gotten some much needed rest. Felicity knows I am strong enough to handle her job till her fatigue lifts. Come on baby, show me how Felicity makes this suffering I see in your eyes settle to the dull roar," he whispered into my ear as he lightly kissed it.

I shuddered as I blubbered out. "Nein, Byron. I need my Lamb. Please I beg of you. Take me to her. Only she knows how to help me. I must go to her, or I will die. My chest hurts. It is the heart attack. I cannot breath. Mercy, please Byron. I do anything to see her." The watershed broke and I fell into the inconsolable crying jag right there locked in Byron's arms.

Byron shook his head wildly as he let me go. I tried to rush away but he grabbed my right upper arm and spun me to face him. Before I could even whimper he came forward and enveloped me into his forceful hugging. My face was crushed into his massive chest while he locked his arms around my own. I struggled uselessly as he held me hostage to his unwanted affectionate snuggle.

I heard the Voter calmly pant out, he was having to work this time to hold me, "Felicity said I am to stand in for her in this most important duty to you. I already told you this. I don't dare to disobey her Maxx, and neither should you. You must accept this is the way it is going to be from now on. You only have Byron to attend to your inner wounds. Let me do my job. Now you listen to me. Whatever Felicity does for you, take it from your Byron right this minute. You better hurry love. That pain in your chest and soul won't do anything but grow until you take your relief. I am waiting." He squeezed me harder.

I wailed out in misery. "Felicity! Felicity, hear me please. Don't do this to me. I beg your forgiveness for abandoning you. I need you, my heart. Grant me mercy and I swear I never will hurt you again as long as I live." I increased my writhing trying to gain freedom of Byron's hold.

He pulled me along after him to the witness chair in the back of the electro-playroom. I was helpless to stop him from dragging me into his lap as he sat down in it. I was as tall as this man, but he had me by yards in girth. The big man grabbed me around the head and held it to his chest while wrapping the other one around my waist. He was behaving like the caring mother to her grieving kid. Yikes! It was like being cuddled by the Jolly Green Giant.

Byron sighed loudly as he said, "Let it all out baby. Your Byron has got you. I won't let anyone hurt you anymore, that I can promise you. You know I tell the truth of it. I killed Reece and punished that low-life Kilian. Peter lays there near death himself because he dared to hurt my sweetheart. From now on you are never alone anymore. If they come for you, they come for Byron. Your pain will go away if you can accept that you and me are together forever as the honest lovers. You must face the facts. Felicity belongs to me Maxx, and so do you." He rubbed the side of my head and kissed my ear affectionately with slowness.

I trembled and cried even harder, "I don't want to be your lover, Byron. I can claim you as the close friend, maybe even best one, but I don't love you like you want me to. I cannot do that. Please tell Felicity she makes an error. She will understand if you explain it to her, ja?" I whimpered out like the little bitch I was swiftly becoming.

Byron shook his head and whispered, "You stop this silly talk that your lamb made a mistake. You know better than that. Felicity knows what is best for you, ja? I think you will find a bit of peace if you quit fighting me and give in to what your lamb has commanded. Come on love. Treat me like you would Felicity." He leaned down and nuzzled my head softly.

I couldn't take the pain within any longer. I stopped trying to push away from him. I wrapped my arms around his waist and buried my face into his neck weeping like the disturbed kid. Byron moaned out in obvious thrill. He responded to my holding him in my agony by rubbing my back and whispered soothing words "everything is going to be alright now."

I shuddered and wept till I was nearly exhausted from the emotional upheaval of it all. I clung to him as if he were indeed my Felicity. Just as I had done with her hundreds of times after the many rough rapes of my past, I continually begged Byron to make the pain stop. The Voter repeated over and over that "I was safe with him for all my life." No matter how many times I disputed that he couldn't save me; Byron maintained his unruffled composure of loving assurance.

I finally gave up the pleas for mercy, like I always did. I fell limp in his arms crying silently till no more tears could be found anywhere within the boy. Byron rocked me in the chair petting my hair and back without saying a word. I closed my eyes and to my astonishment I found the horrible agony that was threatened to split me into pieces had done as he said it would. It was gone having fled back into the dark shadows of the boy's most hidden places in his mind. Before that moment, only my Felicity could make that nightmarish pain go away.

I pulled back from his embrace with suddenness and stared into his eyes with suspiciousness, "How did you do that? This is a trick. Did you hurt Felicity to get her magic powers? I warn you if my lamb is injured I will make you sorry for it. Ask that fucking Kilian. He threw my lamb into the bucket of bleach and melted her. I sent him to the dungeon to have acid flung in his face. He has repaid the debt he owed Felicity. You better hope not a bit of her fur is even ruffled, or I do worse to you in retaliation."

Byron smiled then chuckled as he stroked my cheek with tenderness. "Always the paranoid one, aren't you? Felicity is safe and sound in her haus in your room at our home, my heart. I wouldn't dare to hurt her. She is the soul of the man I love. That means she is more precious to me than my own flesh, baby. She taught me this thing I do for you in her place. Felicity knows only her Byron can take care of her beloved Maxx the way he deserves. Tell me love, did what she teach me work? Is the inner pain gone?"

I looked down at his lap and nodded begrudgingly. "Ja, it is. Felicity is the fine instructor. I thank her for the mercy of it."

Byron grinned even more widely as he rubbed his hands across my upper arms. "That is better Maxx. Anytime you feel the heart aching you come to find your Byron. I will stop everything and make it go away just like this time."

I shook my head feeling nervous for some reason. "Uhm, that is okay. I don't want to be the bother. If you don't mind I would request you allow me to leave your hold. I am no longer in need of any comfort. I thank you again for the mercy you give to me, but I am okay now, I swear it."

Byron frowned and grabbed my chin forcing me to look at him. "Wait, you take a service without an offer of return? That's not fair now is it."

I winced believing he was ready to stop playing the game with me and demand what he truly wanted. "Nein, it is not. You are right. I know better. Nothing ever given to the Mad Maxx is free. I suppose you demand the oral services or some type of the special services for the kindness, ja?"

Byron jerked my chin hard. "Maxx. You stop that thinking all I want from you is sex. I told you I am your honest lover, not a rapist like that trash stretched out on the floor over there. You are playing the perverted slut as usual. I am truly sick of it. Stop trying to get me to fuck you. It is not going to work. You think me weak? Well, you have another thing coming if you really believe your demonic seduction is working on Byron. I am immune to your disgusting wiles. I warn you, insult me like that again and I will leave and never come back. You will be on your own to deal with the monsters that use you for the sex toy."

I gasped and trembled unsure how I had angered him. "Nein, don't go Byron. I didn't mean to be the slut. It slipped out I swear it. I won't insult you anymore. I beg forgiveness for the disrespect I show you." I tried to fall from his lap into the kneel.

Byron held me tightly to prevent me from getting out of his lap. "Stop, no kneeling. You sit here in my lap like a lover should. You don't go to your knees to grovel and beg. That is the slut way to justify your desire to suck my cock like the mindless submissive. When you beg me for such a privilege it will be because you honestly desire to do it with me. Not because you think that is all I want. You listening Maxx?" He glared with fury.

I whimpered in fear and nodded. "I hear you Byron, but I don't know what you want me to say or do. Please, you have to stop playing these mind games. I do what you want without quarrel. I know I owe you for the many things you have done for Felicity and me. I only wish to give you the equal service return to see the balance paid." I looked quickly to the floor and began to wring my hands to control the rising anxiety.

Byron grabbed my twisting palms with frustration in his expression. "Stop that Maxx. I bet you didn't realize that I know what causes you to engage in this nervous habit. You are thinking of ways to placate me without sacrificing too much of yourself in return. You better understand right this minute the folly of trying to figure out a manipulation to use against me. Because it isn't going to work. Byron is not what you are accustomed to dealing with. I won't buy into your lies and half-truths, not especially the ones you tell yourself. Equal service for equal service are words you use that justifies the parasitic life you have been living. Byron won't led your slutty beast feed from him then infect him with the sickness of it. I am not like the idiots Jonas, Peter, Lucus and all the other foul men that can claim knowledge of your favors. Maxx dammit. If you know what is good for you then I suggest you start standing on your own two feet from this moment further. I demand you stop accepting gifts, mercy, or promises of future pleasures as the excuse to let men other than your honest lover Byron fuck you. That equal service for fair return is the bullshit Peter taught a frightened little boy that didn't know any better. How has that been working out for you? I see the evidence of its failure just a bit ago. He brings you the books to study and hold back his cruel lust because why? You suffer at the hands of many before him in line. Now that your schedule is clear of a few brutes he comes to demand you pay him for being a decent fucking human being and you think you are obliged to bend over at his command? Christ, Maxx, which is so wrong. Well, you are not a kid anymore. You are a brave grown man, Maxx, who broke his metal. Yet, you act the collared victim without a choice."

I quit wringing my hands and stared at him in disbelief. "I don't have a choice, Byron. Peter, he has that contract. I refuse him then he can see that metal weighs me to my knees forever. As for Jonas, well he is my Guardian and Mann. To deny that bat means he can lock me away in the padded room or worse, I am sure. The Mad Lucus, that motherfucker he locked this fucking gold collar around my neck. Gretta and him will see me back in chains below the moment I am more trouble than I am worth to them. If you really think I am able to deny those men their demands then you are more deluded than you are claiming me to be," I yelled at him in pure frustration at his refusal to see the truth of my shitty life as the Dominant in name only.

Byron bellow back in retort. "That is not the complete truth, and you know it. I don't ignore that Peter, Jonas and Lucus have you at the disadvantage for the moment, but I remind you in a short while you can be free of all three. All you must do is accept that you do have the right to willingly choose Byron to love. I won't take less than honest desire to be with me, without keeping a constant measure of who gives what. Do it or you find yourself without my company for good this time. I mean it, Maxx. I have waited a long time for you to be old enough to be capable of the honest affection only a man can feel. It is about time you behave as the adult you have become, Gott damn you. I am not willing to spend the rest of my life in this hell hole hoping one day you to come around to wanting me the way I want you. I have to get the fuck out of here and back to the world of sanity outside these walls. You either get your shit together and make ready to join me or get the hell off my lap. Then you can go wake Peter up and stroke his cock so he can finish mounting you like his bottom bitch. If you are lucky, and show him enough suffering during his cruel disgracing of you, maybe he won't beat you, torture you or invite all his friends to take you for a free spin, ja? Ask yourself Maxx, is the fucking you're getting from all of them worth the fucking you're getting? Yes or no."

I winced in a startle at his cryptic words of underhanded threat. "I don't want to get off your lap, Byron. I apologize for asking. It was an honest error, I think. I desire to go with you when you leave this Haus. If you say I must choose you willingly to be able to go with you then I say ja I do what you say to do."

Byron shook his head and sighed loudly. "Christ, did you hear anything I just said? What the hell is in that skull of yours? Bubble gum and shoestrings. Fuck, I waste my breath on the daft."

I gasped and grabbed him around the waist hugging tightly, filled with sudden fear I had angered him again. "Nein, I listen to you Byron. I give you no cause to quarrel with me. I say I choose you like you want me to. Please take me with you. Don't leave me here in the Haus, I beg of you." I whimpered out in complete terror.

Byron tried to pry me off him. "Get off, Maxx. You are doing it again. You only say what you think I want to hear. Gott dammit, this is fucking useless. You are the hopeless catamite slut. I take you with me and in a week you will sucking cock on the street corner for nickels to feed that beast this Haus created in you. I think maybe you are simply too far good to save from such a disgraceful fate," he bellowed just as he managed to push me back.

I shook my head wildly. "Nein, I am not hopeless to the dishonorable lifestyle. I swear it, I can love you and only you the way you want. Please, Byron, give me a chance. Don't give up on me." I pulled him into an honestly eager passionate kiss. Ja, honestly scared that he was going to leave the Haus without me.

As before in the hallway with Reece and Kilian, at first, he tried to fight to keep me from plying him with my lips and tongue. Within a few moments, also as before, he gave up his struggle and returned the heated mouthing. I turned off all abhorrence for sex with the man. I accepted my fate as Byron's lover thinking this was my only hope of freedom.

It was not easy, but I strengthened my resolve to do whatever it took to get this man to be unable to live without me. If it required, he believed I loved and desired him for truth, then so be it. By this time after years of failure to do it on my own, I was willing to sell my soul, ignore my nature, and play the hopelessly enslaved lover to this brute Byron. That is how bad I wanted out of the nightmare that was my life within Der Kaiser Haus.

Byron panted and moaned as I worked my magic around his neck and ears. "You are trying to trick your lover, Maxx. You don't really mean any of this adoration, do you?" He ran his hands across my back pawing and kneading the flesh under my blouse with wantonness.

I whispered into his ear. "I mean it Byron. I love you and no other. I want you to take me here on the floor. Let me show you that I am being honest with you."

He groaned in ecstasy. "Oh, if only that were truth. However, you do lie Maxx. The flesh, it tells on your mouth." He reached into my lap and gripped my flaccid cock.

I wailed in agony and pulled out of the kissing as Bryon applied brutal pressure to my manhood. "Ah, damn it. Please, I am injured. Surely you can understand when I am healed, my flesh will agree with the honest words I say to you. I beg of you to let me go." I nearly threw up from the pain of his rough treatment of that sensitive part.

Byron stared into my eyes that were stinging with tears from his torture. "Ah, maybe you tell the truth of it. Or maybe you find the opportunistic excuse for the lack of physical response expected by one's lustful lover. We will see, won't we Maxx? You are the young man. Those cuts will heal quickly. I am willing to wait a little longer to see if your interest in me and cock grows in the next few days or so. Now get the hell off me as I told you. Peter hasn't stirred. I thought him merely glanced by my blow, but I fear I may have sent him to his grave at this point."

I gasped and wiped my eyes with sudden joy filling my chest. "Do you think he is dead for truth?" I got off Byron's lap and shot a hopeful glance at my father still laying there motionless on the floor.

Byron stood up shaking his head. "Nein, I can see he is breathing. However, I don't know how much longer. We need to try to rouse him from the unconscious state. Go to the sink over there and wet a rag with cold water. Bring it to me and let's see if we can wake him."

I hesitated for a moment. "Wait Byron, uhm, if he does regain consciousness he is going to be really angry at you. I worry he may be." I trailed off as I looked to the floor trying to hide my fear of Peter's retaliation.

The Voter smiled as he leaned down trying to catch my downcast gaze. "What is this? Is this concern for your lover Byron I hear in your words Maxx? You are not worried he will punish us both when he comes to his senses?"

I shook my head. "I am used to his punishment Byron. He will beat or torture me no matter what I do or don't do. You though, maybe you should get out of here and led me handle this. I can deny you ever came here. Maybe he is so addled he believe me when I say you were a hallucination caused by head trauma. I will tell him I am the one that knocked him out. It could work, ja?"

Byron come at me with suddenness causing me to startle and nearly run away in terror. "I don't believe it. You are showing the signs of honest affection for me. You would be willing to lie and take the pain in my place. Aw, my heart, whatever trouble I get into for hitting Peter will be worth it. I get the joy of hearing you voice love and concern for me that is not a fake for the first time ever. That deserves a reward." He grabbed me and re-engaged me in the heavy kissing for a few moments.

I didn't fight him, and I was careful to appear the thrilled participant. I could feel his manhood responding as he rubbed his flesh into my own. I closed my eyes and silently thanked Gott that I had been training to appear the wanton sex partner for years.

Meine Liebe, beware. I give you this warning about dealing with men like this brute Voter. Byron is a highly intelligent man. This kind of opponent should never be underestimated. That said, he is still an arrogant asshole with a huge ego like all the rest of the men I have ever known. It is there only weak spot. If you must outfox one remember, it is not hard to fool them into believing what they already know. That they are Adonis and irresistible to anyone they feel entitled to hold.

If you need to fool a smart fellow like him, it will take you to the limits of all your skills as the pleasure submissive. You must make damned sure to follow their every move with double the feigned eagerness. Hang on there every word, be overly conscientious, and appear the doe eyed fool. They will be watching for the mistakes in your attempts to fool them so the entire world must become your stage. The acting you do better be worthy of an award from the professionals of the actors actress's guilds.

Understand Meine Liebe, if you fail even once, you lose. This kind of horrible situation I found myself caught in with Byron is a game of the highest stakes. These men like him, if they believe for even a moment they cannot have you completely, they will kill you to prevent anyone else from gaining what day see as theirs.

Becoming their murder victim is not the worst thing that can happen, believe me. The worst of fates is to end up their truthful bitch, helpless to break their dare spell over your will. To avoid that, it is much harder than you can imagine.

The real trick is to not to do what your idiot Master did. Never forget you are the actor, not the fucking role you play. It is easy to get lost in the fakery, glitz and sleights of hand you employ to keep this dangerous kind of master criminal and foe at bay. If you let them, they will get into your head and crush you to your knees for truth. Once you begin to believe their lies, you will fall for the ones you tell yourself with ease. Before you know what hit you, it is game over. Life without them seems impossible, and life with them a special kind of Hell you never want to experience.

That day in the electro-playroom, I knew that I was playing the loving boyfriend to Byron. I was in control and faking the behaviors he wanted to see me demonstrate. I was the willing only in the fact that as the desperate nothing was beneath me in my effort to gain his favor. I honestly had lost hope of getting out the front door without the aid of anyone dumb enough to risk their life to see me freed without the permission of the Queens, Elders, Voters and collars. Byron's deal seemed like the dream come true to the young man that knew nothing but pain and darkness. I thought, so what if I had to be the bottom partner to the humongous, stalking, scary, love struck brute. I had sure done worse for far less by then. Yuck!

I was capable of pretending to be eager in the kissing but the one thing I still didn't have a grasp on was the appearance of wantonness in the sexually tinged actions. As before in the closet earlier, Byron was disappointed to find my hands stayed firmly on his waist as he explored my mouth with vigor. I never pawed a man for sexual thrill, except for Leo, in my entire career as the pleasure sub and beyond.

I am ashamed to admit even at the advanced aged of seventeen I only did what my sex partner commanded without offering to do anything more. It was truth that I was the cold machine when it came to the actual acts the comprise all stages of intercourse even if well skilled at performing them. I really shouldn't be too hard on myself for this nasty fact. Except for a handful of romps with Leo, every single situation, no matter how numerous, had been forced. I didn't want to be fucked by any of them, not even Leo. Ja, so there is the sad truth of it.

Only Annette and that minor incident with Karsten can I boast to be the willing participant. That long history of traumatic sexual assault had created the appearance of me being barely better than a fucking mindless sex toy. I would perfectly position, kiss, spin, suck, lick, stroke, wail, repeat words, or hell whatever they wanted done but only on command. I would not stop whatever thing they told me to do or say non-stop until either they ordered the next behavior or finished with me. There was absolutely no spontaneity to me at all. Well, unless you counted all the damned blubbering I did before, during and after the sex acts.

I tell you all that because despite my demonstrating my best skills at the art of kissing, Byron wasn't fooled by my acting job. If I wanted to convince this predator that I was falling for his charms, I was going to have try a lot harder at it. The old follow the leader shit that had always worked in the past to placate the Masters or attackers was useless against the wily Byron.

He shocked me when he pulled away with force and grabbed my hand forcing it to his erection. "Do you feel that Maxx? That is proof of your ability to drive me to desire. I kiss you and my zipper nearly busts. You kiss me and nothing. You are like the corpse from the neck down. You don't cuddle, explore with the eager touch, or do anything other than go along for the ride. You are still behaving just like a fucking parasite. I was the idiot to believe you had finally started to feel something for me other than what I can do for you." He pushed me backwards nearly knocking me to the floor from the force of it.

I panicked and tried to come back at him. "I am not using you, Byron. Here kiss me again. I will try hard to make you the happy man. I will learn if you give me time."

He blocked me from re-engaging in another kiss. "Forget it, Maxx. I may give you another chance to prove your love to me later. For now, go get that fucking rag like I told you. If Peter dies on the floor than you can expect I will need to flee this very night. If that happens you can be assured I take Felicity but not you. You better start praying that asshole pulls through and you get the second chance ja?"

I gasped at the idea he would run off with Felicity and leave me behind to my fate,. "Okay I do what you ask. Peter won't die Byron. He is stronger than he looks. If he lives will you stay? Will you really give me another chance to win your heart for truth? Do you swear it?"

He grabbed me by the jacket and shook me with fury in his eyes. "I don't have to swear to do anything for you. It is you that are the lying, selfish, abandoning, slut, not Byron. I was stupid to make that contract with you Maxx. I already gave you many chances and still you play games with me. If Peter pulls through, then I can assure you I chase you no more. If you want my love, you going to have to work damned hard to earn it back. We clear on that?"

I nodded with a frightened whimper. "Ja, I understand Byron. I thank you for the mercy of it." He led me go.

He grabbed the back of my hair as I tried to head for the small sink in the room. "What mercy Maxx? I already tried showing you that and got the lies spit into my face for it. Maybe if I am cruel then you will finally find honest affection for me. That is the way you like it, isn't it, you disgusting pervert." He flung me toward the wall.

I fell face first to my knees hard. I groaned in agony as Byron barked at me to hurry up with that wet rag. I got back to my feet quickly as possible given the sorry state of my failing health. I thought I was somehow throwing my voice when I heard my sounds of pain seem to grow louder though I didn't seem to be making the noise with the boy's mouth.

Peter wailed out all the sudden. "What the fuck? Oh, my Gott. My head is killing me." I shot a frightened look toward my father.

He was trying to sit up. Byron hand signaled me to be silent as he rushed forward to aid the Voter off the floor. Peter was swooning and holding his hand over his eyes groaning out that his head hurt like he'd been hit by a truck. I rushed to the sink and got a rag damped before returning to the join the Voters. Byron took the moist cloth stealing a glance of caution at me. I backed away trembling, sure that Peter was going to see his brute brother punished severely the moment he got his wits back about him.

Peter allowed Byron to wipe him down, clearing away some of the blood from his face. "Oh, thank you, Byron. Can you tell me what happened? My memory seems to be stalling me."

I gasped and Byron shot me a quick grin. "You mean you don't recall anything, brother? Easy there. That's a hell of a knot you got on your forehead Peter. Don't try to move

205

too quickly. We don't want you to fall again. This time you may not get as lucky."

Peter looked up with a startle at Byron then at me. "Fall again? What? How the fuck could that have happened? The last thing I recall is taking my rights with Maximillian and you rudely busting into the room." He shook his head trying to jog his faulty memory.

Byron feigned concern. "Ja, you were balls deep in the boy when I came in to see what all the screaming was about. You generously offered to share in the thrill. I thanked you for being the generous brother by the way. Anyway, I was patiently waiting my turn at the fun when you decided to change the position of your mount. Apparently, the floor was slick with something. The next thing I knew you slipped and fell on your head hard. You passed out from the force of it. No matter what me and Maxx did we couldn't wake you for the last several minutes. Maxx here was just about to go for help when you started coming to your consciousness. Do you want me to send him to fetch the Haus physician just to be sure you are not injured seriously?"

Peter took the rag from Byron and held it to his eyes. "Nein, that won't be necessary. The quacks around here can only give me the aspirin anyway. I could have the mild concussion. I would appreciate it greatly if you and Maxx could aid me back to my apartment. I also ask both of you to keep this incident to yourselves. I don't want rumors rolling around the hallways that I am a clumsy man ja?"

Byron looked at me with eagerness in his expression. "Sure thing, Peter. We are happy to help you home. You can feel confident what happened in here stays between the three of us. Me and Maxx didn't witness a damned thing amiss, anyway, did we boy?" He swatted my arm and I nodded with quickness in response.

Peter nodded then chuckled weakly. "Great then let's get this man back to his bed, ja? Just one thing Maximillian." I held my breath in fear as Byron took one of his arms and I grabbed the other to help him to his feet.

I barely whispered out. "What is it, Peter?" I was terrified he had recalled that Byron hit him, and we were the liars.

I shot me a diabolical grin. "Did I at least cum before I tripped? If not then the moment I am feeling better I think you owe me a makeup."

I led out my breath in relief even if he was the asshole for asking that disgusting question. "Ja, you did like the bull, Peter. You taught me a powerful lesson with your vigorous punishment. I can assure you that in the future I won't be defying any of your commands." I winced hoping that he wouldn't discover this was a second lie I had just told.

Peter staggered along between me and Byron seeming a bit lightheaded. "Ah, well you can defy me all you like, Maximillian. I told you that is my pleasure. You stand up and I beat you back down. Hahaha. That is the way it works

207

right, Byron? We cannot have the ex-silver thinking he is the truthful Dominant, can we?"

I winced as Byron nodded and chuckled. "I am with you brother. Got to keep Maxx here in his place. It is absurd for him to even think he has a choice."

Peter nodded. "Oh, he has the choice alright. He can do as I tell him and do his duty to me by our contract, or he can deny my commands and have his dick knocked into the dirt for it. Either way he ends up the same way only one with less bruises." He and Byron laughed.

I kept my head down and pulled my father along next to Byron. I was deep in thought about the things that Byron said to me before Peter rejoined the nightmare, I called my life. I wondered if Byron was playing along with Peter to keep him from discovering the truth of his falling to the floor or if he had really meant that he was going to stop chasing me as his love interest. I found it ironic that either way, it was not a good thing for Maximillian.

Byron and I got Peter to his apartment without further incident. The Voters chuckled and said a few cruel things about the moron collars that fell to their kneels as we passed them in the halls and stairs. Peter said that only fools would show respect to the useless psychotic. Byron agreed with his saying and added that I was a nothing but a used up twink to boot. That really made my Vater howl in spiteful mirth.

I kept my tongue silent. I made no effort to dispute the mean things the two men nor did I disagree that they were factual in their assessment of me. I had to admit I am the schizophrenic. Let's face it, I had been engaged sexually with up to seven men a day for years. Having to put up with the Voter's vicious humor over the pathetic situation I found myself in, there is no pain on Earth like facing the truth, you know?

To my despair, I found that with each callous statement they made, whatever small amount of positive self-esteem and/or dignity I had left, plummeted to near non-existent levels. If I had any strength left within me for a battle to prevent Byron, or even Peter for that matter, from hijacking my will, it was completely sapped by the time we reached my father's apartment.

Byron had done a perfect job at destroying all my defenses and lowering all my boundaries. He had moved in on me, taking over my life before I ever knew what hit me. Like Peter when Byron punched him, I was side swiped by Byron. I had always feared and hated that brute thanks to his vicious misuse of me in that hell closet when I was the collared Priceless.

That day as we said goodbye to Peter, all I could think of was how much I needed Byron in my life. Worse, I believed I couldn't survive without his adoration. Somehow, the brute Voter managed to turn the tables on me. To put it into easier words, the unwilling prey had become the calculating predator. Byron's plan to convince me of my slutty perverted nature had been a resounding success. I thought if I was the hopelessly twisted motherfucker, then what was stopping me from doing whatever necessary to gain any comfort wherever I could find it.

Byron had demonstrated his willingness to protect, reward, and even punish me for the price of my honest desire for his love. Well, at the time, it seemed like a pretty reasonable price to pay to have all my dreams of escaping and a real life to come true. This is where the line between faking and falling for the lies I told myself began to blur.

I am ashamed to admit as I watched Byron head to his apartment, after Peter went inside, all I wanted to do is chase after him and beg him to love me. The ache of needing him was not so unlike the desire I had felt for Annette or Karstin. The confusion of this odd mixture of lust and obsession was threatening to drive me back into a psychotic break.

The push to hear him tell me he wasn't leaving me behind and he was taking Felicity pushed me to chase after him to his apartment. Byron surely knew I was right on his heels, but he pretended that he was ignoring my desperate attempt to get him to notice me.

When he reached his door and began to unlock it I stopped dead in my tracks. I didn't know what to say or do as I watched him start to step inside. He didn't say a thing as he began to close it behind him as if I were not exactly right there wringing my hands in pure panic that he was about to be out of my sight.

I whimpered as I came forward blocking him from closing the door with my own flesh. "Nein, wait. Byron please. Can I come inside? I beg of you to speak to me."

The Voter glared at me halfway through his entry preventing him from retreating to the sanctuary of his home. "Maxx, get out of the way. I am tired of this game dammit. I need to be free of you and your drama once and for all. I am never going to find my true love if I keep fooling with you. You need to understand I am not blaming you for being the ungrateful bastard you are. You told me that you are straight, though the evidence suggests otherwise, but never mind. I should have realized you were not playing hard to get. You really don't want me, nor do you find me attractive as the candidate for an honest lover. Go back to Lucus, or Jonas, or Peter or hell, any of the hard dicks around here you can't seem to get enough of. Leave Byron the fuck alone. I deserve better than a perverted slut like you anyway. Haunt me no more, I banish you from my life forever." He shoved me backward with force and slammed his door in my face.

I wailed in pure terror as his words rang in my ears. I couldn't face the idea of never getting to hold Felicity again. Worst of all, and I can't believe I am going to say this, gulp, I didn't want to lose the feeling of safety his cuddle in the electro-playroom brought to me. The overwhelming grief of agonizing loneliness washed over me in a wave of heart stopping misery.

I fell to my knees and began to pound on the door like a loon. I didn't care who saw or heard me sobbing uncontrollably at the brute's door. All I could think about was that I was losing everything that made continued survival worthwhile.

Looking back on the incident, this had always been part of his plan to enslave me to his control. I don't know how long Byron would have allowed this wildly dramatic display to continue before he would relent. I am sure the brute intended to make me suffer a bit. Then, when he finally opened the door, he could enjoy the copious plying of grateful kisses that he had decided to give me one more chance. No doubt, the relief of knowing I was still in the running for the place as his lover would have resulted in his gaining the access to my willing, though misguided, sexual favors.

However, his first attempt at nailing down his position of full control of my mind was thankfully thwarted by a most unexpected interloper. Jonas happened to be headed down the steps of the back stairwell and heard my wild fit throwing. The Vampire thinking I was having a psychotic episode came running to subdue my railing before Gretta or the Guard, he was unaware that I now owned Ivan, were called to have me picked up and then returned to the Palace.

I was in such a panicked state by the time he got to me I was literally clawing at the wood of Byron's door. I wailed loudly but the words I screamed were so obscured by my tearful state Jonas couldn't make them out. Honestly, I was begging Byron to let me in and swearing to love him like he wanted me to. I felt the Vampire's arms wrap around my neck just as he forced me to the floor in a sleeper hold. I tried to struggled but the sneak attack put me at the severe disadvantage. Jonas had cut my air off sufficiently to quickly send me to a faint before I could barely acknowledge his attack.

I don't know how long I was out before I opened my eyes to see the Vampire kneeling next to me. I was still in the fifth floor hallway in front of Byron's door, but Jonas had rolled me to my back. I gasped as he leaned in close to my face. His own was badly bruised and cut from our earlier battling. He wore a concerned expression and I dare say I thought I could sense great fear in him. That confused me since I had not often seen the man worried, except in the beginning when I shattered while in his apartment. I couldn't understand what had happened to upset him so badly.

Jonas shook his head as he chewed nervously on his lower lip like he often does when thinking hard. "Maximillian, you are very ill. I thought I told you to go to the clinic for assessment. Why do I find you acting like a crazy man in front of the Honorable Byron's apartment? What if that bastard had been home? He would surely have called in a complaint and then where would you be? I would think you are in no hurry to be returned to the Palace. If you can stand, then you do it and follow me. No arguments. We are going to see the medic. If you won't mind me on your own, then I will have to drag you down there myself, Gott dammit." He signaled me to rise.

I wanted to argue with the Vampire that I didn't need a doctor, nor did I want to ever see another one for the rest of my life. What I really wanted to do was kick in Byron's door and demand he love me for all my life. I shot a glance at the Voter's apartment and recalled that contract with him. I was sworn to secrecy of our association. He demanded I be even more clandestine than the one I have with Leo. I let out a breath of frustration as I took to my feet. I knew to refuse Jonas would only result in more questions about my odd placement and behaviors. More than that, Jonas likely would call in for aid himself. It seemed best to just do as the man told me and live to fight him another day, ja?

Jonas seemed surprised that I quietly minded his command without conflict of any kind. He narrowed his eyes in suspiciousness as I stood there waiting to take my high protocol position behind him. I didn't look up from the floor as the Vampire examined me from head to toe. He was apparently giving me a moment to offer complaint.

When I continued to appear subdued after a few minutes he led out a long sigh. "Alright, come with me Maximillian. Today is your lucky day. I normally would kick your ass for refusing to answer me when I ask you a fucking question, but I am giving you a pass this time. I am pretty sure whatever is infecting you is the likely culprit in this weird shit I have seen you pulling today. That fucking Lucus should have his ass kicked for letting your run around the Haus, psychotic as hell and full of some nasty illness. To be honest I am really not surprised for all his hubris, the man is the failure at demonstrating worthy leadership skills. Hell, he cannot even get his fucking well trained collar to behave. I fear for the Haus's future if that sonofabitch does gain the regency of the Mortar throne."

I gasped and shot a look of shock at Jonas. "Huh? You speak like there is the possibly he won't gain the metal crown by proxy? What do you mean by if he gains the regency? He has control of the Mortar King by rule of the gold collar, and a contract with the Silk Queen to take possession of my leash for good next year when I end my minority. How the fuck can you not believe him to be the future voice of the Master of the Haus?" Now this was something I wanted to hear. If Jonas knew a way to end Mad Lucus's accent to the top, I was all ears.

Jonas chuckled as he motioned me to follow and took off with speed, forcing me to nearly run and I had broken my cane. "Ah, the creature can speak. Well, for your information Maximillian, nothing around here is assured until it is. Lucus and Gretta think their plan to overtake this Haus is iron clad. That is their weakness. They put all their eggs in a basket with many holes poked in it."

I winced thinking he was making a cruel innuendo to my position as the pincushion. "I don't have many holes Jonas, thank Gott. I wish I didn't have the two I do if you must discuss this disgraceful topic. I didn't have sex with Gretta. The rat bastard that said that is a dirty liar. Even if I was forced into granting her my favors, I was unaware she had a hodensack to be poking into any of my holes. For that matter of all the gross shit I endure in the special service I have never known even that perverted Mad Lucus to put his balls in my so-called basket. He uses the wurst, not the eggs like all the rest of you fools. What that hell is wrong with you to spout such insane lies, Jonas. Surely, you don't believe any of it."

Jonas stopped with suddenness, I nearly ran into him before I too could halt and turned to stare at me. "Are you kidding me? Holy hell, you are the comic today as much as you are the insolent asshole. If that was not an attempt at humor then let me say, damn, you are the simpleton. For your information, I was referring to the holes in your brain fool not the ones everyone uses to fuck you. The eggs I speak of are Gretta and Lucus's plans, not the man's hodensack. Get your mind out of the gutter boy. Not everything is about sex you know." He started laughing till he was red in the face as I stood there hanging my head in embarrassment at my misunderstanding what he was saying.

He slowly recomposed himself and took off with speed to the first floor. I followed as he told me to remain in the proper high protocol, but I was fuming silently as I traveled. I really hated Jonas for always pointing out every single flaw I ever demonstrated. If only he could be so vigilant in his noticing the good qualities I possess as vigorously, then maybe assholes like Byron would have a harder time hijacking my feeble psyche, ja?

We reached the clinic rather quickly. Other than being pissed at Jonas for his rude statements earlier I was not ruffled. I expected the trip was a folly since I had killed the

Haus doctor only the night before. You cannot receive the medical treatment from the dead.

You can understand my astonishment when Jonas and I found the room unlocked. It was an amazement to me that the clinic was actually open for business. The moment we went inside a young man in a white coat came into the receiving area to introduce himself to his patients. It was then I realized to my horror the Haus had already obtained a fucking replacement for that sicko Noethan.

The Vampire shook the man's hand as he stated his name was Dr. Attila Borlan. This man was even more youthful than Noethan. He appeared to be in his late twenties with dark black hair and deep set dark eyes behind a pair of thick lensed glasses. The physician listened intently as Jonas rattled off symptoms he claimed he was seeing in me. It really angered me the way the Vampire spoke to the man as if I were not standing right there capable of using my voice.

Jonas pointed at my cheeks. "See there, that hue of grey is not normal for this boy. His eyes are redder than the sunset, and there is a strange smell he emits. Like, I don't know, old death? He is the verified schizophrenic, but his cycle is calming to residual. Yet today I notice unstable moods, irrationality, babbling, and acute violence that overshoots the cause of his anger. You see the open wound on his head? Well, I happen to know there are many more like it covering the boys entire pelvic region and backside. I wonder doctor, is it possible he is infected with a virus or bacteria from all these exposed cuts?"

Doctor Borlan narrowed his eyes and peered at me through his spectacles. "Ja it is a valid concern you voice for your ward, Mister Weiss. Maximillian is your name (I nodded). Ah, good, as I said I am Doctor Borlan. Will you follow me into the exam room young man. I would like to get a closer look at your injuries and visible symptoms. We can assess this, then go from there, ja?"

I glared at him full of hatred. "Nein, I go nowhere with you pervert. You want to look at me you can do it out here in the open. I am not going to let you take me into the room and tie me down for your gross lusts, asshole. Forget it. I warn you right now freak, you fuck with me, and I can assure you I will send you to visit with the last doctor that abused his station. The yard dogs are going to be the fat, lazy hounds with all this extra meat the Haus idiots keep providing them."

Jonas nearly fainted dead away at my rude words. "Maximillian, you be still. Oh, my Gott. Doctor Borlan I apologize for my son. As I said, he is not himself at the moment. It is quite worrisome."

The doctor lowered his glasses and whispered appearing afraid. "Oh dear. He mentions yard dogs and my predecessor Doctor Noethan I believe was his name. Mister Weiss, tell me, is the boy telling the truth or does he merely intend to bully me with such horrific claims? Oh wait, silly me. I seem to recall the name of the man that killed the last doctor was Mad Maxx die Brutale not Maximillian Weiss. I should have expected with the boy being a verified schizophrenic, the delusion of grandeur may be present, ja?" He chuckled as he lifted his glasses back up his nose.

Jonas covered his eyes and shook his head while groaning. "Nein, Doctor. Maximillian is not delusional in what he says. He is known around the Haus by the residents as Mad Maxx, not by his legal name Maxmillian. The rest of that moniker, die Brutale, is sometimes added when the those with loose tongues have nothing better to do but breed rumors in the hallways."

Doctor Borlan gasped and backed up. "Nein, this is the beast that cut up Noethan, then fed him to the yard dogs? You are funning me. Why do you bring him here? I am in no mood to set this madman off, Mister Weiss. Take him somewhere else for treatment. I intend to live a long, peaceful life."

I yelled back at him, "Then you should have stayed in private practice outside these walls, motherfucker. You know Gott damned well what kind of nightmares happen in this Haus when you took the job opening. If you are her so quickly after I dispatched the last cocksucker calling himself a healer, then I must assume your perversion is likely a rival to the one before you. I repeat, you keep your nasty hands off me or you will not live to regret it."

Jonas threw himself between me and the railing doctor. "Both of you shut the fuck up a minute. Shit, doctor I can assure you're safe from any foul deeds this boy threatens you with. I will make sure he minds his manners. He needs treatment and that is your Gott damned job. Do it or I will have Claus hire someone else. You hear me? Maximillian, you stand the fuck down or I will send you below to the chains for behaving like an insolent prick."

Doctor Borlan bowed his head then nodded. "Ah ja, you are the Elder Jonas, correct? I apologize to you Herr Weiss. I wasn't thinking clearly. I will treat this patient without quarrel. I shouldn't allow fear and rumor to taint my practice nor react as the coward when faced with the difficult cases. I thank you for reminding me of my duty to Der Kaiser Haus. Come with me young man, let's get you straightened out and feeling better, ja?" He pointed at the door of one of the examination rooms.

I laughed loudly at that bullshit. "You are the cowardly fool. Jonas is only the Elder and you quake in your boots. Now you dare to speak to the Master of this Haus as if he were the commoner? Jonas can get you fired from this Haus, but he doesn't have the power to see me whipped. He again forgets his station is beneath the Mortar King. I on the other hand can kill you without citing a reason other than you fucking piss me off. Believe me, when the King Maxx terminates employees it is final, motherfucker."

Jonas turned with speed and backhanded the hell out of me. "Enough of this. You go with the Doctor, Maximillian, or so help me Gott, I don't care who the fuck you are. I have had all I am going to take of your insolence at every damned turn. Now get in that room and let this man fix your sickness." I took his blow, as I had earlier, without flinching.

Doctor Bolen's expression was one of terror as I glared at him full of the rising demons. "You heard me, motherfucker. I don't repeat myself to nothings. Jonas, you are not the insignificant worm like this Doctor Turd. Therefore, l am going to give you a bit of advice before you push me to the limit of my tolerance for seeing you live another day. You may be my father and Guardian on paper, but you are neither my Dominant nor my master. Not anymore. You keep your big nose out of my business unless you intend to see me outside the Haus door. Out there in the real world I have to do as you tell me, or you can destroy me. In this hell hole I am forced to call home, you are nothing but my old, ugly, nitpicking wife. Now if you will excuse me gentlemen, I am going to find my thrill in the bed of a hot young studly lover. Don't wait up for me, honey. This is going to be an all nightery." I tore off out the door of the clinic leaving both of them stunned in shock.

I took out my cigarettes and lit one up. I took a long drag as I rushed down the long hallway. Residents scattered to kneel as I passed them. I repaid their acts of reverence with my cruel laughter and when one didn't move quick enough, a boot to the backside. I didn't understand what that fucking bat was all upset about. I had never felt better in my life.

Sure, I noticed the strange halos of light and flashing orbs that floated down from the ceiling. I giggled in childlike thrill as I watched them dance wildly in every direction I looked. When the ground began to tilt under me, it caused me to howl even louder in my maniacal mirth. I was amazed at how loud my noise was as the sounds of it echoed off the walls behind me.

I was unsure how it came to be that the world seemed to have morphed into a type of colorful circus that somehow balanced on the top of a merry-go-round. I stopped my rapid limping towards the staircase to gaze at the marvelous sights erupting all around me. It was really something to behold. The excitement I was feeling at watching that cool scene turned to horror with suddenness. I could hear, in the distance, the barking and growling of frenzied dogs.

The canines sounded like they were coming my way at high speed and from every direction. I whimpered in terror and took off running fast as my legs could carry me. I knew I had to get to safety fast before the hounds could take me down. I headed for the staircase, knocking collars and Dominants alike out of my way. The sweat poured down my temples, my heart was charging at full throttle. No matter how fast I moved, the yard dogs pursued me relentlessly. Soon so close several were nipping at my heels as they tried to knock me down for their vile attack.

Nein, I couldn't handle the dogs getting me, not again, never again. I needed to get to Byron. I was sure he would save me from the abomination those animals were planning for me. After all,. he told me he loved me. I believed that with all my heart. I knew he would hide me in his apartment. He would protect me from the hell hounds in his loving embrace. I wailed and thrashed in mindless terror just as one of the dogs leapt on me. I fell face first to the steps. I tried to get up to resume my flight, but found I was surrounded by dozens of the vicious yard dogs of my nightmares.

Chapter 52: The Beauty and the Beast

I opened my mouth and began to shout in terror. "Ah, nein, nein. Help me. Someone help me. Get them off me. Please, I beg for mercy." I dropped my face to the step hiding the boy's eyes from the nightmare unfolding. I couldn't defend myself you know. I was hopelessly surrounded.

The hound on my back was putting his paws around my neck readying himself for his disgusting attack on me. I wailed in pure misery thinking I was finished. The yard dogs had hunted me down and this time they brought all their friends. I couldn't believe I was going to be disgraced like this in front of the entire fucking Haus. I clawed at his paws but for some reason he ignored me. My legs were pinned by one of his strong dog brethren. I was unable move to escaping this nightmare come to truth.

Suddenly from the distance I heard Bryon call out to me, "Maxx, hold still. Fighting will only make it worse for you. They are here to help. Listen to me boy, be still dammit."

I didn't look up but instead covered my head with both arms. "Nein, they come to hurt my, Byron. Please, you have to help me. I apologize for being the asshole to you. If you show mercy and get them off me, I will change my slutty ways. I swear it," I screamed in response.

Byron reached down over the backs of the hounds blocking my path. "I am here to make sure they don't hurt you Maxx. Let me have your arm, boy. You are very ill. These men are trying to get you some help. Stop this refusing what they offer. Be still and it will be over quickly. You must trust me. Take my hand, I am helping them to do what they came to do."

I hazard a look up and saw his face wearing a frightened expression and his outstretched hand. "You won't leave me here if I let them do this?" I trembled in disgust at what I thought he was asking me to do, but if he was going to take me out of the Haus I was willing to endure anything, I hoped.

Byron shot me a worried smile. "Just take my hand, Maxx. I am not going anywhere, till you tell me to leave you be. We are friends, ja?" He reached toward me with urgency.

I nodded. "Ja, the best of friends, Byron. You hold my hand through the entire horror? If you say ja, then I do as you say." I tried to swallow, but my mouth had gone dry.

He nodded back. "Ja, Maxx. I stay with you and hold your hand if it will make this easier for you. Unless Jonas or the doctor have a problem with that?" He looked behind me at the dogs waiting in line to have their way with me.

I shook with full blown panic flowing through my veins but took his hand. "I cannot stay here, Byron. Not after this. Forgive me for being the useless slut. I don't have the strength to fight them off. You won't like me anymore. I know you won't." I started weeping as he pulled me to my feet with ease toward him.

The hound on my back was thrown from the boy as the huge brute lifted me. The second I was within grabbing distance I latched onto him and hid my face in his chest crying like the baby. He gently stroked my back as I mumbled incoherent apologies for my perverted nature to him.

To my surprise the hounds had halted their attack. All of them appeared unsure what to do with Byron there holding me. They stood around casting glances of confusion at each other. Byron stood there doing his best to comfort me and ease my anxiety over this thing he thought I should endure.

I heard his deep voice barrel out, "Okay, I have the boy. Lead the way Jonas. Tell the Guard to clear the fucking path. He is upset enough without having to worry about tripping over a pack of idiots, ja?"

I head one of the dogs speak in the Vampire's voice, "You heard the man. All of you get the fuck out of here. There is nothing to see now. Go on about your business or find yourselves hauled down below for the lashing. Ivan, move those people over there. The King is not well. Byron, come with me and Doctor Borlan. Don't loosen your hold for even a second. He is violent as hell and out of his mind. If you don't desire to wear the bruises like I do, then mind what I say. The boy is far stronger than he looks."

I whimpered in fear. "Byron, the hounds, they are speaking. How did they learn to do that? That one sounds like the Vampire Jonas. Tell him to shut up. If Jonas hears of it he will have that hound put down." Byron began to drag me down the steps with me clinging to him like a leach.

The brute cuddled me closer to him as we began to travel towards the clinic. All the hounds allowed us to pass unmolested. "Be still, Maxx. I will tell that hound stop mocking the Elder later. Right now, you come along without quarrel. We go somewhere the hounds cannot get you."

I mumbled out nearly insane from gratitude over his saving me from that horrid rape. "You are not mad at me anymore then? Do I still have the chance to please Felicity? I swear you won't regret this second chance you give to me. I do whatever you say. Thank you for the mercy of it." I squeezed him tightly.

Byron chuckled. "When you are well, we will discuss this change of heart you have Maxx. For now, you keep that mouth shut. Do what the doctor tells you to do. If you mind well, then the answer to your first question is nein, and ja to the second. I won't leave you. I am here by your side." He squeezed me back.

I couldn't understand why he was telling me to mind that new doctor. I also couldn't figure out why the hounds stopped their assault but continued to follow the two of us closely in a pack. That said, I didn't dare disobey Byron's orders to be silent.

I feared if I said another word I would set off his nasty mood. If that happened maybe he would go ahead and abandon me, taking Felicity with him. I limped alongside him without hesitation. The entire journey I kept my head close to his flesh as possible. It took a few minutes, but I finally understood we were headed back to the clinic. This further confused me.

I wondered if Doctor Borlan was like that pervert Noethan. It was then it occurred to me that Byron must have agreed to aid him in getting me subdued for the doctors perverted voyeurism. I began to tremble from the fresh fear that washed over me at the thought of that.

To my horror we went through the door of the clinic moving right into the exam room without stopping. I shot an anxious glance behind us and saw to my horror the hounds were eagerly trailing us inside. I wailed out and tried to struggle out of Byron's hold. I was absolutely sure that Byron had saved me only to turn me over for a semi-private gang raping of the most unnatural kind.

Byron held tightly. "Maxx, stop this now. Do you hear me? Be still."

I yelled as the big Voter picked me up with ease throwing me onto the exam bed. "Nein, don't tie me up. Take me with you. We can go back to your apartment. I make you happy. Please mercy." I flailed with vigor as Byron and one of the hounds began forcing my limbs into the straps to keeping me from escaping their cruel sport.

One of the big yard dogs approached the bed and caressed my cheek while whispering gently, "Be still, Maximillian. I know you are very confused and frightened right now. The doctor is here to help you come back to us. It is going to be okay, I swear it to you." The hound again used Jonas's voice to speak to me.

I stopped my kicking and screaming to stare at the dog in disbelief. "Jonas? This is you? I thought you said the Vampire cannot shape shift. You lied to me again. You get your fleas away from me. Tell your buddies I am not interested in them. I swear to Gott I will kill all you mongrels. I hate you. You are all going to be sorry for this. You don't know who you messing with. No matter what the rest of you do, you will never be men. You are nothing but worthless hounds, the lot of you. Only Jonas has such permissions. I will kill him too one day though he doesn't believe me when I tell him. Get off me, I mean it." I tried to sound tough, but I actually sounded like the weepy bitch that I had become.

It was too late. The hounds worked together with Byron and the dog form of Jonas to get me adequately bonded to that bed. I pulled strongly at the straps, but I was stuck. Whatever their plans for me no matter how disgusting, I was going to have to endure it. I saw one of the hounds stand on his hind legs. I gasped in awe and terror as he undid my beeches. He pulled them down to expose my hips. Another of the dogs came forward and bit the shit out of my exposed flesh. I wailed in agony when the hound didn't release his teeth quickly. It both hurt and burned at the same time.

My breath got shallow, and my muscles began to rapidly lose strength. The world started to melt into a puddle. I felt something slide into the boy's hand. I tried to lift my head to see what the wet, warm thing was. Well, you know what I thought it was, yikes! I wailed in misery thinking the raping had begun. Tears and drool poured from my face soaking the pillow beneath me.

Byron's voice rocked the crumbling world, "It is okay, Maxx. I have your hand just like I promised. Sleep now. When you wake, it will be all over."

I nodded as the darkness began to close in on my sight. "I thank you for the mercy of knocking me out, Byron. I won't forget your kindness." I swooned into the faint, with the vision of a hound crawling on top of me, a huge evil smile spreading across his muzzle.

I opened my eyes to the sound of a man's voice calling me from the peace of the nothing. "Maxmillian? How many fingers did you say I am holding up?"

I groaned as I tried to open my stinging eyes. "Did you enjoy yourself, pervert? Be aware you are going to be sorry for daring to fooling with me. I won't feed you to the yard dogs like the last motherfucker that forced this abomination. I am going to skin you, then bury you in an anthill for the evil you do to me," I mumbled out weakly.

The doctor's voice trembled slightly. "Maximillian please. Tell me how many fingers I am holding up."

I narrowed my eyes trying to protect them from the overly bright lights. "Ten you hold up and ten I will chop off. You nasty bastard. That shit you do to me, that is illegal. Are you stupid? I killed the last doctor for enjoying such disgusting sport with me. I guess you expect you are blessed. Well, tell you what asshole. You untie me this minute or I will show you the blessing of a fast death. You hear me, pervert," I yelled out struggling against the restraints.

The Doctor frowned as he leaned his hand, with two fingers lifted, closer to my face. "Try to focus, Maximillian. Can you count my fingers? Please listen to me. You are very ill, son. I know that you don't understand what you say. I hope you can believe me when I tell you it is the hallucinations you remember, not the reality of it. I have done nothing perverted or cruel to you other than treat you for a serious infection. Your fever was very high from a vicious infection that plagues your flesh. I give you a heavy sedative and IV fluids with powerful antibiotics to help calm the high temperature before you expired on us. You should be feeling better in a couple days." He said sounding very afraid.

I growled back at him full of fury. "You liar. I already take the medication for that infection in my head. I have no fever. I know what you did. I am going to kill you for it too."

The doctor gasped, then leaned in close while he whispered. "Ja, I know you received treatment for the infection in your headwound. However, there was a secondary infection that was missed by Doctor Noethan. One that is, uhm, not typical for the human species. Do you have a hound, Maxmillian?"

I was startled at that question. "Huh? Why do you ask that? I do have a hound. Well, I share a hound with Elder Leo. What does Der Makellos have to do with your brutal sport? I swear to Gott if you bring him here to hurt me I will not kill you. I will keep you alive and torture you forever."

He frowned at me then looked around the room which was empty of everyone but the two of us. "Look Maximillian, I don't know what you are speaking about. Or shall I say I don't want to be made aware. I am trying to tell you the infection that I find in your blood stream is common in the canines but not the humans. You must have picked it up from not washing your hands after playing with your hound or perhaps when cleaning up after him? Ja, that is what happened, right?" He locked eyes with me and nodded with an expression of extreme caution on his face.

I stared at him unsure what the hell he driving at when suddenly he repeated himself.

This time he leaned in real close to my face. "I am writing down in your medical records you pick up this bacteria in your blood by accident from handling your pet's care. You understand me, Maximillian? That is what everyone will think. That said, whatever you are really doing with your hound to manage to acquire such a deadly infection I suggest you stop it immediately. I give this good medical advice to you only. My words are between us and no one else. Accept my mercy and refusal to acknowledge the truth that I cannot bear to think or speak of. You

232

understand me this time?" He glared at me with great sternness.

At last, I got it. "Oh, ja, that must be how this illness came to be. I promise to be more careful when feeding my hound doctor. I thank you for the sound advice. I had no idea owning the pet could be so troublesome."

He nodded without changing his expression of caution. "Ja, engaging in, uhm, the daily needs of a canine can result in serious consequences. I am happy to hear you understand the risks and are willing to assure you never end up in this clinic with this illness again."

I nodded. "Ja, I can swear to you it will never happens again. I uhm, gave my hound to Leo for keeping. I don't want to be anywhere near him anymore."

Doctor Borlan frowned bitterly. "Ah, okay so this situation was not due to your, uhm, purposeful lack of caution. I am to understand the fault lay in your last doctor's love of the canine more than his concern for his patient's safety?"

I looked away while I nodded. "Ja, you understand correctly. Doctor Noethan was a bad doctor. A true quack and shame to all that wear the white coat. He loved the hounds too much. He chose to be the physician but was better suited to be the veterinarian. Well, I corrected that problem by giving him to the animals he seemed to be so fond of." I swallowed hard waiting for this man to destroy me with the knowledge he now possessed on me from my blood testing results.

Doctor Borlan blew out his breath while shaking his head in disgust. "Publicly, I must pretend I find your killing of my predecessor an unjustifiable act of depraved criminality. I must say privately that you did the right thing to see Doctor Noethan permanently terminated from his employment as Haus Doctor. Abusing one's position as the trusted physician is inexcusable in itself. Being a party to, uhm, enforcing poor medical practices should be a crime punished by death. We shall never speak of this shameful business again. That I swear to you. Instead, I remind you if you ever pet or care for any animal then wash your hands and use careful hygiene practices." He winked at me then cleared his throat asking me again to count his fingers.

This time I answered his question without quarrel. Doctor Borlan, despite being the Haus doctor of a den of criminals, had proven he was not like the ones before him. He lied in my medical records about the bacteria ravaging my system, saved me from dying of it, and more than that pretended it never happened at all. to this day, the man has kept the secret, and because of that, his life. I never have had the need to push him down any staircases or feed him to the yard dogs. *Master Maxx laughed hard at that, and I joined him as he ruffled my hair playfully.*

After asking me a lot of questions to determine my grip on reality, the doctor determined I was safe enough to untether. I was grateful that he, unlike that asshole before him, seemed to dislike the bondage of his patients. I, of course, had to promise him I would offer no resistance to his treatment if he led me free. I had no issue with keeping that agreement given that I didn't desire to die from a canine borne illness.

You see, Doctor Borlan could hide the sorry truth of it only if I lived. To die of it, well he would have a lot of tap dancing to do, or everyone would know that Doctor Noethan managed to murder me from beyond the grave.

Once I was untied, he gave me more antibiotics through the IV that I had missed when I first awoke. I listened politely as he told me I had many visitors during the last twenty-four hours while I had been under heavy sedation.

Doctor Borlan said that three of them – Jonas, Mad Lucus and Byron – had been particularly pushy. He told me the trio were hell bent to sit at my side while I made that long trip back from the banks of the river Styx. He had made them leave by stating that any amount of stress could send me back to resume my attempt to take that boat ride.

I thanked him for the extreme mercy he showed me in both keeping the buzzards at bay and for his confidence. I was more than a little grateful for everything he did to offer me a shred of comfort and dignity where none should have been found. I admit, I started to like the fellow with each passing word he said.

Over time I can safely say, Doctor Borlan and I became distant friends, or at the very least I can profess we are not enemies. I was a bit miffed he kept Byron out. *Yikes, did I just say that. Ja, I did. I am dumber than you thought Meine Liebe.* I thought maybe having him there would allow me a chance to gain a bit of pity from the brute. I was not above any edge I could gain to see myself back in his good graces. I really wanted out of the Haus and thought he was the only one that could make that dream come to truth.

Aside from that brainwashing shit that Byron was pulling on me, my physical and mental health was most foul. The doctor explained that even with heavy antibiotics I could expect my symptoms of a grey hue, red eyes, lack of appetite, and insomnia to name a few, to persist for many weeks. That bacteria had gained a solid hold on my immune system as no treatment for over two weeks after the initial infection is not a good thing, you know. It was settling in for the long haul.

My acute cycle had been in retreat, but thanks to severe stressing, as if I were not always under that shit, I had backslid a bit. I was not fully acute, but I was not fully residual either. I had more lucid moments than had been witnessed in months or so Doctor Borlan thought.

However, the psychotic violence and mood swings were persistent. He increased my antipsychotic dosage and hoped it would be enough to take off the edge. I was most unhappy to hear that shit. If I was to convince Byron I found interest in him, extra sedatives in my blood stream would be a real problem.

I already found no lust for the men, especially Byron and Mad Lucus. This added bad news brought me much misery. I decided secretly to cheek the meds at least until I had adequately seduced the brute Voter.

I know, that was not the smart thing to do when fighting my way back from the tapestry. I was a desperate man, Meine Liebe. You have to bear in mind that in my long battle to escaping the Haus, I had chronically failed.

By this point, I was willing to hold still on the staircase for another assault from the hounds merely because Byron told me to. He had completely blinded me to any kind of rational thinking. The man didn't know it or maybe he did, but I was completely under his spell. All he had to do is attach his leash and your idiot Master was his little bitch.

Th only thing about that entire incident on the steps is I still don't know how he managed to hide his obvious meddling with my psyche from the wise Jonas. It has always been the mystery to me. It is beyond weird that the Vampire let it slide past him that I wouldn't mind his commands after all those years of his bullying, but did whatever Byron told me to do.

Then that snuggling to Byron like he was my loving surrogate mother stand in, all I can say is wow. You would think Jonas, being the hunter for warm blooded rodents that he is, could smell that rat.

Well, for whatever reason, no one questioned that public display of submission I showed to Byron. Maybe, they all assumed my mind was so far gone I didn't really know what I was doing. I find that reasoning a bit hard to believe because Byron sure as shit understood my compliance to him, and to him only, meant he was winning his game. He knew victory was near, and you can be sure he wasn't going to let his prize slip away.

Now before I continue, I have to add that while Jonas didn't seem to realize Byron was fooling with my head, he did notice that I was a bit too cuddly with a male. That of all things was the only thing that bothered him of my crazy behavior that day. I know this because of what happened soon after I was released back to Mad Lucus from the clinic's care. We get ahead of ourselves in the story but do remember I said that, Meine Liebe.

Back to the day I awoke from the heavy sedation. It seems that Byron was hell bent to be the first notified of my return to consciousness of the three pushy men looking to visit with me after I was put in Haus inpatient clinic. Doctor Borlan told me a few years after this incident of the things that happened that led to Byron being the first notified of my survival.

He said that when he finished attending my medications and vitals check he came out of my room to find the big brute sitting in the waiting area. He had apparently come in right after the doctor unlocked the clinic door that morning but had not been spotted. Doctor Borlan said the brute hailed him and demanded to be granted information on my well-being or find himself joining his ancestors.

The doctor was aware that Jonas is my guardian and adoptive father while Mad Lucus was the holder of my collar. That of course put both of them far above Byron on the list of persons that should be granted access to visit with me in my perilous state.

That said he told me that he allowed Byron entry not only because he cared enough to sit waiting all morning, but also because of my weird minding him when psychotic with high fever. He thought someone that could break through a disturbed mind at its worst had to be someone that could be good for aiding me in staying calm. Boy was the Doctor wrong and right at the same time.

It was most unfortunate that Byron was given a private audience before Mad Lucas or Jonas could visit and likely break his weak hold. It was also lucky since there was no one I wanted to see more than the Voter. Though not for reasons that were good for me in the long run.

I heard the door come open. I had been laying there staring at the ceiling listening to the sounds of the vortex whirling in the distance. I turned my head quickly thinking it was Doctor Borlan returning with another shot or pill. The smiling Byron stood there looking me over as if I were a steak to the starving man.

I felt a chill run down the boy's spine when he stepped in and closed the door behind him. "You are looking better already, baby. I don't know what that sawbones put in that needle, but it must have been great drugs. Wow, you are so handsome I can barely contain myself. I wonder how long it will be before you can get out of here and come home to visit me." He winked and came towards the bed chuckling at his barely hidden wanton statement.

I shrugged and used all my inner strength to keep from flinching as he leaned down and kissed me. "Uhm, he said a few days? I am not sure Byron. I guess I am seriously ill with some bug. He says he can cure me, but I will need rest." I said as he pulled back from the kissing and sat down beside me.

Byron nodded. "Ja, you were burning up with a fever. I should have noticed it when down in the torture chamber earlier. I suppose I thought you were merely hot for me." He chuckled again at his inappropriate attempt at humor.

I forced a light chuckle back. "Well, I must confess I could understand that belief. I was doing a bit of sweating from your charms." I wanted to gag. y attempt to flirt back was mediocre at best.

Byron stopped laughing and glared at me. "Stop the teasing, Maxx. You were anything but interested downstairs and we both know it. You are barely conscious and already you attempt to tell me lies? I guess I am the fool to believe the ranting of the sick man. You make promises you never keep about your willingness to change your slutty ways." He started to get up to leave.

I grabbed his arm with swiftness. "Nein, Byron. Stay, I beg of you. I apologize for the attempt to tease you. I won't do it again."

He turned back and stared at me menacingly. "Alright, I am going to sit down for a moment, but you watch that mouth of yours Maxx. One more bullshit lie, and I leave. No more chances."

I nodded and blew out my breath in relief. "Thank you for the mercy of it Byron. I won't speak unless you tell me to."

Byron smiled and leaned in caressing my cheek. "There you go. Good boy Maxx. You are finally starting to get it. You cannot be trusted to know what is best for you. Given the chance you will always choose the way of the slut. Give your control over to your lover Byron. I look out for the both of us now, ja?"

I nodded as I kept my eyes locked into his thinking he was right. "Ja, I do what you say. I am the idiot slut that fucks up everything I touch."

He sighed. "That doctor really is good. He cures your illness and clears your mind of stupidity too. Remind me to tip him well. He brings my boy to a place where I can finally save him from himself."

I nodded, "He is a great doctor. I am doubly glad I killed that fucker Noethan."

Byron chuckled. "You are the vicious little cunt, aren't you? Kind of turns me on. I wonder, if I were to slip into this bed, do you think we have enough time to consummate our relationship before the man comes to do a bed check? What do you have on under this clinic gown? Nothing, I hope." He slid his hand from my cheek down to my chest with eager slowness.

I held my breath as I squeaked out. "I do have the underwear and socks on Byron. I think the doctor said he must tell Mad Lucus and Jonas I am alert. If you were to demand special services this minute he is the least of our troubles if you desire to have me without being caught." His groping stopped with suddenness on my stomach.

He led out a shudder and closed his eyes. "Oh, my Gott I do want you Maxx. This waiting is killing me. I hear what you say but I am almost beyond giving a shit. You belong to me, and those assholes are the interlopers. You broke that fucking collar. You earned the right be leveled the Dominant and are the Master of the Haus to boot. These fools don't give you the proper respect. You have a choice, and you chose Byron. What I wouldn't give to flaunt that fact in their arrogant faces." He pulled back his exploring hand much to my relief. Close one there, yikes!

I took a deep breath. "You could tell them that Byron. Maybe they will let me go and I come to live with you?" I couldn't believe I just said that shit, but hey, better one brute than the nasty Mad Lucus and Jonas, ja? If only I could get rid of Peter as well.

Byron smiled with adoration in his expression. "You would come to live with me for true?"

I nodded. "Ja. If that Mad Lucus would let me. I don't want to be in his Haus nor have him pawing at me and worse. He is the pervert. I told you that already."

He sighed as he reached back out to fondle my chest and stomach again. "You being in my home, me waking up each morning with your flesh in my embrace, ah what a beautiful dream that is. I could have you anytime I wanted without having to sneak around or wait my fucking turn. It sounds like heaven. That said, only fucking Lucus can unlock that collar. I checked the law. Not ever the Master or the Haus or Silk Queen can force his hand to undo what you willing agreed to engage in."

I groaned as I thought of the horror at having to endure the constant coupling with Byron, yuck. "I didn't realize this collar was that serious. I thought when I am not in the psychotic cycle he would have to relent if I say to. I swear I would never have agreed to such a damnation had I been told the truth. Mad Lucus, he lied to me Byron, you have to believe me. He said he would take the collar off when I an competent. Yet, I fear that is a lie too. He is never going to remove it or his power over me. I need to run away from the Haus. Then that dream of yours can be the reality, ja?"

Byron frowned as he rubbed on my flesh through the clothing more vigorously. "I want to believe what you tell me Maxx, I really do. However, you are the lying slut by nature. You say the things you think will get you what you want but have no feeling or regard for what it does to another. It is always about you. I know you take that collar because you thought Mad Lucus could bring you power and a better lot in the Haus. You make that contract with Peter because you thought of getting the free education after you break your metal. Jonas, well you blood bond to him to keep Peter from collecting on your ass in case you failed. You think the powerful Elder can save you from the powerful Voter. I see clearly what you have done even if you thought yourself clever making these chess moves. I think you are trying to play me too. I think you plan to use me to get out the Haus door, then run off with the education Peter must pay for, and money Jonas gives to you now that you realize Mad Lucus isn't going to share his fortune with you. You need the ticket out to make good use of all the things you have stolen from those men I speak of. Byron, ja, not your truthful lover but the bus ticket to the easy train right out of East Germany. You are not fooling me, boy." He pulled back his hand with suddenness.

I trembled as he said those words and shook my head. "Nein, that is not true Byron. I was twelve when Peter tricked me into his contract. I didn't even know what a collaring meant much less the special services. I was only a child and an inexperienced idiot. Jonas? He fooled me too. He lured me to his place promising to protect me from Peter. He tied me up and forced the blood couple. I didn't agree to his marriage. He tricked my mother into marrying him, stole my custody papers from her, and now takes any money I earn to keep me broke. I get no fortune from him. He is the liar like Peter and a fucking thief. I told you Mad Lucus he trick me too. He used my fear of the Altergotts and led me to think the gold collar a fake to have his way. He stole my apartment, my freedom, my life. I am the fool not the manipulator you accuse me of Byron."

He glared at me with disgust. "You are expecting me to believe the Mad Maxx of legend is not fooled once but thrice? I think that is too farfetched for anyone to buy. I know you are trying to seduce me into yet a fourth situation. Admit it, Gott damn you. You are a stupid slut. Say it or I break your fucking arm worse than that brain of yours." He grabbed my upper arm and jerk it hard causing me to cry out in pain.

I gasped and panted in fear. "Okay, I am trying to trick you. I am the stupid slut. Please, mercy. Let me go. I apologize for daring to try to outfox the brilliant Byron. I am no match for your skill at discovering this fool's game."

Byron applied more pressure on my arm as he growled out, "You going to try to fool me again, ever?"

I shook my head and wailed out. "Nein, I will never try to play games with you again. Please, mercy."

He dug in his nails as he squeezed even harder. "Look me in the eyes and tell me you love me for truth, and no lying. I can tell if you are. If you say it and don't mean it I will know. Then you already know what will happen. You will have far more to worry about then a broken arm, ja?" He stared deeply into my eyes.

I whimpered as I looked back at him full of terror. "I, I love you Byron, for truth. I swear it. I love no other. I don't lie. Please, mercy, I beg of you. I do anything you say." I could feel my heart about to beat out of my chest as the brute leaned in closer to my face trying to see into the wheelroom.

I was shaking so bad I could barely hold on to the wheel. I shot Mad Maxx a glance of fear. He gazed back wide eyed frozen to the spot full of his own fright. We couldn't do anything to stop Byron from taking possession of the boy's will. If we dared to maintain any amount of free choice the man would abandon the boy to the fate of the Mortar King.

That Palace hell loomed in the screen and all the horrors that came with incarceration within that prison. Our only sure escape was through Byron. No matter what he did to the flesh, we had to comply with all his demands or be damned. This was an intense moment of danger. It was not just the nightmare Palace that could end our struggle to survive anymore. Byron held our Felicity his willing hostage.

Without our lamb the boy won't live long. She is our guide to a world we could no longer understand. Felicity knows what is best for the boy and warns us when trouble is coming. We are unsure but it has occurred to us, that once a long time ago, she was a part of Christian Axel. How she ended up outside the wheelroom or why she morphed into a lamb is still a mystery to this day. None of the shards can recall it, not even the oldest of us, Der Hund.

All we know for sure is she keeps the boy from making fatal mistakes and translates the gibberish that comes in from the real world. When she ran away to Byron we had become blind in a way. We were wandering around in the darkness of the nothing, unsure of our location. We were no longer capable of understanding what was happening around us. The demon of insanity within the boy was breaking loose his bonds because the lamb was not there to strengthen his cage. Our senses were in constant chaos, and it caused devastating confusion.

Byron was acting as a type of faux Felicity. He was capable of clearing our mind, and making the unexplainable makes sense thanks to his affiliation with our Felicity. When he was present, the pain of our disease was lessened like with Felicity. That was quickly causing us to become addicted to his presence despite our long term hatred and honest fear of the man. His constant demands that the boy love him for truth, drove our disordered thinking backward.

This along with his stroking the inner fear that we were unworthy of life, was quickly subduing our confidence that we needed no one or anything to function. That slowly had eroded our faith in our ability to understand right from wrong or truth from lies.

Eventually, it had led to the belief within that we did love him but had incorrectly judged him the perverted predator. It was the other way around. We thought ourselves the monster and he was sent by Felicity to save us from ourself. This was the moment where the line not only blurred but crumbled. Byron had effectively hijacked my willpower.

This is important because the brute had managed to do what Peter, Jonas, all the Elders, and even Mad Lucus had failed to do. I was truly brought to my knees as a real submissive, not merely faking my way through the role as I always had done. To my complete misery I found I was unable to resist his commands, but even worse I believed I wanted nothing more than to mind and please the sonofabitch.

You must understand the being unable to say nein, and desiring to please a Master doesn't bring happiness or pleasure when the match is like this one. I didn't choose him because I thought myself incomplete as the honest submissive does. I was essentially given four choices that I never asked for and no one would want. Byron was chosen for all the reasons I gave you (Felicity, his protection, etcetera) but more than that was the least of the very worst probable outcomes.

I had already been made painfully aware of what Mad Lucus, Peter and Jonas had planned for me. They all told me lies, used tricks, and were brutal in their punishments for even the most minor of infractions. The way I saw it, at that time, Byron had so far kept all his promises, and his plan for the future included things I wanted too.

I was most unhappy I would have to tolerate his horrible pawing and coupling with me. That said, at least, unlike the other men mentioned, he wasn't saying he planned to just selfishly use me to meet his lusts. I wasn't interested in letting the man fuck me, but I assumed I could endure that nightmare to receive his favor of something worth having in return. Namely, freedom from the Haus.

That morning, as Byron sought his answers in my eyes, Mad Maxx and I agreed. We loved Byron because he said we did, end of story. Mad Maxx die Brutale stayed in his spot next to wall in silence. He didn't have any better ideas. The boy was the cornered animal, who was ready to throw itself at the captor hoping for mercy, and if lucky, a chance at a life that till that moment had been the unobtainable dream.

The Voter narrowed his lids and then a big smile pulled at the corners of his mouth. "Oh, my Gott. You aren't lying. You have finally grown a man's heart. Say it to me, Maxx. You know what I want to hear. The words I have waited to be repeated to me since I first beheld the sight of the beautiful boy covered in scars many years ago."

I shuddered and tried to swallow but my mouth had gone dry from anxiety. "I love you, Byron. I love only you. You are my world. You ask and I will see it done. I cannot exist without you by my side." I held my breath hoping this was the correct answer, if not I was ready to find my peace through death. I had enough. I didn't have any fight left in me, you know.

Byron led go of my arm and stood up with such force he knocked the chair over. I gasped and covered my head. I was thinking he was going to hit me. My flesh trembled uncontrollably as the huge man's frame took a full stance towering above me.

He bent at his waist and leaned down. I felt his arms tunnel under me on both side. Byron lifted me up and embraced me with careful gentleness. I was panting in terror, but he misunderstood this to mean I was romantically swept off my feet. Well, I was laying down, but you know what I mean. He smiled with complete thrill at that idea and kissed my forehead lightly.

Then he laid his head on my shoulder. "Thank you Maxx for making my wait worth all the pain. I swear I could die right this moment a happy man with your words of love echoing in my memory. You focus on getting better. When you are well, we will work out how to proceed with this true love affair together. In the meantime, I go to allow your needed rest. When I come back later today, I will bring Felicity with me to cheer you up." He rubbed my back and kissed my neck with affection.

I gasped. "You will bring her to see me? You mean this Byron? I do love you. Thank you for your mercy. I am the grateful man." I thought I had never felt more relieved in my life when he said I could see my lamb.

He chuckled as he nuzzled my neck playfully. "You heal up quickly, then you can show me how grateful you are to your Byron, ja?"

I nodded "Ja, of course Byron. You honor me by accepting such a shoddy payment in return for the adoration you show me."

Byron laughed even harder. "Shoddy you say. Oh, I think not. I have coupled with you many times as the boy and once as the man. In all those cases the situation was one sided with you the truthfully unwilling participate to the acts. This time, I get the real sex with you for the very first time. I dare say no other can boast such a coveted experience with you. Not since you were brought into the knowledge of sex most brutal. Is this not the truth of it, Maxx? You maybe the overused slut, but when it comes to the heart you are the virgin."

I nodded, mostly because I was too scared not to agree with him. "Ja, which sounds right Byron. I confess I don't understand what the difference would be though. Sex is sex. Why would love cause there to be any difference in the performance of it?" That was the honest question that I didn't know the answer t0.

Byron raised his head and grabbed my chin while still holding me in the hug with one arm. "That, my spatz, you will have to wait to find out. When the feelings are real, lust takes the backseat to its high class cousin love. Then the behaviors are no longer the act of sex but the art of love making. The urge to unite as one is unquenchable and no matter how many time you reach the orgasm, there is never complete satisfaction. Instead, the need to try to merge again increases with each encounter. Ah, there are no words to fully describe it. You will understand soon enough. Be patient. You are in no condition to fulfill me nor gain your own at this moment. I want our first time as lovers to be special, not rushed or eclipsed by poor environmental situations. Maybe, in our bed as I always dreamed, ja?"

I had to use all my strength to keep from shuddering at the horrible idea of wanting to be used as the pincushion by any man. "Oh, I see. Well then, I suppose I will just have to experience this love making myself to understand the difference. I thank you for your mercy Byron. Ja, ja, sure in your bed Byron. I want nothing more than to see you happy, my love. I only go where you go and be there to aid in making your troubles flee from the overabundance of happiness." I led out my breath in relief. Damn, I was pretty good at this flowery speak shit. Whew, that was easy.

I was feeling more confident I could please this man with every smile and each tender touching of his hands. He was nuzzling and gently exploring my facial outline when a knocking began at the door. Doctor Borlan called out asking to be let in.

The Voter released me as if I were on fire and lifted his over turned seat with speed. I watched him sit down quickly and then nod that I could tell the doctor to come inside. I saw him flash me a smile and wink as I yelled out to "enter."

Doctor Borlan opened the door and was followed in by the Vampire Jonas and my father Peter. I felt the air leaving my lungs as if punched in the gut. These two didn't look happy as they eyed Byron appearing suspicious of his being there alone with me.

I began to wring my hands but stayed sitting up as the two men approached. Doctor Borlan asked me if I was feeling up to speak with the men. I certainly didn't want to see either of them, but I dared not say nein. I knew it would look bad and both would question why Byron was except from my visitor fatigue. I nodded and mumbled I felt strong enough for the communications with them.

The doctor lowered his glasses and looked at each man. "Maximillian is still quite ill. I politely ask you gentlemen to keep your words peaceful and keep your visit with him brief. He needs rest and nutrition. If you have any stressful news you think deals with him, I warn you now. It will keep to another day when the boy is strong enough to tolerate it. Thank you gentlemen in advance for minding my good advice. Maximillian, if you need me, push that button on the bed. I will come to see you're attended in seconds." The gutsy doctor then strode from the room shutting the door closed behind him.

Jonas and Peter watched him leave then shot a humored look at each other. Byron sat there in the chair with his arms crossed, his own expression darkened to one of irritation. I wrung my hands faster and stared at the blankets that covered my lap.

The Vampire cleared his throat. "So, what you doing here Byron? It is awfully early to be out trolling for young men that don't belong to you, isn't it?" He lightly chuckled at his attempt to insult the Voter.

Byron frown and shook his head. "I beg your pardon honored Elder. I am the early riser. I was headed down to the gym for the work out when I noticed a nasty crick in my neck. I stopped by to have the doctor check it out and heard he had untethered the boy. I decided to come in to check that this sawbones wasn't prematurely letting the little psycho go free is all."

Peter scoffed. "Well, isn't that mighty good of you to take it upon yourself to check on our property."

Byron shook his head again. "Nein, I came for my own personal aches and pains, but was killing time. I was curious too, I confess, to see if the boy had calmed."

Jonas snorted and chuckled. "Your aches and pains mean you are getting old, pal. As you can see the boy's guardian and contracted supervisor are here now. You may go on about your business."

Byron stood up and glared with fury at the Elder. "Okay, sure. I am glad you fellows got here. The boy was starting to bore me anyway. Oh, and if it is not too much to ask, how about a fucking thank you. Shit, I didn't have to lower myself to sit here staring at your sperm pocket when I could have been doing something of worth."

Peter put up his hand to calm the Vampire that was about to yell back another insult. "Easy there brother. Ignore Byron. He is just being difficult to get your goat. Brother, you really need to cut back on the steroids. That shit will cause your balls to shrink, and your moods to turn dark. I say thank you for the aid. It is most appreciated. I think however, it is time you go before that good deed you do is forgotten by your larger mouth infractions." My father looked back at the door with mild anxiety in his expression.

Byron nodded and headed for the door. "Sure thing, Peter. Just so you both know, the boy is about to blow. I wouldn't get anywhere near him if I was you. I am serious. Watch your asses. If you ignore my warning then get your

254

asses kicked by this insane slut, well don't say I didn't warn you. See you fellows around." He shot me a quick look and silently ordered me to attack the brutes the second either tried to touch me.

I nodded back that I understood his unsaid instructions. He smiled and went out the door without another word.

Jonas turned his attention back to my father with a shocked expression on his face. "Damn, you should get your brother Voter a lesson in proper manners. Peter. He is one rude motherfucker."

Peter shrugged. "I told him to leave the drugs alone. The man is hardheaded as hell. Shoots that shit up so he can be sculped into the bullish brute you know. He cannot help that insolent mouth. That is a side effect of his poison, along with violent mood swings and impulsive aggression. I am unsure why you let what that nothing Byron says get to you anyway. You should be used to dealing with the irrational by now, Jonas. This boy I dare say has done plenty over the years to give us all the lessons of madness, ja?" He pointed at me.

The Vampire snickered. "If that isn't true then nothing is, Maximillian. Do you know who I am," he shouted at me causing me to flinch from the noise.

Peter chuckled. "Shit ask him something harder, Jonas, like does he know who the fuck he is?" They both started to laugh wildly.

I stopped wringing my hands and glared at them filling full of anger. "Shut the fuck up, you stupid bastards. I know who you are. Tweedledee and Tweedledumb, pull out the plug and stick in your thumb. Only interested when next you get to cum. I dare you to try to force your fun. Step any closer and I will give you some." I doubled up my fists and threatened to hit the two with them.

Theu brutes stopped laughing as Jonas bellowed out, "Fuck, he is worse than ever. What the fuck is this quack even doing? He looks like shit, sounds like a loon, and the rhyming, I cannot take that again."

Peter put up his hand requesting silence once more. "Easy there brother. Maximillian is fucking with you. He is improving. You must overlook his foul appearance. That is to be expected given the severity of infection raging within his flesh. Trust me when I say, I can see this doctor has done a marvelous job."

Jonas gasped as his eyes went wide. "You call this improvement? I have seen healthier looking corpses Peter. And at least they didn't babble bad poetry."

Peter chuckled at that. "At least he doesn't think we are the yard hound anymore, Jonas. His aggression is directed this time instead of general. He also couldn't have been so damned eloquent in his stanza delivery if he were completely psychotic. This boy is nearly lucid, and his hue has turned a bit pinker compared to the other day. Look closely. There is the rose color to his cheeks."

Jonas crossed his arms and scoffed. "Oh, sure I see that now that you point it out. I must have missed it because that bright red in his eyes. Controlled insanity is that what you observe Herr doctor Schmidt? Well far be it for this uneducated Vampire to know a thing of good complexions or mental stability when I encounter it. Tell me Maximillian, is what the honorable Peter spouts truth or is he trying to blow wind up my tailcoat?"

I narrowed my eyes at the Vampire. "What do I care if you blow each other? Less work for the Mad Maxx, ja?"

Peter really started laughing as the Vampire snorted in mild irritation. "Damn it Maximillian, you know Gott damned well what I asked you. Stop feigning daftness and answer me or so help me your ass will match the color of your eyes when I am done with you."

I snarled at him. "It already does Jonas. Do your worst, I dare you. Then when you are through acting the asshole, I am going to return the service motherfucker. I am most thrilled to have a roomie. You know what? It will be nice to have you sharing my bed for a change. I can assure you that I am most delighted to have you resting in my brutal cuddle and sharing my breakfast." I pointed to the IV bag.

Peter grabbed the Vampire's arm as he started to take a run at me. "Jonas, what the hell, man. The boy is already in a fucking hospital bed. I have to wonder who is the nut if you intend to attack him while he is on the medical tubes. Calm down. Maximillian, enough. You got your point across. Drop it, I mean it."

I shot Peter an angered look. "Where is my master? I want to see Mad Lucus right this minute. You two are the nothings. I miss my master. Someone call him to come be with me. He will send you both out of my sight."

That caused them both to startle. Jonas stole a glance at Peter, then back to me his mouth nearly on the floor from shock. I crossed my arms as best I could given the IVs. I held my furious glare on them without showing any signs of fear.

Almost like he heard me, the door opened and Mad Lucus entered the room. He saw me sitting there looking like the pit viper and his brothers standing in silent confusion. I watched him stop his fast gait toward our group as an expression of confusion came over his face.

I led out a loud yelp as I shouted, "There you are my lord. Please lover, will you get these nothings out of my hair? I desire to be alone with you. I have missed you so bad." I did my best to appear eager to hold him as I opened my arms enticing him to come to embrace me.

You could've knocked all three men down with a feather. Mad Lucus stood there appearing unsure if he wasn't hallucinating for a moment, but then came to himself. He dashed across the room and leaned down to enjoy what he thought was his lover's thrilled reunion with him. Peter and Jonas were left scratching their heads in disbelief of their straight Priceless appearing excited to be cuddled by the unattractive Mad Lucus.

I stole a glance over the hugging Mad Lucus's shoulder and saw the look on the ex-Masters' faces. That incited my next perplexing behavior. I lowered my arms that held Mad Lucus and grabbed his backside as if trying to pull him into me wantonly. Mad Lucus moaned out in surprised delight, while Peter and Jonas nearly fainted in shock.

I groaned out in a breathy voice. "Oh, I have really missed you, my Lord. Can you throw them out, lock the door and spare a few minutes to remind me why I love you so much? I swear I will make it worth your while, baby. I am feeling very snuggly at the moment, but who knows when the sickness comes back on, ja?"

Mad Lucus couldn't believe his good fortune. His hijacked ward appeared to be finally giving in to his brainwashing techniques. I am pretty sure at that point he would have been willing to fight off pride of lions to bask in the spoils of his, or so he thought, winning the mind games.

He led me go and pulled from my eager embrace appearing overwhelmed with lust. "Get the fuck out, both of you, now." He turned and pointed at the door yelling in a deep voice full of authoritative tones.

Peter railed back at him while the Vampire stood there appearing too startled to know how to respond. "You dare to tell your betters to leave? Just who the fuck do you think you are?"

Mad Lucus frowned as the fires lit in his eyes. "I am the voice of the Master of this Haus. His words are law. He says to leave, then you fucking do it, or I will see you sent below to take it up with the dungeon masters. Go now, I will not warn you a third time honorable brothers."

Jonas grabbed Peter by the arm. "We better go, brother. Lucus is right. He is the voice of Maximillian, like it or not. We can take this out of the boy another time when that bastard is not around to make his words audible. I don't desire a fight with Gretta, and something tells me neither do you. Besides, there is more than one way to skin a Priceless, ja?" Peter nodded begrudgingly but followed the Vampire from the room.

Mad Lucus turned to me with a huge smile on his face. "Holy shit, that actually worked. Wow, now that was exhilarating. I just tell them to go away, and they go. I think I am going to love this being the Lord to my King more than I ever imagined. Now, where were we? Oh ja. You said you miss my company, my King?" He reached out and grabbed me forcing his lips to mine, planting a tongue filled kiss on my mouth.

I held back the urge to vomit as I tolerated his wandering hands and slobbering across my face, ears and neck. I thought of Byron only a few moments before then this man. I had tried to entice two men to fuck me while viciously ill and confined to the hospital bed. Shit, Byron was right. I am the slut.

Mad Lucus continued to try to remove my bed gown as I did my best to block him from it for a few moments. It took him that long to realize he was kissing, but I wasn't responding in kind to his advances.

He pulled off me with his eyebrow raised inquisitively. "What is this? You come on to me strong and now you are the limp noodle. Have I done something to upset you?"

I nodded. "Uhm, ja, my Lord. I do believe it will be hard to bend over this bed to see to your desires with all the tubes restraining my movements. There is also the problem of the cuttings. I thought you said you feared scars. Well, I find it distasteful that you tease me when we both know not only is this not going to happen today, but it shouldn't happen."

He scoffed. "Ja, you have valid points there Christian. However, I wish to say you came on to me, not the other way around. I came here to check on you. See if you needed anything, my heart. I had no intention of taking advantage of you in this poor state of health. I swear it."

I reached down and grabbed his erect cock and jerked hard making him wince and thrill too "Oh? Then what is this for? You worried that you would skin your nose tripping over your boots? Is that your safety gear to prevent it?"

Mad Lucus chuckled as he blushed. "Uhm, I don't apologize for finding you sexy Christian. I never lied about my honest desire for you. You been having sex with the men for years and you are a man yourself. You are well aware that rubbing and kissing with tenderness is going to cause that side effect. I won't allow you to chastise me for that natural response. Hell, you should be flattered your lover finds you attractive even in your worse state, ja?" He pushed my hair from my face with a loving look in his eyes.

I groaned at that. "I would be flattered if I wanted to play the female to a man. However, I don't. In fact, I don't want a man anywhere around me when my side effects occur."

He chuckled and dropped his gaze. "Ja, I know that Christian and I cannot apologize more than I already have for not being the partner of your true desire. That also is not of my design."

I glared at him with hate. "Nein, it is not that is the truth, but you sure as shit are not above abusing the sad fact I am forbidden the woman. Why couldn't you just be a decent fucking human being and treat me like a brother and not your unwilling lover? Will someone please explain to me why it is so hard to keep their dicks to themselves. You know in all my days as the catamite I have never once wanted to fuck a man. I have never been that horny in my life, Gott dammit. Why can you schwulers not just find a man that is all for this shit, like Jakob or hell any of the fellows from the FBL. Can't you assholes leave the straight boys alone for Christ sakes."

Mad Lucus sighed then took my hand into his, kissing the knuckles. This made me shudder in disgust. "Christian baby, you are never getting out of the Haus. I admit it would have been more merciful to leave you alone for me. Not for you though. Like it or not, one of the so-called schwulers are going to put you on their leash. You were born to be the Mortar King. That position requires the regent and with that powerful Peter blocking the FemDoms it was by default ruled to be a Dominant instead. Sure, I could have stepped aside and turned a blind eye as all the brutal men desirous of your leash fought to take you for their own. Maybe Jonas would have won the right, or Peter? How about Malfred? Oh, I know, your pal Claus or worse, Osvin. You see, sooner or later one would have cornered you. Do you think they would overlook the rights thy possessed to your special services skills? Better think again, Christian. Your ability to please the man sexually is not only legendary in this Haus, but the truthful rumor. I thought about it. It occurred to me that if you are without a choice in the matter, then why not have a Dominant that will use the power you possess to make sure this place never hurts another innocent soul. I may not be the lover of your dreams, my love. I certainly am the wrong gender of your preference. That is more than a little obvious. I must tolerate for all my days living with a man that merely minds my commands, but who will never feel anything but resentment for me even if I never lay a finger on him. I happen to know if I never touch you again, that won't stop Jonas, or Peter or even Claus. You are not going to escaping this sorry fate you are forever trapped in. I can only tell you that I am truly sorry, my dove, for the evil they have done to you. That said, if you will allow me to enjoy all the benefits along with all the drawbacks of being your regent, then I think maybe I can at least offer comfort. I can give back the special service return I take from you if you can only open your mind to a love that is not about the part, but the heart."

I shook my head "What? Am I to understand you are willing to play the bottom in our relationship?"

He laughed hard, until he coughed. "Uhm, well I wouldn't go that far, Christian. At least not yet. I mean if you were gay like me, then surely over time both of us would enjoy the full possibility of our couplings. However, you are never going to be schwuler. I know for a fact I don't like to be the bottom in anal sex. I have tried it and found no thrill in it. I am a pure top. You my love are not either top or a bottom, but you are trained to handle what I cannot find sexually stimulating. What I am saying is I am more than happy to engage in the other types of stimulations for you to find release other than the full intercourse. I do enjoy bringing my lover to orgasm if only my lover would find his lust for me. You did it in the Great Hall. Maybe once you see that I am not like the other Masters you have known, you will give in to the only release you are allowed. I want to give you my heart and my mercy Christian. I wish you could understand I am not your enemy. I love you. I don't want to hurt you. I want to please you. Nothing in this world would bring me more peace than to know you are as happy as possible given the restrictions of this abomination called Der Kaiser Haus."

I rolled my eyes at him. "You are a liar, my Lord. I am not some dumb twink that just discovered the horrors of special services anymore. You sell something I no longer buy. My happiness is your goal as long as it doesn't prevent you from finding the full extent of your own."

Mad Lucus frowned and dropped my hand as he looked at his boots. "Christian, if you don't listen to another word I say then please, I beg of you to hear the next ones. Jonas, Peter and Malfred intend for you to have that Frau you have groused about since I can recall knowing you as the little boy. Beware my heart. The second you blood bond that poor girl you condemn her to a fate far worse than your own. Those men intend to use her as their breeding mare. She will be forced to endure couple after couple with you and them plus others. All to ensure a steady supply of Priceless children. The Haus will then confiscate your children and force them to do all you both have done, and likely far worse in time. Your legacy and bloodline will fertilize this Haus for generations to come. Any female you couple with is in grave danger of this nightmare I speak of. If there is any soul left in you after all they have done to destroy you, Christian, then I beg of you not to act as their bait to lure in another innocent along with countless more yet unborn. If you listen, you can hear the weeping of that Frau they promise you. You will hear the screams of your sons and daughters as they haul them to their beds for defiling."

I looked up at him with fear crushing the air from my lungs. "You lie, Lucus. Peter told me that when I blood bond and make the first child I am free. I will be allowed to…" I trailed off as I heard Jonas say he intended to blood bond my Frau.

Mad Lucus nodded as tears began to cloud up his eyes. "You know I tell the truth, my love. They have been preparing you for this horror all your life. Everything they have done was to push you to make this fatal mistake. They want to make you so desperate you would be willing to risk the life of another. Please, don't become the Priceless of the legends, Christian. Accept your fate as my lover, where no child is possible, and no innocent female is forced to take your place as the damned. I will treat you with love and respect all your life. It is not what you wanted, but it is merciful in its own way."

I sniffed back the cold tears as his words cut into me. "My Lord, can you tell me something? Answer a question for me? If you do, then I swear I will take what you say to heart."

He nodded. "Sure Christian, ask me any question and I will answer it with honesty."

I took a deep breath. "What is the address of this Haus? Where am I?"

Mad Lucus nearly choked. "Huh? What? You want to know the address of the Haus? Why?"

I glared at him with fury. "You want me to trust you, but you stall in answering this simple question. Now tell me the fucking address. Where the fuck am I being held the captive."

He shook his head. "I cannot answer that question Christian. I am honor bound. I swore an oath."

I interrupted him. "To the Haus? To Grett or another of the so-called Silk Queens? You are a fucking asshole that abuses a man that never had a choice. I told you nein. You didn't listen. You tricked me and use me for your nasty lust. You tell me now that I should trust you, believe in you. You want me to accept my fate as your unwilling catamite. I ask you to give me one good reason. You deny me that reason by saying 'oh, I swore an oath to the very pigs that abducted you, raped you, tortured you, and abused you, but hey, I am your friend.' Well fuck you Lucus. I am not your friend. I am not your lover. I am nothing more than your cock warmer. Get out of my sight. I do believe that sickness I was speaking of earlier has returned. I wish to suffer as I always have, and always will, alone." With that I flung myself into the bed and turned my back on him.

He stood there several more minutes trying to speak to me. I closed my eyes and blocked his voice out. Doctor Borlan came into the room and asked him to leave because I pushed that button he told me about, ha. I spent the next two days alone. I refused to see anyone but Byron.

However, he didn't come visit again. I was hurt deeply that he didn't bring Felicity like he promised. That is, until on the third day I asked for the thousandth time if Byron had come by. Doctor Borlan told me that Jonas had put Byron on a list that forbid him from any visits. I was beyond angry when I found that shit out. The Vampire had no right to interfere with my private business, or so I thought anyway.

On the fourth day the doctor thought me well enough to be released. I asked him to keep my discharge to himself. He was not inclined to do as I asked him, but with a bit of threatening, mild trust me, he relented. The good doctor made me promise to check in with either Mad Lucus or the Vampire within two hours or he would be forced to tell them himself.

I took his offer of two hours of freedom and decided to use them carefully. The first stop was to see Matz. The wolf was shocked to see me eager to have him line up a list of clients to begin the next day for the second time. He was happy to do as I asked but made me swear this time I wouldn't leave him trying to explain to angry customers why their whore wasn't there to suck their cocks, yuck.

My second stop was in the torture chamber. Poor Samual had been in the holding cell since I had the Guard haul him away from the Great Hall. I felt kind of bad he got stuck for that entire five days, but shit, that's the life of the collars in the Haus. He was not tortured other than the five tawse strikes. I released him and saw him compensated for the extra days he had been unable to attend his jobs. The man was grateful for the mercy. To this day he has never denied any order I have given him since. I made him and all the black collars of the Haus a believer. It only cost Samual a few swats and five days in a cell. In the long run, it was worth the overly dramatic display of false brutality.

My next stop was to see Felicity. I was hauling ass up the staircase thinking of ways to apologize to Byron for Jonas's unacceptable behavior when I ran smack into Peter.

My father had been headed to the Great Hall and noticed all around him the collars had gotten nervous. He then saw many fall to their knees several moments before he even saw the one he knew caused this odd behavior. The Collar King himself, me.

He called to me before I could turn tail and run away. "Maximillian, you come here a minute, boy. Follow me. There is something we need to discuss immediately."

I groaned under my breath but limped up the steps to obey his command. "Ja, I know. You are pissed off that you have sprained your wrists and back manually dealing with your own urges." I snickered at this crude statement.

Peter glared at me with fury. "You must be feeling better. I hope your ass is as healed up as your tongue seems to be. I have a feeling I am going to remedy that return to health shortly. It is good for a man to keep up his skills with the tawse. I am happy you are eager to volunteer to keep my aim strong."

I scoffed,. "You don't scare me with that little piece of leather anymore, Peter. Beat me all you like. You will wear yourself out old man. Then Mad Maxx is the winner when you are too tired for your lusting. I will thank your tawse when your thrusting is as weak and gentle as the kitten."

Peter raised an arm to strike me but thought better of it at the last moment, which surprised the shit out of me. "Enough of your bravado. I can beat you all day and fuck you all night. I am fit as the fiddle. I will not be misled into causing a scene here for all the Haus to see. I know you boy. There is always a reason you pull the tricks you do. If you desire me to backhand you, then I can assure you I am able to control myself. I told you to follow me for this discussion. I am politely asking you to do it in silence or maybe you desire that I call in for help to see that tongue of yours stilled by use of the spider gag?"

I shook my head and looked to the floor. "Nein, I am in no need for restraints. I thank you for the mercy of it." He smiled as he motioned me to stay high protocol behind him.

That angered me but without Mad Lucus around I was viewed as the King without a voice. I did as he commanded grumbling to myself about all the bad things I wanted to do to Peter. Of course, I dared not do any of them. His death assured me a one way ticket to the cell in the Palace. I really hate that man you know. He is a clever bastard.

I was shocked to see him lead me right up to his front door. I looked around the hallway hoping to spot Byron. The place was devoid of any people as usual. The fifth floor was forbidden to anyone other than the specially trained black collar staff, the Elders, and invited guests of the Voters. I could hear the many voices of the Haus residents below us in their daily hustle and bustle. It seemed so odd to have that silent, reverent hallway echo the faint voices of so many like ghosts in the distance.

Peter opened his door and hand signaled me to follow. I immediately felt sick to my stomach. You know what I was thinking. It had been almost five years since my father had forced himself on me in his own bed when he was still my Master. I was in no hurry to revisit those evil days.

I took a deep breath to brace myself and went in after him. He closed the door just as I gasped. I could see from the receiving area into his fancy living area. Though my view was partially obscured by a wall, I clearly saw Jonas and Mad Lucus sitting on his couch speaking to each other quietly. I thought that Doctor Borlan must have betrayed me and told them I was out of his care and on the loose. That didn't explain why all three of these men were hanging out together in Peter's apartment.

I narrowed my eyes at Peter. "What the fuck is this about? A foursome? Really? Come on man, I just got released from the fucking hospital. Give me at least the morning to relax, would you?"

Peter chuckled. "Ah, you have always made me laugh with your crazy humor Maximillian. Nein, you are wrong. This is not a three man tag team you are here to serve. This time it is us that intend to grant you a pleasure. Come with me. Jonas, Lucus and I have a gift for you."

I blew out my breath, grateful it wasn't what I feared it was then fell in behind him as he led me into the living area. The moment we were completely inside the room I saw a small girl child wearing a silver collar. She was kneeling across from Mad Lucus and Jonas with her eyes to the floor. The female couldn't have been more than twelve, maybe thirteen. Her hair was the color of hay, and she was like all silvers breathtakingly beautiful even for her immature age. I could tell she had been weeping heavily and in the light coming through the window I could see her shadow trembling. There was no doubt the girl was scared to death for some reason.

I was completely unsure what to make of this weird scene. I stole a glance of confusion at Mad Lucus. He dropped his gaze to his lap. Jonas on the other hand was beaming a triumphant smile at me as if he just caught the juiciest rat and was satiated with its blood.

I shook my head as I looked at that silver with concern. "What have you done to the poor girl? You are all a pack of monsters. She isn't even legal, is she? How dare you bring me here to gloat over your cruel sport with one of my court? I will call Gretta and lodge a complaint. You are not allowed to abuse the children of this Haus wantonly just because they wear the silver."

Peter and Jonas began to laugh wildly at my angry rant. Mad Lucus covered his eyes with his hands and sighed deeply. That only managed to make me even more furious.

I stomped my boot. "You won't be laughing when I see you all whipped for this. Girl, get off your knees and leave this minute. These brutes had no right to defile you. I will see them suffer for the crime."

The silver shook her head and squeaked out, "I beg your mercy, Master. I cannot obey your orders to leave. I must attend my Master's every whim but leaving his side." She shook so hard she almost fell over.

I gasped. "One of you rat bastards own this poor girl. Who is it? Wait, Jonas you cannot own the silver nor can you Peter. Lucus? You motherfucker. Why? Are you trying to prove a point by defiling a female? Christ, you are sick in the fucking head."

Mad Lucus removed his hands from his eyes and glared at me with sternness. "Nein, Christian, this girl is not mine. She is yours, fool. Jonas and Peter have selected her for the blood bonding with you. This is to be your wife."

Chapter 53: The Beauty and the Beast, Part 2

I stood there in shock so bad I couldn't even blink my eyes. "What? This is to be my…" I trailed off as I shot a look at the silver that trembled on the floor.

Jonas laughed loudly as he crossed his arms. "Look there Peter. I told you the boy is not gone schwuler on us. He is so overcome by the thought of finally being the married man he cannot believe his good fortune. Tell Peter, Maxmillian, you find this girl beautiful, ja?"

I couldn't take my eager eyes off that object of my forbidden desires. "Where does she come from? I never see this silver before. Did she agree to this union? Does she even have a name? Why does she wear a true collar? This girl is how old?" I felt my feet carrying me across the floor to get a closer look at the gorgeous female that was all mine. Hell, yes.

Peter wore a huge smile as he walked over to join me. "Her name is Motte. You never seen her before because she has belonged to a nothing fourth floor Dominate since your return from Heslach. The man was most unhappy to part with this glorious prize, but Jonas managed to rip her from his greedy paws. As for choosing you as her husband, not that it matters to the submissive, but what girl wouldn't be desirous to be at your side on the Mortar Throne. Motte, look at me girl. Tell your Master Maxximillian of your joy to be his blood bonded Frau." Peter slapped my back with a chuckle as he said this to me.

Motte raised her tear drenched face keeping her eyes to the floor. "I am grateful for the honor to be your blood bonded Frau, Master. I thank you for the mercy of it." I saw more tears flowing as she dropped her head back to the floor.

I winced upon seeing that sadness where there should be joy. "She is weeping, Peter. That doesn't seem to be the behavior of a willing bride. I think the girl finds me repulsive." I backed away feeling suddenly quite anxious.

Jonas sat forward his expression of glee beginning to darken. "The girl is crying the sweet tears of thrill, Maxximillian. Stop being stupid. What the fuck do you even care if she does find you repulsive? Not like she has a Gott damned choice. You tell her what to do and it is her duty to fucking do it. Peter, tell that dumbass to shut up her blubbering. Not like she is the stranger to intercourse. Shit that idiot Master of hers already broke every law in the Haus with the little twat. Fuck her anyway you want. She is well trained. That is why I picked her, you know. You my boy have no skills with the women. Motte here will teach you all you need to know, plus Peter and I will enjoy her well-honed talents far more than any unseasoned virgin. I personally prefer the professional to the fresh any day of the week. I have been told her oral skills are exquisite. I can barely wait to find out for myself. Oh, but of course, she is yours Maxximillian. You go first. Take her back to Peter's bedroom. When the deed is done yell. I am happy to witness the marriage."

I gasped as I shot a stunned look at Jonas. "What? The girl is not fresh. No virginity at all? That is why she wears the honest silver and has the submissive name, isn't it. Shit, she is a Gott damned baby. What pervert raped a little baby in this Haus? I want that fucker's name, Jonas. I will see him put to the yard for such criminality."

Peter scoffed. "Ged off your high horse, boy. Hell, Maxximillian, I was fucking you ten ways to Sunday at the age of not even twelve yet. That is far younger than this girl of nearly fourteen and you turned out fine. Besides she is still mostly unused. Her virginities were not tapped till a couple months ago. She has shown great promise in the art of special services and is beautiful to boot. I am usually against bothering with the women before age fifteen, but this girl is already broken in. No harm done if I do enjoy all she has to offer, ja? Hell, boy you should be thrilled. You not only get this lovely girl for all your pent up lusts, but you save her from the circuit. Thank your Lord and Master for the extreme mercy he grants you this day, Motte." He kicked the girl lightly.

She sobbed out. "I thank you for the extreme mercy, Master." She covered her eyes trembling so hard I thought she was going to fall over. Poor little thing.

I watched the little silver with an aching heart. I knew very well how much it hurt to hear everyone discussing your disgrace as if it meant nothing to them. I stole a glance at Mad Lucus. He had covered his eyes with his hands. I thought I heard him sniffle loudly. It was then I realized he was trying to hide his own tears at this most horrible scene.

I thought of what he had told me that day in the clinic. I saw the way Jonas and Peter were looking at Motte with thrill in their eyes and erect cocks in their jeans. That poor girl was about to endure what I had feared, the grotesque three-man tag teaming. I assumed Mad Lucus, the only real gay man there, would refrain. *I am a lot of things Meine Liebe, and given what I did to you, one would think this horror was not above me. I refused to do to Motte the same shit that often was pulled on me.*

I swore to myself I was not going to be just another nightmare to my own fucking wife. I waited all my life for the wife and children. I couldn't risk that Mad Lucus told the truth of it. Nor did I desire to be only one of a long list waiting to fuck the mother of my babies. The disgust of it made me want to vomit as I watched the heaving chest of that frightened little girl at my feet.

Master Maxx stopped his story with suddenness and turned me around in his lap. "Meine Liebe, I warn you. Don't say a word about what I just said. I will get to why I refused to do the evil I do to you to this girl Motte when the time comes. I know hearing this story may hurt your feelings. Maybe you will wonder why I cared so much for Motte's welfare, but not your own? If that be the case then stop it now. There is a huge difference between what happened that day and the one where you and I met. Do me the favor of withholding your judgement till I finish my entire story and I will see you rewarded greatly for it. I swear it on my honor. Do you agree to this?"

I nodded feeling a bit fearful at his apparent irritation though I had not said a word, I swear it. "As you wish Master. If I may add, I think I already know why you wouldn't accept Motte but then took me. I have been listening to the story. Motte didn't match the female priceless of legend."

He nodded as he narrowed his eyes at me. "You think that is the reason for truth? Don't lie to me."

I looked at his lap with unease in my chest. "Nein, I know it is not the reason Master. You don't believe in the legends of the Priceless."

Master Maxx scoffed. "Then why did you give me that bullshit reason? Tell me with honesty why you and not Motte."

I winced. "A couple of reasons, Master."

He grabbed my chin and held it tightly, forcing me to look at him. "Then give me a couple."

I shuddered. "Uhm, well for starters Motte was completely soiled Master. You could argue that the lack of virginity was a problem to keep from having to fuck a girl old enough to get pregnant."

His eyes lit up with thrill as he nodded. "That is very good, Meine Liebe. Why did that matter, her getting pregnant? Isn't one of my goals to have the children?"

I shook my head. "Yes and no, Master. I heard you say at the time you worried Mad Lucus told you the truth. You *didn't want to find out if he was being honest. I also remember you almost left me behind when Debbie told you I had no girl part virginity. You came back when you found out I still had the one, you know, in that other place. Well, that is because, if you put a boy thing in there no babies get made." I blushed.*

He chuckled. "I fucked you how many times 'in that other place' and still you blush? Damn, Meine Liebe, you are funny. Okay, I say you are correct but is that the only reason?"

I shook my head. "Nein, you pretended to be interested when Debbie said I had an anal virginity. You came back to think about me twice because you wanted Peter to think you are gay. A gay man only wants that place. Plus, I am so little you thought it would be a long time before you even had to worry about making any babies with me. Then that accident happened, but it is okay. I kind of like it when you do it to me. Oh, my God, I didn't mean to say that. I mean I want to make you happy Master." I blushed again.

Master Maxx hugged me tightly while laughing hard. "You make me laugh. Kind of like it. I know you do because the flesh doesn't lie, my demonseed wife. Oh, how I do love you, Meine Liebe. Intelligent and completely forgiving. I truly don't deserve such a prize. I fear I will have to spend the six months away from you in Almut's chains every fucking day at this point. The only way I can ever be worthy of such joy is to pay the price for the rest of my life."

I hugged him back. "I don't want you to be beaten up by Almut, Master. Why can't we just love each other without having to pay for it with all the pain?"

He pulled me back and looked into my eyes appearing bewildered. "There is no agony on Earth worse than true love, Meine Liebe. The emotion brings sublime thrill so great one believes for a moment in Heaven. Yet, the price tag for such joy is sacrifice so hellish you will rue the day you ever felt cupid's sharp pierce. To be in love is the promise of pain by its very definition. However, you have misunderstood what I say. The honest love that I have for you is why I must go to Almut when I return to the Haus, but not to pay for it. That happens without being thudded, trust me. You see I go to the chains to remind me of the horror I inflict upon you my Frau. I fear that engaging you in the training will harden me to the deep empathy I feel for my little victim. You must understand to fool with things like the thudding or torture changes the soul. It is an infection that if not treated with swift harshness can completely take over. One day I hope to hold you in my arms and be able to swear that I will never lay a hand on you again with any motive other than loving gentleness. I cannot be sure that will be a promise I can keep if I develop a taste for your blood and screams. The Mad Max and Mad Maxx must always be in balance within the man. Neither can ever be allowed the right to rule exclusively without fear of the others retaliation. This you understand?"

I nodded. "I think I do, Master. I thank you for the mercy of it. I look forward to the day when you don't have to hit me anymore."

He stroked my cheek lovingly with sadness in his expression. "So do I, Meine Liebe. You have no idea how much I want to just be your husband, not your Master, monster, nightmare nor rapist. All I ever wanted was a quiet life without drama or fear. That my Frau is our goal. We will find this peaceful paradise together or not at all. Now since you don't take offense to my reasons for sparing Motte what you have to endure, I go on with the story, ja?" I nodded as he flipped me back around in his lap holding me tightly to his chest.

The lust that had been overcoming me for that pretty silver suddenly receded like the sea water before the tidal wave. There was no telling the horrors this Motte had endured at the hands of her child molesting Master before that morning. I didn't want to know of it. I only wanted it to stop. I couldn't bring back her innocence, but I could spare her more of the same and even give back her power of choice. To do that would require more strength than I, Maximillian possessed alone. I needed all my brothers for this horror show I was about to unleash.

I closed my eyes and called to my brothers Mad Maxx and Mad Maxx die Brutale. With a deep breath the monstrous shard approached and wrapped his arms around me. Mad Maxx took up the wheel at my side. They nodded in silence that they were ready for this dangerous game we simple couldn't afford to lose. A little girls life was on the line and so was ours.

All five of the shards in the boy melded into one dangerous, cruel, but merciful creature. The wheelroom quaked and the sound of loud shattering rang out in the distance. We could not hold like this for long without setting off eternal insanity. Come what may, we only had this one shot to do the right thing. I silently hoped that despite my foul perverted nature, as pointed out to be my Byron, would take a holiday for a change.

I opened the boys lids ready to do what had to be done, for Motte, me, and the unborn Priceless children that should never be. Jonas had taken to his feet and was rapidly approaching Motte, Peter and me. He was no doubt ready to try to force me to drag that girl down to Peter's room.

I couldn't allow even a moment for me and the female to be out of sight of credible witnesses. If I did, it could be said that I had completed the act of blood bonding, and the girl would be tethered to me for life. I knew that Peter and Jonas were just the kind of assholes that would be willing to lie and say they saw the evidence of the blood couple whether it was really there or not.

Jonas's grab my upper arm smiling with wickedness. "Well? What the fuck are you waiting for fool? You surely are ready to see those pent up urges attended. If you get started now, you maybe have time to get your thrill a few times before that idiot Master of yours hauls you off for his own nasty interests." He shot a humored look at the weeping Mad Lucus.

I glared at the Vampire as I shook off his hold violently. "Get your filthy paws off me, dog. How dare you think me so depraved I would want the nasty leftovers of a nothing. This silver is beneath me and female to boot. She possesses used holes and is too feminine looking for me to even pretend in the dark she is of the proper gender for my interest. Yuck! I think I may be sick just thinking of even having to be in the same room with her. You fellows are idiots to believe I would desire this whatever the fuck this thing is." I pointed at Motte that immediately fell to her face openly wailing in terror at my words.

Jonas backed away, his eyes wide open in stun. Peter stood there with his mouth hanging in pure confusion at my angry rant. Mad Lucus dropped his hand from his face to stare at me with an expression that was the mixture of relief and disbelief. I was loudly announcing my disinterest in females and believe me when I tell you that man couldn't have been happier to hear it.

Jonas cleared his throat and glanced at the freaking out silver girl. "Maxximillian? This girl is, well, I mean that lack of virginity, it don't matter I swear it to you. That is all hype spewed by the no nothings of the Haus. This Motte can satisfy you fine without any of it. You don't mean what you saying. Peter, you are the doctor. Is this boy suffering another psychotic fit? That is what is going on, ja?" He looked to Peter with desperation in his eyes.

Peter shook his head and crossed his arms as he re-composed himself. "Cut it out Maxximillian. No one in this room is going to fall for your tricks. You are not a schwuler. All you are going to do is piss me and Jonas off. This girl, another, they are all the same. As long as day have the uterus and vagina then you have no business being so fucking picky. In the end, you are still able to claim the Frau you always wanted. The way I see it, you also have no right to be complaining of this girl's sexual indiscretions of the past. She has known only one cock. How many have you had in you, boy? Can you even count that high I wonder? You are a Gott damned used up catamite trying to call this nearly innocent girl soiled. What a joke. You should be on your knees thanking Jonas and me for the mercy we grant you like your wife is. I suggest you shut the hell up and take this fucking cunt to the back to do your duty, boy."

Without hesitation I reared back my arm and backhanded Peter. He was so startled by that move he fell to his ass. Jonas backed away appearing unable to wrap his mind around what I had just done to my father.

I turned my sight to the Vampire. "Do you have something to say to me, hound? Go ahead. I am listening. Don't you desire to inform me of my own Gott damned sexual interests? Are you going to agree with Peter and say I lie about being the schwuler for true? Well? What I want to know is how the fuck do either of you dare to think you know a fucking thing of what makes my cock hard? I don't seem to recall any of you assholes being the least bit interested in finding that out. This girl is not going to be my wife. I thank you both for nothing. This bullshit is not mercy, or at least this silver will not think so when I am through with her." I reached down and grabbed Motte's long hair holding it tightly in a wad.

The girl wailed, "Please, Master, I apologize that I don't thrill you. I swear if you give me the chance I will do whatever you want to see you satisfied."

I pulled the little girl to her feet and held her by the hair forcing her to look into my face. "Is that so? Well, now you are speak my language Motte. I thought you completely useless for my sport but since you are so interested in seeing me the happy man, then hell, how can the Mad Maxx resist your charms, ja?"

She feigned a weak smile. Damn, she was beautiful. "I thank you for reconsidering, Master. I am grateful for your mercy." Her tears continued to fall in great number.

I nodded. "Humm, you are grateful for what mercy, madam? I think you speak before you know what it is that will satisfy your Master. Tell me Motte, are you familiar with the Torture Chamber below?"

Motte's fake smile turned upside down as she trembled. "Ja, Master."

I nodded. "Ah the fear in your eyes tells me you are indeed aware of the pleasures of that incredible place. Tell me something, which room is your favorite? Don't be ashamed to admit your secret desires to your Master. I am quite the twisted motherfucker myself. In fact, I can safely say there is nothing I am not up for when it comes to the taboo thrills. Hurry my dear. I wish to see if you and I can come to an understanding. You know they say all great marriages are built on the foundation of commonalities. Let's see if you and me are the compatible, ja?"

Motte barely breathed out. "I am thrilled by whatever pleases my Master. I desire only to serve him with perfection." Her tears came even faster as she began to pant in full on panic.

I raised my eyebrows. "Oh? Then I am to understand you love all torture then."

Her face drew up into the weeping jag as her mouth opened but nothing came out. After two tried she dropped her wet gaze and nodded. I watched her shoulders slump as she came to accept her doom and likely worse nightmare come to truth.

I chuckled as I watched the abused girl try to find that place far away from the reality she couldn't bear. "That is good to hear, my beauty. I think we are going to get along famously. Tell you what. I am not interested in your for the carnal pleasures, but I think instead I will pretend you are a pretty boy. I desire to take you below and beat the silver called Motte to death. How does that sound? I warn you girl, careful how you answer me. I assure you it is the only way you will every please this man of yours."

Motte shuddered and sniffed back her tears keeping her eyes to the floor. "I thank you for the mercy of it, Master."

I leaned in closely as she trembled and whispered into her ear. "Ja, you understand don't you. If I kill you then you truly would have received mercy. Come with me little nothing. Time to die." I jerked her hair hard forcing her to the floor.

She wailed and unconsciously grabbed at my hands. Jonas and Peter, who had regained his footing, came running after me as I dragged the kicking, screaming girl to the door. I turned around when I saw they were attempting to interrupt my thrills.

I glared at Mad Lucus that appeared frozen in complete terror at what he was watching. "Tell these mongrels to back off, my Lord. They have no right to interfere with me taking my pleasures from my own submissive. I do believe you said she belongs to me, ja?"

Mad Lucus stammered out, "Ja, Motte is yours by paper but Christian please. What are you doing to that girl. Let her go. You are not really going to kill her are you?" He wrung his hands nervously.

I glared to him and the two thugs that had stopped their chase. "I am going to kill Motte. You see I don't want this disgusting creature in my bed for life. I am not stupid like Jonas to blood bond without thinking it out. If I find her this gross now, then what about a few years from now. I learned to be careful of the consequences of breeching unfair contracts from Peter and you my Lord. She has no virginity to seal her contract with me. That means I don't have to agree to take her and no one else will either. I understand that means she gets sold off to the circuit. They will slowly rape and starve her to death. Her horrific end could take weeks, even months. This way she can serve her function to make me happy and I equally serve her back. She gets the honorable, quick death and I get to hear her scream. You call these brutes off me, my Lord, or I will lodge a complaint with Gretta that you don't do your job as the regent in training."

Peter and Jonas shot a look of shock at Mad Lucus as he said, "Honorable brothers, I may not agree with what my King says but he has the right to do what he demands. You both must stand down. You gave him that silver. She is exclusively his property. He is also the Master of this Haus and the Collar King. If he desires to murder this poor, innocent, sweet little girl then he has the right."

Jonas bellowed out angrily, "Are you fucking kidding me? I just spent a fortune on that collar. I am not going to sit back and watch this idiot waste perfectly useful silver flesh. It is an abomination. That girl could pleasure a man for years to come yet. Nein, I will not allow him to do this."

Mad Lucus came forward with fires lighting up in his expression. "If you wanted that girl to warm your bed you shouldn't have given her to him in the first place. It seems to me that Peter and you picked a female of your own desires. As usual, you didn't ask the boy what he wanted, did you? Nein! Well, too bad for you both and for that little girl. Stand down. Christian, I beg of you to let that child go, but I defend your right to do with her as you wish."

I scoffed at Mad Lucus as Peter and Jonas backed off me. "Always the gentlemen aren't you, my Lord. Tell you what. The moment I am through killing this little bug, I come home to you. I have been thinking about what you said. I have decided you are right. I should be granted a release during our couplings. You better go brush those teeth because when I get back you can suck my cock. Ciao boys." I opened the door and dragged the weeping Motte out behind me.

I headed right for the banister. Motte kicked and screamed as she saw me looking over the side of it to the bustling crowd below. I held the tiny girl tightly by her locks preventing her from doing anything more than appearing silly in her weak struggling.

I turned back to look at her in my grips. "Settle down idiot. You make too much noise. You want me to drop you off here instead of taking the long trip below? If not then I suggest you shut the fuck up."

Motte ceased her struggling as she took to her knees. "Please Master, I beg of you. I don't want to die. Is there not some other way I can make you happy? I swear I won't give you quarrel if you take the special services from me. You can put a bag over my head or turn off the lights."

I glared at her in full blown fury. "I don't want to fuck you with the lights on or without them, girl. You are a fucking mess. You speak like a dirty slut to trade your dignity to the likes of me for what? Years of suffering in my chains? Gang raping? Do you really think death is worse?"

She shuddered and wiped her nose with her sleeve. "I don't know, Master. I am just so scared. I want to live. I don't want to be tortured or killed." She trailed off as the water dripped from her eyes to the carpet below.

I nodded. "You don't want to be fucked by man after man, night after night. Say it."

Motte sucked in her breath. "Nein, Master, I don't want that. It is horrible. I never knew it could be so. Please, mercy. I hate it but I do whatever you want to see tomorrow, even that."

I sighed loudly as I jerked her hair harder forcing her head forward. "Bow when you speak to me. You know like when you give head or get like the dog. You better get used to that movement sweetheart. A beauty like you will be servicing the eager cocks in this Haus round the clock, ja? You say you don't like the special services. Too bad for you. These Dominants around here don't take nein for an answer. You give me whatever I want now. In an hour, you will do the same for that Vampire and another hour for Peter. They will tire of you. Then a new group of men come to defile you some more. Tell me Motte, what is all that suffering for? What do you think is the outcome of my granting you mercy today? You ready to live the life of the sperm pocket? Do you think you can escape or perhaps you hope I fall in love with you. Then maybe I can stop the others from hurting you like they do. Will you love me for loving you or will you look at me as the least of the worse possible outcomes?"

Motte shrugged/ "I know there is no escaping, Master. I did hope you would fall in love with me, then keep the other men from their raping me."

I snorted. "Did you hope to love me? I would merely be the cock that invades you, blocking the other out, ja?"

She began to sob again as she nodded. "Ja, I admit it aster. I am afraid of you. I heard the stories of the terrible things you do. I know about what you do with the men too. You are our King, but you are like the Haus, twisted and scarred. I don't want to be the wife to such a brute."

I sucked in my breath and stared at her with wickedness. "Now you tell the truth to your Master. I thank you for the mercy of it."

She startled at my words and stole a glance at my face. "What? You are not angry with me, Master? I assumed you would punish me for being insolent and rude."

I shrugged. "Call me the fool but I don't believe it is insolent to tell the truth. It is rude to lie, my beauty. This Haus has fucked up your vision of right and wrong. You lie to be rewarded and tell the truth to no one, not even yourself. Motte is not you name. What is it really?"

Motte looked down with a bitter smile. "My mother called me Amanda. She named me after her own mother. They took away my name when my Master, well, when he collared me."

I nodded. "Ja, I know Motte. They take everything, don't they? Tell me, do you believe there is anything left of this girl once called Amanda? Does she still live somewhere within these hallways or is she in her grave?"

Motte looked at me with confusion in her expression. "Master, I don't think it is okay to answer that question."

I jerked her head harshly by the hair causing her to wail out in pain. "I asked you a fucking question, Motte. I am your Master, and you dare to refuse me? I am above all as your Gott damned King. You tell me what I want to know, or I will throw you off this motherfucking banister."

Motte sputtered and trembled. "I apologize Master. Yes, I am still her. They can call me whatever the fuck they want. That doesn't make it the truth of it. I am Amanda. I will always be Amanda. They soil my flesh, but they cannot touch my soul. That belongs to no man. You can toss me over the banister. I want you to. I don't care. I won't beg anymore. You intend to kill me anyway. Then do it, Gott damn you. You will burn in hell for the evil you do to me, and I will be there laughing as you scream in eternal agony." She stared at me in open defiance.

I let go of her hair and grabbed her by the throat with both hands hauling her to the railing. The girl clawed at my me, her eyes wild with terror. I laughed with great humor as I began to tilt her over the side of the banister. If I let go she would fall five floors to her gruesome end.

I yelled to her. "Stop fighting me, Motte. You are going to die right this minute. However, if Amanda wants to live, she better heed my warning. If her hands break my hold on the girl's neck, she will go over the edge. You hear me, Amanda? You let me kill Motte, stay out of this. Learn to trust your king. When it is over you will have to carry on in Motte's place." The girl stopped her struggling and closed her eyes.

I purred out to her. "There you go. Led that poor submissive die. She has earned her freedom from service. You have no right to keep her from it. You tell me when you feel she is no more. Then I take you to a place where they remove the deceased Motte's collar. Amanda will rise from the grave wearing the color that will stand as the reminder of where the memories of Motte should stay, black as the darkness of a grave."

I felt Motte gasp and shudder in my hands as she finally understood what I was telling her. "I am Amanda, Master. Motte is dead. I am forever grateful for your mercy. I am ashamed that I speak without truthful knowledge of your honest nature."

I pulled the girl back from her precarious vantage into my gentle embrace. "Hush, now you need not be ashamed anymore, Amanda. You are the innocent kid. You cannot be held responsible for being inexperienced, ja? Now come with me, be still, look frightened. I take you to that place where they will cut that nightmare off your neck. You have the second chance. Live it well, forget the false start. That silver collared called Motte is a ghost now, she never existed. You believe that and find your destiny is cleared of obstacles. The next time a man holds you in his arms, it will be one of your own choice. Amanda, the black collar owns her own flesh. Sex is the gift only Amanda can grant to her lover, ja? Swear to me you kill any that dare to try to taking what is not theirs dares again." Amanda nodded but

293

wept loudly as I said the words every pleasure submissive desires to hear, your flesh belongs to you, and you have the freedom to choose to say nein.

When the girl had composed herself enough to feign fear I grabbed her roughly by the wrist. She gave no quarrel and did well appearing terrified as I dragged her without tender care down the stairs to the third floor. All around us the collars fell to a kneel, the Dominants and FemDoms bowed. The looks of pity on their faces as they stole glances at the hapless Amanda caused me great mirth. I broke out in maniacal, evil sounding laughter halfway to our destination.

Amanda played off my insane sounding noises by whimpering, looking about wildly as if seeking aid, and even wailing once in a while. The girl missed her calling on the stage, ja?

At last, we arrived on at the door of Almut and Blume. I knocked on it with furious vigor setting my expression to one of extreme irritation. Amanda stood quietly behind me. I could tell she was confused and holding her breath. She most likely was thinking I had betrayed her, and this was a drop off to see her further defiled by some cruel Dominant.

Blume answered rather quickly and dropped to a reverent kneel the second she saw it was her King. "Master, you honor us. How may we be of service?"

I glared at her with fury rising. "You will be of no service to me on your fucking knees woman. Get the fuck up. Is Almut and Jaison here or have they already headed below? Hurry and answer me, damn you. You are wasting my time"

Blume rose with quickness,. "Oh nein, Master. They are still here finishing their breakfast. Do you desire I call them for you?"

I blew out my breath in frustration. "Nein, Blume. I just was taking the stroll around the hallways and decided to stop by to take the census of how many Torture Masters are still at home at nine am. Ja, idiot, call them."

Blume startled as she yelled for the fellows to come at once. I turned to shoot a look of cruel humor at Amanda. She saw me catch her gazing in awe at the handsome Jaison that was rapidly approaching the door with his father Almut. She dropped her head blushing.

I nodded and winked at her as I whispered, "Be careful there, Amanda. Jaison is about to be your brother in more ways than the history of silver. You will work with him all your days. Beauty wains, but the heart can grow stronger with each year when tended properly, ja?"

She whispered back, "You are giving me to the famous Almut and his Frau, the torture Masters of legend?"

I nodded, purposely ignoring Jaison, Blume and Almut who were all standing there in silence waiting for me to state my business with them. "If you desire to be the Torture Mistress trained under the heavy hand of the infamous Almut then the answer is, ja. If not, we could return to the banister. You are my submissive a few more moments, my beauty. The submissive is the power in the D/s couple. I am helpless in your hands. Move me to do your bidding sweet Mistress and see it done to your satisfaction."

Amanda smiled so beautifully it truly took my breath aways. "Ja, I desire this more than anything Master. I can never repay your kindness. I understand why they say you are the King of the legends. Your magic is almost unworldly. You give me back all that was stolen from me in only one moment without asking for anything more than truth as your payment."

I chuckled as I grabbed her roughly by the upper arm and leaned into her ear to whisper, "Ah you are wrong there, Amanda. Nothing this wonderful is that cheap. You owe me equal to what I give you, your life. I expect payment in full too. I had to kill a girl to get you this chance. You will live it to the fullest and remember your vows to me. You keep a smile on those gorgeous lips, or I will come to repossess all the favor I show you. Beware, I am always watching you. You piss with me, and I make sure you join Motte in the grave, hear me?" She nodded with a shiver unsure if I was teasing or deadly honest. Either way she was in no mood to find out.

Finally, I turned my attention to the confused but patient black collar family. "Almut and Blume, this is Amanda. I noticed you have the son without a daughter. I have come to rectify this oversight of nature. You are blessed this day with another kid. I am tarnishing her silver to black. If you find this girl worthy, I turn her care and training over to you. She told me of her love for everything about the Torture Chamber earlier when I ask what was the best room there. I think one with such an interest would serve you well. Is it too much a burden to add her to your already busy business training of that other nothing, oh, what was his name. Oh, ja, that idiot apprentice of yours called Jaison?"

Almut and Blume did their best to hide their joy at receiving the thrill of a daughter for all their own. Jaison, that was eyeing Amanda with eagerness equal to that of her own gaze, also tried to appear the stoic. They all failed miserably. I could see the glee in their eyes as Almut nodded, and Blume put her hand on Jaison's shoulders in a loving hug to squeeze him with excitement.

The big Torture Master's voice boomed out. "It will be a pain in the ass, but for you Master, I will make provisions for this worthless creature. I am sure my Frau Blume can find space for her to join us in the apartment."

Blume nodded., "Ja Master, if it is your wish then we are honored to see it done." Jaison's face broke out in a beautiful smile and Amanda blushed as she dropped her eyes coyly to the floor.

My eyes danced with mischievousness as I saw that Jaison was as attracted to the beautiful Amanda as she was to him "Well, then I expect you can take this unworthy silver to the black collar Mistress, Almut. You have my permission to claim her as one of your kinsmen. I wash my hands of her. She has been the most miserable pleasure submissive. I hope she is more skilled to handle the whip as a Torture Mistress or perhaps the Frau of another of your level." I shot a humored glance at the handsome Jaison that quickly looked away blushing from his being caught looking at his new sister with carnal interest.

Blume smiled as she too realized I had brought a perfect match for her beloved and most talented son. "We thank you for the mercy, Master. Consider it done. When the time comes, I will take responsibility for matching the girl to the correct mate for her black collar level."

I nodded. "Good. Then I bid you ciao. I have far more important things to attend then this bullshit. Amanda, you go with Almut. Mind him well or be sorrier than you ever could have imagined in your worst nightmares."

She nodded then just as she went by she turned and embraced me leaning into my ear before I could stop her.

Amanda quickly whispered, "I will pray for you, Master. I had given up hope but now I know God does listen. He sent you to save me, now I will lobby him day and night till he saves you too." She kissed my ear lightly then released with speed.

I watched the beautiful girl disappear into the apartment as the three black collars welcomed her into her new home. Her soft lips caressed my memory for several more moments as I took off back the way I had come.

Her words of belief in the divine intervention bothered me greatly. I knew it was my ass, not God's, who intervened with her sorry fate as the tarnished silver sold to circuit. Or even worse as my Queen trapped with me in the beds of many violent men.

However, it was not the misguided faith in God that caused me discord. It was that she thought I needed help to be rescued. This made all that Byron said about me seem even more honest. Even that young, abused silver girl had been able to see the evil deep within me. I couldn't understand how I had managed to continue so damned long never realizing the truth. I headed back to Peter's apartment believing it was my perversion that attracted the worst of the worst to see my demonic urges filled.

By the time I reached my father's Haus, I had managed to convivence myself I got everything I had ever deserved. Worst still, I thought I was deficit in what was truthfully owed for being the creature of nightmares. I felt a trembling within just as Mad Maxx die Brutale unlatched from me. Mad Maxx led go of the wheel as well. I watched him stepping back to shake off the trance we had all been overcome by during that difficult extraction of Amanda from the claws of destruction.

I was shocked to notice he was bigger than he had been when taking up his place on the wheel next to me. He saw me shooting him a look of confusion. A big smile broke out on his face as he crossed his arms glaring back with apparent humor at my discovery.

I took a trembling breath. "Brother, forgive me for saying this but you seem stronger? I don't mean disrespect nor accuse you of being weak."

Mad Maxx nodded as he chuckled,. "I am stronger brother, by a lot. You don't offend by noticing but would have if you had gone much longer making no comment of it."

I shuddered. "You control the intelligence and seeing that increase is a good thing. However, you also are the one that holds the…" I couldn't say it.

Mad Maxx die Brutale grumbled out angrily, "Maximillian are you so over fucked by the men you have actually taking on the nature of the pussy they use you for? Say it and show you still have a pair, fool. Mad Maxx is stronger because the boy is loading up on guilt. Der Hund banned that emotion a long time ago and yet here is our brother gobbling it up. He has become fat and healthy from the abundance of fuel laying all around the boy."

Mad Maxx chuckled even harder. "What's the matter Mad Maxx die Brutale? You jealous I am well fed while you grow weak from starvation?"

I shook my head. "Brother you and I have always been close. True friends I would hazard to say. But this time I have to side with Die Brutale. You must stop taking in the guilt. If you don't then I fear what will become of the boy. It is not good to hold that emotion within our intellect. It will destroy us all in time."

Mad Maxx stopped laughing as he looked at the floor suddenly saddened "Ja, I know what you say is right Maximillian. Though I admit it is good to have the meal after so many years without a single bite, survival is not assured if I grow too fast in size. I suppose I will need to resort to the old ways of working off the extra calories."

I groaned. "Shit, trips to the chains are not something I wish to endure brother."

He frowned. "You won't have to Maximillian. I will take the wheel when Egon or Almut torture or thud the boy at our request. It is the only way to keep me fit and in shape. I apologize for it, but it is the way of things, you know that."

I nodded. "I am aware brother, but when you finish your workouts I am left to manage the results. I have enough pain in the ass from the intercourse situations without adding stripes, welts and cuts. Dammit, why does everything have to be so fucking complicated," I wailed out feeling overcome with a sudden urge to jump from the banister yet again.

I was called out of my internal worries by the voice of one I was happy to hear, "Maxx? Where are you going baby? Come here. Hurry up before Peter, Jonas or Lucus see you." I glanced up the steps to see Byron standing there big as Goliath.

I immediately cheered up thinking that maybe he had Felicity with him. "Byron, I was just on my way to come see you. I wanted to apologize for that shit Jonas pulled. He had no right to keep you from seeing me." I rushed up the steps almost tripping over the kneeling collars and my rushed words of explanation for his being banned from seeing me.

Byron nodded as he caste a nervous look behind him. "Never mind, all is right now Maxx. Look, we better get out of here. What you say we go to the gym for the work out? Surely, even Lucus would agree that would be a great activity to see you back to health, ja?"

I reached him standing there on the steps between the fourth and fifth floor. "Uhm, well I don't know Byron. I just got out of the inpatient treatment for illness. I am not sure Mad Lucus would think it safe for me to work out yet?" I tried to steal a look around his middle, without him noticing, to see if Felicity was hiding in his pockets.

Byron snorted. "I don't really expect you to work out, Maxx. I mean we go to the gym and that way if Lucus asks you are being truthful. I wish to speak to you. You know we must be careful in our associations. Jonas is already blocking me on visitors lists. I don't desire to have everyone watching and keeping us apart. Do you," he whispered to me to avoid the many people around us from eavesdropping.

I gasped and shot a frightened look behind him. "Can Lucus, Peter and Jonas actually ban you from seeing me everywhere, not just in the clinic or Palace? Nein, I am the King. I visit with who I want. Fuck them." I tried to sound tough but the idea of not getting to see him, and Felicity, scared the shit out of me.

Byron blew out his breath as he grabbed my upper arm. "You are the King with no tongue, Maxx. Here don't argue with me. I thought we already decided you don't know what is best. Do as I tell you, not as you think. We must hurry. The fellows will be looking for you any minute. You did rush off with a female they expected you to bond to after all. No doubt they will be seeking the proof it has been done." He began dragging me back down the stairs after him.

I gasped "What? How did you even know about the silver Byron, much less be aware they wanted me to marry the girl. Did they tell you about that nasty trick? Am I always the last bastard to know anything around here?"

He growled out in irritation as he tightened his grip on my arm. "I told you Maxx, I make your business my concern. Where is that little bitch now? You didn't do anything stupid with her did you?"

I groaned as he pulled me faster after him. "Nein, you know better than that Byron. I never laid a hand on the girl. I tarnished her to black and gave her papers to Almut. She is safe from the claws of those three idiots and every other cruel Dominant in the Haus. I took her straight to the third floor."

Byron stopped with suddenness and turned to me with a huge smile. "You tarnished her? Oh, my Gott. You had the chance to gain sex with a woman and you send her

303

away. Why would you do that? She was yours, Maxx. You didn't have to blood bond, but you could have fucked her at least. You didn't even touch her? Not once?"

I dropped my gaze to the floor feeling more than a little miserable at losing such a coveted chance to have the proper sex with a woman. "Not even once, Byron. I did it because I love you. I told you so and I mean it. The girl was nothing to me when I am already promised a lover of the finest quality." I lied while doing my finest acting job to that date.

You and me know the truth of why I tarnished Amanda, but I thought Byron would not understand. I decided to use this unfortunate incident to try to lobby the man to believe I did love him and only him). I really thought if I could get him to stop questioning my interest in him then maybe Felicity would come back to me. It was a calculated risk but with everything to gain by the lie, I finally stopped bothering with always standing up for what was right.

I was known until that day for my brutal honesty even at the threat of punishment. That was a thing of the past. The new Maxximillian would say whatever would get him where he wanted to go and if necessary even lie to himself.

It shouldn't be such a surprise that I would take up the habit of spinning the truth and engaging in falsehoods. All I ever got for being the honest heart was my teeth knocked out, beaten and raped most foully. Not that I had never told a single lie before that day, but I didn't make a career of it.

Most of the time, stupidly, I would defend the truth to near death.

As Byron grinned with thrill I kept my eyes to the floor. I saw Mad Maxx grow even larger. Lies, brutality to the innocent, perverted behaviors, foul words and loss of pride all were feeding my brother shard to a near gargantuan size. I made the mental note that before that day was up I needed to head below.

You see, we had discovered after I birthed Mad Maxx that without intervention he could easily become the humongous shard of guilt. If that happened even his controlled intelligence would be overshadowed by the useless emotion. You see guilt is like a piece of chocolate cake. It is desirable to the taste but without healthy benefit and full of useless calories.

Everyone, except the psychopath, loves to engage in it as the pleasure of self-blame even though they don't admit to it. There is a little martyr in each of us (hahaha). Few are strong enough to accept they don't control their world as much as they wish they did. No one is a God. Yet, from time to time, most will find a reason to believe they are at complete fault for things that were simply not within their power to cause or stop from happening.

Well, thanks to the horrors I was forced to endure both as the boy and young man, the one thing there was a plethora of was guilt. There were so many reasons to feel shame in our sorry life and so few excuses to absolve us of any wrongdoing.

I was often forced to say I wanted to be injured, raped, or worse to keep from heavier tortures from being inflicted upon my flesh. Hearing your own voice yell or beg for the terrors to be levied on you fucks with your head.

In time, you start to believe you really did want them to hurt you like they did, even though you only said it to end the pain. It is a vicious cycle as you have been most unfortunate to learn the hard way, ja Meine Liebe. I nodded that I had learned it.

We quickly realized it would take no time for the guilt shard's girth to become so heavy it would paralyze the boy. Early on we figured out that after a session in the chains, Mad Maxx had lost weight. To counteract the feelings of terrible shame, we made sure that the boy was beaten regularly. It worked perfectly to keep Mad Maxx's weight from getting out of control. It is the sad truth, but it takes beating it out of him to keep him small and manageable.

Master Maxx pulled me close in a hug as he said, "So, now you know why he is the masochist, and why I have the tawse custom made for you, Meine Liebe. If the man Christian Axel doesn't suffer for the terrible things all us shards are forced to do to survive, and as you saw to save others, he would be overwhelmed by Mad Maxx's guilt almost within a week. Yikes! It is you my Frau that I feel the most guilt over these days. The only cure is to allow you to give me equal punishment back for what I must do to you. If you and I work together, then one day maybe Mad Maxx will have a reasonable diet without all the junk food, ja?"

I nodded that I understood because even at age nine I did.

He patted my head. "Good, you be strong and so will I. The two of us are one from today to eternity. If you are ready, then on with the story we go, ja?" I nodded again and he cleared his throat loudly, which I knew meant something bad was coming, like he tends to do when he is getting nervous.

Byron, to my relief, appeared to buy my act. He let go of my upper arm with a grin on his mouth and adoration in his expression. I kept my eyes to the floor just in case the man could read the lies I was hiding from him through my soul portals.

He was barely breathing as he whispered out, "You seriously turned away the thing you have wanted all your life so you can be with me?"

I nodded. "Ja, which is what I am telling you Byron. Should we not be getting to the gym? I don't think Peter, Jonas and Lucus are far behind us at this point. It took me a moment to get that silver securely passed to Almut and safety painted black."

Byron nodded as he again shot a nervous look up the crowded staircase. "Ja, you are right. I can bask in the glow of your love once we are alone in the gym. Come on, baby. Hurry I do believe I saw Lucus behind that tall Dominant a few flights above us." He turned and began to move with speed.

I didn't look behind me as I tore off in pursuit of the Voter. I was well aware that all three men were no doubt scouring the fifth, fourth, and third floors looking for me. It wouldn't be long before they expanded the search to the second and first.

The two of us practically sprinted the second our feet hit the first floor. I followed like the faithful pup on his heels as we rushed down each winding hallway till at last we reached our destination, the work out gymnasium. He pushed open the doors and held them as I flew past to the sanctuary we both thought we would find inside. Like him I believed no one would think to check this of all places in the Haus, especially since I just got out of the fucking hospital. Well you know, the Haus's version of the hospital anyway.

To his irritation the gym was already inhabited by a small group of lower Dominants. The men looked up from their work out machines and weightlifting briefly as we came inside. Byron shot me a glance of caution and pointed at the locker room. I nodded as I took off with him to see if our bid for privacy would be met in the dressing areas.

Once again our chance at quiet discussion had an audience. Another couple of lower Dominants were changing their clothes and showering as we entered. Byron blew out his breath in increasing frustration. He glanced at me, and I shrugged. There was nothing we could do but whisper or wait till the men were finished. I saw immediately, Byron was not the patient man. He pointed at a door off to the right of the shower room. I narrowed my eyes in wonder of what lay behind that entry. There was no marking on it to describe to where it led.

He put his finger to his lips to signal my silence. I nodded and followed him as he rushed to his locker. I stood there holding up the wall watching the entry to the locker room with anxiety. I just knew that Peter, Jonas or Lucus would bust in any moment and catch me with Byron. The Voter dug around in his messy cubby hole, eventually pulling out a black gym bag. once he secured that item he motioned me to come after him.

We again moved with stealth and speed headed for that unknown door he had pointed out to me. I wondered if there was a sauna or secondary weight room behind it that I had never been invited to visit before this day.

Though I knew most of the Haus far better than I ever want to boast, I was aware there were many secret passages and hidden rooms that only the most privileged had access to use. I assumed this was one of those situations.

That thought was compounded when I saw Byron pull a lock picking set from his gym bag and begin working on the doorknob. It was obviously barred closed for a reason and Byron didn't have a key.

The fact that someone locked everyone out of there made me anxious. I didn't desire to be caught by the trio chasing me, but I also didn't want to give Gretta reason to send me below. Though I am the Master of the Haus it didn't allow me to just ignore the property rights of other Dominants or FemDoms at will. If this secret room was a private workout area that belonged to a prominent Elder or Voter and I got caught trespassing without permission, that could be a serious infraction.

I slipped up close to Byron and whispered out in fear, "Byron, what if we get caught in there. Maybe we can just wait out here for these men to finish their tasks. Soon enough we will have the privacy to speak without others listening in. I don't want any more trouble than I am already in."

He shot me a glance full of irritation. "Shut up, Maxx. I'm not going to tell you again to trust my judgement. If I say to come with me, then you do it without daring to question me. What would Felicity say of your showing misgivings of her wise counsel?"

I startled at that. "Felicity? Huh? I wouldn't question her judgement, Byron. She knows when there is danger. She has that kind of power to see into the future, but she isn't here. You are a mere man like me. I don't think you would lead me into trouble on purpose, but since you cannot see what is coming any more than I can, I think it fair to ask if it wouldn't be safer to speak in here and not in the room you are breaking into."

Byron stopped his work on the lock and glared at me. "Felicity is supposed to meet us in there, Maxx. Now if you want to stay behind go ahead. You will miss her meeting with us, and I don't think that will set well with her. She is already upset that she was blocked from visiting you in the clinic. She was so looking forward to seeing you that day when we were rudely turned away thanks to that damned Jonas. Tell me, do you desire to break her heart yet again? If so, then sure we stay in here to speak if that is really what you want to do."

I nearly fell over when he said Felicity was behind that door. I grabbed the lock picking tools from his hands and pushed him out of the way with vigor. He was doing it wrong, you know. I heard the click as the mechanism let go it's bolt.

Byron patted me on the back with a soft chuckle "Wow, which was fast work Maxx. You ever think you missed your calling in life? I believe you would have made one hell of a cat burglar." I opened the door and peeked inside with excitement rising within me at getting to see my lamb.

I turned back to him with a scoff. "I gained the skills of breaking out of locks by spending all my life in them, Byron. I couldn't be one without the other and to be honest I am disinterested in both. I wish to be the doctor not the criminal."

He chuckled as he pushed me through the door coming in behind me. "A schizophrenic doctor. Now that would be something to see. I wonder, do you think they will let you hold the scalpel to a patient when you are so insane you think a toy is alive and can see into the future?" He closed the door and locked it behind us.

I winced when he said that. "Byron, I would ask you to not say another word if you are insinuating what I think you are. I am going to be a doctor, and Felicity is not a toy."

He grinned with humor as he pointed in front of me. "Okay, sure Maxx. You will be the world famous Mad Doctor of Messalina. Why not? Shit, weirder things have happened, ja?" I looked and saw we were at the bottom of a stairwell I had never known existed. I wondered where it ends.

That caused me to startle. "What did you say Byron?" I lost interest in the stairs when I heard that word Messalina.

He pushed me gently trying to get me to go up the steps. "I said you can be the Mad Doctor of Messalina. I am agreeing with you Maxx. Why are you not going up the steps? Do you want to be caught down here? Move damn you. The further up the stairs we get the safer we are, and Felicity is waiting."

I nodded as I began to climb the steps with him following behind. "Byron, can I ask you a question?"

The Voter led out his breath sounding irritated. "Ja, sure Maxx. Ask me anything. I will answer it best as I can."

I stopped on the step and turned to him forcing him to stop too. "I want to know if you really are my friend or if like all the others you lie to me and play tricks. Tell me Byron. What is the address of the Haus? Where am I being held the hostage?" I glared at him with fire lighting in my eyes.

Byron pulled his black gym bag up onto his shoulder as he looked at the ground appearing nervous. "You are in East Germany, about seven kilometers north of a little village called Meissen in the Saxony region, Maxx. The exact address is for the post office only. The physical description I just gave to you. Is this what you want to know?"

I stood there with my mouth open in disbelief. "I am prisoner in occupied Germany as I suspected. Then if I tried to leave the Haus I would be shot by the police for being unable to prove my right to be here." I felt my heart stop in horror that everyone from Matz to Rolf had been telling the truth. More than the fucking Haus trapped me.

He nodded as he pushed on me lightly urging me to get back to climbing the stairs. "Ja, Maxx. You are without papers to prove your identity. You would be at least taken to an East German prison and at the worst shot on the way to that jail. The only way you are getting out of here is with my help. That is why I need my mother's money. Lawyers and bribing local politicians to look the other way cost a mighty sum, my love. To see you safely out of this Haus will not be cheap."

I began to walk up the steps wringing my hands in fear. "What if you cannot get enough money or someone won't take the bribe, Byron? I would then be trapped in this hell hole forever."

He sighed loudly. "Ja, unless the fucking country re-unifies, and it is most unlikely those rat bastard Russians are going to just give up their hostage. You led me worry about the details to see you freed. That is my burden."

I reached an open landing that had a set of stairs that continued further up. There was a window far up the wall that allowed the natural light to illuminate the area. I briefly enjoyed the luxury of that sunlight before headed for the next steps to trudge ever upward in the murky darkness. Byron grabbed the back of my jacket and told me to rest a moment. He needed a breather.

I nodded with a bit of discontent. I was in a hurry to see Felicity, but he was panting pretty heavily. Plus, he had proven he was truly my friend. I had asked everyone that question but only Byron was willing to betray the Haus, and his own oath, to answer me with honesty.

I admit that won me over to complete loyalty the second he told me what all others had denied that truth of my sorry situation. I thought whatever ill will that had been between us in the past should be forgotten. *I was ready to follow that man wherever he wanted to go. That Meine Liebe was a very stupid mistake. I would come to regret it in time, too much time as far as I can see it.*

I leaned into the wall and pulled my cigarettes from my pocket. I lit one up and took a long drag. Byron chuckled and asked me if I was enjoying the smoking. I of course nodded that I did. He unzipped his bag and took out a fresh pack then handed it to me. Good thing as I was down to my last three cigarettes. I thanked him for his generosity. The Voter leaned into the wall above his bag appearing completely worn out from our wild flight to avoid my pursuers.

As he gasped, coughed and panted, I smoked that cigarette and went to the mysterious steps. I stood there at the bottom craning my neck to trying to see if I could get a view of what it was above us that Byron saw as our destination.

I didn't even look back at him as I asked, "How far do these steps go, Byron? It seems thy maybe go all the way past the seventh floor. Is Felicity up the steps a little further or maybe waiting on the roof?" I started to turn around when suddenly Byron leapt on me.

In a single smooth movement, he slid his right arm through my own at the elbows. He used his left to grab me around the neck from behind. I was effectively helpless to do anything but try to kick before I even knew what the hell was going on. My lit cigarette fell to the floor and Byron stomped it out with a loud pop. He was no doubt beyond furious over something I had done but what I had no idea.

I whimpered in fear as Byron dragged me back across the little area towards the wall he had been leaning on. "Byron? What is going on? Have I angered you? I don't understand. Please, whatever you're mad about I beg your mercy. I swear I don't intend to incite discord between us." He held my neck but let go of my arms as he bent us both down toward his black bag.

He panted into my ear sounding more the a little pissed. "I saw you cuddling with that fucking silver you swore you never touched. At the banister right after you threatened to throw her off, like you should have. Where did you really take her Maxx? To a closet to fuck her I bet. You put her with one of your men so you can have access to her charms whenever you want, but don't have to worry tongues will wag of it ja? I know you. Sneaky fucking bastard. Low life pervert. Fucking twisted up freak." I gasped and clawed at his arm that was cutting off my air as I heard the clink of metal behind me.

He led go of my neck and quickly grabbed my right wrist twisting it behind me. I wailed in pain as he pulled it beyond its comfortable angle. I felt him snap a pair of handcuffs shut on me. with a loud growl he demanded I give up my other arm or lose the first one when he broke it off.

I did as he told me trembling in terror. "Please Byron, it is not what you are thinking. I didn't hug that girl she hugged me. I pulled her off me. I did take her to Almut but not for the future use as my whore. I swear it to you. I don't even find that girl attractive. I certainly didn't ask for her. This was all the doing of Jonas and Peter. You have to believe me." Byron forced me to my knees and chained my arms to an exposed pipe that ran up along the wall as far as the eye could see.

He was sweating bullets and panting with fires lit in his eyes. "Shut the fuck up Maxx. I already told you I saw you, Gott dammit. You may not have hugged her first, but she was kissing your ear. You sure as shit didn't stop her when she did that. I was not so far I didn't notice that cock of yours didn't agree with your words of finding no interest in her. I thought you were going to bend that twat over the railing and bone her right there for all the Haus to see. You are a rotten liar and a dirty slut. You are a twisted pervert. How old was that girl? Twelve or thirteen? You wanted to fuck a baby."

I felt the tears break from my eyes because he was right, I did want to fuck Amanda and would have too if she had kissed on me another minute. "Please, mercy Byron. She was not the baby. She is fourteen nearly and not fresh. I didn't fuck her. I cannot help that her unwanted kissing caused my nature to rise. I ignored that instinct for the loftier emotion I share with you. Do you even think of the crime you say I committed? Do you need to be reminded that I was only fourteen when you first took me for your intercourse. It is unfair to accuse me of baby rape when you don't see it that way between you and I. Truth be none of this matters anyway. I didn't fuck that girl and am not going to ever fuck that girl. Don't you understand? I was straight but I gave up the girl to be with you, the man. Forgive my moment of weakness I beg of you. It won't happen again, I swear it." I pulled on the makeshift bondage device that held me to the pipe looking around wildly for a place to flee. I was scared out of my mind. Byron was crazy mad, and he is fucking huge, you know.

Byron leaned down into my tear drenched face with an evil grin. "Damn are you one stupid motherfucker. You want me to show you mercy? Then I would suggest you think before you go calling me a baby rapist. I do believe it was you that offered me that contract when you were

317

fourteen. If taking what was given freely makes me the rapist then what does that make you, boy?" I gasped as he grabbed my face and squeezed it.

He repeated his question. "Well, Maxx? What does that make you?"

I whimpered out, "A slut."

Byron smiled widely as he nodded. "I think you said the correct answer, but I didn't hear you. You better say it loud enough for me to hear it or maybe I leave you here to rot in this abandoned stairwell. How long you think before you starve to death, or the rats eat you alive?"

I sobbed loudly. "That makes me the slut, Byron."

He chuckled as he led go of my face and began to undo my shirt buttons. "There you go. You are a slut. Nothing but the dirty pleasure hole for whoever wants to use you for their orgasms. Now, I wanted our first time out together as the lovers to be special, but you insisted on behaving like the wanton sexpot despite your promises to me. Since you are in such a hurry to fuck I have decided to help you out. When I am done with you this morning you will decide you don't like this life you lead of disgrace. I know how to treat the heartless nymphomaniac. You have no respect for yourself, so I won't have any for you either. Cry all you like. I know you are merely acting Maxx. You live for this rough raping. That bag of my has all the tools I could ever need to pick your lock boy. I am about to open your eyes with as much skill as you did that door below us." With that he ripped open my shirt and began to undo my beeches with the expression of brutal thrill on his face.

I could barely see through the tears as he tore down my trousers and rapidly flipped me to all fours. "Please don't do this Byron. It doesn't have to be like this. I am your honest lover for truth. I am neither into this rough sex nor torture. You misunderstand. I beg you. I will give you what you want without hurting me."

Byron laughed as I heard him spitting. "Shut up, Maxx. First you see to my needs, then I will make sure to return the service just the way you like it." He forced himself into me with harshness causing me to wail in incredible pain. He is a big man, you will find out, and no lube.

Byron was brutal in his intercourse. He offered no comfort nor concern for the pain he was causing me. I didn't even bother to hide the tears or wailing as he fucked me without a moment's rest. The steroids must have prevented him from his apex, or he was purposely holding back because it went on and on. I was nearly mad from the constant thrusting forcing my face to smack into the wall, and the horrible splitting sensations in areas one doesn't want to feel that.

Half-way to where I wanted him to hurry and go, he stopped and forced oral services. My throat was already sore from all the screaming. He didn't care. He was just as harsh in his taking this service. All through it he said the most revolting things about me, and if I didn't nod that

319

what he said of me was true he would grabbed the back of my hair to hold me still while he impaled my head with his cock. I learned real quick it was best just to agree with anything the man said.

When he was satisfied he had humiliated me enough with this nasty game he returned to his cruel mount. I endured at least another fifteen minutes of his horrific intercourse before he yelled out that he was cuming. I never been so fucking relieved to hear those words in my life. Okay maybe all my life I hear those words with relief but that kind of goes without saying, ja?

As he bucked and moaned out in ecstasy, I wept silently thanking lady luck that this nightmare was finally over or so I thought. I was thinking I wasn't going to be able to handle this deal I had made with Byron. I knew being his bottom in intercourse was a terrible fate. If I wanted to avoid painful intercourse with a large male then steering clear of the overly endowed Byron was number one on the checklist. No matter how many times that man had taken me it had never gotten any easier.

Yet that morning I found out he had always been gentle with me in the past. Holy hell, which was not a good thing to discover either. I trembled while drooling and blubbering as he uncoupled me. I rolled off my knees backing into the wall slowly while wincing from the burn and biting in my backside. Byron stood there towering above me breathing hard and readjusting his manhood back into his jeans with a big smile on his face.

I kept my eyes to the floor wishing he would unbound me so I could do the same. I hated being exposed like that. I watched him bend down and start to dig through his bag with a determined expression on his face. I shuddered and decided that now that he got what he wanted maybe he would be more reasonable and willing to take me to see Felicity. I really needed my lamb after that horror.

I sniffed back the tears and called out to him calmly. "Byron, can I see my lamb now? Please, I beg your mercy."

He chuckled as he pulled out a long stick object that had small nettles pointing out everywhere. "Nein, she doesn't want to see a little slut like you, Maxx. I already told you that. I promised my lamb that I would keep all the riff raff away. We wouldn't want her innocence to be shattered by being exposed to a pervert of the worst kind now do we." He got up and started coming my way still carrying that nightmare stick thing.

I wailed nonstop and began to pull wildly trying to break my wrists to get away when I realized he was going to use that thing on me. Byron found great thrill in my terrified kicking and screaming. None of them did a thing to even slow him down. He pinned me to the floor and raped me with that horrible tool till I was near unconscious from the torment and pain. Through the whole incident he demanded I yell I am the slut and that I loved being used as the cock pincushion.

Byron finally tired as I slowly lost my fight against his sexual assault. I was worn out, bleeding and numb from the waist down. I mercifully began to faint for a few minutes at a time from the stress. While the nettles on the stick were terribly painful and ripped me up, they were too small to cause permanent, and if the area was treated properly, deadly damage.

He managed to gain a fresh fight as he did this cruelty I had become quite used to by that time. He poured alcohol down my backside to sterilize the tiny bleeding wounds. I hallucinated that I was in hell and Byron was the Devil putting the red-hot poker up my ass. Well, sure felt like it let me tell you.

Byron finished his brutal punishment and rolled me to my back and straddled me. "There you go little slut. I believe I have proven to you that I can keep up with your perversions just as well as any of your big boys. Tell me Maxx, did I please you in a way that brought you pleasure? Now do you finally love me the way I love you?" He held my face forcing me to stare at him as I answered.

I could barely breath from the horrible pain as I looked into his eyes nodding. "I do love you, Byron. I thank you for the mercy you show me. Now can I please see Felicity? Please Byron, I need my lamb." I broke down weeping hard as I watched Byron shake his head nein.

Byron jumped off me with suddenness. I gasped as he reached for me with a wild look in his eyes. I thought he was going to attack me again, but instead he undid my restraints. His hands were shaking, and he kept looking down the steps nervously while he unlocked the cuffs. He snatched the metal bracelets off my wrists and grabbed his cruel tool from the floor where he threw it. I backed into the corner rubbing my wrists sobbing and trembling as the big man crammed all his torture items into his bag. He shot me a look of anger and said "Remember your vow Maxx. What happens between us is a secret. You tell and I will leave with Felicity."

With that he rushed up the stairs leaving me there on the floor never looking back. I gasped in agony as I tried to rise. Then I heard the sounds that had set Byron running in terror. A tongue popped and a familiar high pitched voice rose from the stairs below. "I swear to Gott I saw Maxx go into the locker room and that lock has been picked Matz. You can go back if you want but Jakob knows he came this way. Why the fuck do you think he is headed to the roof. Oh shit, Matz, you don't think, hurry brother, we have to stop Maxx before he jumps."

Chapter 54: The Ascent of the Dove, Part 1

I panicked when I heard Jakob's voice float up the steps. It took all I had, but I ignored the horrible pain caused by Byron's cruel punishment and stood up with speed. I reached down pulling up my breeches and grabbing my lighter at almost the same moment. I threw the fire making device down the steps before attempting to button and readjusting my clothing.

I heard the lighter make a loud snapping sound as it landed on the series of steps below. My pursuers Matz and Jakob heard it too. As I hoped they let out a yelp and called my name. They stopped their ascent thinking somehow I had gotten behind them on the steps. I heard their bootsteps retreating as they rushed back down the stairs headed for the area they heard that lighter land.

That bought me a few more moments to try to try to hide all evidence of Byron's sexual assault. I looked at the floor as I hurriedly buttoned up my blouse with a gasp. That brutal alcohol bath had left the floor all around vet. I winced realizing I had no time to figure out a story to explain why there was red tinged liquid on the light-colored concrete. I knew it wouldn't be long before Matz and Jakob resumed their climbing the steps.

I felt my heart near pounding out of the boy's chest when in mere moments after throwing the lighter, I heard Matz yell out to his partner. To my horror he had rapidly located the item that fooled them to head the wrong direction. I nearly fled in wild fright when I heard him call out to Jakob there was no doubt I was above them somewhere on the staircase. He urged the Queen to move faster before they lost my trail.

I cannot stress how upset I was that the two of them had already discovered my trick. I was trapped with nowhere to run looking very much like the rape victim. I looked up the steps wondering if Byron was up above me watching and listening to see if I would betray the vow to keeping our associations a secret. I shuttered as the chill of fear ran down my spine. I felt his eyes on me and knew that if either Jakob or Matz figured out this horror show, then my ass was going to get far worse than he already done to it.

I turned to the wall and without a second hesitation slammed the boys head into it with force. My knees buckled and I fell to my knees as the lights of consciousness flickered like a candle in a breezy room. I was sort of aware that Jakob had reached the top step when I felt his hands cradle my back as I swooned heavily headed for the floor.

In the distance I thought I heard the Queen say, "Hurry up, Matz. Maxx is having the fit brother. Help me hold him from slamming himself into the wall again. Gott Dammit, why does Lucus let him wander unattended when he is clearly unwell." I think I fainted for a moment.

The next recollection I have is that of Matz lightly slapping the boy's cheeks. I opened my eyes and tried to focus the softened borders of the pimps form. He looked worried and was saying something to me, but I couldn't understand him for several more minutes.

Jakob's high pitched voice tumbled into my ears discombobulated at first then, "Maxx honey, can you hear me? Nod if you are in there." I groaned as I nodded my aching head slightly.

He squealed with thrill "Oh, Matz. Look he understood me. Maxx. Maxx. Listen to your Auntie. Can you tell us what you are doing up here? Why did you pick the lock and hide in this abandoned stairwell? Did Jonas and Peter's threats frighten you?"

I mumbled out trying to focus on the Queen's face. "Jonas and Peter? I am not scared of them. You tell them to kiss my ass, nein, don't do that. The fuckers likely would take me up on it. Where the hell am I?" I turned my head realizing I was laying on the floor still on that nightmare landing where Byron attacked me.

Matz was kneeling next to me on my left, the Queen was hovering over me on the right. "You are in the abandoned stairwell behind the door of the locker room in the gymnasium. Maxx. Don't you recall how you got here?"

I shook my head and lied. "Nein, I didn't even know there was such a place Matz." That last part was not a lie.

He sighed. "You were having the psychotic fit, then? Maybe?"

I shrugged. "Well, I wouldn't know that now, would I? Psychotic means the person is out of their fucking mind. Why the hell are you two bothering me? I don't recall looking to visit with either of you. State your business and move the fuck on. I have more important shit to deal with than a couple of idiots that think they are my mother or something." I sat up with rapidness and nearly fell back to the faint from the sudden drop in blood pressure. Stupid of me but hey I was trying to appear unaffected the way a psychotic would, you know.

Jakob popped his tongue then responded sounded mildly irritable. "You are just as ugly behaving as you were when last we met. What the fuck has gotten into you Maxx? Where is that sweet boy I love hiding these days? Tell him to come back we miss him."

I chuckled with bitterness. "Sure thing, Jakob. I find that little bitch I will tell him you are seeking his company, right after I bend him over and fuck the hell out of him the way he likes it."

Matz choked on his spit as Jakob gasped and grabbed his chest dramatically. "Christ, you are crude as you are cold Maxx. What the hell. Matz, help me get him to his feet. We are hauling him to the clinic. They let him out too soon. He isn't any better at all. I think they gave him the wrong meds." He snatched at my upper arm motioning Matz to do the same.

I jerked out of his grip with a growl. "Keep your filthy paws off me, dog. I go nowhere with either of you. Why do you bother me? I don't recall asking for aid, nor do I need company. Get out of my way. I need to be getting back to my Master. I mean it, you move out of my way, or I will knock you down the stairs for daring to follow me, you nosy bastards." I pushed Jakob in the chest knocking him into the wall.

The Queen came unglued at my continued bullying of him. He recovered from my shove and flew at me with the speed of the cat. I fell to my ass as he leveled a harsh backhand to the boy's face. Without pause or hesitation the angry Jakob kicked me in the chest sending me to my back gasping and struggling for air.

Matz grabbed Jakob with a yelp of terror. He held the skinny brute at bay begging him to get himself under control. The Queen squirmed out of the Pimp's grip and slapped Matz with a loud smacking sound. I watched helplessly, clawing for air, as the wolf backed away from the railing Jakob. He realized too late that the Queen was more than a little fed up with my continued rudeness toward him.

I braced as Jakob dropped down on top of me and leaned down into my face. His expression was one of pure fury. I expected he was going to either strangle me with his bare hands or at the very least backhand me several more times. To my shock he grabbed the sides of my head by my ears and pinned me to the spot.

Jakob's eyes shown with inner fire as he growled to me in loud whisper, "You are an ungrateful sonofabitch. I shouldn't give two shits about what happens to your worthless ass after that bullshit you pulled on me and my beloved in the hallway a few days ago. That said, I find I am forever the idiot. I tend to love the bad boys that are good for nothing. Jonas and Peter are on the hunt for you Maxx. I saw you running this direction just behind Byron. I thought maybe my brother was trying to aid you in escaping the ass kicking that, no doubt given your behavior of late, you have coming. Yet, I find you here alone hiding in the abandoned stairwell trapped with no escaping if those two monsters were to locate you. Surely, you realize Matz, and I are tempting being pulled into punishment ourselves merely by trying to save you from your own."

I glared back at him defiantly. "Oh? You thought that brute Byron was helping me escape punishment? Whatever gave you such an impression, Jakob? That man wouldn't care if I was flayed and served for brunch in the Great Hall. You should have figure out a long time ago, no one is going to aid the Mad Maxx. While we are on the subject of my being left out to dry, why the hell do you claim to be here when by your own say I am not worth the efforts much less the anger your being found with me would incite? I am just dying to hear the excuse that you think will cause me to feel like I owe you something more than my deepest resentment, you dirty liar."

Jakob led go of my right ear and backhanded me to silence. "Gott damn you, I am no liar. You stop calling me that, I mean it, Maxx. I am the closest thing you have to family, and I do fucking care about you despite your foul attitude as of late. I know you are suffering the mental illness, but I am only human. I cannot be expected to tolerate your continued attacks on me and those around me as you have been doing. For your information I came looking for you with Matz to deliver a message. I am so worried about you that I took it upon myself to contact your favorite uncle, the Elder Leo, about your changed personality. He demands an audience with you immediately."

I gasped when he said that. "Leo, you say. He wants to see me. Funny, he didn't bother to grant me audience when I went seeking him several times in the last few months. I wonder why. Oh, wait you already told me. Sorry I wasn't really listening to your whining, Jakob. I am to understand Leo didn't give a fuck that I needed him, but his favorite bitch ca.me crying about me giving him what he had coming. Suddenly, my loving uncle is concerned enough to want to see me. If I had been aware all it would take to get a little attention from his Highness Leo was to smack around his princess a little, shit I would have knocked your useless dick in the dirt far sooner." Jakob backhanded me so harshly at that he busted my lower lip open. Damn, that Queen did have a wicked backhand. Who knew.

Jakob snarled out. "I should cut your heart out the way you have my own for daring to show cold indifference to sweet Leo. That man loves you like his own blood kinsmen, and you act like he is nothing but gum on your shoe? Not on my watch, you cocksucker. For your information Leo didn't answer your attempts to visit with him because he has been away receiving treatment for cancer. The man battled for his very life for the last three months. Thank Gott the last specialist he saw managed to put that beast illness into remission, but you listen closely Maxx, Leo's survival was in serious peril. He assumed he was the dead man."

I felt my stomach fall through the floor when Jakob said the word cancer. "What? Nein, you are fibbing to me, Jakob. If Leo had cancer he would have told me. You are a bigger lying bastard than I ever thought possible." I heard the words I said but deep inside I knew Jakob was telling that truth of it. For a change I really hoped someone was lying to me.

Jakob shook his head with bitterness in his expression. "I don't lie. Leo loves you so much he swore everyone that knew of his situation to keep it secret. He feared knowing of his struggles would push you further into the madness that overtook you than is already going to happen. He assumed since you could not help him, the least he could do is help you by granting you the mercy of ignorance."

I felt the tears trying to rise in my eyes as I swallowed hard. "You say he is better?"

The Queen sighed sounding very sad. "Well, they say he is in remission for now. However, the cancer will likely return at some point Maxx. If it does, and they cannot get it under control like they did this time, he will not survive for long."

I nodded feeling all the fight leaving the boy at hearing that my lover Leo was possibly terminal. "What, where is the cancer or was the cancer?" I stammered fighting hard to keep the tears from falling.

Jakob got off me and offered his hand to see me to my feet. "The brain, Maxx. He has an inoperable brain cancer. For now, they have appeared to shrink the tumor and kept it from growing, For how long no one knows. A year, five years, maybe a little more but not forever the say."

I took his hand and winced from the pain in my hindside unconsciously as I stood up. "Brain cancer? It started there or has it come from somewhere else, Jakob?" I looked at the floor already knowing the answer to that question.

Jakob shuddered. "Metastasized Maxx. He has had a surgery or two to remove the original site and many lymph nodes."

I nodded and wiped my eyes before the tears could escaping their holding cells. "Uhm, stage four is what he has. It is terminal."

The Queen shot a worried look at Matz. "Nein, you shut that up Maxx. Sure, it looks bad, but there are all kinds of new things happening in the medical world. Leo is not dead yet, and for now I told you they have the cancer on a leash. Leo is still a young man and tough as the bear. He can beat this, you wait and see Maxx. You better not count him out. That said, I don't believe I need to tell you that whatever beef you think you have with him, you let it go without voicing it to him. I don't care what you say or do to me, or anyone else for that matter. However, you hurt

Leo's heart like you have my own, I don't give a fuck if you are mad as the hatter I will not stop till I personally dig your grave at the foot of the first tree I come to in the yard." He glared at me with extreme irritation in his expression.

I softly chuckled at his attempts to appear tough. "You have nothing to worry about, Jakob. You are right to call me a bastard and even the sonofabitch. I am not however the asshole that cannot admit when he is in error. I apologize to you Jakob and will to your Jäger when next I see him. I didn't know that the friend you referred to that split your time attending me was Leo. I assumed it was, never mind what I thought. It was the wrong thing to think anything without knowing for sure. There is no excuse for my childish behaviors of jealousy and resentment. I had no right to call you a liar and oath breaker. I throw my self upon your mercy and beg your forgiveness for the evil I do to you and Jäger without the right." I fell to my knees and bowed low at Jakob's feet feeling very much like the little slut Byron had pointed out I had become.

Jakob gasped and put his hand gently on the back of my head rubbing my hair with affection. "Get up, Maxx. I should have broken my word of promise to Leo. Your hurt at thinking he and I abandoned you did far more damage than if we had just been honest with you. I can see that now, but there is no undoing the damage on either side. Tell you what. Let's forget all that happened and pretend those nasty months of illness never happened. I will be your Auntie again and you my favorite nephew as it should be," he whispered out sounding full of regret.

I nodded and looked up at him. "I thank you for the extreme wisdom and mercy you grant me, Jakob. I surely don't deserve any of it, but I am grateful. I must ask you a favor, despite my unworthiness of the right to ask any kind of favor, great or small, from one I have so ignorantly injured."

Jakob smiled as he caressed my cheek. "You ask me anything Maxx and see it done. I told you I forgive you and forget what we even quarreled about. That is what family does. They let the bullshit go, ja? My heart for you doesn't change because we misunderstand each other. The honest love between us is stronger than that, my Taube."

I closed my eyes with sheer gratitude filling my chest that Leo survived, and Jakob was my friend despite my cruelty to him. "I ask if Matz and you can sneak me to see Leo? I know the Guard, Elders and Voters are seeking me but maybe one of you know of a secret way to bypass them all? I swear to you Jakob, I never question your feelings for me again if you can do this mercy for me or even if you cannot. I fear I am too inexperienced in matters of the heart to be anything more than the bull in a China shop, unable to tell the quality from the trash with any validity."

Jakob giggled as he popped his tongue and put his hand on his hip. "You stop that silliness right now Maxx. You keep up the groveling I swear you will make me cry. I don't wish to ruin my make up. Come here and give me a hug sweetheart. You will always be my first love forever. You can be assured nothing is going to change that. Not even my deepest affections for Jäger or your being the horse's ass once in a while. Of course, Matz and I will take you to see Leo at once. You are already halfway there in fact." He winked at me as I rose and embraced him full of truthful eagerness for his re-bonding cuddle.

Matz, that had been uncharacteristically quiet through this whole show, cleared his throat upon seeing our hugging going on a bit long. "Well, ladies, if we intend to get the King to see his Uncle then it would be best to get to it. The night is growing a bit long in the tooth, you know."

Jakob led out a loud whooping noise and laughed. "Ah, I forget myself when a hot young man rubs on me. I apologize for that gratuitous snuggling Maxx. Matz is right, though he is a bastard for interrupting my fantasy love affair with this gorgeous hunk of man in my arms." Jakob led me go and shot a dramatic look of irritation at the pimp.

Matz giggled and dropped his gaze to the floor. "Jakob you are the funny one. Maxx here adores you and still you choose to be with Jäger. I think you two are the most adorable couple. Maybe if you can overlook his unstable nature you could make an attempt to be the truthful lovers?"

Jakob slapped at Matz playfully. "Oh, my Gott. Do you hear this Maxx? This nasty boy is insisting that I seduce you and run away to some warm beach for continuous adoration. He would have me rob the cradle without a thought for the fact I am already halfway to hagdom."

I chuckled at that insane thought. "Matz tends to drink early and often Jakob. He means well but the man's judgement leaves much to be desired."

Matz frowned and crossed his arms. "That was uncalled for Maxx. I am not the drunk and you fucking know that. We lived together many months, and did you ever see me drink other than that one time that we both lived to regret. Jakob is a fine catch, and it is obvious that he loves you with all his heart. What is so insane about wanting the best for my friends. I see that his love is requited. You love him as much as he does you. He is full of shit regarding that getting old business too. Look at him. Jakob is beautiful Maxx. Can you stand there and truly say you never thought of running off with him. I know I sure as hell would if I liked the more feminine type of lover. With all the reasons I give, name one that precludes him from making you truly the happy man Maxx."

Jakob swooned and nearly fainted over the many flattering compliments Matz voiced as I shook my head. "I will not dispute the truth that Jakob is a marvelous catch. There is no argument from me that he possesses enough beauty to make the finest artist's brush tremble with fear they cannot capture the honest radiance of it. I have actually been witness to that." Jakob covered his mouth and giggled as he recalled my having his portrait done. "However, I can give you two reasons that Jakob and me are never going to happen, Matz. First, I owe a kid to see my contract with Peter broken. I dare say for all his amazing qualities, my dearest Auntie cannot provide me with one. He may have the walk, talk and more style than

336

most girls I ever seen, but he doesn't have the right equipment to see my debt paid. Second, and this is most important my dear Matz, we are both strict bottoms, you fool. What are we going to do? Play scissors in the bedroom? There sure wouldn't be any proper coupling now would there be. Hmm."

Both Matz and Jakob choked on their spit when I said that. I guess they expected one of my points of argument against me and Jakob being the lovers would be my status as straight. Well, by this moment I no longer believed I could claim such a thing with any honesty. Byron was right. I had only truly been with Annette and Gretta (not sure if that was real or hallucinated). I had indeed been most interested in Karstin but when given the chance to fuck her without strings, I had turned it down.

I had thought of many reasons for walking away from the eager FemDom's attentions except the obvious one. You see, I had developed an unreasonable fear for women. I had nothing but bad experiences with them. To be fair I had bad ones with men too.

Annette had begged me to stop, then refused to ever sleep with me again thanks to the bad performance. Gisela and Sigerd had attacked me, rape by strapon is the accurate description, causing me much humiliation. Gretta had used me (maybe) while I was under the heavy influence of drugs and unable to even know the identity of my lover or even what was going on at all.

Mad Lucus told me that any female that I slept with was subject to being used as the pincushion by the horrid men that already used me for that purpose. I was in no hurry to watch my beloved Frau be passed around or see her fucked by another man other than myself. Worse if she bore children than it was brought to my attention the Haus could take them away and do far worse to my own babies than done to their parents.

I had every reason to deny my internal urges to mate with the opposite sex and almost no argument anymore to deny my fate as the catamite I had always been. I had resigned myself that a schwuler relationship was the only chance I had to find someone to provide affection and companionship. I didn't find the man sexy or attractive in any way. Afraid or not, women still caused me to go right into rutting mode. That no longer mattered to me. I decided I was a gay man and a slut bottom at that even if the evidence suggest that couldn't be farther from the truth. Damn Byron that motherfucker really confused me, I confess it.

Though in time, *with you my little Frau*, I would find I am straight. At that time all the confusion that Byron put into the boy's head had led me to ignore my honest sexual preference for the female. That in turn had set me on a path that would lead to nothing but terrible stress, guilt, shame, internal rage, and complete dissatisfaction. Damn I still cannot believe I was so stupid.

It was not that I wasn't already being sexually used against my truthful nature. My taking on the belief they were correct to do such horror added a new dimension of hell. Nothing worse than thinking something is wrong with you when you still don't find a thrill but believe you should.

After a bit of time, besides feeling sick each time I lied to myself, I also found terrible humiliation that I asked for the misusing of me for their sick pleasures in the first place without having to be threatened or beaten over it. This created a deep self-loathing and fear within that I couldn't be trusted to know what was best for me.

My once strong self-esteem didn't recover from such a terrible blow. It didn't take long before, thanks to the lack of faith in myself, I became easily controlled by my sexual abuser, Byron, as the dependent submissive. If I had broken that oath to Byron and told Jakob, Matz, hell anyone, maybe I could have been saved.

However, by that day in the abandoned stairwell I had fallen to my knees. I couldn't find the strength to rise on my own anymore. Nor could I bring myself to ask for help. Not even from my beloved Leo. I actually no longer believed I needed aid. I believed the answer to all my questions had been given to me by that predator Voter of all fucking people.

Byron had said with plenty of what appeared to be proof I had to be a gay, submissive, bottom that was deluded in his thinking himself the heterosexual, Dominant, top. There couldn't have been that serious a mistake made far beyond my breaking of the metal. He told me I was so obviously the slut twink and that is why everyone kept treating me in the fashion to which such a creature would be appreciated. It made perfect sense that no one could be so unlucky, nor so easily conquered, especially a brute of my huge size.

It no longer mattered to me that I couldn't really think of a time when such brutality or schwuler sex turned me on. Saying that I complied with things I didn't want to happen because of threats or worse were not good enough to justify my always bending over and just taking it. A real straight man would have chosen death rather than the pathetic life of a catamite, right?

Well, before you wonder why I didn't argue harder against this change of heart I was having, do recall in our lifestyle there are no excuses allowed. I gave up and accepted that I must have asked for all the evil that had been done to me all my life. I even told myself the lie, and believed it, that this horrible existence was the way I wanted it. Byron had won and I was his prisoner of war. I was a man without a country or hope for living independent of the victor's rules.

Matz's eyes were huge as Jakob slowly recovered from my oddly not standing my ground as the straight man. "Oh, well honey, if you wanted to give it a go with your Auntie, I am sure one of us could learn to rise to the occasion." He giggled into his hand trying to appear superficially calm, but I could see the confusion in his gaze.

I rolled my eyes at that. "Maybe so Jakob darling, but the arguments every morning over the makeup and lip gloss would be epic. We'd spend more time fighting over the latest Spring fashion gowns and cute, but comfortable pumps to get anything else done. Think sweetheart, how will we decide which of us is to play the top when we struggle constantly for who looks better in the lacy tops. Nein Jakob, we couldn't be the couple. Besides, I would be cheating on you the second you introduce me to the latest hunk that was looking for love in all the wrong places, right after your lusty Queen ass had already been ridden to broken. Not to mention I don't think there is a medicine cabinet in this whole Haus big enough to store all the fucking witch hazel the two of us will run through."

That made even the often grouchy Matz bust out in laughter. "Holy hell, I never considered all of that. Two bottoms trying to live together as the lovers would create one hell of a soap opera."

The Queen popped his tongue and grabbed his chest. "Oh, you are the brute to accuse Maxx and me of drama equal to daytime TV stories."

I put my hand into Jakob's face and popped my own tongue. "You better stop it girl. We don't have time for your attempts to get Matz to flatter you further. Damn bitch, why you always so needy? Doesn't that man Jäger cuddle your fancy ass to your satisfaction. If not, then perhaps you are wearing the wrong flavor of lip gloss. Why don't you try mint? That way you can set his loins on fire with your mouth instead of his ears with your constant cries for attention."

Jakob gasped and then snapped as he rotated his arm in that cliché Queen movement they are known for. "Oh no you didn't just throw the shade insults at me, miss thing. I will have you know my man Jäger is smiling and walking with a high step thanks to his girl keeping him well attended. You got a lot of room to say this to anyone, Maxx honey. You want to point out flaws in your Auntie? Well game on, bitch. Everyone knows that ass of yours literally smokes from all the fires it has put out. Tell me sister, is there any cock you don't treat like the honored guest in your Haus?" He threw his hand on his hip and smiled with wickedness.

I flounced and crossed my arms in a most Queenish fashion. "Jealousy makes you look fat, sweetheart. I am sure in the day many a stud enjoyed gazing at your boyish good looks and no doubt you entertained scores of them with your charms. However, that day has long passed away. Along with your fitting into the size four. Honey you really should either eat more salads or accept you are the size six. If you did, then maybe you could have your pick of the desert menu and eat it to your filled like I do."

Jakob led out a loud sound of indignation. "Ah, the kitten has grown up to become the wild cat. Get your claws out of your Auntie you little cunt. Damn, I trained you well, but it is bad form to practice your techniques on your teacher, bitch." He snapped and swished over to stand near Matz for pretend protection.

I scoffed as I snapped my finger and popped the tongue. "I think you must have cum blocking your ears from all the dick you have sucked when you were still the over hustled slut. I repeat to you bad form is something you should be concerned about, my honey. Those leggings you are wearing, what the fuck were you thinking? Didn't you get the dear Jakob letter that color left you when you were twenty-five? Look sweetie, I hate to be the one to break it to you but white is not your friend anymore. Well unless your man has impaired sight and needs an obvious target to hit your bullseye. In case you missed what I say to you this time, unlike seconds at supper, your ass is blinding me Jakob. Get some damned style or buy a fucking clue and along with it a new wardrobe, bitch." Matz had been standing there appearing confused by this battle of the Queens for a moment.

Jakob flounced and snorted loudly beginning his retort insult when Matz burst out laughing. "Stop it, both of you. The two of you are killing me. There is far too much bottom salt for this helpless top man to handle in such a small a space. Christ Maxx, Jakob has a point. You have gotten the acting job of the drama queen bottom to perfection. If I didn't know you better, I would swear you are the real thing."

I glared at my pimp as I popped my tongue. "You deny I am not the honest bottom. I find that rude. I heard no complaints from either you or that switch lover of yours when you enjoyed my favors with vigor. Sure, seems you both found me to be the perfect twink when the mood hits Roland to be seeking a role as the top man."

Jakob gasped and covered his mouth as if in extreme shock. "You and Roland have tasted this delicious meal for truth. Matz, you bastard." The Queen smacked Matz hard on his shoulder with a girlish limp wrist though.

Matz winced and backed away from the angered Jakob. "What? Shit, Jakob, Maxx was my boyfriend once, remember. Hell did you think I would live in the apartment with him and never sleep with that beautiful creature?"

Jakob twirled his hair feigning a pout. "I tried not to think about it, to be honest Matz. I hoped he would refuse your advances."

Matz glared, now it was his turn to appear insulted. "Oh? Why would you hope that Jakob? Because I am not good enough for the Mortar King, right?"

Jakob scoffed and rolled his eyes. "Nein, that is not what I thought, and you fucking know it, Matz. You know damned well having Maxx as my truthful lover is my darkest fantasy. I have always been an idiot for the sadistic bad boy type with the secret heart of gold and none are more brutal than that lovely man. Nor is there a purer heart in the world. I pretended that he is untouched by any man but Jakob, but I know damned well it is not the truth of it. I guess now that this little tidbit is out in the open, I am more pissed you never shared your knowledge of the experience with this girl." He swatted at Matz again, playfully this time.

I groaned and snapped my fingers. "Oh, shut up Jakob. Matz ignore her. She is being the greedy bitch yet again.

344

That lusty slut was there when her buddies, all of them, enjoyed my favors a few years ago in the storeroom closet. Hell, at every ballgame in there she played the fucking goalie with her buddy Rolf. Jakob tries to pick your brain about our sex life only to stroke her fires that thanks to the boring life of loving only one man, she finds have cooled to embers."

Jakob laughed into his palm. "Gott damn. Matz is right Maxx. You fool even me, the one that taught you that act. I swear you are a natural or something. When did you even have time to practice?"

I started down the steps. "I been practicing being the bottom since I was a twelve year old boy Jakob, you know that. The whole Haus knows that. The only thing I learned from you dear is that despite having more than my fair share lined up to make sure I do the job, advertisement as the bottom schwuler is still expected of me. It is pure silliness, but it is what it is. What you think is the natural skill came from thousands of hours of painful training. If you two ladies are through wasting time with your girlish chattering about nothing, I would really appreciate you sneaking me in to see my favorite Uncle." I snapped my fingers to demonstrate my sincerity at this request.

Jakob yelped out dramatically, like someone heavy had stomped on his toes you know. "Ah, Maxx where you going honey? The secret way to Leo's apartment is up, not down." He pointed to the staircase that Byron had used to flee.

I stopped with a shiver as the biting from his cruel nettles reminded me that going after Byron was not wise. "Uhm, I don't think I am willing to use this route you offer. Is there not another way to get to the sixth floor undiscovered?"

Matz groaned. "There is only the back staircase and this one that can get us up there without half the Haus seeing you. This one is completely devoid of people. If we try the back steps, there is a real chance of running into the Elders or Voters. This is the only sure way to go Maxx. We can take these steps to the sixth level then you pick the lock like you did to get in here."

I interrupted him. "When you need to pick the locks Matz, that means the troubles are far deeper than my slipping out of Jonas and Peter's grips. For that matter, how the fuck did you and Jakob get in here? I refastened the security on the door when I came into this place for the peace and quiet it offered a tired man. Which of you bitches has my fire? I would thank him to return it to me." I pulled my cigarettes out of the jacket and put out my hand waiting for the lighter to be returned to me.

Matz frowned as he stepped in my direction while handing the requested object to me. "I am not real good at breaking and entering but what kind of thug would I be if I couldn't do a bit of it? I got me and Jakob this far, but I expect the locks to enter the Elder's floor would be far more advanced than I am capable of picking. You on the other hand seem to have the knack for it. When did you start smoking? You realize those things will kill you, right?"

I took a hard drag as I lit the tobacco. "Well, for your information mother, nicotine takes about twenty years to destroy it's host. So, tell you what. If I live to be the old man, which is unlikely given the list of fellows looking to send me to the yard, I promise I will rethink my long term suicide planning. Until then I would thank you to mind your own fucking business. I dare say I do far more risky things than smoking the second I get out of the bed every morning. Oh, I apologize, the second I get into the bed every morning I meant to say."

Matz shook his head and flashed a disgusted look toward Jakob. "You know Maxx, smoking makes the breath bad, and I must tell you brings down the level of sexy by many points."

I blew my smoke at him with a chuckle. "Shit, if only someone told me that sooner. I would be smoking two or more cartons a day since I learned to walk. So? Are we done with this latest attempt to distract me from my goals? Are you two going to come with me to the back staircase or nein?"

Jakob put up his hand into Matz's face before the pimp could respond. "Nein we are not. All of us are going to climb up these steps to visit with Leo. I agree with Matz that this is the safest way to do this, besides we are already halfway there."

347

I scoffed. "I already said I am not going any further up this path, Jakob. I go by myself if you do not wish to aid me. However, I suggest you come along. A long walk down, then up the stairs would do you good, or at least that huge ass of yours would benefit from it."

Jakob roared. "That is it. This is war, you little bitch. Fine, come on Matz. We all go to the back stair. When Jonas and Peter catch that twat, I want the front seat view of his fall from that high horse he is riding."

I chuckled loudly as I took off with speed down the stairs. "Well, don't count on that my honey. You see I am the high horse Jonas and Peter be riding not the other way around. Not likely they will cinch my nose too roughly and if they did, even bedder. Ask Matz, brutal is just the way I love it." The sounds of my insane laugher echoing up the narrow corridor was all that was left as I rushed with anxiety down those stairs.

I assumed Byron was not far above us listening in on every single word of that exchange. I was moving like my ass was on fire because, dammit, it was. I worried that anything I were to say to any other man or woman maybe would be taken as the insult by my viciously jealous lover. I trembled with growing anxiety that Byron was going to rush back to his apartment to report to Felicity all the terrible things he had overheard being discussed among the three of us. Not to mention I was in no hurry to become familiar with his raping stick again.

I couldn't go up the steps for fear of leading those men right to Byron. It would look more than a little sinister if the two of us were found lurking on that abandoned stairwell at the same time. I knew neither Jakob nor the savvy Matz would believe finding Byron there was accidental or innocent. I feared that his threat to leave with my Felicity could come to truth if I didn't do all in my power to avoid his being discovered.

I was two flights down and beginning to worry when I didn't hear any bootsteps following me. Then just as I was about to flee back up to knock both the men out before they found out the real reason I didn't wish to go the easy route, I heard Jakob's signature tongue popping not far above me. I led out my breath and slowed my journey so they could catch up. The relief would have been complete if not for the terrible pain I was suffering. Moving quickly like I had been was not a good thing trust me.

I lit another smoke and considered the likelihood of Jonas or Peter catching the three of us heading up to visit Leo. It was simply too dangerous to try to see my lover with so many looking to grab me. If they found out about my long term affair with the wily Leo, the punishment for both of us would be far worse than the simple nettles raping I already endured.

When the two men reached me I took a deep breath then headed down in the lead as I said, "Matz do you not have work you need to be doing? I heard the rumor you are running a new game in the Haus beginning tomorrow. Surely, you have better things to do then tag-a-long with a

349

couple of Queens seeking a visit with another of their kind."

Matz chuckled when I referred to the Elder Leo as the third queen, "Ja, actually, I do have a lot of phone calls to make and debts to collect. I don't mind putting it off if you ladies need a man to escort you up the steps safely."

Jakob snorted and popped his tongue. "If we ladies needed a man, then I sure as hell wouldn't have come to find you Matz."

The pimp glared at Jakob with irritation. "Just what the hell is it you are trying to say to me, Jakob?"

I didn't even look back as I snapped my fingers and said, "She means you are only a few whiskers away from being the pussy. That has always been your problem Matz. You think having the equipment makes you a bullish man automatically, when really it merely makes you the male. The real creature uses his horns to do battle as often as he uses them to fuck. Your horns wouldn't even scare a matador nor even offer the crowd a thrill if you were to gore the fellow with them."

Jakob led out an approving yelp and swatted my shoulder blade while chuckling in approval. "Oh, my Gott. You are the bad boy Maxx. Matz honey don't you mind what he says. That little twat is unable to say anything nice to anyone these days."

I chuckled and popped my tongue. "Jakob is right. Don't mind my sourpussing. Hard to make the butterflies

350

come out of the orifice that has nothing, but the worm put in it, ja?"

"Is that so Maxx? You been forcing down a lot of worms lately, have you? Well, that is not good. You tell your buddy Byron all about it and I will make sure you never have to dine on such deplorable cuisine again." The voice of the Voter rang out from just behind the three of us with suddenness causing the blood to freeze in my veins.

Jakob led out a dramatic scream. "Christ, you scared me out of my panties, you brute. Where the fuck did you come from? How did you get in here?" The queen grabbed his chest breathing shallow and rapid as if near to fainting.

Matz's eyes were wide in terror. He didn't have any better a history when meeting up with Byron in the past than I could boast. "Honorable Byron, forgive Jakob for his rudeness. You surprised us, is all. Surely, he realizes you are looking for the same man as we have been and possess a key to checking all possible hiding places." He swatted at the panting queen and shot him a look of caution.

Byron came down the steps into our view. His eyes locked onto me, and a small cat grin tugged at the corners of his mouth. Jakob had managed to get ahold of himself. Matz moved to try to flatten himself against the wall of the steps as best he could. I dropped my gaze and took a drag of my nearly spent smoke. I wondered what game the brute was playing by risking that these two, who were not stupid, would realize he was not a newcomer but with me the whole time.

Byron nodded slowly as he stopped on the steps. "You got it right, Matz. I was sent by Peter, Lucus and Jonas to find Maxx. I see you boys beat me to it. I have to assume you were taking him to his Master, Guardian and trainer, ja? If you don't mind me tagging along I would be most grateful. I been searching for this wayward boy for some time now. You don't know how happy I am that he has been located before he managed to do something we all would regret. The worry that the mad King would harm himself made me near sick you know. I am not the young man I used to be. The anxiety has gotten to me a bit. I am in need of a little rest and good company. I can think of none better than my buddy Jakob and you, what was your name again?" He tore his eyes from me to feign a bit of interest in Matz.

Matz backed into the wall further appearing most anxious. "Uhm, I am Matz, honorable Voter."

Byron grinned in a wicked fashion. "Ah, ja, that is right. I really am getting worn out to forget the name of Mad Maxx's ex-boyfriend. You moved out of his apartment with that other wolf from the first floor, ja? How long ago was that?" The brute crossed his arms.

Matz's stammered out, "Oh something like two months, I think. I admit I haven't been keeping count."

Byron nodded still smiling with that toothy grin of mischief. "Well, I can understand your moving on with speed from Maxx. That boy is one cold hearted bastard. To be honest I was pretty surprised you held his fickle favor as

352

long as you did. He bores so damned easily and let's face it, he isn't exactly the marriage material for anyone with hope for a real future. I don't intend to sound so coarse over that failure you made with him. After all, everyone knew you never intended to use him, errr, fuck him, oh I mean stay with him for him very long. You can be honest here among us friends, Matz. Maxx was really nothing but a good time that lasted more than a single night, ja? Roland, now there is a fellow that is going somewhere. You are certainly the lucky one to have the true lover that wants you for more than a quick mount when his schedule is at a lull."

Matz flashed a frightened look at me then back to Byron. "Nein, I don't know what to, what exactly are you wanting me to say honored Voter. The relationship between Maxx and I was not that of the predator and slut as you seem to be insinuating. I did, do love Maxx and always will. It just happened that our paths were not headed the same direction is all. I won't lie and say I don't think of him every day and wish things could have been different." He looked at the floor with what appeared to be true regret.

Byron glared at me with barely restrained anger, more like jealousy. "You give Maxx the mercy of discretion, Matz? Well, I stand corrected. You and Maxx were the real lovers after all. I apologize for my cruel statements. I had been misled to believe there was only the smoke screen between you two. I didn't mean to step on your broken heart that I swear."

Matz gasped as he began to sweat and pant. Even he could sense something was wrong here. "Nein, again honored Voter, you misunderstand what I am trying to say. I love Maxx in the brotherly way not like the lover. I wasn't using Maxx nor was he me. We were a little more than caring roommates is all."

Jakob popped his tongue and shot Byron a baleful glance. "You know what Matz? Don't say another word of your private business with Maxx or Roland for that matter. I think my brother Byron is overstepping his bounds here. What did or didn't happen between you and the King is no one's right to know. Besides, it is ancient history. Byron, I don't have any issues with you traveling back to the door out of this stairwell, but once we are back to the gym I suggest you seek your rest and company elsewhere. Dominants of our status shouldn't be seen mingling with one of your level. It sets the tongues wagging around here."

Byron nodded while flashing me another nasty look. "Mad Maxx is the Master of us all Jakob. None of us should be witnessed surrounding him by your standards, not even me. If you want to see me gone than you will have to come up with another reason for it."

I growled out sounding more irritated than I intended to. "Enough out of all of you. I don't need the fucking babysitter. I can walk myself back to face whatever bullshit Peter, Jonas and Lucus think I have done this time. You all are released to attend your own business. I won't be impolite and not thank each man for attempting to do what he thought correct. Your mercy is appreciated even though not necessary." I began to head back down the steps with speed praying that Byron wouldn't follow this time.

Matz yelled out after me, "Maxx, you better not fuck around with the Elder and Voter. They are really pissed at you for some reason. If you wish to go unattended than I beg you make sure you give them no further course to see you punished."

I didn't turn around as I shouted back at the three of them. "I am going to see my Master, not the brutes that seem to think they own me. I don't see their collars around my neck. Mad Lucus will keep the Vampire and Peter from doing anything other than the dirty looks at me. I will make that man happy and then I will be back on the floor in two hours. Just wait and see if I don't tell the truth of it. Matz I see you another time. Jakob, come by the apartment in a bit. Mad Lucus wanted to visit with you and hear all about that trip you took to Tahiti. Byron, it has been nice to see you. Say hello to Rolf and Friedrick for me please. Ciao." I was moving so fast I almost tripped over my own feet in my efforts to escape further troubles with Byron.

I wanted more than anything to rush to see my beloved Leo, but I couldn't demonstrate that eagerness in front of Matz and the Voter. I knew Jakob would understand my message to come visit with Mad Lucus was bullshit. He was not a fan of the man, not since he tricked me into that gold collar anyway, and Mad Lucus had no tolerance for the Queen's company either. I knew that my only shot to sneak off to check on the ailing Elder was to run to seek shelter under the wings of my love struck Master Mad Lucus.

It was going to be a bit stressful trying to make it to the fourth floor. It would practically take the magic trick to do it without being spotted by the vicious Vampire and my nasty father, or any of their associates surely seeking me as well.

However, it was imperative that I manage it somehow. Neither Peter nor Jonas had the right to punish me for sending my own submissive, Motte, away. Once they turned that girl over to me, whatever I choose to do with her was no longer their right to insist. That was the Haus law. Since I am the Master of it, I was ready to see any argument the two wanted to lodge with me over Motte go right to the ears of Gretta. I was sick and tired of those brutes bullying me at every turn, you know.

I was ready to fight back in any way I could. If I reached my Master's care before they could catch me then Mad Lucus would be capable of voicing my wishes legally. With Mad Lucus the regent in training, he was now my best hope for fair treatment among those that still held power over my life and future. Watching his reaction to the dirty trick Peter and Jonas pulled on me with that poor submissive Motte made me believe that Mad Lucus truthfully loved me.

Now that I had accepted my status as the slut submissive bottom schwuler, I was ready to use that knowledge of Mad Lucus to full advantage. I told myself as I tore down the hallway out of the gym that Leo was worth whatever I had to do or promise to Mad Lucus. I needed to gain a little private time out of his sight so I could slip up to the sixth floor to see my true lover.

All around me the collars, Dominants and FemDoms made a fuss. With all of them falling to the kneel or stopping their journeys to bow I knew I was sure to alert my pursuers to my whereabouts. This dramatic display of reverence was not only getting on my last nerve but had always worked against me when I was trying to go about my dark dealings undetected.

I growled in fury as I grabbed a skinny black collar male kneeling next to me on the right. "You stop kneeling to me. You are blocking my path, motherfucker. Nein, what a minute. You and all these idiots within my sight, gather around me. Your King needs protection. I command my subjects to form the human shield this minute. We will move in unison and in silence. I wish to be escorted to the fourth floor. Hurry the fuck up everyone. I haven't got all day, dammit." I tossed him backward just as every silver and black within hear distance of my command stood up.

I felt suddenly claustrophobic as within only seconds all the submissives, Haus and pleasure, took up places around me making not a single sound. I was surrounded by four walls made of living flesh. At least twenty of my collars stood there waiting patiently for me to hand motion that I was ready to start this unusual procession.

I wondered if this was actually going to work to see me safely to Mad Lucus's apartment. I thought it more likely the sight of many collars traveling together in a pack would

357

defeat my purpose. Whatever the outcome, my loyal subjects were ready to see their King's orders followed without quarrel no matter what dark things they truly thought of me.

I took a deep breath, braced for failure and gave the signal to begin the march. I admit I was astounded at how smoothly the many men, women, boys and girls moved through the crowded hallways and staircase. It was as if each had practiced for this all their lives. Not a single one got out of step the entire way. It was a much appreciated mercy that they managed to keep me hidden deep in the center of the moving creature with more than twenty heads. We made it to my destination without a single incident nor anyone spotting me to alert the angered Dominants hot on my tail.

When the group arrived at Mad Lucus's door, though I never told them that is exactly where I wanted to go, they all just seemed to know, they all dropped into the reverent kneel once more. I stepped through them careful to avoid stepping on any fingers or toes. I reached Mad Lucus's entry and turned to gaze upon my champions with gratitude.

I raised a hand to release them from their knees as I said, "You made your King the happy man. I reward each of you with a special favor. Go this moment to the Great Hall. Tell the Haus submissive Samuel that the Mortar King Mad Maxx orders that his loving collars be seated at the finest table. Order any and all that you like. Dance, feast, laugh, speak of better days. Hold your heads up in pride. For the next two hours each of you are free Dominants or FemDoms and will be treated as one. If any of your Masters or Mistresses have issue with my directive, or if Samuel doesn't provide for all your pleasures, I will be notified of the insult immediately. The punishment for denial of my commands will be severe. Do all you understand?"

I saw the incredulous smiles and thrilled glances ripple through the crowd faster than a juicy rumor through the hallways. My ears were assaulted with the loud and excited words of thanks and eager shouts of "long live King Mad Maxx" from each of them. I must say to be granted such a coveted pleasure for doing nothing more than walking up four flights of steps definitely was unanimously well received.

I once again hand signaled the release than began knocking on the door with vigor. Anxiety rushed down my spine as I watched my temporary protectors moving with eagerness to collect on their reward at the Great Hall. I prayed Mad Lucus was back home, or all that drama was for naught. I was trapped now with nowhere left to run, nor enough collars hanging around to guard me from attacks.

You cannot imagine the relief I felt when I heard the locking bolts of the door being undone from within. Mad Lucus was there. I had been saved for the moment from the vicious wrath of my father and the shady Vampire. That is if I had read my Master correctly and he wasn't angered for the same reasons as them.

Mad Lucus had appeared upset that I said I was killing Motte, but I was hoping he would forgive me for doing what had to be done. Even he knew Motte was a goner whether I blood bonded her or nein. Sending her to the grave was an honest mercy, and besides I gave the Haus a wonderous black collar named Amanda to compensate for the loss, ja?

The door opened and my Master stood there wide eyed staring at me like I were the specter of a lost lover. "Christian? You have returned to me? Oh, my Gott. where have you been? He looked around me wildly trying to determine if I was alone. Oh nein, where is that little girl the brutes gave to you? Please, I beg of you, tell me you didn't do what I think you did to her?"

I shrugged. "Depends on what you think I did, my Lord."

Mad Lucus glared at me as he snatched me by the wrist pulling me inside with force. "Don't play with me Christian. You act stupid but you are anything but that. Where is Motte? What have you done to that kid? You fucking tell me or so help me Gott I will call Gretta and see you put below myself." He tossed me so roughly I nearly fell face first onto the floor as he slammed the door shut enclosing me in the apartment with him.

I recovered my footing and reached into my jacket for another cigarette as I responded, "I told you I was going to kill that silver. I did as I promised. Motte is no more. I tossed that poor soiled creature off the banister. Her death was fast and merciful, I swear it. I then resurrected the girl called Amanda and give her black collar to Almut for his care. After that, I went down to the gym to do the light workout. All that murdering of little girls made me a bit nervous. I needed to blow off the steam of it before returning to attend to your services, my Lord." I lit the smoke taking a long, careless drag as if I were merely discussing the weather with my Master and not the brutal murder of a kind.

Mad Lucus gasped. "You threw that sweet little Motte off the banister? Christian, she was only a baby. How could you? Wait, if you had done such an evil thing the Haus would be buzzing about it for days. I heard of no one being flung from the fifth floor today. Are you sure you didn't hallucinate killing that child. You resurrected a black collar called Amanda? Fuck, you speak in riddles, my King. I must insist to ask you once more, where is Motte?"

I snorted with irritation. "I already told you, my Lord. I tossed her off the fifth floor to her doom. I don't know why you even care what I did with that trash lover. She was a nothing. I had no use for her and neither did anyone else. No loss. I pay back the debt owed the Haus by giving them Amanda in her place. I am many things my Lord, but I am no thief. I make the equal trade, one worthless silver for a prized black collar to service the residents. Why are you still harping on this useless subject? I do believe you promised me the blow job. I am ready to be adored." I pointed at my zipper demanding Mad Lucus keep his promise to see my needs attended for a change. *Quit shaking your head Meine Liebe. I had decided I was the*

361

schwuler man, so why the hell shouldn't I get a little something, ja?

Anyway, Mad Lucus stood dare with his mouth open. Too high in the air for it to be any use to me, ha. "Are you saying you painted Motte black? Is that what you did Christian? Oh, please let this be the truth of it and not some delusional statement from the mind of a madman."

I was getting perturbed that Mad Lucus wasn't doing what he said he would. "Uhm, you dare to insult me, my Lord? I am not a madman. I am the horny man if anything. I am more than happy to grant you the oral service return for the one you give to me, but that means you got to pay up first motherfucker. You are going to do what you promised, or should I go out looking for someone else that will?" I tossed the half-spent cigarette at his chest.

Mad Lucus appeared confused by my sexual aggression toward him. "Christian, I cannot just turn on the lust because you say you are interested. Christ, I have been worried out of my mind for the last several hours that you were going to fuck up and blood bond that innocent kid. Then you take off threatening to kill her and disappear into thin air. Now you return demanding to have sex with me. What the hell is going on inside your head? I thought you hated me and found sleeping with me repulsive."

I chuckled as I approached him with slowness, my wicked gaze locked onto his own. "You can thank Peter and Jonas for my change of heart, lover. There handing me that disgusting female for marriage and sex proved to me that I have been the mistaken schwuler all this time. Try touching me and see if I you are incorrect that I find you gross. You that said in time I would get over my reservations of being your kept pet? Well, revel in your win, my Lord. I am all yours. Come and get it." Mad Lucus didn't move a muscle as I grabbed him with suddenness around the waist and began kissing his mouth with wantonness, feigned to be honest. I really didn't suddenly find the man attractive at all. I merely wanted to satiate his calls to service quickly so I could be ready to meet Jakob in two hours as we agreed.

Mad Lucus gasped and shuddered in my embrace as he panted out into my ear, "Why are you toying with me like this Christian? What have I done to you recently to deserve such cruelty? I beg you to relent this torture you force on me."

I increased my kissing and added aggressive foundling to my acting job. Despite his words, his flesh didn't find my caresses cruel, that was for sure. "I don't understand why, when you finally have all that you thought you wanted you suddenly turn the doubting Thomas, my Lord. You say you wish to demonstrate equality in our love affair. Well, than come with me to the bedroom and prove it. As you see I give you no quarrel. I cannot escaping your gold nor your carnal interests. Only you can free me, and you say you are not going to anytime soon. You said if I give into your demands and learn to accept what is my fate, you will be fair in your service returns. Be fair then. Without threat I offer to you the orgasmic release. I demand you grant me the same." I ran my tongue into his ear setting off a full flesh quiver from the Dominant.

Mad Lucus could take no more with his quarry appearing to be more than the willing partner. I gasped as the man pushed forward like the bull. I offered no resistance as he held me tightly in his embrace rushing forward while forcing me backwards toward his bedroom and that horrid cock bed. I continued the heavy, tongue filled kissing on his mouth, ears and neck. It was without a doubt driving the man insane with passion.

He got me through the bedroom door and practically tackled me to the mattress. I held him tightly as he wildly pawed and moaned, kissing my flesh anywhere he could find it. I was heavily dressed in the blouse and jacket still. I ran my fingers through his hair and began to construct a pornographic fantasy of a most beautiful and buxom woman within the wheelroom. I felt my manhood began to respond to the images of the gorgeous girl of my dreams. Mad Lucus noticed the sudden stiffening in my breeches and led out a thrilled yip believing he was the one turning me on.

He began to undo my breeches with eagerness as he dropped to his knees. I focused all my thoughts on the target of my most unbridled lustful desires. It maybe should have registered that while Mad Lucus was giving me head, it was not a hairy brute that I was thinking of, but the soft, well-endowed female. How the fuck I still could think myself the truthful schwuler with the evidence pointing, okay that is the wrong word to use in this situation but there it is, to straight on the gaydar dials is beyond me. I am such an idiot.

Needless to say, in my mind the ugly Mad Lucus became the big boobed, lusty bride of fantasy. That disgusting cock bed was the goose feather marital bed that me and the Frau would share for all our lives. I imagined I was far from the Haus, cuddled deep in the bedroom of a little cottage nestled in the green fields. For those moments, I was the happiest man in the world. My wife couldn't get enough of me, and I never wanted to let her go. I fell to my back moaning in pure ecstasy as she brought me to the apex of the place between life and death. All the pent up frustrations, fears, pain and loss were forgotten for that brief few seconds there in her arms.

I nearly puked when reality hit me like a ton of bricks when I heard the sounds of someone spitting several times and gagging as they did it. I opened my eyes in the startle at that most obnoxious sound. I felt overcome with the sudden sickness. I glanced around the room recalling that this was not my beautiful Frau sucking my cock but the brute Mad Lucus. He was on his knees hocking out the contents from his mouth into the small trash can by his lewd bed.

He apparently didn't believe that equal service included swallowing when it came to dealing with the results of bringing a man to orgasm. I stared at him in disbelief, feeling a bit of anger as I watched him taking a mercy I was always denied. I wanted to kick him in the fucking head and force him to endure my taste as he had made me do on many occasions.

He looked up and noticed me glaring at him. "Oh, sorry about that, my dove. I never could stand the texture of the jizm, you know. Never mind that though. This is so wonderful. I cannot believe this magnificent thing is finally happening to us. You do love me, Christian. I thought you were trying to fool me, but the cock don't lie." He didn't get off his knees as he came forward and wrapped his long arms around my hips pulling me closer to him at the edge of the mattress.

I scoffed. "Sure, I love you my Lord, but you spit. You don't love me back apparently."

Mad Lucus frowned as he rested his chin on my bare knee. "You cannot base such a lofty emotion on the frivolity of one choosing to spit or swallow during oral sex, Christian. The fact that I gave you the blow job at all should be the true clue as to the honesty of the way I feel about you."

I shifted my leg so his chin was displaced with suddenness. "Bullshit, my Lord. You and every other motherfucker I ever known make me swallow that nasty shit you put in my mouth. None of you cared if I don't like the taste, texture, quantity, that I find it beyond disgusting, or even when it is my own seed. I always get told the same thing when I ask for the mercy of spitting it out, true love is to swallow. Now you say it doesn't matter either way. Who is lying? You or all the others?"

Mad Lucus stood up and glared at me appearing mildly irritated though still glowing with what he thought was a win for his bid to gain my love. "Some men find pleasure in knowing their lover swallows their orgasm, Christian. It is a fetish of mine to see you engage in the consuming of your own from time to time. You have been doing this for years, so it should no longer be something that bothers you." He sat down next to me as he reached out to message my tense shoulders.

I reached down and pulled up my breeches with a huff. "Thank you for correcting my deep held belief that only I can decide what is the burden to me or not, my Lord. I suppose you are interested in your service return. If so then I will attend that immediately, but can I beg the mercy of one small request before I engage you?"

Mad Lucus removed his kneading hands with a loud sigh. "Nein. You may not have permission to spit out my cum if that is what you are about to ask me."

I glared at him full of hatred. "That was not what I was going to implore, my Lord, but thank you for making damned sure I remember who the bitch is around here and who is not. I wanted to know if I could have an hour or two in a bit to head for the pool. The doctor says swimming to regain my health and vigor would be good to see me heal faster."

Mad Lucus chuckled as he caressed my check with a smile. "Well, that depends on if this is really what you want to do. I warn you love, I have not been able to see you for several days. I wanted to spend the quiet night snuggling as the couple Christian. Can you not begin your attempt to recover tomorrow?"

I held back the urge to vomit at the idea of having to endure his cuddling with me for hours, barf. "While that sounds just heavenly, my Lord, I am eager to feel strong once more. I swear I only swim for an hour or so if you could find it in your heart to spare me for that long. If you allow me this mercy I swear to return without quarrel or argument to see to your pleasures sated to completion."

Mad Lucus smiled with a light blush as he pulled me closer to him and kissed my ear. "My pleasures to completion you say. Well now that is a tempting offer indeed, Christian. Tell you what. You go to take the dip right now, and when you come back then I get my service return anyway I want it. Deal?"

I tried not to shudder, but I think I may have anyway, as I nodded. "Okay, that sounds fair, my Lord. Uhm, can you give me a bit of privacy for a moment? I need to use the restroom." I didn't really have to go but I needed to check on the damage, and fix it if possible, Byron had done before daring to show up as nothing but a teaser to a surely wanton Leo.

Mad Lucus shook his head as he pulled me into another series of deep kissing then said, "Nein, that bathroom and whatever you do in there is a team effort from this point forward, Christian. I appreciate that you are willing to think of my needs well in advance of offering the service, but I will be in charge of the enema treatments."

I pulled away from him with a startle. "What? Are you fucking kidding me, my Lord. I don't need nor want you to aid me in that personal hygiene ritual, dammit. I haven't required help doing that simple process since I was the boy."

Mad Lucus frowned then grabbed my upper arms with mild harshness. "You shut that arguing with me right this minute my King. I told you that I have certain pleasures that are not maybe what you are accustomed to. You will do as you are told and see to all my service needs without the drama or find yourself punished for it. I am an easy going Master, and as you realize now most generous in the service return. However, I am still the Dominant in this Haus, and you may be the King, but to Mad Lucus you are the submissive bottom. You may not like it, but I enjoy attending your grooming and hygiene needs by my own hand. You will endure my tender care in these areas and that is final. You need a shave, the enema, and after that likely the shower. You can go to the bathroom and wait for me to see these things done this moment or when you return. That is the only choice I give you. Make up your mind Christian, which will it be?"

I lowered my brows and snarled back at him. "I choose later. You likely demand I take another shower and enema the second I get back from the pool to clear off any false dirt knowing you. I must say Mad Lucus, I try hard to meet you halfway with this arrangement you have me trapped in. I thought we could work out our differences, but I no longer think that possible thanks to your nasty fetishes. Bad enough the disgusting things you stick into my orifices without having to also suffer having you there to witness the things that come out of the same places. Christ, you are a sicko. Coming from me that really means something." I got off the bed and tore out of the room buttoning my trousers while cursing Mad Lucus to death.

He yelled out from behind me. "You will get over it Christian. In time you won't even recall why it bothered you. By the way, be back here within two hours. If I have to come looking for you I promise it won't be pleasant for you. I mean it. Oh, and where the hell is your cane? Did you misplace it already?"

I lifted my middle finger to point at Mad Lucus as I stood at the door checking the time and lighting a smoke. "The cheap thing broke before I even ended up in the clinic. You'd think with all your riches you could buy more than the pauper's walking stick, you bastard."

I heard him chuckle loudly from the bedroom as he responded. "If you didn't go smacking people in the head with the tools necessary to see you keep those pretty hips in good health I would buy you an expensive cane. Until you can learn to take better care of your things the cheaper versions is all you get, Christian. Grab the spare from the closet by the door before you head out. Break that one and I break your ass."

I grumbled but searched the coat closet till I came across an exact replica of the cane I broke over Peter's back. "I am leaving, my Lord. Do me the favor of calling off the dogs Jonas and Peter will you? I don't desire to end up being used as there London bridge tonight, nor do I think you want that either. I be back sooner than I wish that I assure you." With that I took off out the door slamming it hard behind me full of fury.

I knew I had told Jakob to wait for me for two hours. It had only been less than one since I left the trio in the staircase but in my life, you take any release you can get when you can get it. I rushed to Jakob's apartment and knocked with urgency. He answered right away for a fucking change.

His eyes went wide when he saw me as he grabbed his chest dramatically. "Maxx, what the fuck are you doing here? I thought you were going back home to Lucus. If Peter and Jonas see you, honey they are not playing. Those brutes are pissed. I fear they plan to hurt you."

I nodded with a dry expression of boredom on my face. "Ja, they likely are hoping to do that, but if they do it is their funeral. I did go home as I said I would. My Master granted me permission to be out in the Haus unescorted by him. I only have a short time, Auntie. If you wish to come with me to see Leo, you better grab your purse and worry about your lipstick later."

Jakob giggled into his hand as he swatted at me. "Oh, stop the teasing, Maxx. Of course I come with you to see Leo, honey. Led me grab my shoes real quick. Do you want to come in and wait?" He shot a nervous look down the hallway.

I rolled my eyes. "Nein, I wait here. Hurry up sister. I am serious when I tell you I have only a bit of the reprieve. I come inside and likely you will try to seduce me. I am not the doe eyed twink you think me to be, sweetheart." I winked at him.

Jakob lowered his face coyly and smiled with mischievous. "When you say shit like that to me Maxx, I feel like it is time to rise to the top, if you know what I mean."

I laughed. "You are a cock tease Jakob. Get your shoes before you end up riding up the stairs on the end of my boots after I kick your sweet ass."

He slapped me playfully and flounced off inside his apartment to grab his pump high heel shoes. I stood there watching for danger. I wasn't sure Lucus would call off Peter and Jonas, you know. It was at that moment I saw a glimpse of someone rushing to hide behind one of the stone pillars that held up the roof. I craned my neck trying to see the identity of the stalker though I already knew deep inside who it was. Fucking Byron had changed places with Lucus in the constant trailing of the Priceless Mad Maxx.

Jakob came out with a loud yelp and a pop of his tongue. "Alright, I am ready honey, unless you have reconsidered allowing me to give you a tour of my boudoir." He giggled and twirled his hair in the open flirtation.

I shook my head as I put my arm through his own to lead him next to me as my partner. "Sweetheart, we already established I am the submissive bottom like you. I cannot tour your boudoir any more than you can my own. That is unless you are willing to become the Lesbian with me? Just think, we could move in together and buy her and her towels. Maybe then we could toss the witch hazel and stick to mouthwash."

Jakob's high pitched laugher could be heard several floors when I said that. "Gott is such a bastard, Maxx. You are funny, handsome, loving, loyal and young. You are the perfect man of my dreams. Only the cosmic joke is you are no more a man than your Auntie. If I thought it would bring you to my bed for all time I swear I would call the doctor tomorrow and have him change my religion."

That made me laugh as hard as him. "Seriously? Now that is the most flattering thing anyone has ever said to me Jakob and perhaps the dumbest too. You would be willing to get a vagina to capture my heart? Really? Did you somehow forget what being the submissive bottom means? I don't do the penetrating my love any more than you do. What the fuck am I going to do with a vagina?"

Jakob turned bright red with a blush at his being caught in error as he sashayed wiggling his rear with a wide dramatic swing. "Oh, ja, I guess that would be a problem, wouldn't it? I guess I forgot you recently came out of the closet."

I scoffed. "You didn't forget sister. You were trying to test me. Stop trying to bullshit the King of bullshit. Well, there you have it, honey. I am the gay bottom just like you and there is no more confusion about it. So, if you desire to be with me you have to either grow a pair or at least a beard."

Jakob swatted me on the shoulder "Stop. I am going to pee my pants you are making me laugh too hard. We both act like we are off to the Strubenfarm rather than visiting our sick sister. Wipe that smile off your face before we arrive at Leo's place. The man has suffered terribly you know. Oh, and Christian, Leo's beautiful locks, they…"

I nodded as I interrupted. "Fell out from the chemotherapy. I know the ravages of cancer, Jakob. I may be ignorant of the outside world, but I do have the medical books. I realize he will be frail and probably still quite sick from the rough treatments."

Jakob suddenly became somber. "Good that you are prepared, honey. I have difficulty not breaking down in tears each time I visit him. I pray that stone heart of yours can fare better than that of your Auntie."

I shrugged. "I love Leo, Jakob. I never cared what he looked like, trust me. If the man were nothing but the torso in a wheelchair, I would still think him the most beautiful man on earth."

Jakob sniffed loudly as he reached out and ran his finger through my hair. "Such a romantic. Like I said, Gott is a bastard. Leo is one lucky Queen thanks to it. I think seeing you is exactly what he needs to find the strength to keep fighting."

I nodded as I began to knock on Leo's door. "The feeling is completely mutual Jakob. I have missed my Leo more than I can say."

Jakob opened his mouth to say something, but I never heard it. Leo answered our attempts to hail him without hesitation and so did Der Makellos. The hound saw his buddy Mad Maxx and came running at full speed. Mad Maxx saw the dog too and after nearly ripping Jakob's arm out of his socket, scrabbled to get away. Mad Maxx took off running down the sixth floor hallway screaming in complete terror as the eager hound gave a friendly chase. Der Makellos thought it all a game until the panic stricken Mad Maxx missed the first step and flew head over heels, tumbling at breakneck speed to his likely death below.

To be continued in book eight of The Collar King Series: Chocolate Dreams

About Author: Alexandria May Ausman

Alexandria May Ausman in her 16th year was diagnosed with Schizophrenia. She was quickly abandoned by her foster parents. While still only a teen, she was forced to battle this devastating illness alone.

Alexandria has struggled with lack of a support system, numerous psychotic episodes, exploitation, homelessness, and an uncaring mental health system.

Alexandria raised two healthy children. After obtaining her bachelor's degree in psychology she worked as a child abuse investigator and became a diagnostic psychologist while acquiring her Master's in psychology. Alexandria never forgot the experience of 'slipping through the cracks.' Her life's goal is to help people suffering abuse and/or mental illness have access to necessary services. By accident, she became a model of 'gothic attire' and the World Goth Queen.

She began writing a fictionalized account of her life experiences after a catastrophic return of psychotic symptoms. Today, Alexandria is retired, and homebound due to crippling symptoms of Schizophrenia. She currently lives in Tallahassee, Florida, with her loving husband and a loyal support dog.